THE PAINTER'S DAUGHTER

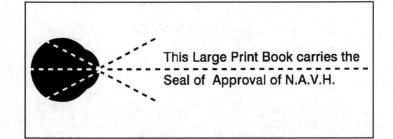

This Large Print Book carries the
Seal of Approval of N.A.V.H.

THE PAINTER'S DAUGHTER

JULIE KLASSEN

THORNDIKE PRESS
A part of Gale, Cengage Learning

GALE
CENGAGE Learning·

Farmington Hills, Mich • San Francisco • New York • Waterville, Maine
Meriden, Conn • Mason, Ohio • Chicago

GALE
CENGAGE Learning®

LIBRARY OF CONGRESS CATALOGING-IN-PUBLICATION DATA

Names: Klassen, Julie, 1964- author.
Title: The painter's daughter / Julie Klassen.
Description: Waterville, Maine : Thorndike Press Large Print, 2016. | © 2015
 |Series: Thorndike press large print Christian historical fiction
Identifiers: LCCN 2015042258| ISBN 9781410485694 (hardback) | ISBN 1410485692 (hardcover)
Subjects: LCSH: Large type books. | BISAC: FICTION / Christian / Historical. | GSAFD: Love stories. | Regency fiction. | Christian fiction.
Classification: LCC PS3611.L37 P35 2016 | DDC 813/.6—dc23
LC record available at http://lccn.loc.gov/2015042258

Published in 2016 by arrangement with Bethany House Publishers, a division of Baker Publishing Group

Printed in Mexico
1 2 3 4 5 6 7 20 19 18 17 16

To Anna Paulson,
with love

Reader, I married him.
A quiet wedding we had:
he and I, the parson and clerk,
were alone present.
— *Jane Eyre,* by Charlotte Brontë

The one . . . who keeps an oath
even when it hurts,
and does not change their mind
. . . will never be shaken.
Psalm 15 NIV

CHAPTER 1

March 1815
Devonshire, England
Infuriating artists . . . Captain Stephen Marshall Overtree grumbled to himself as he walked along the harbor of the unfamiliar town, looking into each shop window.

He glanced down at the crumpled paper in his hand, and read again his brother's hastily scrawled note.

> . . . I will let a cottage as last year, though I don't know which yet. If the need arises, you may write to me in care of Mr. Claude Dupont, Lynmouth, Devon. But no doubt you will manage capably without me, Marsh. As always.

Stephen stuffed the note back into his pocket and continued surveying the establishments he passed — public house, harbormaster's office, tobacconist, and cider seller. Then a stylish placard caught his eye:

9

CLAUDE DUPONT

Painter, Royal Academy of Arts

~

Portraits by commission,
also local landscapes.

Instruction and supplies
for the visiting artist.

Inquire within.

Stephen tried the door latch, but it wouldn't budge. He cupped a hand to the glass and peered inside. The dim interior held easels, framed landscapes, and shelves of supplies, but not a single person.

He bit back an epithet. How could he *inquire within* if the dashed door was locked? It was not yet five in the afternoon. What sort of hours did the man keep? Stephen muttered another unflattering comment about artists.

From the corner of his eye, he saw a frowsy woman step from the public house, dumping a bucket of water. He called, "I am looking for Wesley Overtree. Have you seen him?"

"That handsome Adonis, you mean? No, sir." She winked. "Not today at any rate."

"Know where he's staying?"

"One of the hillside cottages, I believe, but I couldn't tell you which one."

"Well then, what of Mr. Dupont?" Stephen gestured toward the locked door.

"Mr. Dupont is away, sir. But I saw his daughter pass by not fifteen minutes ago. Walking out to the Valley of Rocks, I'd wager, as she does nearly every day about this time." She pointed to the esplanade, where a path led up the hillside before disappearing from view. "Just follow that path as far as it goes. Can't miss it."

"Thank you."

For a moment Stephen remained where he was, looking up the hill — thatched cottages and a few grander houses clung to the wooded slope, while Lynmouth's twin town of Lynton perched above. Perhaps he ought to have remained in the coach for the half-mile climb to Lynton. He sighed. It was too late now.

He walked along the seaside esplanade, then started inland up the path. He was glad now he'd brought his walking stick — a thin sword cleverly concealed inside. One never knew when one might meet highwaymen while traveling, and he preferred to be armed at all times. His military training was well ingrained.

The steep path soon had him breathing hard. He'd thought he was in better condition than that. The month of soft living, away

11

from drilling his regiment, had already taken its toll. He would have a few choice words for Wesley when he found him. Stephen should be with his regiment, not at home doing Wes's duty for him, and not here.

He ascended through the trees, then out into the open as the rocky path curved westward, following the cliff side, high above the Bristol Channel — deep blue and grey. The steep downward slope bristled with withered grass, scrubby gorse, and the occasional twisted sapling. Little to stop a fall. If a man were to slip, he would instantly tumble four or five hundred feet into the cold sea below. His stomach lurched at the thought.

His old nurse's recent pronouncement echoed through his mind. *"You won't live to see your inheritance. . . ."* He could still feel the wiry grip of her hand, and see the somber light in her eyes.

With a shiver, Stephen backed from the edge and strode on.

The cry of a seabird drew his gaze upward. Gulls soared, borne aloft by strident wind. Black-and-white razorbills and grey-tipped kittiwakes nested among the rock outcroppings.

He walked for ten or fifteen minutes but saw no sign of the young woman ahead of him. He hoped he hadn't missed a turn somewhere. As he continued on, the temperature seemed to drop. Although spring came earlier on the southwest coast, the wind bit with icy teeth, blowing across the channel from the north, still held in the grip of winter.

He tugged his hat brim lower and turned up the collar of his greatcoat. In less than two weeks he would again exchange civilian clothes for his uniform, return to duty, and make his grandfather proud. But first he had to find Wesley and send him home. With Humphries retiring, someone needed to help Papa oversee the estate. Their father was not in good health and needed a capable spokesman to keep the tenants happy and the estate workers on task. As a captain in the British Army, the role had come easily to Stephen. But his leave would soon be at an end, Napoleon exiled or not.

The role of managing the estate should have fallen to his older brother. But Wesley had again gone south for the winter, in spite of their mother's pleas. His art came first, he always insisted. And he preferred to leave practical, mundane affairs to others.

Rounding a bend, Stephen saw a craggy headland — rocks piled atop one another like castle battlements — with a sheer drop to the lashing currents below. He looked down to assure his footing, but a flash of color caught his eye and drew his gaze upward again.

He sucked in a breath. A figure in billowing skirts, wind-tossed cape, and deep straw bonnet stood atop that high precipice. Wedged between a rock on one side, and the cliff on the other, her half boot extended over the edge. What was the fool woman doing?

She fell to her knees and stretched out a gloved hand . . . trying to reach something, or about to go over? Did she mean to harm herself?

Pulse lurching, Stephen rushed forward. "Stop! Don't!"

She did not seem to hear him over the wind. Leaping atop the summit, he saw she was trying to reach a paper entangled in the prickly gorse.

"Stay back. I'll retrieve it for you."

"No," she cried. "Don't!"

Taking her objection as concern for his safety, he extended his walking stick to reach the paper and drag it back up the slope. Bending low, he snagged a corner of the thick rectangle — a painting. His breath caught.

He turned to stare at the tear-stained face within the deep bonnet. He looked back down at the painting, stunned to discover the image was of the very woman before him — a woman he recognized, for he had carried her portrait in his pocket during a year of drilling and fighting, and had looked at it by the light of too many campfires.

A gust of wind jerked the bonnet from her head, the ribbon ties catching against her throat, and its brim dangling against her back. Wavy strands of blond hair lifted in the wind, whipping around her thin, angular face. Sad, blue-grey eyes squinted against a dying shaft of sunlight.

"It's . . . you," he sputtered.

"Excuse me?" She frowned at him. "Have we met?"

He cleared his throat and drew himself up. "No. That is . . . the portrait — it's your likeness." He lifted it, also recognizing the style — clearly his brother's work.

Instead of thanks, her face crumpled. "Why did you do that? I was trying to toss it to the four winds. Make it disappear."

"Why?"

"Give it back," she demanded, holding out her hand.

"Only if you promise not to destroy it."

Her lips tightened. "Who are you?"

"Captain Stephen Overtree." He handed over the paper. "And you must be Miss Dupont. You know my brother, I believe."

She stared at him, then averted her gaze.

"That is, he let a cottage from your family. I stopped at the studio but found the place locked. Can you tell me where to look for him?"

"I should not bother if I were you," she said. "He is gone. Sailed for Italy in search of his perfect muse. His Dulcinea or Mona Lisa . . ." She blinked away fresh tears, and turned the painting over, revealing a few

15

scrawled lines in his brother's hand.

He read:

My dear Miss Dupont,

That visiting Italian couple we met invited me to travel with them to their homeland. To share their villa and paint to my heart's content. It was a spur-of-the-moment decision, and I could not resist. You know how I love Italy! We sail within the hour.

I know I should have said good-bye in person. I tried to find you, but could not. Thankfully, as a fellow artist you understand me and realize I must follow my muse and pursue my passion. Must grasp this opportunity before it leaves with the tide.

We shared a beautiful season, you and I. And I shall always remember you fondly.

Arrivederci,
W. D. O.

Thunder and turf, Stephen inwardly raged. How was he to send his brother home now?

"He left no forwarding address?" he asked. "Or even a specific port or town?"

She shook her head. "Not with me. I believe the couple he mentioned was from Naples, but I could be mistaken."

"Did Lieutenant Keith go with him?"

"Carlton Keith, do you mean? I assume so. They seemed to go everywhere together."

Stephen nodded. "Do you happen to know

16

if my brother took all his belongings with him?" He asked the question to determine if Wesley planned to return to Lynmouth.

Again she shook her head. "When I looked in this morning, I was surprised to see he'd left many of his paintings behind, as well as his winter coat."

"Did he not tell your father he planned to leave?"

"My father has returned to Bath on a portrait commission. We thought your brother planned to stay on through the spring. That's why I was so . . . surprised . . . to receive his note."

Was that why she was surprised? The only reason? Stephen didn't think so. Her tears and Wesley's apologetic letter painted a telling picture. Miss Dupont was in love with Wesley. No doubt he had worked his legion charms on her and then left when he grew bored. Perhaps Wesley had loved her, for a time. Or at least admired her. How far had it gone? Had Wes done more than break her heart? Dread rippled through him at the thought.

Stephen asked, "May I see the cottage?"

She reared her head back. "Why?"

"I'd like to look around — see if I can find any indication of where specifically he's gone. I'll have to try to get word to him in Italy somehow."

"Oh . . ." She paused in thought, then said

17

briskly, "You might ask the harbormaster, see if he knows where the ship was bound."

"I shall do that. Thank you. Even so, I'd like to take a look."

She bit her lip, then faltered. "I . . . don't think Bitty has been in to tidy it up yet. Perhaps you —"

"No matter. I am pressed for time, so if I could see it now . . . ?"

She drew a deep breath. "Very well."

Miss Dupont clambered off the precipice, as nimble and surefooted as a girl, though she looked to be in her early twenties. She gestured toward a path on the other side of the headland. Not the way he had come. "This way is more direct," she explained.

He fell into step beside her, feeling like a brawny brute next to her willowy figure.

She led the way into Lynton, the higher of the twin towns, past its blacksmith, livery, and old church, and then followed a cobbled path partway down the hill. There, three whitewashed cottages huddled along the hillside, overlooking the Lynmouth harbor and sparkling channel beyond. At the first cottage, she unhooked the chatelaine pinned at her waist and sorted through the keys until she found the correct one. She unlocked the door and stepped inside.

Stephen was surprised at the young woman's apparent aplomb in entering a bachelor's cottage, when she seemed so ladylike in her speech and demeanor. Entering after her, he left the door open behind them for propriety's sake. He walked around the single room and noticed her survey the chamber as he did, as if looking for something. Was there something she didn't want him to see? He saw remnants of art supplies: an easel, used paint pots, canvases, and sketchbooks. A table and chairs and a simple stove huddled along one wall, an unmade bed against the other. Her gaze flicked to it and quickly away.

She swiped a lacy glove off the arm of a chair and tried to make it disappear up her sleeve. Noticing his look, she murmured, "Must have dropped it when I looked in earlier . . ."

He glanced at the pair of matching kid gloves she wore but said nothing. Instead he fingered through the paintings propped against the wall, then paged through a sketchbook on the table. That same familiar face — her face — looked up at him wearing different expressions. Solemn and reluctant at first, progressing to increasing confidence, shy half smiles warming to full blown brilliance. Her clothing varied as well — prim lace collars giving way to round, open necklines and, eventually, one bare shoulder.

Reaching past him, Miss Dupont shut the sketchbook, her cheeks mottled red. "Yes, I posed for him several times." A defensive note sharpened her tone. "He was most insistent.

I had never done so before — not even for my father — and was quite uncomfortable with it. But as you might guess in such a remote place, his choice of models was extremely limited."

Inwardly, Stephen groaned, his stomach sickening. Oh yes. It had gone too far. And Wesley had done more than break this girl's heart. An otherwise innocent girl, if he did not miss his guess.

He asked, "Did Lieutenant Keith lodge here as well?"

"Yes. We offered to bring in another bed, but he said he preferred his bedroll." She looked around the room. "I don't see it. He must have taken it with him."

Sounded like Keith, Stephen thought. "I don't suppose my brother made arrangements to store his belongings, nor paid sufficient rent to keep this cottage until he returns?"

"No. He paid only to the end of the month."

Stephen mentally calculated. A sea voyage to Italy could take two or three weeks each way, depending on weather and the winds, not to mention whatever time Wesley planned to spend there painting. What had Keith been thinking to let him go? To leave without sending word? Or perhaps a letter was even now making its way to Overtree Hall through the post.

Stephen sighed. "I will have to pack up his

belongings and somehow transport them home."

She nodded absently. "We probably have a suitable crate in the studio. Come. I will ask Papa's assistant to help you make arrangements."

"Thank you."

She offered him the use of the cottage overnight, since his brother had already paid for it. He politely declined, having secured a room at the Rising Sun, where a warm supper awaited him.

He gestured for her to precede him. "I'll escort you back."

As the sun set, they walked down the switchback path and into Lynmouth.

"Do you know . . ." she began. "Your brother never mentioned a sibling named Stephen. Only a 'Marsh.' Something of an ogre, apparently."

Stephen pulled a face, knowing the act would only serve to pucker the scar on his cheek and make him more ogre-like yet. He explained, "My second name is Marshall. He calls me Marsh — one of several nicknames he reserves for me. Including Captain Black."

"Oh. I'm sorry, I —"

"No matter. It's an apt description."

When they arrived at the studio near the harbor, Miss Dupont used another key to open the door. She frowned at the dim, silent interior. "Maurice is supposed to keep the

21

lights burning and the door open until five at least. Looks like he's been gone for hours."

"Is this where you live?" Stephen asked.

"We have a house in Bath, but when we're in Lynmouth we live in the apartment upstairs. Although, with my father gone I'm staying with a neighbor, Mrs. Thrupton."

He read between the lines. "Is your father's assistant a lad or a . . . married man?"

"Neither."

"Ah." He nodded, illogically relieved she cared something for her reputation.

A man of about twenty trudged down the stairs in stocking feet. He wore trousers, rumpled shirt and waistcoat, but no coat. His dark hair stood askew, as though he'd just rolled out of bed.

"Bring me any supper?" he asked her. "I'm starved."

"You're on your own, I'm afraid," she replied, setting down her bonnet and gloves.

"Who's he?" The young man lifted an insolent chin.

"This is Captain Overtree, Mr. Overtree's brother. Captain, Maurice O'Dell. My father's assistant."

"Another Overtree? It's my lucky day," he said sarcastically. "What does this one want?"

"Simply to transport the belongings his brother left in the cottage. I would like you to help him."

"I . . . heard he left," O'Dell said. "And

22

good riddance, if you ask me."

Miss Dupont said coolly, "I didn't."

Stephen sized up the young man as he would an opponent. He was barely more than Miss Dupont's height, though stockier. His prominent dark eyes and upturned nose put Stephen in mind of an ill-behaved pug yapping at a larger dog.

O'Dell turned to him, thick lip curled. "I am not merely an assistant. I'm family. Claude Dupont's nephew."

"By marriage, yes," she clarified. "My father married Maurice's aunt a few years ago."

"I won't be making prints forever," O'Dell asserted. "I'm an artist in my own right. I'll be famous one day. Just you wait."

"Sadly, I haven't that much time," Stephen said dryly. "Now, if I might trouble you for a crate and the name of the local drayage company . . . ?"

"We have several crates in the storeroom," Miss Dupont said. "Maurice, if you will see the largest delivered to the first cottage."

"Very well, but don't expect me to help pack up that fop's leavings."

"Then, please mind the shop in the morning while I do."

She turned to Stephen. "What time shall I meet you?"

"I am an early riser. Shall we say eight — or nine, if you prefer."

"Eight is fine. I'll see you then."

23

Stephen hesitated. "Are you . . . all right here, or shall I walk you to the neighbor's you mentioned?"

"I'm all right on my own. But thank you."

Sophia Margaretha Dupont watched the black-haired, broad-shouldered stranger stride away, barely believing he could be related to Wesley Overtree. Beautiful, heartbreaking Wesley.

She'd had no inkling that things had changed between them — for Wesley at least. She had shown up at the cottage that morning as usual, smiling, stomach fluttering with happiness, eager to see him again, wondering how best to tell him her news. Only to find the farewell note he'd left and the cottage abandoned. Her smile had quickly fallen then. Her stomach cramped with dread. What had she done wrong?

She knew men did not like to be pressured, so she had not pressured him. Had he simply lost interest, or had he realized she was not beautiful enough for him — either as a model or a wife?

She read the rescued note again, and the conclusion seemed unavoidable. Wesley had not only abruptly left Lynmouth, but he had also left *her*. She turned the note over, struck anew that he had written it on the back of one of the dozens of likenesses he'd painted of her. A dozen too many apparently.

Sophie sagged against the studio counter, feeling weary and low. It had been the worst day of her life, except for the long-ago day her mother died. At the thought, she gently clasped the ring she wore on a chain around her neck, close to her heart.

Not only had Wesley left, and her last hope of happiness with him, but then she'd had to endure that mortifying interview with his own brother. The man's hard, knowing expression left her with the sickly feeling that he'd guessed the truth — that posing was not the worst of her indiscretions.

She remembered Wesley describing his dour and disapproving brother Marsh. And saying *"Captain Black would sooner strike a man than listen to him."* She had formed an image of a foul-tempered, hardened warrior. A man who had seen terrible things. Who had probably *done* terrible things.

Captain Overtree certainly looked fierce, with that jagged scar, which his bushy side-whiskers and longish dark hair did little to conceal. Had his coloring spawned the name Captain Black or had it been his brooding personality? Perhaps *black* described both. He was taller than Wesley — several inches over six feet — and his strong-featured face boasted none of Wesley's fine bone structure or handsome perfection. His eyes were striking though. Blue, where Wesley's were light

25

brown. She would never have expected blue eyes.

Her fleeting comparison of the brothers faded as the reality of her situation reasserted itself. This was no time to think of trivial things. Not when her life as she knew it hung in the balance and was soon to change forever.

She had not given God a great deal of thought since her mother's death. Church had not played a significant part of her childhood. But during these last few weeks she had prayed very hard, hoping what she feared wasn't true.

Now her prayer changed. She had been so certain Wesley would marry her. But now he was gone. Even if he came back, would it be in time to save her and her reputation? *Oh, God, let him return in time. . . .*

CHAPTER 2

In the morning, Stephen arose early and breakfasted. Feeling unsettled, he asked the innkeeper to direct him to the nearest church, and then walked there to pray. As a younger man — and a younger son — he had once hoped to make the church his vocation. But his grandfather had other plans for him. In some ways, the military had brought Stephen closer to God than a career as a clergyman ever could have. Even so, he yearned to serve his fellow man in some significant way.

In the solemn silence of the empty nave, he asked God for wisdom concerning what to do about Wesley . . . and Miss Dupont. He also prayed for the grace to accept God's will, if his old nurse's prediction was indeed correct. She had made the unsettling remark just as he was leaving Overtree Hall. Now the scene ran through his mind yet again. . . .

Coming down the stairs, Stephen drew up short, taken aback to see Miss Whitney stand-

27

ing at the open back door. His former nurse usually remained upstairs. Had she come down to say good-bye?

He walked toward her. "What is it, Winnie? Is everything all right?"

"No. But there's nothing you or I can do about it." The woman sighed, then looked at the valise in his hand. "Heading off to bring Wesley back?"

"Yes. But don't worry. Kate will look after you while I'm gone. Everything will be fine."

She shook her head. "I don't believe it will be. You won't always be able to save him, you know."

She looked out the door again, and he followed her gaze, surprised to see his childhood friend and neighbor, Miss Blake, stalking off across the garden.

"There is a change in the wind," Miss Whitney said. "I feel it in my bones."

Stephen winced in confusion. "I don't understand, Winnie. But I'm afraid I have to go now."

She inhaled deeply and blew out a long breath. "It isn't right."

"What isn't?"

"That Wesley should be heir when you do all the work."

He had heard the same lament before. "Don't trouble yourself. And don't forget I'll have that trust from Grandfather when I'm thirty." He chuckled and teased, "If I live that long."

"No. I don't believe you will," she replied, expression somber. "You won't live to see your inheritance. I know things I wish I didn't. The world's turned topsy-turvy."

Stephen frowned. "What are you talking about?"

Her eyes took on a faraway, distracted look. "He shall reward every man according to his works."

"My reward in heaven, do you mean? Don't rush me." Again he tried to brush off the woman's strange words with a joke, but the eerie light in her eyes made him uneasy.

She grasped his arm. "Be ready, my boy. Your time is coming."

His sister wheeled into the hall at that moment, waving emphatically. "Stephen! Everyone is looking for you. Roberts says you must leave now or you'll miss your coach."

Stephen dragged his gaze from Miss Whitney's and called back, "Coming!"

For a moment longer, his old nurse kept her hold on his arm.

Stephen patted her hand. "I'll be back soon, Winnie. And everything will be fine — as it always is."

"No, my dear Stephen. I don't think things will ever be the same again. Are you prepared to meet your fate?"

His throat constricted. Was she saying what

he thought she was?

"Yes, I am," he whispered, and gently extracted himself from her grip.

As he sat in the unfamiliar church, Miss Whitney's words echoed once again through Stephen's mind, *"You won't live to see your inheritance. . . . Are you prepared to meet your fate?"*

His former nurse had never claimed to have second sight or any special revelation from God. But he would be lying if he said her words didn't give him pause. He recalled countless instances over the years when she had known things she logically should not. Or predicted outcomes that had later come to pass. He trusted her — and had never known her to be wrong about anything. Even so, as a man of faith Stephen knew his fate was in God's hands. He told himself not to give credence to her words. But he *was* a man about to return to active duty, where life was always at risk.

Unbidden, a verse went through his mind: *"Greater love hath no man than this, that a man lay down his life for his friends."*

He did not take it as a good sign.

A few minutes before eight, Stephen walked up the hill to the cottage. He arrived before Miss Dupont and waited outside. Near the door lay a large crate. The door, however, was locked. He checked his pocket watch, then reminded himself Miss Dupont was not one of his privates who deserved a tongue-lashing for keeping him waiting.

Five minutes later, she came hurrying up the steep path, looking weary. "I'm sorry. I'm not quite the thing this morning. I'm not usually late."

She unlocked the door, entered, and began opening the shutters. But somehow the cheery morning light only served to make the abandoned belongings and wrinkled bedclothes look more forlorn.

He carried the crate inside and said, "I'll begin with the larger canvases if you'd like to sort through the supplies. Keep anything that belongs to your father, or any paints or oils that will spoil in the interim. I'm guessing your father or his assistant might have some use for them?"

"Yes. Thank you."

"No sense letting them go to waste."

Stephen gathered Wesley's coat and a few personal items left behind, then turned toward the paintings.

"I am surprised he didn't take this easel with him," he commented.

"That is an extra one from the shop." She wiped her hands on a cloth and suggested, "We ought to wrap the canvases first, to protect them for travel. These landscapes are quite good."

31

Stephen lifted one from the easel. "I like this one. Quite a different style for Wesley."

"Oh, um. That's not one of his. It . . . was done by one of his pupils."

"Ah. If you would be so good as to see it returned."

"Of course."

He lifted another. "And this one of Wesley? Not a self-portrait, I take it?"

"No. Another by . . . that same pupil. I shall see it returned as well."

He reached for another canvas, one Wesley had painted of Miss Dupont in Grecian robes — windblown hair escaping its pins, coppery highlights among the gold brushstrokes, her face thin but lovely, lips full, eyes large and searching. He wondered why he'd not seen any full-size paintings of Miss Dupont among the landscapes Wesley had brought home from Lynmouth the previous year. Apparently the miniature portrait Stephen had found was one of only a few small paintings and sketches Wesley had done of the painter's daughter last year. This year, however, he seemed to have painted little else. Stephen wrapped the canvas with care, then picked up the image of her with a bared shoulder. Looking at it, he felt a stab of . . . What was it? Reluctant admiration? Resentment? Jealousy?

She glanced over, and a frown line appeared between her blond eyebrows. "Must you take that one? Any of me, really?"

He shoved the illogical feelings aside. "What would you suggest I do with them? Are they not Wesley's property?"

"I suppose. But certainly you can understand why I loathe the thought of them sitting out in plain view somewhere in your family's home?"

"Perhaps you ought to have thought of that before you agreed to sit for him."

She ducked her head, and he immediately regretted his cutting tone.

"Of course, you're right," she allowed. "I wasn't thinking clearly, and I certainly didn't think it through."

"What *were* you thinking?"

She shrugged. "I was simply helping a fellow — helping an artist with his work. I didn't foresee finished paintings that might someday be sold or hung where his own family would see."

He laid the final canvas in the crate. "There, that's the last of them."

She nodded. "I'll send Maurice up with a hammer and nails to close the crate and carry down these supplies. I . . ."

Her face suddenly paled, and her eyes shot wide. She pressed a hand over her mouth, whirled to the door, and ran outside.

Through the window he saw her bend between two bushes and retch.

His own stomach clenched in reply. *Oh no.* Did it mean what he feared it did? Enough

33

soldiers' wives had accompanied his regiment for him to recognize the telltale sign. He thought again of her tears, her uneasy glances at the bed, that bare shoulder . . . If he was right, what should he do? Ignore the evidence of his eyes? Or offer some money to the poor, ill-used girl? But this was no London light-skirt. This was a respected artist's daughter. This was the woman whose likeness he had secretly carried with him for nearly a year. . . .

Miss Dupont entered on shaky legs a few moments later, trying to look nonchalant, probably not realizing he'd seen.

He handed her a clean handkerchief, and her eyes flew to his, then to the nearby window before her sickly green countenance reddened once more.

"I'm sorry. I'd hoped to spare you that. Not a pleasant thing to witness." She forced a weak smile. "Must have been something I ate."

He asked, "Are you feeling better now?"

"Yes. Now, where were we?" She turned toward the crate.

"Miss Dupont, wait."

She slowly turned back.

"It wasn't something you ate, was it."

Her lips parted, then she said briskly, "Well, I can't be certain, of course. But it's nothing catching, I'm sure. Never fear."

"Oh, but I do fear."

"Excuse me?"

34

He gestured toward the chairs at the table. "Please. Sit down."

"I don't wish to sit down. We are here to pack up your brother's things, and that is all. Then I shall have Bitty put the place to rights for the next lodger, if there is one. It's not likely this early, but —"

He pulled out a chair with a whining scrape and gave her his most imperious look. "Sit."

"I am not a soldier in your command, sir."

"Sit, please."

"Very well. For a moment." She sat, fingers folded primly in her lap. "I am feeling a little queasy still, I admit. But it shall pass."

"Yes, in about eight or nine months, I imagine?"

She gaped up at him, eyes wide in shock. "How dare you . . . ? It's . . . it's . . . none of your business."

He grimaced. "But it is, I'm afraid. Family business." He ran a hand through his coarse hair. "Look. I'm sorry to be so blunt. But it's not in my nature to speak in polite generalities when there is a specific problem to solve. Nor have I the time to mince about."

"It is not your problem."

"Is it not? I came here to find my brother. To send him home to help our father before I must return to my regiment. Instead I find he has sailed for Italy, leaving a young lady in a serious predicament. He is the man responsible, I take it?"

Her full lips thinned to an offended line. "You, sir, are presumptuous beyond belief."

"No. That was Wesley. I am the one trying to help. What do you plan to do?"

For a moment she stared at him, eyes glittering and face set. Then she released a long breath and sank back against the chair. "I don't know. It's early days yet. I don't know what I *can* do. Please don't tell anyone — it would kill my father."

"But you won't do anything . . . dire, I hope? When I saw you on the cliff's edge, I feared you meant to do yourself harm."

She shook her head. "I confess the notion went through my mind. But, no."

"I am glad. Life is precious. A gift from God."

"I am surprised to hear a military man say that. Are you religious, Captain?"

He shrugged. "When a soldier knows he might die at any moment, he either ignores God to 'eat, drink, kill, and be merry,' or becomes very aware of the brevity and blessedness of life."

She nodded thoughtfully. "I suppose I might go away and have the baby in secret, and surrender it to a foundling home. But I don't want to give up my child."

Her eyes rested on the top portrait lying in the open crate. "Once again, I didn't think through the consequences in advance. I thought Wesley would marry me. I suppose I still hope he will return in time. . . ."

She probably believed Wesley would realize his mistake, beg her forgiveness, and vow his undying devotion. Stephen would like to believe that too. But he had known his brother all his life, and he doubted it. It was possible that personal resentments colored his opinion unjustly, but he didn't think so.

He recalled his prayer in the church that morning, and the verse that had gone through his mind. Surely this wasn't what God had been prompting him to do. Was it?

Stephen was accustomed to taking care of his brother's responsibilities, and covering for his mistakes. But it was more than that. Foolish or not, he felt protective of this woman whose face had smiled softly at him through nearly a twelvemonth of deprivation and battles. He'd become strangely attached to her. And he wanted to do something good with his life — make some sort of recompense for what had happened with Jenny. Especially with Winnie's morbid prediction hanging over his head.

Should he? Would Miss Dupont reject his offer outright? Be offended? She was in love with his brother, after all — golden boy Wesley, far more handsome and charming than Stephen had ever been, and all the more since the Peninsular War had left him with a long scar across one cheek.

But Wesley wasn't there.

Hands behind his back, Stephen paced in front of Miss Dupont's chair. He stated his case as resolutely as a general laying down battle plans.

"Wesley has gone to Italy. Who knows when he will return, or if he would do his duty by you if he did. I don't say this to hurt you, but at this point neither of us can afford the luxury of wishful thinking. We must be realistic."

He paused. "May I ask how far along you are?"

Again she reddened. "About two months."

He nodded, silently estimating. Might Wesley return in time to wed her himself? Would he, even if he knew? It would be risky to wait.

He paced across the room once more. "It should be Wesley offering to marry you. But he is not likely to come back for several months, if not longer. I haven't time to wait that long, and neither have you. I cannot offer love, of course, as we are barely acquainted. However, I can offer you marriage in name only, and moreover, it may be a short-lived marriage, as I have reason to suspect I may not be long for this world. But even if that happens, you will have born your child with benefit of marriage — and he or she will be legitimate, bear my name, and the protection of my family."

She stared at him blankly, then her face curdled in incredulity or repugnance. "*You*

38

are offering to marry me? You yourself?"

"As I said. Did I not speak clearly, madam?"

"Your words were plain but difficult to fathom. Why would you do that?"

"I hold no dishonorable motives, if that is what you fear."

"I . . ." She hesitated, then frowned. "What do you mean by 'may not be long for this world'? Why do you think you won't survive, especially now with Napoleon in exile. Are you ill?"

"No. But military service is always risky." He decided not to expand on that topic. "So let me be plain about what I am offering and what I am not. Maybe not a long future together. Definitely not wealth — I am a second son. Although if I die you would have a widow's pension and my family would see you and the child provided for."

Her eyes widened. "But you cannot know you won't come back. You aren't God, after all. And what happens if you do? You would be saddled with a wife you don't know or care for, and a child who isn't your responsibility. What will you do then?"

He nodded gravely. "We shall cross that bridge if and when we come to it. But I am a man of my word. If I vow before God to love, honor, and protect 'til death do us part, then that is what I shall do."

Could Sophie say the same? She stared at the stranger before her, mind whirling. She could not deny that she was desperate for a way of escape from her predicament. But which would be worse — to marry a stranger, or to be discovered with child without a husband? She'd not been exaggerating when she said it would kill her father. And how her stepmother would gloat and rail. Perhaps even insist her father put her out. Maurice, nearly two years her junior, might marry her. But once he found out about the child, he'd never let her forget what she'd done. He would make her life — and the life of her child — a misery. Would Captain Overtree do the same — make her live to regret marrying him?

Her heart twisted. And what if Wesley came back, realized he loved her, and asked her to marry him? It would be too late — she would be married to his brother. Would Wesley feel betrayed, or relieved that someone else had fulfilled his duty for him? Even if Captain Overtree did not live long, as his widow she could *not* marry Wesley. The laws of England didn't allow in-laws to marry. Saying yes to his brother now would mean giving up Wesley forever.

She asked, "May I have some time to think about it?"

He ran a hand over his scarred face. "I am afraid I must ask you to decide quickly. I return to my regiment in less than a fortnight. Which reminds me — if we proceed, we shan't have time to post banns in our home parishes and wait the usual interval before marrying. We shall have to elope."

"Elope?" The word inspired thoughts more scandalous than romantic, and would spark the very rumors she wished to squelch. "All the way to Scotland?"

He shook his head. "Too far. But marriage laws are more lenient in the Channel Islands as well."

"I didn't realize . . ." Sophie murmured, considering. She knew her father would not approve of an elopement. But he would forgive that more readily than an illegitimate child.

She thought again of the brief parting note from Wesley. No words of love. No promises. Sophie stepped to the window, unable to meet his brother's forthright gaze. Quietly, she said, "He isn't coming back, is he. For me, I mean."

She felt him focus on her profile and steeled herself for his answer.

"I don't claim to be a prophet," he said gently. "But knowing him as I do . . . No. I don't believe he is."

The captain drew himself up. "Well. I will give you until tomorrow morning to decide. Let you sleep on it."

Sleep? Sophie doubted she would sleep all night, even after she paced the rest of the day as she was certain to do, thinking about Wes-

41

ley . . . and his brother.

Wesley Dalton Overtree sat alone in the parlour of an inn overlooking the bustling port. The schooner had reached Plymouth that morning, and soon he and the Italian couple would board the larger merchant ship that would carry them on to Italy. He had two hours to kill. Two hours to remember . . . and regret.

His traveling companions seemed to sense his desire to be alone and retreated into the dining room without him. A young servant knelt before the sooty embers in the hearth nearby and coaxed a reluctant fire to life. Smoke stung Wesley's eyes and made them water. He swiped a hand across them, wishing he could wipe away his remorse as easily.

He should have said good-bye to Sophie in person.

When the opportunity to go to Italy had first presented itself, he had been tempted to simply leave a note and slip away. A selfish part of him had thought it would be easier. Wiser. Cut all ties before anyone tied him down. But in the end, he could not do it. He was still a gentleman, after all, no matter what Marsh said about him. And so he had gathered his courage and gone to the Dupont studio.

But only that surly assistant, O'Dell, had been there to greet him.

"She's not here," O'Dell said, his tone barely civil.

"Gone out to Castle Rock again, has she?"

The young man hesitated, perhaps reticent to tell him her whereabouts. Then he said, "Not this time. She's gone with Mrs. Thrupton to Barnstaple for the day."

"When will she be back?"

O'Dell shrugged. "Too late for you, I reckon."

Something about the way he'd said it gave Wesley pause. Was that malice glinting in the young man's eyes, or was it a figment of Wesley's guilty conscience? Because a moment later, O'Dell was all smiles and well-wishes for the journey.

It turned out the man was right — it was too late. Wesley asked the schooner captain if a later departure might be possible, but the crusty salt invoked the old saying "The tide waits for no man." And apparently neither would he.

Wesley had felt torn. The ship and his new friends were leaving with or without him. And with them went his chance to return to his beloved Italy, share their villa, and paint in the land of Michelangelo, Raphael, and Caravaggio. How he longed to see Italy again. Naples. Rome. Florence. And hopefully be inspired, and rediscover the elusive muse.

So he'd scribbled a note to Sophie after all, left it in the cottage, where he knew she'd

43

find it, and departed without seeing her.

Sitting there in Plymouth, Wesley reviewed the words he'd written. In hindsight, his rushed few lines seemed dolefully inadequate. So cold and impersonal.

Sophie deserved better.

He imagined her reaction upon reading the letter — her smile falling into crestfallen lines, disappointment washing over her — and guilt pinched his gut. How disillusioned she must be, when she had thought so highly of him. In her sweet company, he had felt a hero, as if he could do no wrong. Now he had tumbled off that pedestal.

His eyes watered again and he winced.

Wesley knew he'd acted selfishly. He thought of all the intimate, loving things he'd said and done in the heat of passion, and another wave of remorse struck him. He had not lied to her. The feelings he'd expressed were true at the time. But then, as had happened before, the walls had begun to close in on him. He began to feel his life, his opportunities, narrowing. The visiting foreign artist and his sophisticated wife seemed to represent everything he wanted, everything he would miss — carefree living, travel, adventure, new experiences, inspiration, success. . . . He was an artist, after all, he reminded himself, and Sophie knew him well. She would understand.

Wesley had told himself all this and thought

he could sail away from her with an easy conscience, or at least that the guilt would quickly fade. But even now his spirit remained troubled. His heart was not in the journey, but it was too late to turn back. The voyage was paid for, his companions expecting him. He must make the most of this opportunity while he could.

He would make it up to Sophie when he got back. They had time, had they not? She'd said nothing about the future. No coaxing. No pressure. He liked that about her. So refreshing compared to those who seemed determined to prod him into a declaration, with coy smiles and thinly veiled manipulation.

Wesley ran a hand over his face. The truth was, he'd been afraid. Afraid as he had been only once before in his life. Again a woman held his life in her hands, and the vulnerable position unnerved him. But this was different, he realized. This time, he was in love.

Wesley made a decision. He would write Sophie another letter. A better one. He would apologize. Beg her forgiveness. Ask her to wait for him.

Would she welcome him back?

She would, he believed. For she was a kind, gentle woman, and she loved him.

Warmth flowed over Wesley at the thought, and he rose to seek out the innkeeper. He borrowed pen, paper, and sealing wax and sat back down to write.

Dear mia Sophia . . .

As he composed the lines, he prayed that she would forgive him, and that she would be there waiting for him with open arms when he returned.

CHAPTER 3

Sophie's mind spun with questions. Could she trust Captain Overtree? Must she accept on blind faith that he was a good man? She remembered again Wesley's descriptions of "Captain Black." A soldier who had probably killed men with his bare hands in combat. Could she put her life in those hands? And how would he treat her child — Wesley's child — whom the world would see as his, though they would both know better?

Having met him now, she wasn't sure what to think. Stern and blunt, yes. But dangerous? She wasn't sure. She'd been surprised by his gentlemanlike reserve and religious convictions. Were they genuine?

In her mind's eye, she saw again his striking blue eyes — glinting in determination, hard and officious, icy in irritation — and a warmer look she thought she'd glimpsed once or twice but could have been mistaken. It was too early to try to form her impressions of this man, and certainly too soon to consider binding herself to him for life. If only she had more time!

She decided she would go and talk to Mrs. Thrupton. Hopefully she could help her decide what to do.

Mavis Thrupton sat in the armchair near her sitting-room window, sunlight spilling over her face, softening the lines around her eyes and across her forehead and giving her skin a golden glow. At that moment, Sophie could imagine the beautiful young woman Mavis had once been, with a fine complexion, well-shaped features, large dark eyes, and thick brown hair piled atop her head. Actually, she had seen Mavis looking very much like that once, in a portrait her father had pointed out in the home of a wealthy patron. Mavis had worked as a painter's model in her earlier years. Several artists had vied for her attention, and the opportunity to paint the striking brunette.

Sophie felt a twinge of sadness as she now looked at the former beauty. Which was worse, she wondered, to have been beautiful once but faded, or to never have been beautiful at all?

No one had ever extolled Sophie's beauty, pursued her, or asked her to pose for him. Until Wesley . . . But even he had acknowledged that she wasn't the feminine ideal. Her pale skin lacked brilliancy and tended to look

sallow in certain light. Her face was thin —
as was the rest of her. She was not endowed
with the apple cheeks and rounded arms and
bosom men seemed to praise. But Wesley had
admired her in spite of those flaws, which
endeared him to her all the more. He liked to
tease her, saying she reminded him of a sad,
half-starved Madonna. She could still see his
golden-brown eyes, shining warmly with
humor and admiration.

Now Mavis listened as Sophie confessed
her predicament and Captain Overtree's
astounding offer.

"Oh, my dear!" Mavis breathed, eyes round.
"But what about Wesley? I know how you feel
about him."

Sophie nodded. "I love him. Body and soul.
But . . ." She shook her head in regret. "What
you must think of me. You did try to warn
me, I know."

"Never mind that now. We have all made
mistakes. I would be the last to condemn you.
In fact, I feel responsible. What sort of a
chaperone have I been? Your father will be so
disappointed in me."

"It isn't your fault."

"Wesley is a very handsome man, and he
paid you such marked attention. I can easily
understand how you might be tempted. But I
thought him a gentleman, so I was not as
vigilant as I should have been." Mavis clucked
her tongue. "Still I never guessed he would

49

leave you like this, to face this alone."

"Don't blame him too harshly," Sophie defended. "I didn't . . . exactly . . . tell him."

Mavis cringed. "Oh, Sophie."

"I hoped he was about to ask me to marry him, and I didn't want him to feel forced. I told myself I would wait just a little longer, and then if he did not ask, I would find the courage to tell him. I thought he loved me. I still do, in my heart of hearts. He is the one I want. Not his brother. Not a stranger I don't know. And what I *have* heard about him does not bode well."

"What do you mean?" Mavis's brow furrowed.

"Wesley spoke of his foul temper, his disapproving and cold manner. His tendency to strike first and ask questions later."

"That could be his military training — not necessarily his natural disposition. You . . . don't think he would hurt you, do you?"

"I don't think so, but what do I know? I have only just met him."

"You are in an awful predicament, my dear. But what other choice do you have? Tell me you aren't thinking of marrying Maurice."

Sophie's stomach soured at the thought. "Never." Her father might think highly of the young man, but Sophie neither liked nor trusted him.

"Good. Then what will you do — wait for Wesley?"

"I don't know. As his brother points out, unless Wesley reaches Italy and immediately takes the next ship back, I shall be well past the point of hiding my condition."

"But . . . would that be the worst thing? If you really thought he would marry you as soon as he learned the truth?"

"I don't know. His parents no doubt hope for a more advantageous match. But I *think* he would marry me if he knew."

"Are you confident enough to risk your life on that? Your future and that of your child?"

Sophie thought again of Wesley's blithe parting words. And his brother's regretful conclusion that he would not be coming back, at least not for her. Captain Overtree would have no reason to mislead her, would he?

"I don't know," Sophie admitted.

"I'm glad you're not considering the drastic course women sometimes take." Mavis nibbled her lip, then tentatively continued, "I once . . . knew a woman — a former painter's model, like me — who found herself in a similar predicament, and felt she had no other choice."

Sophie had heard of the dangerous things desperate girls sometimes did to avoid losing their respectability, loved ones, marriage prospects, or livelihoods. She shuddered. "I could never do that. Not to an innocent babe." *And especially not to Wesley's child,* she added to herself.

Mrs. Thrupton nodded. "I have to say that relieves my mind."

Sophie asked, "What happened to that woman — do you know?"

Mavis nodded, eyes distant in memory. "She went on to marry, her secret never becoming known. But years later, I . . . saw her, and she admitted she deeply regretted it. I tried to comfort her, reminding her she had done what she'd thought she had to. But they were hollow words."

"Poor woman." Sophie sadly shook her head and pressed a hand to her slim abdomen.

Mavis inhaled deeply and drew herself up. "I can't tell you what to do, Sophie. You know enough of my history to know I married a man I didn't love. Mr. Thrupton was not a bad man, but he didn't love me either. I wouldn't wish that sort of life for you, my dear. But plenty of people marry for reasons other than love. It's not the worst fate. I survived, and so can you."

Sophie thought of her father, who had enjoyed a loving relationship with her mother, while she lived. Sophie still didn't understand why he had married Augusta O'Dell a few years ago, a widow with a cruel tongue and three small children. Had he thought he would grow to love her? Or had he believed any marriage would be better than loneliness?

Sophie asked, "Did you ever come to love Mr. Thrupton, or he you?"

"Honestly, no. But over the years, I found that the more respect and kindness I showed him, the more respect and kindness I received in return. I know not everyone is as fortunate. Some men repay kindness with cruelty. But hopefully Captain Overtree is not that sort of man."

"How am I to know?"

Mavis pressed her hand. "Perhaps pray about it and ask God to show you. I hope that isn't hypocritical of me. I admit I have not given God much thought lately. Nor prayed as often as I should."

Sophie nodded. "It almost seems wrong to beseech Him for help when I have ignored Him all these years. But I confess I have been praying like never before. I don't know if He hears me, but I hope He forgives me."

"I believe He does, with all my heart," Mavis assured her. "Now, may I meet this Captain Overtree? I am no infallible judge of character, as I've already proven, but I would like to at least meet the captain and convince myself he is a decent man. I will have to answer to your father, you know, and I can't have you running off with someone I've never even met."

"Yes, of course you may meet him. I would like that. But he says I must give him my answer by tomorrow morning, and that if we

53

are to marry we must elope to Guernsey without delay."

"Does he indeed?" Mavis's eyes sparked with ire. "As if I shall let you sail away with a strange man without a chaperone! I have learned my lesson, better late than never. I will escort you and confirm his intentions are honorable before he has you alone and in his power."

"Oh, I don't think you have to worry about that," Sophie said. "He made it clear it would be a marriage in name only."

"What?" Mavis gaped at her. "Is the man not flesh and blood?" She shook her head. "Lofty promise, but difficult to swallow. I'd believe a man's actions before his words. I think we've both learned that the hard way."

Sophie managed to eat a little something at Mavis's insistence, and then left the cottage and headed down toward her father's studio. Thoughts in a whirl, she walked through Lynmouth, past shops and public houses, barely seeing what she passed. Then a familiar face caught her eye and she drew up short. There, through the window of the Village Inn, she was stunned to see Wesley's friend, Carlton Keith. She had thought he'd left with Wesley. What was he still doing in town?

She pushed through the inn door and slid onto the bench across from the man before he could say a word. He paused, glass raised halfway to his lips in his one remaining hand. He might be attractive if he were sober and groomed — and if he wiped the ever-present smirk off his face.

She abruptly began, "I thought you went with him."

He shook his dark head, eyes bleary with drink. "I wasn't invited. No — that's not fair. I had insufficient funds for the journey, and for once my generous friend was disinclined to pay my way." He smirked. "Wesley went without me, so I plan to return to Overtree Hall without him." Mr. Keith lifted his pint. "As soon as my ale money runs out."

She didn't fully trust the man, so she asked indirectly, "You are acquainted with Mr. Overtree's family?"

"That I am."

"And . . . his brother?"

"Yes. Better than most, I'd say. I fought with him in Spain. Saved his life, at the cost of my arm."

She leaned forward. "What can you tell me about him?"

A wary look entered his eyes. "Why do you ask?"

"I've met him. He is here looking for Wesley."

Carlton Keith sat up straighter and glanced over his shoulder as though the captain might be right behind him. When he spoke again his demeanor changed, his tone less cocksure

55

and more respectful.

"I may have bragged a bit about saving his life. Truth is, he saved mine. After I lost my arm, I was invalided to England and later discharged. While he was on leave, he took me under his wing, so to speak. Got me on my feet again. That's how I met Wesley in the first place. The captain asked me to keep an eye on his brother, and I've been doing so ever since. 'Til now." Mr. Keith tipped his head back and drained his glass.

"He was your commanding officer?" she asked.

"Aye. Poor sot was stuck with me. I had about as much business with a gun as Gainsborough's *Blue Boy.*" He laughed. "Green boy, more like, still wet behind the ears. My father purchased my commission, sure it would be the making of me."

She regarded him seriously. "Was it?"

He flipped up his empty sleeve. "You tell me."

She was about to feel sorry for the man, until she remembered her own situation.

She decided to keep her reasons for asking to herself, because Carlton Keith knew she and Wesley had spent a great deal of time together alone in his cottage.

"Is he . . . a good man? Can I trust him?"

Speculative light sparked in Mr. Keith's green eyes. "Trust him . . . with what?"

When she made no reply, he watched her

face a moment longer, then ordered another pint. "Does he know I'm here in town?" he asked.

"I don't think so. Is it a secret?"

"No. Though he won't like to hear I've abandoned my charge." He gave her a lopsided grin. "He has his nurse, and Wesley has me. Or he did have, until he left without me."

She didn't understand what he meant about the captain having a nurse, but the publican appeared with a fresh pint, so she didn't ask.

Keith drained half of it, then set down his glass with a decisive *thunk*. "Stephen Overtree is stern, stubborn, and self-righteous. Humorless, and about as much fun as a guilt-ridden puritan. He has a bad temper, little conversation, and is infamous for his black moods and black looks. We soldiers called him Captain Black. And Wesley the same, as well as Marsh. Or sometimes, Blister, because he considers his younger brother an ever-present pain. Of course, Wesley has a nickname for everyone. I'm CK or sometimes Flap, on account of my wing here." His eyes glittered with challenge. "Do you want to know what he called you?"

"No." Sophie exhaled. "I don't think I do."

Mr. Keith rose to leave, and Sophie's heart sank at his grim assessment of Captain Overtree's character.

Then the man turned back. For a moment

the ironic humor faded from his florid face and he said earnestly, "I could bear a year in Wesley's company better than a week in his brother's. But if I were in trouble, the captain's the one I'd turn to."

Late that afternoon, Sophie sat at Mrs. Thrupton's kitchen table with a cup of tea.

Mavis looked at her in concern. "You've made your decision, then?"

Had she? Sophie had let herself get swept away by romance with Wesley, and look where it had gotten her. She couldn't afford to let her heart rule her any longer. She had to think practically about her welfare and the welfare of her child.

She took a deep breath. "Yes. Captain Overtree may never love me, but I hope he will care for, or at least provide for, my child." She pressed a hand to her midriff. "This is his niece or nephew, after all."

"Are you sure this is what you want, my dear?"

"Want? No. But it seems the lesser of evils." Better to be an unloved wife or even a war widow, she had concluded, than a shamed woman shunned from society and her family. She hoped she was doing the right thing — for the baby's sake and her own.

The kindly woman leaned forward and grasped her arm. "Then I shall pray that he will treat you kindly. And never give you cause to regret it."

"So shall I."

"And I will accompany you. At least to the coast. That way, you may report to your family and his that you were chaperoned on the journey. Besides, my dear, it will give me time to observe him. Assure myself he is of good character and will not ill use you."

"At least while you are with us."

"Well. Hopefully never. He is Mr. Overtree's brother, after all. He would have mentioned if the man were a criminal or a notorious rake, would he not?"

"I suppose so. We shall have to ask his permission, I suppose, about your going along. As he is hiring the chaise and driver."

Mavis lifted her chin. "I'd like to see him try to refuse me."

Sophie bit back a grin. Mavis Thrupton should be the one marrying Captain Black — they would be better suited, despite their age difference.

"I suppose I must tell Maurice," Sophie said, dreading the task. "I don't want to risk him sending word to my father that I've disappeared — or worse."

"Perhaps you might leave him a note. And you will write to your father as well, I trust?"

"Yes, I had better. Heaven help me work out what to say. . . ."

Mrs. Thrupton supplied paper, quill, and ink, and Sophie sat down to write.

The few, impersonal lines to Maurice came easily. But when she began a letter to her father, she was surprised to find tears blurring her vision. She reminded herself that she would have happily moved away from her family if she'd married Wesley. And that she would be ostracized from them if she married no one. At least as a respectable officer's wife, she could still visit and be received in their home — and not lose contact altogether.

Dearest Papa,

I have some surprising news. By the time you read this, I shall be a married woman. I know this is sudden, and unexpected. I met my intended after you left to fulfill your commission — though I have known of his family for more than a year. His name is Captain Stephen Overtree. You are acquainted with his brother, Mr. Wesley Overtree. At all events, everything between us happened quickly, and because Captain Overtree must depart soon to return to his regiment — too soon to allow time to ask your blessing, or post banns — we plan to marry on the Island of Guernsey as soon as may be. I know this will come as a shock to you, Papa. I am sorry for it, and hope you and Mrs. Dupont will not be overly disappointed.

The captain and I plan to travel to Bath as soon as we return, so you may become acquainted with him. I hope that will not be inconvenient. In the meantime, I have left the studio in Maurice's care. I know you have great faith in him, so I trust you won't mind. Mrs. Thrupton will serve as chaperone for our journey, but promises to help Maurice manage the cottages when she returns to Lynmouth.

Until we meet again, I remain,

Your loving daughter,

Sophie

She blotted, folded, and sealed the letter, preparing it for the post.

Mavis had disappeared into her own bedchamber while Sophie wrote her letters, but now she came out, carrying several things in her arms.

"I don't know if you have given any thought to what you will wear for the wedding, my dear. Of course, you would be lost in any of my gowns, but I do have this silk shawl, and a cap you might wear, along with one of your finer muslins."

Sophie fingered the soft silk shawl, white shot with primrose, with embossed satin flowers, and very handsome fringe. "It's lovely," she breathed. "I would be honored to wear it. The cap as well. I like the lace trimming. It's smarter than anything I own."

Mavis handed her a small bunch of silk flowers, "In case the captain doesn't think to stop for hothouse flowers. If only it were later in the spring we could pick a fine bouquet."

"That's all right, Mrs. Thrupton. These will do very well."

Mavis sucked in a breath, then clapped a hand to her cheek. "Oh no! I completely forgot about a ring! He does not wear one on his little finger, does he, that might suffice until he can replace it? I have a plain silver band, but if it fits my sausage fingers, it shan't fit you. And there's no jeweler for miles."

"That's all right. Don't worry." Sophie tugged gently on the chain she wore around her neck, fishing out its end from within her bodice. "I wear my mother's ring as a pendant. There is no other ring I would wish for."

CHAPTER 4

Sophie decided not to wait until morning, but to seek out Captain Overtree that very night so Mavis could meet him before the journey.

Together the women walked to the Rising Sun. There they found Captain Overtree finishing his supper in the inn's dining parlour.

No welcoming smile broke over his somber face when he saw them, though his low voice when he greeted them was perfectly polite. "Hello, ladies. Will you join me? I am afraid I have just finished, but I would be happy to ask the innkeeper to bring you something, if you like."

"No, thank you," Sophie replied. "Captain, this is my friend and neighbor, Mrs. Thrupton. Mrs. Thrupton, Captain Overtree."

"How do you do, sir."

"Mrs. Thrupton." He acknowledged her without warmth, then turned to Sophie. "I did not expect to see you until tomorrow morning. Have you a question, or am I to understand you have come to a decision already?"

"I have, sir."

His stern expression threatened to steal her courage. Did he hope she would refuse him, so he could wash his hands of her and the whole sordid mess?

"And . . . ?" he prompted.

She swallowed. "I have decided to accept your offer. If you are still willing."

"I said I was. And I am not given to changing my mind, as I believe I mentioned."

"Yes, but I wanted to be sure."

He nodded. "Very well. The hired chaise will be waiting in the mews at nine in the morning, if that will be convenient?"

So soon. She forced a wooden nod. What had she expected? Smiles of pleasure? Whoops of congratulations? An embrace? Glancing at his flinty expression, she knew none of the above would be forthcoming.

In her mind's eye, Wesley's affectionate gaze appeared. She blinked it away, along with the stab of pain that accompanied it. This was certainly not how he would have reacted.

Mavis spoke up. "I would like some assurance that you have honorable intentions toward my young friend here. How do I know you will follow through on your promise to marry her?"

His eyes glinted. "I suppose you shall have

to take my word for it."

Mavis swallowed. "Then I wish to come along as chaperone, at least as far as the coast. Plymouth, is it?"

"Yes. We will find a ship to carry us the rest of the way from there. If Miss Dupont wishes your company, I have no objection, Mrs. Thrupton."

Sophie hoped the dear woman had not expected gratitude. After all, the time to save her reputation, or at least her virtue, was long past.

Mavis added with a timid smile, "And will not your family approve when they learn Miss Dupont traveled with a chaperone?"

He pulled a face. "Considering the circumstances, Mrs. Thrupton, I doubt they will approve of our nuptials in any case. But the gesture can't hurt. I might ask where this urge to chaperone Miss Dupont was a few months ago, but I shan't."

Mavis breathed, "Well, I never . . ."

"And therein lies the problem." He laid his table napkin beside his plate, and asked coolly, "Any other questions, ladies?"

Sophie looked at Mavis, a part of her hoping the woman would find a reason to object to their marriage, another part of her afraid she would. But the usually outspoken woman seemed as intimidated as she was and remained silent.

When the women left, Stephen sat there a few minutes longer, his heart beating dully in his chest. He could hardly believe he was soon to marry a woman he barely knew. An attractive woman, yes, but one who loved his brother and carried his child. His stomach knotted at the thought. Had he done the right thing? God forgive him if not. *If this not be your will, Lord, show me. . . .*

He settled his bill with the innkeeper, then walked toward the stairs leading up to his chamber. He glanced into the taproom as he passed, the long counter lined with men bent over pints or glasses of something stronger. The smoke of cigars, pipes, and several cheerful fires hung hazy in the lamplight. There was a time when he would have joined those men — sat too long and drank too much. But those days were over, thank God.

A familiar face caught his eye, and Stephen paused, scowling.

"Keith?"

His former lieutenant looked up, then raised his hand in surrender. "Sorry, Captain. You know how your brother is. Off on a whim without so much as a by-your-leave. He's gone to Italy, to paint in the land of Michelangelo."

"So I've heard," Stephen said dryly. "Why didn't you go with him?"

"I found myself with insufficient funds for

the journey, and Wesley disinclined to pay my way."

"I gave you a hefty purse. . . ."

"I know you did, sir. I know you did. But the expenses here — everything must be carted in from Barnstaple. Very costly to eat and drink and well . . . everything."

Stephen sat on the stool next to Keith's and waved away the barman's offer of a pint. "Did Wesley leave an address with you, or tell you when he would return?"

"No, sir. All he said was, 'I'll be all right on my own, CK. You go on home to Overtree Hall, and let my family know where I'm bound.' "

"So why are you still here?"

"Oh, I will be on my way soon, Captain. But first I aim to win back the money I lost here. My luck is about to change — I know it. Unless . . . Do you have another commission for me? I hope you don't want to send me off to Italy now, sir. Not on my own."

"I suppose not." He glanced at the empty glasses at Keith's elbow. "Something tells me you would drink or gamble away the passage money before the next ship sails. Had we Wesley's direction, perhaps, but as it is, no."

Did he really even want Wesley to hurry home now? Now that he was about to marry Sophie Dupont? For his parents' sake, he should want his brother back in Overtree Hall. For himself? Not so much.

Keith sipped his ale, then asked, "And what about you, sir — returning to Overtree Hall as well? Shall we travel together? You still have a few weeks leave, if I'm not mistaken."

"Yes, but I'm not returning directly. I have something to attend to first."

"Oh?"

"I travel to Plymouth tomorrow, and from there, sail to Guernsey."

"Guernsey? Whatever for?"

"A personal matter."

"Shall I accompany you, sir? Or do you prefer to travel alone?"

"I shan't be alone. Miss Dupont goes with me."

Keith's eyes widened. "Miss Dupont?"

"Yes."

He clucked his tongue. "My, my. I am surprised. First one brother, then the other. I can't say I appreciated having to leave the cottage for hours at a time, while Wes 'painted' her, but I didn't take her for a light-skirt."

Stephen clenched his jaw, stifling the urge to throttle the man. Nearby, a trio of sailors guffawed at some joke, and Stephen leaned closer. "She is not. And I will not hear a word against her, spoken in my hearing or anyone else's. Do you understand? Miss Dupont is to be my wife."

Keith's eyebrows shot to his hairline. "Your wife? That's why you're going to Guernsey?"

"Yes. As you pointed out, I haven't much time before I must rejoin the regiment. A wedding on Guernsey seems the most expedient option."

"Expediency, ay? Not the romantic quality females seem to long for in a wedding. How do you think Mr. Dupont will feel about you eloping with his daughter?"

"I don't imagine he will like it."

"And Wesley?"

Stephen met the man's challenging gaze directly. "What about Wesley?"

"How do you think he will feel about you eloping with his . . . with Miss Dupont?"

"You tell me. He isn't here to ask."

Keith grimaced in thought, ending with a shrug.

Stephen asked, "Had he any *honorable* intentions toward Miss Dupont?"

Carlton Keith opened his mouth to reply, then shut it again, seeming to think the better of whatever he'd been about to say. He shrugged again. "May have done. But it seems to me he made his choice. His art came first."

Stephen nodded dourly. "And his own pleasure second and third and fourth."

Keith's eyes twinkled. "Doing it again, are we?"

"What?" Stephen snapped. Impertinent fool knew him all too well.

"I told Miss Dupont how you saved my

life." Keith smirked. "I think I recognize the signs."

In the morning, Sophie reached the innyard a few minutes before the hour and stood alone, valise in hand, waiting for the captain. Mrs. Thrupton had offered to take her note for Maurice to the studio because she had a list for him as well — tasks he would need to take care of in her absence. Mavis jested that she would tuck Sophie's letter somewhere Maurice was unlikely to see it for several hours — among the cleaning supplies he so rarely used. Sophie was only too glad to leave the errand to the stalwart woman and hoped she would manage to slip out before Maurice read the note.

Instead, a few minutes later, Maurice himself wheeled into the yard, open letter in his hand, face an angry mask.

He shook the page before her nose. "Is this a joke?"

"No."

"What do you mean you're getting married? I thought that scapegrace left."

Sophie willed herself to remain calm. "Are you speaking of Mr. Overtree?"

"You dashed well know I am."

"I am not marrying Mr. Overtree."

"What? Then who?"

"I . . . don't know if that is any of your business."

"Rubbish. Of course it is." He gripped her wrist. "What are you playing at? You don't know anyone else here. Don't tell me that one-armed man twisted your arm."

"No one twisted my arm, but you." Sophie tried to wrench herself free, but he held fast. "Let go."

"Not until you tell me who you are supposedly marrying."

"That would be me." Captain Overtree appeared at Sophie's side like a menacing shadow, towering over both her and Maurice. She glanced up and saw anger glinting in his eyes, his jaw clenched.

"You? But she has just met you." Maurice's grip loosened, and Sophie yanked her arm away.

"Clearly you don't know everything," the captain said. "Miss Dupont is under no obligation to acquaint you with her every decision. Nor is it any of your concern how or when we met. But let me make one thing perfectly clear. If I ever see you lay a rough hand on her again, I will break that hand. Is that understood?"

Maurice's lip curled in disdain. "Her father shall hear about this."

"Yes, he shall," the captain agreed, unconcerned. "I shall tell him myself when we see him in a few days. And I shall also apprise him of your disrespectful treatment of his daughter."

Maurice swallowed. "I meant no disrespect. Worried about her, that's all. And why wouldn't I be — planning to run off with a stranger as she is?"

Captain Overtree formed a humorless smile. A dangerous smile, it seemed to Sophie.

"Your concern is touching, young man. But I am hardly a stranger. I am soon to be Miss Dupont's husband. Now wish us happy and be on your way. It is time we took our leave."

Leave . . . The thought of setting off with this man toward an unknown future filled Sophie with trepidation. She was suddenly very glad she'd accepted Mrs. Thrupton's offer to accompany them.

When Maurice stalked off, the captain stepped away to speak to the coachman.

Mrs. Thrupton hurried into the yard, huffing and puffing. "Sorry, sorry! Ran into a neighbor. She's going to feed my cat for me. . . ." Mavis looked at Sophie's face and frowned. "What is it? What's happened?"

"Maurice was just here."

"Oh no."

"Captain Overtree dispatched him — never fear."

Mavis *tsk*ed. "Sorry about that. He must have seen me leave your note."

Sophie looked at her wrist, relieved to see no mark there. "Oh well. It's over now."

Captain Overtree finished speaking with the coachman and joined the ladies. "Are we ready?"

"Yes," Sophie lied and forced a smile.

The groom opened the door for them, and the captain handed in Mrs. Thrupton, then offered his hand to Sophie. She glanced at it as though it were a coiled snake.

Noticing her hesitation, his blue eyes grew icy again. "Afraid of me, are you? Thank heavens you have a chaperone to protect you."

Sophie swallowed and allowed him to help her inside. She sat beside Mrs. Thrupton on the front-facing seat, leaving the opposite bench for him.

"Do you mind, Mrs. Thrupton?" he said. "I prefer to face forward."

"As do I."

"So you can keep your eye on me?" he asked.

"I didn't say that."

"Tell you what. Sit here straight across from me and I shan't move a muscle without first announcing my intention to do so. That way I needn't see Miss Dupont looking at me like a frightened rabbit the entire journey."

Mavis sniffed. "Very well. He that pays the piper calls the tune, I suppose."

"Thank you for understanding," he said sardonically. "You are all goodness."

He sat next to Sophie, leaving as much

73

distance between them as the narrow bench allowed. Seated on his left as she was, she could see the unmarred side of his face when she sneaked a glance at his profile. Was that his intention?

He certainly kept his word to sit quietly and paid neither of them any attention, staring out at the passing countryside with a vague expression.

As the journey began, Mrs. Thrupton tried a few times to engage him in conversation. He responded civilly but remained aloof. Mavis soon wearied of his terse replies and lapsed into silence.

Hours later, they passed a mile marker and few buildings, and Captain Overtree announced they had reached the outskirts of Plymouth. Suddenly the carriage lurched violently to one side and careened to a halt. Sophie, half asleep, lost her balance and pitched forward. The captain's arm shot out and stopped her from falling off the bench.

"Thunder and turf!" he exclaimed.

"Are you all right, Sophie?" Mavis asked.

"Yes, perfectly well," she murmured, straightening her bonnet. Though she'd likely feel the impact of the captain's hard arm against her shoulders for days to come.

"Must have hit quite a hole," he said, pushing open the door. "Hopefully we did not break an axle."

He stepped out to survey the situation, and Sophie followed, needing to stretch her legs. The groom hopped down as well.

While the men checked the carriage underbelly and wheels, Sophie walked a few steps away.

"Stay close," the captain warned. "Rough area."

"I won't go far."

She had walked only a few yards, when she passed a wheelwright's shop. How convenient for him to have a nasty hole in the road so near his door. Or perhaps it was no coincidence at all.

A young man leaning against the building pushed himself upright. She had not seen him in the shadows.

"Hello, love. Can I interest you in this fine gold watch fob?" He held up a tarnished brass chain. "A gift for your husband? Only a bob for you, pretty lady."

She almost replied that she had no husband but bit back the foolish words. "No, thank you."

A second youth leapt from an alleyway and snagged her reticule. Its ribbons around her wrist bit into her flesh as he jerked it away.

She cried out in pain and alarm. "Stop!"

In a flash of black coat and gleaming brass, Captain Overtree struck the young man with his sword stick, knocking him to the ground. The second youth turned to run, but the captain grasped him from behind, one arm across his throat while twisting the youth's arm behind his back.

"Give the lady her reticule."

"You'll break my arm!"

"I said . . . give it back."

The youth extended it to Sophie, who stood trembling nearby.

The coachman jogged into the fray with his blunderbuss and held the men until the constable could be found.

Sophie walked unsteadily back to the coach, rubbing her wrist, the captain beside her. She noticed Mavis's face in the window, staring wide-eyed.

Although relieved to be safe, and have her bag returned to her, Sophie was stunned by his violent strike. "You needn't have done that," she hissed.

"I should have let him take your reticule?"

"No. But they are only boys — not more than eighteen."

"I have killed men even younger." The captain jerked open the carriage door. "Now, wait inside."

She climbed back into the carriage as bid, legs trembling.

"Are you all right?" Mavis asked.

"Did you see that?" Sophie whispered, feeling torn. "Of course I am grateful, but . . . such violence. What sort of man is he?"

"He is a soldier, Sophie. A hardened one,

by the looks of it." Mavis squeezed her hand. "Were you frightened?"

"I was more frightened by his reaction than I was of those boys."

Mavis bit her lip, brow furrowed. "It's not too late, you know. If you are afraid of him, I could . . . take you to my sister's in Bristol. You could have the child there, and then perhaps find a nice young couple to —"

"No. I want to keep my child. Going to Bristol would not solve my problem."

The captain entered the carriage a few minutes later, the equipage lurching under his weight.

He sent her a sidelong glance and asked darkly, "Having second thoughts?"

Mrs. Thrupton spoke up, "Captain Overtree. Thank you for protecting my young friend. But I'm afraid we find your violent behavior quite shocking. It makes one wonder if you are able to control your temper. Can you give me some assurance that you will treat Miss Dupont in a gentlemanlike manner?"

"If by 'gentlemanlike' you mean slow to act, servile, and soft, then no. I'm afraid I cannot oblige you. In my profession, that sort of behavior gets one killed. I haven't the luxury of a tender conscience."

"Let us not mince words. I need to know that you will not ill use her."

"I will not ill use her. You have my word. I

shall even promise not to touch her if that will chase the frightened fawn look from her eyes."

"Not touch her? I would not ask that. You shall be husband and wife, after all. Is that not so?"

"That is up to Miss Dupont."

Sophie made no reply, and the carriage starting moving again.

A short while later, they reached the Plymouth docks, where they would buy passage on one of the boats waiting there to carry eloping couples across the channel.

When the carriage halted, Captain Overtree grasped the door latch and said over his shoulder, "I shall go and check with the harbormaster about a ship. That will give you five minutes to talk about me between yourselves. Please finish before I return."

CHAPTER 5

Sophie bid Mrs. Thrupton farewell at the bottom of the gangway.

"You're certain?" Mavis asked one last time.

Sophie braved a smile. "Yes. Quite certain." She embraced the woman and resisted the urge to hold on too tight or too long.

She released her friend, avoided meeting the captain's brooding gaze, and preceded him up the gangway.

Together they crossed the deck, passing two other couples and half a dozen crewmen busy with ropes and baggage. He led her down a steep set of stairs toward the cabin he had purchased for the trip.

"Be forewarned. Even the best cabins are small." He opened the door for her, set his own kit on the floor, and surveyed the room.

The cabin held a narrow bunk and a porthole high on the outside wall. His broad shoulders seemed to fill the space. Very close quarters indeed. Did he mean to share it with her? He would not fit in that bunk with her

— unless their limbs were completely en-twined. She swallowed at the thought. The ship tilted as it left its berth and moved toward open water. Her stomach roiled, and she pressed a hand against the wall to steady herself.

"Try to get some sleep," he said. "I'll go up on deck and leave you in peace. Lock the door behind me."

She breathed a sigh of relief when he left. A relief that was short-lived when the ship lurched to the side and then rose and fell. Her stomach lurched in reply. It would be a long night.

The bedclothes looked dingy and smelled less than fresh, so Sophie laid her cloak over the bed and lay down fully clothed. Eventually she fell into an uneasy sleep.

A few hours later, she rose, feeling ill. Bile soured the back of her throat. She quickly scanned the room, swiped up the basin, and held it in her lap.

Someone knocked softly. "Miss Dupont? It's me."

She recognized his low voice.

"Don't panic. I've only come to bring you something to eat."

She rose on unsteady legs and unlocked the door. Captain Overtree stood there, candle lamp in one hand, a bowl of something in the other.

"Thought you might be hungry . . ." He

studied her face by candlelight. "Are you all right? You look unwell."

"Sea travel doesn't agree with me."

"Ah. Sorry to hear it. Maybe eating something will help?"

She took one whiff of the fish soup and her stomach wrung. She turned and retched into the basin. How mortifying! At least she need not worry he would find her attractive and be tempted to rush the honeymoon.

"I'll see if I can find some bread or something plain." He left, taking the offending soup and the basin with him. Her ears burned in embarrassment to have him do so.

He returned a short while later and handed her a hunk of crusty bread wrapped in brown paper.

"Better?"

She nodded and accepted it gratefully. "Thank you." She nibbled a piece, then said, "I have managed a few hours of sleep, if you would like a turn." She gestured toward the bunk with a nervous hand.

He removed his hat. "Perhaps I'd better, or I shall not be fit for anything tomorrow."

He stretched out on the bunk fully clothed, crossing his hands over his chest. Eyes closed, he said, "How can I sleep with you watching me?"

"Oh, sorry. Shall I go up and take some air while you sleep?"

He opened his eyes. "No. Please stay. I

won't sleep if I have to worry about sailors ogling you. Or worse."

"Very well."

He closed his eyes again. She sat on a small stool in the corner and pretended not to watch him. He turned on his side — the scarred side of his face pressed into the pillow. A few minutes later, his breathing slowed and he apparently slept. Sophie leaned her head back against the wall, took deep breaths to ease her nausea, and prayed.

The bed ropes creaked, and her eyes flew open, thinking he'd awakened. But he had only turned over in his sleep. She leaned near, looking more closely at the jagged, angry-looking scar snaking into his side-whiskers. She wondered how he'd gotten it but doubted she really wanted to know.

When they neared St. Peter Port the following day, Sophie tidied her hair, donned her lace cap and shawl, and repacked her valise. Together they disembarked and easily found their way to the stately brown-brick Town Church overlooking the harbor — its tall steeple visible from the docks.

Inside they saw another couple before them, a doe-eyed brunette and her attentive lover. Their adoring gazes and secret smiles made Sophie feel all the more self-conscious, standing beside this stiff, austere man who barely glanced at her and certainly wasted no smiles on her.

They met the Reverend Mr. Partridge, who smiled enough for the rest of them, and who would conduct the wedding for a fee. His amiable wife and grown son, who also served as parish clerk, would act as witnesses.

When their turn came, Sophie and Captain Overtree walked up the aisle to the altar. Sophie held the silk flowers Mrs. Thrupton had given her, chagrined to see them tremble in her hands.

How awkward she felt standing with this stranger, forming vague smiles as the cheerful clergyman explained what would happen next, and asking the requisite questions: had they both come of their free will to be married, their ages, and so on.

Tension emanated from Captain Overtree. Was he having second thoughts? She could not blame him if he were. For her part, Sophie felt oddly numb. Her decision made, she went through the motions without resistance or deep thought, as though performing a role in a play.

With his wife and son looking on, the parson began, "Dearly beloved, we are gathered together here in the sight of God . . . to join together this man and this woman in holy matrimony; which is an honorable estate . . . signifying unto us the mystical union that is betwixt Christ and His Church; and therefore is not by any to be enterprised unadvisedly, lightly, or wantonly, to satisfy men's carnal lusts and appetites, but reverently, discreetly, advisedly, soberly, and in the fear of God . . ."

Sophie's heart beat hard at the parson's words. Were they entering into holy matrimony "unadvisedly, lightly, or wantonly"? A chill went up her neck at the thought.

The parson continued, "First, it was ordained for the procreation of children, to be brought up in the fear and nurture of the Lord . . ."

Would she and Captain Overtree have children together? Sophie wondered. It seemed difficult to imagine when he would barely look at her, let alone touch her. But he was a man of faith, apparently. So might he help her raise the child she already carried to love and fear the Lord? She hoped so — if he lived. Even though faith had not played a role in her upbringing, she wanted it for her own child.

"Secondly, it was ordained for a remedy against sin, and to avoid fornication . . ."

Sophie flinched at the word. What must Captain Overtree think of her?

"Thirdly, it was ordained for the mutual society, help, and comfort . . . both in prosperity and adversity. Into which holy estate these two persons present come now to be joined. Therefore, if any man can show any just cause, why they may not lawfully be joined together, let him now speak, or else hereafter forever hold his peace."

Sophie instinctively glanced toward the door. Captain Overtree gave her a cynical look, his mouth ruefully quirked. He no doubt guessed whom she hoped to see.

The parson now spoke directly to them, "I require and charge you both, that if either of you know any impediment why ye may not be lawfully joined together in matrimony, ye do now confess it. . . ."

Last chance, Sophie thought to herself. She glanced up and found the captain watching her. She blinked and returned her gaze to the parson.

Hearing none, Mr. Partridge continued, "Stephen Marshall Overtree, wilt thou have this woman to thy wedded wife, to live together after God's ordinance in the holy estate of Matrimony? Wilt thou love her, comfort her, honor, and keep her in sickness and in health; and forsaking all other, keep thee only unto her, so long as ye both shall live?"

He lifted his chin. "I will."

Then the clergyman looked at her and asked her a variation of the same questions.

Heart thudding, Sophie ran her tongue over dry lips. "I will."

Then the smiling parson took Sophie's right hand and joined it with the captain's. Would he notice her sweating palms? The captain's fingers were cool and loose, and she might have easily slipped from his grasp.

"Repeat after me," Mr. Partridge said. "I, Stephen Marshall Overtree, take thee, Sophia Margaretha Dupont, to my wedded wife, to have and to hold from this day forward, for better for worse, for richer for poorer, in sickness and in health, to love and to cherish, till death us do part, according to God's holy ordinance; and thereto I plight thee my troth."

Captain Overtree repeated the words in a low monotone, then released her hand.

Mr. Partridge turned to her. "Now take your groom by the right hand and repeat after me. . . ."

Sophie repeated the words, a marionette on a string, her mouth opening and closing while a little voice in her mind cried out, *"What are you doing? How can you vow to love, cherish and obey this man till death, when you love another?"* She ignored the voice, and repeated the words by rote. Words she had heard recited at several weddings in her life — including her father's own recent nuptials. It seemed as if she were listening from across the room, as if someone else were intoning the words, while her heart remained aloof.

Mr. Partridge leaned forward and whispered to the captain. "The ring?"

The captain stiffened.

"Oh!" Sophie exclaimed. She had forgotten to give it to the captain in advance. She fished it from her bodice, unclasped it from the chain, and handed it to him, her face burning all the while.

The clergyman smiled and accepted it, laying it atop the black book. Then he instructed Stephen to place it on her finger and repeat after him.

"With this Ring I thee wed, with my Body I thee worship, and with all my worldly Goods I thee endow. . . ."

How unsettling and embarrassing to hear this man she barely knew pledge *to her* in his low voice, "*. . . with my Body I thee worship . . .*"

Sophie's face heated anew. And he, in his turn, seemed to avoid her gaze.

At the parson's signal, they both knelt as he prayed over them. Then he joined their hands together again, and said, "Those whom God hath joined together, let no man put asunder."

Finally, the man of God pronounced them man and wife, "In the Name of the Father, and of the Son, and of the Holy Ghost. Amen."

There. They were married. Legally, and before God.

The parson blessed them, read from the Psalms, and closed with an additional blessing for procreation. But with her ears already burning and ringing, Sophie barely heard the words.

After the ceremony, Mr. Partridge led them to a table at the rear where they signed the register, and he and the witnesses added their signatures.

All smiles, he asked, "Would you like a copy of the license for a small added fee? Makes a nice keepsake."

"Yes," Captain Overtree handed over the coin, and when the license was delivered, he folded it and carefully, ceremoniously, handed it to her for safekeeping. For proof.

The clergyman's wife closed the register and said, "Now. How about a nice room for the night, and a good dinner, hmm? We have a charming little inn up the lane. Much nicer than the crowded, dirty establishments here along the harbor."

Captain Overtree returned his leather purse into his pocket. "Thank you, but no. We shall leave directly."

"But the next ship for the mainland doesn't leave until tomorrow morning," Mr. Partridge said. "We find most couples are, em, eager to consummate their nuptials, straightaway, you see. Eloping as so many are without a father's blessing." He leaned nearer the captain and suggested knowingly, "Best to do a thorough job of things, you see. Dissuades an offended father from contesting the match. All done, all in. Too late to make a fuss."

His wife added, "So why not share your first night in one of my clean and tidy rooms? Bed ropes recently tightened. Plump new ticking. My maid washed the bedclothes herself. And a good roast dinner with my famous fish stew for starters. Hmm? What do you say?"

Helplessly, Sophie looked at Captain Overtree. He returned her gaze with a bemused expression. "My wife does not care for fish stew, I'm afraid, Mrs. Partridge. But I am amenable to the other arrangements, if . . . the missus agrees . . . ?"

Four pair of eyes looked at her expectantly. She swallowed. "I . . . well. If we cannot sail 'til morning, we shall have to sleep somewhere, shan't we?"

"Very true, madam," Mr. Partridge said. "We all must sleep, wedding night or no."

But Sophie was almost certain she saw him wink at the captain.

An hour later, Sophie and Captain Overtree sat in the inn's parlour. The captain sawed at his roast with relish while Sophie picked at a potato.

He paused and surveyed her full plate. "Is the food not to your liking?"

"Hmm? Oh no, it's good. I am just not very hungry."

He set down his fork and knife with a clank. "See here. There is no need to be terrified. I have no intention of . . ." He lowered his voice. "I will not press you or expect anything from you. You needn't sit there trembling like a cornered mouse."

He wiped his mouth and tossed down his table napkin. "I realize your affections lie elsewhere . . . on a ship bound for Italy. I am not a brute. No matter what you think me after that incident yesterday."

"Th-thank you," she managed.

"Yes, I thought you'd like that. Now eat something, so we can go to bed."

Her gaze flew up to his.

"To sleep," he clarified, eyes hard.

Sophie ate a few more bites before surrendering to her nervous stomach.

"Look," he said. "Go up alone and I'll ask them to send up a maid to help you undress or . . . whatever it is ladies do before bed. I'll stay down here for a while. Give you some privacy."

For how long, Sophie wondered. All night? She dared not count on it. And why should he spend his wedding night alone? They were married, she reminded herself. Like it or not. For better or worse.

Sophie went upstairs into the room they'd been given, which was as clean and tidy as Mrs. Partridge had promised. In a few minutes, someone scratched on the door and opened it. A young maid of eighteen or nineteen entered, all coy smiles.

"Your husband sent me to help get you

ready for your wedding night."

Sophie's heart pounded. What happened to *"I will not press you, or expect anything from you . . ."*? Did he intend to consummate the marriage tonight after all?

Her stomach knotted at the thought.

"Joe's bringing up the slipper bath so you can have a nice soak. Then I'll help you into your night things."

"Oh. Um, thank you." Perhaps it didn't mean what it seemed, she told herself. Perhaps he was only being thoughtful — realizing she'd had to basically live and sleep in the same clothes for two days of traveling and would like a bath before she changed for bed. Yes, that was probably all it meant.

Sophie bathed and then the maid helped her into a nightdress. The cheeky girl winked, then left her waiting nervously. Sophie wrung her hands, listening to the woman's retreating footfalls and expecting them to be replaced by a heavy tread climbing the stairs in reply to whatever saucy announcement of her readiness the maid had delivered.

But the stairs remained quiet.

Was he finishing his drink? No, Wesley had distinctly told her his puritanical brother did not drink — another weakness he disapproved of in others, according to Wesley.

A quarter of an hour passed. Then half an hour. Then an hour. She was growing both exhausted and irritable at once. She was tempted to climb into bed and feign sleep, hoping it would dissuade him from touching her. But how could she sleep when her nerves were wound tight, waiting every second for him to barge through the door and demand his conjugal rights?

Another hour passed. The rumble of voices in the taproom below diminished. Still he didn't come. Had he paid for a second room without telling her? Found some more willing female with whom to spend the night? She grew more vexed the longer she allowed her imagination to play havoc with her peace of mind. Finally, she gave up wondering. She tied a dressing gown over her nightdress and tiptoed down the stairs.

As she neared the archway to the taproom, she heard the crackle of a large fire and the low rise and fall of a pair of voices in quiet conversation — his voice not among them. She peeked around the threshold. The room was empty except for three men. At one end of the counter, young Mr. Partridge sat on a stool talking companionably with the barman, as the older man dried glasses. And there, slumped in an inglenook, was Captain Overtree, the dregs of a pint in one hand, peering at a small oval he held in the other.

She crossed the few yards that separated them, trying to ignore the raised-brow look the barman gave her.

Nearing his elbow, she hissed, "Captain,

what are you doing?"

He tucked the oval frame into his pocket before she could gather more than the faint impression of a face, then glanced up at her from beneath a fall of black hair. "Staying away from you. Trying to, at any rate."

"What were you looking at?"

"Nothing." He finished his pint.

"I was told you didn't drink."

"I don't — usually. But there's nothing *usual* about tonight. It's my wedding night." He chuckled bitterly. "Some comfort was required."

"Come upstairs."

"Why?"

"Because you are embarrassing yourself. And me."

"Because our young Mr. Pheasant, or whatever his name was, and Mr. Thompkins there might wonder why I prefer to spend the evening here than in my . . . your bedchamber?"

"Yes." Was he trying to hurt her feelings? Already regretting their marriage? She thought of the portrait he'd tucked away. Was he mourning the loss of the woman he would have preferred to marry — a woman he loved?

"Come, Captain." She took his elbow and tried to pull him to his feet. He did not budge. She turned to the barman. "Mr. Thompkins, would you please help me get my . . . husband to bed?"

"Ma'am, if I had a wife as young and pretty as you, I wouldn't need anyone to drag me to her."

"Thank you. Now, please just help me . . ." She picked up the captain's discarded coat from a chair nearby.

The man slung one of the captain's arms around his shoulder and helped him off the bench and up the stairs. In their nuptial chamber, they half-dropped him, half-rolled him into bed.

Mr. Thompkins asked, "You can undress him yourself, I take it?"

"I . . . am sure I can manage. Thank you."

The man left, closing the door behind himself.

Sophie regarded her bridegroom — eyes closed, dark hair unruly, legs askew. With a sigh, she wrestled off the captain's boots, glad he had removed his own coat downstairs. She sat on the edge of the bed and reached for his waistcoat buttons, then stopped.

Since he was sound asleep, she studied him closely by candlelight. His face was so much softer and gentler in repose. The scar he tried to hide, more vulnerable. He smelled of ale and smoke, and she wrinkled her nose.

"You don't deserve it," she whispered, "but . . ." She kissed her finger and pressed it lightly to his temple. "Everyone should be kissed on their wedding night."

Exhausted, she lay beside him — her in her

dressing gown and him in his clothes — and soon fell asleep.

Sometime during the night, the captain moaned and turned over. He threw an arm around her, and murmured a sorrowful "Jenny . . ."

Who was "Jenny"? It wasn't a name she recognized. Sophie gingerly removed his heavy arm, wondering what in the world she had gotten herself into, and already beginning to regret it.

CHAPTER 6

In the morning, Stephen awoke with an ice pick in the back of his skull and a stomach full of bile and regret. He was swamped with remorse for his behavior of the night before. For showing weakness to his new wife. For breaking his vow to himself.

The truth was, he was attracted to Sophie, and the very thought of her undressing and bathing in the bedchamber they were meant to share did torturous things to him. Yet he had promised he would not press her, that he expected nothing. Why had he done so? He wished he'd never suggested a marriage in name only. In hindsight, he knew he'd done so to lower her risk in accepting him. To protect himself from rejection if she turned him down. Stupid, proud fool that he was.

How disheartening to find himself married to a woman who loved someone else and wanted nothing to do with him. And that thought had fed a revolting combination of resentment and self-pity that no man should succumb to, especially on his wedding night. It was either have a drink, or go upstairs and make a fool of himself. So he had broken his code of the last five years and had one pint. And then another.

Now he was surprised to find himself in bed, and partially undressed. In the sunlight that jabbed his eyes, he saw her seated at a little table in the corner, sticking pins in a coil of hair atop her head. He would have liked to see it down. Too late. And she was already dressed. He had a tantalizing memory of glimpsing her in nightclothes, so the maid must have slipped in and helped her change while he slept on. Or rather, slept it off. He cringed in regret.

"I am sorry, Miss . . . Dash it, I don't know what to call you."

"My name is Mrs. Overtree," she pronounced without pleasure.

"I suppose it is. Well, Mrs. Overtree. I apologize for last night and promise not to do it again."

"Which part?"

He eyed her warily. "I hope I didn't do anything . . . worse . . . than becoming stupidly drunk?"

"Um, no. Nothing." She stood up. "Well. Mrs. Partridge promised to lay quite a spread for breakfast this morning, and I am very hungry. I doubt you feel like eating, so I will leave you alone to wallow in your misery."

More miserable than you know. . . .

After the door closed with a wince-worthy bang, Stephen glanced around for his coat, and saw it lying over the chair nearby. He dragged it close and dug in his pocket for the portrait, relieved to find it undisturbed. He lay back, looking at it, almost ruing the day he'd found it in the first place. He very much doubted he'd be in his current predicament if he'd never set eyes on it.

On the sea voyage back, Sophie realized their roles were now reversed. Captain Overtree was too ill to eat much or do more than suffer, curse every wave, and now and again to retch. She felt a modicum of pity but decided he was getting his just rewards. And, she admitted to herself, she was relieved he was too ill to make any advances.

She brought him bread and a wet cloth to wipe his face, approaching the bunk cautiously as she did so. He reminded her of an untamed animal, temporarily subdued as though by a sedative that would soon wear off. She felt safe ministering to him now but reminded herself he was still dangerous.

She knew she should be reasonable. It would not be realistic or fair to live as strangers, despite his assertion that theirs would be a marriage in name only. But she was in no hurry to change his mind. Memories of Wesley, his secret smiles and caresses, were too recent, too well remembered, too dear.

Leaving the captain sleeping, she went and stood on the deck, breathing in the brisk sea air, refreshing after the dank confines of the cabin. The wind lifted her hair, just as it had so often atop Castle Rock. And on its current, memory took her back. . . .

That day, more than a year ago, had begun like so many others. She had checked their inventory of paints, brushes, and canvases, then reviewed her father's appointment diary, wishing for all their sakes he had more commissions scheduled. He did have two pupils coming at the end of the month. And one of their cliff-side cottages had been let by another painter due to arrive later that day, a Mr. Wesley Overtree. Probably another of the many young hopefuls who came to the area with dreams of capturing its wild beauty but without the skills to do so. It was a challenge for the most skilled artist. And certainly for her.

She tied her smocked painting apron over her day dress and set about arranging her father's brushes, which she had cleaned and laid out to dry the night before. She then mixed and prepared a fresh palette of paints, so he might continue his work in progress.

Ingrid, their maid of all work, stepped in from the back kitchen, bringing her a cup of tea and another for her father, just as he descended from his room above.

"Morning, Papa." Sophie handed him his palette and tea.

"Morning," he murmured, looking bleary-eyed and in need of a shave. He'd been up late the night before with a party of artist friends visiting from London.

He shuffled to his easel, positioned near the front window overlooking the Lynmouth harbor. There he sipped his tea and continued his portrait of Sir Thomas Acland, Baronet.

Sophie went to her own easel at the back of the studio and set down her teacup, preparing to continue painting the gown of Sir Thomas's wife. Flowing yards of silk in subtle tones of wine — burgundy in the shadows, to claret, to purplish-puce where sunshine had lightened the fabric. Her father had completed the fine detail work of Lady Acland's face, enlisting Sophie's help in adding liveliness to the woman's bright eyes. And now it fell to her to finish the tedious dress and background, according to his specifications.

She did not bother to pull shut the curtain that concealed her work area from the rest of the studio, as they would not open to the public for another hour. And she did not like to be shielded from her father's eyes any longer than necessary when Maurice was near.

Maurice O'Dell was the favored nephew of her father's second wife. He had taken the young man under his wing at his wife's request and had high hopes for him — saw him almost as the son he never had. Sophie could not deny the young man had talent, but he also had a quick tongue that could flatter and cut with equal skill, and had a way of looking at her that made her uneasy.

He appeared suddenly at her side and whispered, "I'm painting Miss Roe's hair today. But it isn't as pretty as yours."

It was the closest thing to a compliment she had ever received on her looks.

"If I were painting your hair, Sophie, I would use old gold, bright gold, and copper."

"What's that, Maurice?" her father interjected. "Old gold for Miss Roe's hair? You must be joking."

The outside door opened and a man walked in. Sophie looked up and caught her breath.

Before her stood the most handsome man she had ever seen. Slightly above average height and slender — his bearing graceful and confident. Wavy dark hair framed a striking face with fine features that were almost beautiful. Sophie was reminded of Guercino's painting of David, except this man's hair was not as long, and a day's growth of beard made him look more masculine than the harp-carrying youth in the portrait. He was in his late twenties or perhaps thirty and was dressed in the garb of a wealthy gentleman, though he disdained to wear a cravat, his

101

white shirt open at the neck beneath his coat and waistcoat.

"Ah, Mr. Overtree!" Her father beamed. "You've arrived early. We didn't expect you until tonight."

"An honor to see you again, sir."

Her father glanced over and gave a less-than-subtle jerk of his head, gesturing for her to close the curtain shielding her work area. He did not like to advertise the fact that she painted his backgrounds, especially to patrons or illustrious visitors.

Sophie drew the curtain but did not miss the knowing glint in Mr. Overtree's eyes.

The two men exchanged greetings and pleasantries and news of mutual acquaintances in the art world.

Then her father summoned her. "Sophie, come out here, if you please."

Sophie removed her apron and complied.

"Sophie, meet Mr. Overtree. Mr. Overtree, my daughter, Sophia." He added, "Mr. Overtree and I met in London, at a lecture of the Royal Academy of Arts."

"A pleasure to meet you, Miss Dupont," he said with an elegant bow, his golden-brown eyes brushing over her face.

He was polite in his address, but his expression revealed no particular interest. Men rarely gave her a second look. They seemed universally to skim over her painfully slender figure and pale coloring in favor of curvy, dark-haired beauties, like the lushly beautiful Countess of Blessington, who epitomized the feminine ideal and had artists vying for the privilege of painting her — her father and his contemporaries among them.

Had the visitor been less august, Mr. Dupont would probably have assigned Maurice or even Sophie the task of trudging up the steep path to their clutch of cliff-side cottages. But in this instance, her father said he would show Mr. Overtree the accommodations himself, having reserved their largest and best cottage for him.

Nothing was too much trouble, and he announced his assistant would carry his bags. Maurice frowned darkly at this but complied.

Her father gestured the man out the door, leaving his tea to cool and his paints to dry. Sophie sighed. She would have to begin all over again when he returned.

Later that afternoon, Sophie donned bonnet, pelisse, and gloves for her usual walk. It was the time of day she liked best. She never tired of watching the sunset from Castle Rock, a precipice high above the Bristol Channel. The wind up there would be brisk at this time of year, but she wrapped a muffler around her neck as she left, taking her sketchbook with her.

She walked at a steady pace up the steep, serpentine path. The Valley of Rocks lay nestled between two ridges of hills, dotted with huge stones piled atop one another like block towers left by giant children. Accustomed to the exercise, she ascended with little effort, her breathing only slightly taxed, to the headland above the valley. To the left, points of land fingered into the sea one after another. Before her, the blue sea to the horizon, and to the right, the faint line of the Welsh coast.

It was her favorite place on earth.

She set down her sketchbook and simply savored the view.

"So this is what all the fuss is about."

Startled by the voice, she turned. She'd heard no one approach over the wind.

It was Mr. Overtree. His gaze not on her but on the rocky fingers fading into the shimmering sunset.

"Your father suggested I walk out here, but I have long wanted to see it anyway, based on another artist's recommendation. Don't tell him I said so." He sent her a grin. "Thomas Gainsborough described Lynmouth as 'the most delightful place for a landscape painter this country can boast.' "

"I know. Why do you think my father began coming here in the first place?"

"Did he?"

She nodded. "He spent his honeymoon here."

"Your father?"

"No." She laughed. "Thomas Gainsborough. And the poet Percy Shelley — I met him here a few years ago."

Mr. Overtree inhaled, looking over the valley, the craggy rock formations, the sea. Then he asked, "It does beg to be painted, doesn't it?" He gestured behind her. "Is that your sketchbook lying against the rocks?"

"Oh . . . yes. I sketch a bit for my own pleasure."

"When you are not painting for your father, that is?" His brown eyes shone with humor.

"I only paint backgrounds and the like."

"And skillfully, by the looks of it."

"Thank you, but don't mention it. He prefers to keep it quiet."

He shrugged. "Very well."

Mr. Overtree didn't ask to see the drawings in her sketchbook, Sophie noticed. She didn't know whether to be relieved or slightly offended.

"He needn't be self-conscious, you know," he added. "Many painters have assistants. Though I thought that Maurice fellow was his."

"He is. Father is training him."

"To take over for you . . . or to marry you?"

She gaped. "Not to marry me, I assure you!"

"Only teasing." He grinned at her again, his eyes lingering on her face in a way that was partly studious and perhaps slightly admiring. In general, she detested when artists looked at her closely — noticing the long slope of her nose. Her thin face. Her thin . . . everything.

"So there is nothing going on between you and Mr. O'Dell?" Mr. Overtree asked.

"Nothing whatsoever."

"He seems to think there is."

"Then he has a vivid imagination."

Mr. Overtree said quietly, "Yes, I fear he does."

She again felt his eyes lingering on her profile, but when she glanced up, he shifted his gaze.

"Ah, the magic hour. . . ." he murmured.

Before them, the sun sunk low, sending shafts of golden sunlight over the sea, the land, over each of them.

"Yes," she breathed. "Why do you think I come out here almost every evening?"

"Because the sunset becomes you?"

She laughed and glanced at him shyly. "If it does, there are only the wild goats and gulls to notice."

"I hope you shan't mind some company while I'm here."

She met his earnest gaze. "Not at all. It isn't as though I own the place. I am willing to share, if you are."

"I am indeed."

She smiled at Mr. Overtree but quickly looked away. He was almost painfully handsome, not to mention charming. She would

106

be wise to guard her heart. A man like him was unlikely to take an interest in her.

Or so she'd thought.

Standing on deck, Sophie shook off her reverie and returned to reality, and to the small cabin she shared with the stranger she had married.

When their ship returned to the Plymouth docks, Stephen led the way to the nearest coaching inn and booked passage to Bath. While they waited in the parlour for their coach to be called, he wrote a few lines to his parents.

Unlike Sophie, he had not sent a letter to his family before leaving Lynmouth. He supposed he wished to shield himself from embarrassment if she backed out of their marriage at the last minute. Now that they'd returned to Plymouth as man and wife, he hoped a letter would give his parents time to lay aside their disappointment that he had not married some well-connected woman of fortune.

As a younger man, he had once thought he would marry someone known to them all. But after she directed her affections elsewhere — and war had wrought its changes — he'd given up the notion. Stephen thought his parents should be glad — if not shocked — that he had married at all, considering he had asserted for several years now that he had no plans to do so.

Dear Mamma and Papa,

I am writing to let you know that I have taken a wife, Miss Sophie Dupont, whom I met in the course of my travels to find Wesley. Unfortunately, Wesley had left for Italy before I reached Lynmouth, so I was unsuccessful in my mission to send him home.

I know my marriage will come as a surprise to you. But hopefully not an unhappy one. Because I have little time before I must rejoin my regiment, we were married on the Island of Guernsey. Miss Dupont's friend and neighbor, Mrs. Mavis Thrupton, acted as chaperone on the journey.

We travel first to Bath, so I may become acquainted with her father and his family. Then I shall bring her home to you. I trust you will welcome her warmly.

Sincerely,
Stephen

He blotted and sealed the letter, preparing it for the post. Would his parents welcome Sophie warmly? Somehow Stephen doubted it.

CHAPTER 7

On the journey to Bath, Sophie found Captain Overtree even quieter than usual and wondered if he dreaded the coming visit as much as she did. Or perhaps he was still suffering the ill effects of drink. The captain had insisted they call on her family before he returned to his regiment, to prove the husband she had written about was no fiction created to explain away a child as some wartime "widows" did in an attempt to establish respectability. He wanted no one to question the validity of their marriage. Besides, there was no point in delaying the visit, he asserted, as Bath lay between Plymouth and his family's estate.

She appreciated the sentiment but did not look forward to explaining their rushed marriage to her father and stepmother in person — or to pretending to be a happily married couple in front of them, even for a few days. She certainly hoped her father had received her letter, so the worst of the shock would have passed.

Beside the captain in the rocking carriage, Sophie lapsed into silence as well, concentrating on breathing deeply to keep her own nausea at bay.

Several hours later, the coachman directed the horses into the yard of the Westgate, an old coaching inn near the heart of the city. There a groom opened the door and offered his hand to help Sophie alight, her legs stiff after the long confinement.

Inhaling welcome fresh air, she looked across the courtyard to the Roman baths and Pump Room to gain her bearings.

Captain Overtree alighted beside her, bags in hand, and surveyed the busy innyard. "Shall we find a hack?"

"The house isn't far. And I, for one, long to walk, if you don't mind."

"Not at all."

She led the way north, up Lansdown Street. The tall, narrow terraced houses stood like books shelved side by side — white, with black wrought-iron gates.

She stopped before Number 6. "Here we are."

He shifted the bags to one hand and opened the gate for her. "Anything we need to talk about before we go in?"

"Well . . ." She hesitated. Should she warn him about her stepmother? The children?

The door opened, and her two little stepsisters dashed out, launching themselves at her legs.

"Sophie! What have you brought us?" six-year-old Martha asked.

Lyddie, the eldest at eight, eyed the captain warily. "Who is this man?"

Oh dear. Perhaps they had not yet received her letter.

Her father stepped out. "Sophie. Here you are, as promised. How relieved I am to see you. We only received your letter yesterday. I could not credit it." He looked up at the tall man beside her. "Captain Overtree, I take it?"

"Yes, sir." The captain held out his hand, and her father hesitated only a moment before shaking it.

"You look nothing like your brother."

"So I am often told."

Her father turned back to her. "And my Sophie. A married woman. Can it really be true?"

"I am, Papa." She held out her hand, showing him the ring on her finger.

He squinted at it. "Your mother's ring?"

"Yes. I thought she would like me to wear it."

"Yes. And so do I. Well, come in. Mrs. Dupont will wish to see you." He said the latter dutifully but without conviction.

Inside, they left their bags in the vestibule

and followed her father into the drawing room.

Augusta O'Dell Dupont sat on the sofa, her prized son, John, four years old and quite plump, beside her. The two little girls crowded around. Mrs. Dupont wore an ornate overdress atop her plain muslin, and a fresh cap in which to receive callers. Stiff, dark pin curls circled her forehead like a second cap.

Sophie neared as if approaching a queen about to sentence her to the tower.

"Hello. Allow me to introduce Captain Overtree. My . . . husband."

"Well, is he or isn't he?" her stepmother asked, her disapproving eyes snapping with questions.

"I am, madam," the captain replied in her stead. "And we have a copy of the marriage license to prove it."

"May I see it?"

Sophie blinked. "Why?"

In lieu of answering, the woman extended a long graceful hand.

Sophie pulled the license from her reticule, unfolded it, and handed it to her.

She skimmed it. "I cannot say I approve of your way of getting a husband," she said. "But everything seems to be in order. Guernsey, hmm? We shall keep that to ourselves."

She handed it back. "I would have ordered a finer dinner, had I more notice you were coming. As it is, you will have to make do with a plain family dinner of fish and vegetables. And it's too late to send Betsy for another bream. I trust you don't mind?"

"Not at all. I'm not very hungry. Captain Overtree may have mine."

"I suppose you will want a room to yourself. If you like, we can take Martha and Lyddie in with us for the night. How long do you plan to stay?"

Captain Overtree spoke up, the edge to his voice barely sheathed in civility. "You are all goodness, madam. But we don't wish to put you to any trouble. We shall remove to an inn, if you prefer."

"An inn? Good gracious, no. This is Sophie's home. Or it was."

Sophie said, "The girls may stay with us. We shall lay cushions and blankets on the floor. We don't mind, do we, Captain?"

He glanced at her, his smile stiff. "Not at all."

She turned away from his ironic gaze to address her father. "How goes the commission, Papa? Have you completed the portraits of the Miss Simons?"

He grimaced. "Not quite, my dear. I had hoped you would finish the backgrounds for me, but now . . . well. I am also struggling to capture the eldest Miss Simon. She is not as pretty as her sisters, unfortunately. I am trying to make her look as well as I can, while

113

keeping it reasonably accurate." He shrugged. "Though she is plain, the shape and brightness of her eyes gave her a certain comeliness. A liveliness, rather like the eyes of Lady Acland, if you recall."

"Yes, I do. Shall I see what I can do, Papa? If you don't like it, you can always paint over my changes."

He seemed about to agree, but his wife frowned and said, "My dear Mr. Dupont, this is an important commission. I hardly think you ought to let Sophie anywhere near it. The background is one thing, but the face, surely . . ."

Her father chewed his lip. "Perhaps your stepmother is right, Sophie. Let's not worry about it now. Tell us about your journey and the latest news of Lynmouth."

They spoke for a few minutes, and then her father showed the captain his studio and offered him a glass of something, which the captain declined. Later, they sat down together to a meager dinner in the cool, starched company of her stepmother and her quiet father.

Soon after, Mrs. Dupont announced it was the girls' bedtime. She clapped her hands, and the girls scurried off to clean their teeth and dress for bed. Sophie supposed it was their signal to retire for the night as well.

The small room, with its single bed, seemed even smaller with Captain Overtree's large commanding presence in one corner, arms crossed, watching her every move as she laid cushions, lap rug, and wool blanket on the floor.

"Is this for your sisters' comfort or for mine?"

"Which would you prefer?"

The housemaid came in to help Sophie with her buttons and stays. When Sophie asked her to step into the small dressing room — little larger than a closet — to do so, the woman looked at her askance. She had not been so modest before.

A few minutes later, when she stepped out in nightdress and dressing gown tied tight, the captain's gaze swept over her without change in expression. He finished washing hands and face and cleaning his teeth at the washstand, then followed her example and stepped into the dressing room to change as she had.

Stephen wedged himself into the closet-sized room with his kit. He was glad Edgar had insisted on packing a nightshirt for him. Stephen didn't usually bother with the long — and in his mind, effeminate — garment. After his years in the army, he'd become accustomed to sleeping bare-chested or in an untucked shirt and clean pair of breeches — ready to leap up and throw on his uniform coat at a moment's notice. But considering he would be sharing the room with little girls, he would have to remember to thank the overeager footman who served as his valet.

The moments alone in the tiny room were a welcome respite. He was relieved to be out of the evil stepmother's company. Poor Sophie. No wonder she went with her father to remote Devonshire whenever she could. Mrs. Dupont's cold dark eyes and blunt features had put him in mind of her nephew, Maurice. The dozens of spiral curls circling her head? Of Medusa herself.

Perhaps he was being unkind. Weariness and hunger made him irritable. He was tired from the night before and still hungry after that skimpy meal. Seeing the dismissive, patronizing way that woman treated Sophie irritated him as well.

Her father seemed a mild man. Slender and handsome with fair thinning hair and a long aristocratic face, not unlike his daughter's. He dressed well and wore a ring on his small finger. That affectation irritated Stephen too. He really should try to get some sleep. But he doubted he would manage it, in such close quarters with Sophie and her stepsisters. Three snoring officers? Not a problem. Three giggling females? Heaven help him.

He had just returned to the bedchamber when the little girls bounded inside, the eldest bouncing on her knees on the bed, and little Martha sitting atop the makeshift pallet on the floor.

"Where will you sleep, Captain?" Lyddie asked.

"Excellent question," he replied.

"We always sleep with Sophie when she's home. She tells the best stories. Don't you, Sophie?"

He looked at her, brow quirked. "I should like to hear one of her stories."

"Oh! Tell the one about the wolf and the sheep, Sophie. No! I know. The one where we are little lambs hiding in a cave."

Martha jumped into the bed next to Sophie and nodded vigorously, smiling up at her in anticipation.

"Very well. Though the captain will think us very silly, no doubt." Sophie tucked her feet under the bedclothes, a girl on either side. "Three little lambs were lost in the wood," she began. "Suddenly they heard someone, or something, coming. 'Quick. Let's hide!' the eldest lamb cried, and all three ducked into a nearby cave."

Martha pulled the blanket over their heads.

Now Sophie's voice came slightly muffled by wool. "Heavy paw treads approached. Oh no! Is it a wolf? Have we hidden in a wolf's den?"

Stephen interrupted, "There hasn't been a wolf in southern England for two hundred years . . ."

"A bear, then."

Martha poked her head out. "You're the bear. A big, hungry bear."

"Don't forget grumpy," Lyddie added.

"A big, hungry, grumpy bear," Sophie repeated.

He crossed his arms again. "Bears have been extinct here even longer."

"You're no fun."

"So I have been told."

"Shh . . . Don't make a sound. Maybe he'll pass by."

"Now what sort of tactic is that to elude attack by a larger, stronger enemy?" Stephen asked, mock serious. "Hiding in silence or making little frightened peeps will not do. I say the three lambs must roar like lions, or French cavalrymen. And scare the hungry predator away."

Lyddie and Martha obliged with their best roars.

"That's better. Now I promise not to eat you."

The door opened and Mrs. Dupont's disapproving face appeared. "What, pray, is going on in here?"

Sophie lowered the blanket, looking — appropriately enough — sheepish.

"Sophie was just telling us a story," Lyddie said. "The captain was a grumpy bear and tried to eat us, but we roared like French lions and chased him away."

Mrs. Dupont frowned. "Well, do keep it

118

down. Baby John is sleeping. And don't keep the girls up all night, Sophie. Or I shall be the one left with grumpy children to contend with come morning."

"Sorry."

The door closed again.

"Well, girls, time to settle down," Sophie said gently.

The little girls complied, nestling in bed together with Sophie.

Stephen stretched out on the cushions on the floor. The bright moon outside the window shone on Sophie in the middle, one arm protectively over little Martha. It caused a tender ache inside of him that he did not like. Such tender feelings would not help him. They would only make it more difficult to stay detached, to leave her, to focus on the task ahead.

He awoke sometime later, the room still moonlit. He glanced at the bed. The two little girls slept peacefully, but Sophie was not there. He frowned, worried she had taken ill.

He rose, tied a dressing gown over his nightshirt, and slipped into his shoes. He let himself from the bedchamber and crept quietly downstairs and from room to room, looking for her. He did not find her in the drawing room or dining parlour and saw no light in the privy behind the house. Worry mounted. He turned the corner and saw candlelight seeping from a door left partially ajar. Her father's studio. He should have guessed. He walked silently toward it and peeked inside.

There sat Sophie on a stool before an easel, surrounded by a half dozen candles and a wall sconce nearby. The female in the painting appeared to be the unfortunate Miss Simon with the troublesome eyes. A swath of fabric lay across a chair back, and Sophie glanced at it now and again as she painted the woman's gown.

After a few minutes, she rose and began cleaning her brushes. Then she paused, rag and brush in hand and simply stood there, staring at the woman's face. At her troublesome eyes, he guessed. He was no expert, but there did seem to be something unnatural about them. Would she ignore her stepmother's edict and attempt to improve them anyway? She approached the easel, hesitated, and then turned away. Apparently not.

He inched open the door with a small creak. She gasped and whirled at the sound.

He held up a placating palm. "Sorry. I tried to be quiet and not startle you."

She laid down the brush and rag, picked up a candlestick, and hurried to the door, forcing him to back from the threshold. She closed the door behind herself, clearly not wanting him to see her work.

"Was there something you wanted, Captain?" she asked, looking uneasy.

"I just wanted to make sure you were all right. I was concerned when I woke to find you gone."

"I am well, as you see. I will finish cleaning up and be back up in a few minutes. You needn't wait."

In the flickering candlelight, Stephen noticed a smudge of paint on her cheek. It looked oddly endearing. He resisted the urge to wipe it away, and to stroke the plait of hair draped over her shoulder while he was at it.

Keep your distance, Overtree . . .

"Very well." He turned, and returned to his solitary bed.

In the morning, Stephen arose early, as was his habit, and breakfasted alone. He then donned his greatcoat and slipped from the house. He walked around Bath to see something of the city, and to inquire about hiring a private chaise to take them on to Overtree Hall in a few days. Then, as he often did, he found a place to pray. He spent a peaceful half hour in the Bath Abbey, asking God for wisdom, kindness, and self-control in his relationship with his new wife. And for patience in dealing with his in-laws.

When he returned to the house late morning, he came upon Sophie and Mrs. Dupont in tense conversation in the drawing room. His defenses immediately rose, and he stepped through the door without knocking.

"Am I interrupting something?"

"Ah. Captain Overtree. I was just asking Sophie what my nephew thought of your sudden nuptials. Did you not think to ask his permission?"

"No," he answered without hesitation.

"I realize he is young. But he was Sophie's nearest male relation in Lynmouth. Did you honestly not even consider asking him?"

Stephen pursed his lips and peered upward as though in serious thought. "I remember that I considered throttling him at one point, but asking his permission?" He shook his head. "Not once."

Apparently, he should have prayed harder.

Sophie glanced up and gave him a secret smile.

He guessed her stepmother would likely retaliate with more hurtful barbs later. But for the moment he relished the minor victory, and Sophie's lovely smile.

Sophie had been embarrassed by the meager dinner their first night in Bath. A man the size of the captain was no doubt used to eating heartier meals. He'd said nothing however, though she'd thought she heard his stomach growl when he'd lain down on the cushions. How odd it had been to share her and her stepsisters' bedchamber with a man — and a veritable stranger in the bargain.

The dinner fare their second night was

thankfully more satisfying — though the same could not be said for the conversation.

"When my girls are a little older, they shall have music lessons," Mrs. Dupont said as they finished their pudding. "Learn to sing and play the pianoforte or harp. Fine needlework too. And French, perhaps. All the accomplishments. Poor Sophie never had the opportunity. Her father let her potter about with his paints and tag along in his studio for hours on end when she ought to have been learning or doing something useful. She helps with the mending, when I ask, though she is not a dab-hand with anything finer. She speaks some Dutch and Italian, though to what advantage I don't know. She is good with the children, I own. But now . . ."

She halted her litany and asked, "Where will she live when you rejoin your regiment, Captain? We haven't much room here, but this is her home, and she is helpful, in her way. . . ."

The captain's eyes glinted. "I am afraid that will not be possible, ma'am. My wife and I journey to Overtree Hall next to meet my family. Sophie is a married woman now. Certainly you can appreciate that she will no longer have the time to spend on your mending and child-minding."

He smiled and continued on casually, "And who knows? Lord willing, she may have her own children one day. Have I mentioned twins run in the Overtree family? You will have no trouble accommodating us all, I trust?"

Sophie pressed her lips together to keep from protesting. Or laughing.

Mrs. Dupont blanched. "Here? Heavens no. Sophie is always welcome, of course. But we have our hands — and rooms — full as it is."

"Then how fortunate that there is plenty of room for us at Overtree Hall. In fact, we shall depart tomorrow."

"So soon?" Mr. Dupont asked, brows high.

Sophie was surprised as well.

"I am afraid so. I must rejoin my regiment in less than a week now, and want to have time to introduce Sophie to my family and to familiarize her with the estate and parish. You understand."

"Of . . . course."

Sophie spoke up, "I'm sorry, Papa, if I am leaving you in the lurch. If you need me in the studio, perhaps after Captain Overtree leaves to rejoin his regiment, I might —"

"Your father doesn't *need* you, Sophie," Mrs. Dupont retorted. "What a high opinion we have of ourselves. He is perfectly capable on his own. After all, he was a renowned portrait painter while you were still in pinafores. Is that not right, my dear?"

Mr. Dupont hesitated. "Well, of course. But Sophie has always been a help to me. Preparing paints and canvases and whatnot."

124

Captain Overtree began to protest, "She does far more —"

Sophie squeezed his hand beneath the table to forestall him.

"And I have been happy to do so, Papa. But as Mrs. Dupont says, you don't need me. And besides, you have Maurice now. My place is with . . . my husband."

"But thank you for understanding and for hosting us," the captain added, keeping hold of her hand as he rose. "We shall trouble you no longer."

He led her from the dining parlour and started toward their bedchamber, but Sophie tugged his hand in the opposite direction, down a quiet passage. She paused before a painting of her mother from when she was young, with fair hair, a broad forehead, button nose, and blue-green eyes.

"I wanted you to see this. My mother, right before she married Papa."

"She's beautiful."

"Yes."

"You look like her. Did your father paint this?"

"No. Look at her eyes . . . A Dutch painter you would not have heard of."

He looked at her instead. "How do you stand to hear your stepmother belittle your contributions and abilities?"

She shrugged. "It's nothing really. She's right. My help is trivial. I am a dabbler —

that's all. Papa is the real artist."

He shook his head. "Your father takes you for granted."

"Please don't speak poorly of Papa. I love my stepsiblings, of course, but really . . . Papa is the only family I have."

He held her gaze and pressed her hand. "Not anymore."

Sophie's heart warmed, but she looked away from his earnest gaze. "Come. The girls will be up soon and want their story."

Reaching the bedchamber, Sophie saw the girls had not yet arrived. She rang for the maid and ducked into the dressing closet, taking down her hair and plaiting it herself while she waited. The housemaid appeared and helped her undress, then stayed to tidy up the tiny room and hang up Sophie's things.

Sophie stepped out alone and saw Captain Overtree's bare back as he pulled his shirt over his head. The muscles in his arms and shoulders rippled as he did so, and his back was smooth and taut. He turned at the sound of the door, and her gaze was drawn to his chest — masculine muscles, coarse hair, and a scar running shoulder to chest.

"Sorry," he said. "I thought I had time to change before you returned."

Sophie swallowed. "No, I'm sorry. That is . . . I . . . finished early."

She averted her eyes, and he quickly pulled

his nightshirt over his head. She wanted to ask about the scar but feared raising a painful subject.

The door banged open and the girls flew in, jumping into bed as usual. "Tell us one of your magic paintbrush stories, Sophie."

"Oh yes, do!"

Captain Overtree raised his brows. "What, pray, is a magic paintbrush story?"

Lyddie supplied, "We tell Sophie what to paint with her magic paintbrush, and whatever we say comes to life, and she tells us a story about it."

"Sophie makes them up as she goes," Sophie said modestly. "And some of them are very poor indeed."

"Not poor. We like them. Don't we, Martha?"

Martha nodded vigorously, curls bouncing.

"I don't know that I should. Your Mamma wants us to be quiet."

"We'll be quiet. Please!"

"Mrs. Overtree," the captain said, sitting cross-legged on the cushions. "I for one would enjoy hearing such a story."

Sophie felt her cheeks warm to hear him call her by that title.

Lyddie smiled. "Me too."

"Me three!"

"Shh. Very well. They're just little made-up ditties. But if you insist, I shall try. You all

must help me. Once upon a time there was
a . . ."

"Beautiful princess!"

Lyddie frowned. "Martha, you always say
that."

"Then how about a plain princess instead?"
Sophie suggested. "A more . . . realistic tale?"

"Very *welllll* . . ." Martha pouted.

"Once upon a time there was a plain princess. One day, while she was . . . ?"

"Outside in the garden."

"One day when she was outside in the
garden, she took her easel and paints with
her. She painted the colorful flowers and
fruits she saw there, wishing she were half as
beautiful as just one of the most ordinary
blooms. Suddenly, whom should she meet,
but. . . ."

"A big hungry bear!" the six-year-old cried.

Captain Overtree gave the child a lopsided
grin. "Why am I not surprised?"

"Oh, Martha. Not that again."

Sophie nodded. "That's fine, Martha. She
met a big hungry bear. So, thinking quickly,
she picked up her magic paintbrush and
painted a . . . ?"

Lyddie stole a shy glance at him and said,
"A brave soldier."

Sophie hesitated only a moment. "Right.
Good idea. She quickly painted a brave soldier."

"A cap'in!" Martha insisted.

"A brave captain. In a red coat, and a . . . ?" Sophie hesitated, encircling her head with her hands.

"A black hat," he supplied.

"And a sword!" Martha added.

Sophie bit her lip. Were they to have violence right there in the little girls' bedchamber, in one of her princess stories? She decided to ignore the suggestion. "The brave soldier came to life, leapt from the canvas, faced the snarling bear and . . ."

She looked nervously at the captain, hoping he would follow her lead, wincing in anticipation of a bloody stab or decapitation.

Apparently ignoring her in favor of their captive audience, he said, "And thinking quickly, the soldier drew his sword and from the painting cut a handful of fruit, which had become real, and offered it to the bear in exchange for the lady's life. The bear gobbled down the fruit, belched, and slunk back into the wood for a nap."

Martha giggled. Lyddie pressed a hand over her mouth in delight.

"The end," Sophie finished in relief.

The girls clapped.

Sophie looked at the captain. He met her gaze, eyes warm with humor.

At dawn the next morning, Stephen was awoken by quiet footsteps. He saw Sophie tiptoe into the room, gingerly lift the bedclothes, and slip into bed with her stepsisters. He guessed she'd been down working in her father's studio again.

He waited until her breathing had slowed into a regular, relaxed rhythm, then rose and quickly dressed. Curious, he slipped from the room and down the stairs.

He inched open the studio door, expecting to find the room empty. Instead Mr. Dupont stood there in dressing gown and slippers, chin propped in his hand.

He glanced over. "Ah, Captain. Good morning."

"Mr. Dupont."

"Do you see the eyes? How alive they look? How natural?"

Stephen crossed the room and stood beside him. "Yes," he agreed. He could not have verbalized specifically what had been changed, but it seemed a marked improvement over the face he'd glimpsed before.

Mr. Dupont mused aloud, "Why is it, Captain, that we only appreciate what we have after it is gone? If only the thought of losing something or someone would cause us to value it while it's right under our nose."

Stephen nodded. He was already thinking about — and dreading — losing Sophie. "I understand how you feel, sir."

Not removing his eyes from the painting, Mr. Dupont said quietly, "Promise me you will take good care of her, Captain."

Stephen drew in a long breath. "I would love nothing more than to make that promise, sir, but I cannot. I will very soon have to leave her. I have rarely wished for the luxury of staying at hearth and home more than I do now. I cannot. However, I assure you that my family will take good care of her. She will have everything she needs at Overtree Hall. The best doctor in the county lives not two miles from us."

Mr. Dupont turned to frown at him. "Doctor? Why on earth should Sophie need a doctor?"

Stephen inwardly cursed his undisciplined mouth. "I only meant . . . should she have some cold or trifling malady . . ."

The man's eyes measured his. "Ah. Well. Considering your talk of twins yesterday, I guess there may be more to the story, but I don't think I ought to ask."

The man was sharper than he seemed. Stephen felt his ears heat at the implication of his father-in-law's words, as though he had done something to be embarrassed about. He did not defend himself. He would gladly take the blame if he could.

Along with her favorite drawing and painting supplies, Sophie packed her best clothes and two evening gowns she had not bothered to take with her to rustic Lynmouth. She imagined she would need her finest things to pass muster at Overtree Hall. She surveyed the room and her dressing chest, wondering what else she should take with her, having no idea how long it might be until she returned to visit.

When she was ready, the captain carried her extra valise as well as his own, and together they went downstairs to the vestibule, where the Duponts had assembled to bid them farewell.

"This Overtree Hall," Mrs. Dupont began. "It is not some remote place far off the beaten path, is it? Not some gated castle or walled estate that we could not visit at some point to assure ourselves Sophie is well looked after?"

Sophie felt embarrassed at the woman's presumption. "But . . . remember I have never even been there myself. It is not my prerogative to invite others."

"Nonsense. You are their daughter-in-law. And if you take up residence there as Captain Overtree seems determined you shall, then we have every right to visit. We are your family. They cannot object to that."

Captain Overtree spoke up. "Of course not. If you wanted to visit for a few days as we have here, you would be most . . . My family would no doubt graciously receive you."

Augusta Dupont's eyes flashed with knowing irritation. Though she was not a pleasant woman, no one could doubt her quick intelligence.

She smiled thinly. "Remember, Captain. Though our acquaintance with you is of short duration, my husband has known your brother for above two years, and hosted him in Lynmouth for many weeks at a time."

"My brother is not often at home," the captain said. "But as you say, Mr. Dupont would of course be more than welcome."

CHAPTER 8

They traveled north in a hired chaise and into
the rolling countryside of rural Gloucestershire. Through the window, Sophie saw
meadows dotted with sheep, charming villages, and stone cottages with thatched roofs.
When they passed through the bustling village of Moreton-en-Marsh and into smaller
Wickbury, Captain Overtree announced they
were almost there. Leaving the cluster of
shops behind, they rounded a bend and traveled up a tree-lined lane. Ahead stood a tall,
old manor of golden-blond stone, gabled all
around. Just to the right of the house, a
battlemented church tower rose through the
trees.

At the end of the lane, they passed through
an arched gateway of the same stone and into
a courtyard. From the carriage window, the
captain pointed out the stables on the left
and churchyard on the right. "And this" —
he pointed upward toward the imposing four
stories — "is Overtree Hall."

Closer now, she admired the full-height bays on either side of the manor's front door, and banks of mullioned windows. He and Wesley had grown up here? How small and ordinary he must have found their terraced house in Bath, not to mention her father's studio in Lynmouth. She felt more out of her element than ever.

The coach halted on the pea-gravel drive. A footman strode out to help them alight, and the captain gestured for her to precede him up the few stairs and through the door, held open by yet another liveried footman.

From the vestibule they passed through an ornate oak screen into a two-story hall with a musicians' gallery high above one end. It seemed familiar to Sophie for some reason, as though she had seen it before.

The footman took their coats and informed the captain that his parents were in the white parlour. "Shall I announce you and your guest, sir?"

"This is my *wife,* Edgar. Mrs. Overtree."

The young man's eyebrows rose high. "Mrs. Overtree!" He blushed and bowed.

She smiled at the nervous young man. She knew how he felt. She was nervous too.

"And no need to announce us, thank you," the captain added. "I know the way."

The captain led her across the hall, down a corridor, and into a nearby room. For all its windows, the dark paneling throughout

135

seemed to drain the light from the place, giving it a grim, melancholy feel. Or perhaps Sophie's opinion was colored by her anxiety.

Inside the small parlour, a middle-aged man and woman set aside their books and rose from matching armchairs.

"Stephen, welcome home," his father said. "And this must be the Miss Dupont you wrote about. Forgive me — Mrs. Overtree. How do you do."

"Sophie, these are my parents. Mr. and Mrs. Overtree."

Sophie curtsied and gripped her hands to keep them from trembling. She had imagined meeting Wesley's parents one day, but never under these circumstances.

Mr. Overtree was a thin man with smallish eyes and long nose set in a mild, studious face. His brown hair was shot through with silver, especially at the side-whiskers. His wife was a tall, handsome woman. Her face was gentle and attractive, though softened with age, her eyes cool and cautious.

"Is it Sophie, or Sophia . . . ?" she asked.

"My given name is Sophia Margaretha Dupont, but I have been Sophie for as long as I can remember."

"Margaretha? That is an unusual pronunciation, is it not?"

"It's Dutch. My mother's family was from Holland."

"Interesting. And your father is . . .

French?"

"Only distantly."

The captain offered, "Sophie's father is a portrait painter of some renown. Claude Dupont."

"Dupont. I believe I recall Wesley mentioning the name," his father said. "So since you were not successful in finding Wesley, you found a wife instead?" The man smiled, attempting a joke, but the smile did not reach his eyes.

"You must forgive us," Mrs. Overtree added. "We have only just received your letter and are still struggling to credit the news."

"It is quite true, Mamma, I assure you."

An older man with excellent posture came striding into the room. "Stephen, my boy. Welcome back. I hear congratulations are in order."

"Thank you, sir." He turned to her. "Sophie, this is my grandfather, Colonel Horton. Sir, my . . . Mrs. Overtree."

"How do you do, my dear. How do you do." The older man's smile was warm and genuine. His skin was weathered, his grey hair thinning, but he was still a handsome man.

He clapped Stephen's shoulder. "Decided to take the plunge with this fellow, did you? Brave woman. I applaud your courage." His eyes twinkled.

"I am afraid you have quite shocked your mother and me," Mr. Overtree said with an uneasy glance at his wife. "I never expected something so impetuous from you, Stephen. Sounds like something Wesley would do."

The captain answered coolly, "Yes, it does."

Colonel Horton beamed at his grandson. "I don't find it so shocking. Passion runs in the family. When we see what we want, nothing stops us — ay, my boy?"

"Something like that." The captain turned to his mother. "I don't want to put you to any trouble. I thought we might give Sophie one of the guest rooms. Or she could have my room, and I shall —"

"Not a bit of it," Colonel Horton said. "It's all decided. You two shall have my rooms." He turned to Sophie and explained, "I lost my dear wife, you see, these three years gone. I don't need all that space, or two dressing rooms, just for me. It's time."

"No, Grandfather, I won't put you out of your apartment."

"Already done. I have moved my kit into your room. The maids are still cleaning, but all shall be in order shortly, Mrs. Hill assures me."

"Really, there is no need," Captain Overtree protested. "Sophie would probably sleep more soundly in one of the guest rooms. Without me, that is. I snore terribly."

"Oh? Since when?" his mother asked.

Sophie wondered if he protested more for her sake or his.

"I am restless at night," he went on. "All my years with the regiment, I suppose. Camping in dangerous places. I'd hate to keep her awake. . . ."

"Nonsense! You two are newly wed," his grandfather insisted. "Plenty of time to sleep later."

His mother added, "You must grow accustomed to one another eventually. Besides, Miss Blake may wish to stay, with her father gone to town so frequently. And one never knows when your Mr. Keith might turn up. So all our rooms are accounted for. Besides, your grandfather has already gone to quite a bit of effort to sort through and box up his things, and I helped with Mamma's."

"It's all right, my . . . Captain," Sophie spoke up. "You are kind to think of me, but I am sure I shall sleep perfectly well. Besides, it shall only be —" She broke off. She had been about to say it would only be for a few days, but what sort of bride would eagerly anticipate her new husband's imminent departure? Instead she finished lamely, "It shall only take a day or two to grow accustomed to my new surroundings."

The captain sent her a sidelong glance, then said to his grandfather, "I . . . don't know what to say, sir."

The older man grinned. "Thank you will suffice. Your boyhood bed isn't much wider than an army cot. You shall thank me in the

139

morning, I don't doubt." He winked at his grandson and slapped his other shoulder.

Sophie felt her neck heat at the implication. Everyone else ignored it.

"That's settled then," Mrs. Overtree said, injecting a cheerful note into her voice. "You traveled without a maid, Mi . . ." She hesitated. "How strange. I don't know what to call you. I am afraid I shall struggle to call you Mrs. Overtree, which has been my name for ages."

"Two Mrs. Overtrees under one roof," the colonel said. "What a bounty of blessings."

"Please, call me Sophie," she offered.

"Very well." Mrs. Overtree stepped to the wall and pulled a cord. In a few moments one of the footmen appeared. "James, please see that Captain and Mrs. Overtree's baggage is carried to the blue bedchamber, if you please. And ask Libby to attend the new Mrs. Overtree. She hasn't a maid of her own."

Captain Overtree glanced around the parlour. "Where is Kate?"

"I believe she is with Miss Blake at Windmere. You must realize that not everyone will be happy about the news, Stephen."

Sophie bit her lip. Did she mean Stephen's sister would not be happy about their marriage, or this neighbor, Miss Blake? She thought again of hearing the captain murmur the name "Jenny" in his sleep. Was Miss Blake's given name Jenny? Might he have planned to marry her? Sophie hoped not. Would it be worse than learning his own sister disapproved the match? She was not sure.

"That is unfortunate," the captain replied. "But the opinion of others was not the primary factor in my decision to marry."

"No? And what was?" his mother asked.

"Well, it will be time for dinner before we know it," the colonel interrupted. "Perhaps we should let these two go up and get settled."

Mrs. Overtree sent her father a knowing glance, then drew herself up. "Quite right, Papa. No doubt they will wish to rest before changing for dinner."

The captain led the way up the stairs and along the corridor. "I'm sorry about that. I had not anticipated this maneuver of Grandfather's."

"It is very kind of him, really. He naturally assumes we would . . . wish to be together."

"I must say, you are handling this well." He opened the door. "Remember, it will only be for a few days."

She reminded herself of that fact by the moment.

The room was large and lovely but somewhat formal, with ornate oak furniture, floral draperies, and bed-curtains of primrose and green.

Stephen looked around. "Yes, I can see why Grandfather thought you might like this room. I am surprised he left it furnished to Grandmother's taste even after she passed away."

"Are you? Apparently, he was quite devoted to her."

"Yes, he was. He is."

Along with a four-poster bed, there were two armchairs, a desk, dressing table, cheval mirror, and — as the captain discreetly pointed out — a hidden commode.

"There are his and hers dressing rooms with separate, outside entrances for valet and lady's maid. Here is yours."

She followed him to the adjoining door and peeked inside. The small room had been overtaken by wardrobes, built-in gown drawers, and deep shelves for bandboxes. There was barely enough space to turn around inside, let alone change clothes. No wonder the dressing table and long mirror remained in the bedchamber itself.

He gestured toward the opposite side of the room. "Mine is not so crammed. And it has a decent sofa. I can sleep there for the time being."

For the time being? Why had he phrased it like that? Did he anticipate things between them would change in future — especially when he'd said he didn't think they *had* a future?

Perhaps she should have objected, insisted he share the bed, but she did not.

A maid scratched on the door and entered, bobbing a curtsy. "Ma'am. Sir. May I help you unpack? Or would you like to rest first?"

"Rest. Definitely," Sophie answered.

"Very good, ma'am. I'll come back in an hour to help you dress."

"Thank you . . . Libby, was it?"

"Yes, ma'am."

When she had gone, the captain went into the other dressing room and Sophie lay down atop the bed. She thought she would be too nervous to sleep but soon nodded off. Lately, it seemed, she was always sleepy.

Libby returned as promised and helped her change for dinner. Sophie chose the less wrinkled of the evening gowns she had brought from Bath, hoping it was not terribly out of style.

As Libby laced her into it, Sophie thanked heaven for the current fashion of high waistlines that came in under the bosom before belling out wide and nearly shapeless past the ankles. Oh, the many indulgences that could be hidden under such frocks.

Then she sat at the dressing stool, while Libby brushed out and repinned her hair. Sophie wondered what Stephen and Wesley's sister would be like. She imagined her tall and imposing like Captain Overtree and his mother, and beautiful like Wesley. She felt intimidated at the thought.

A soft knock sounded, and the dressing room door inched open. There stood Captain Overtree, looking masculine and almost handsome in evening dress. If only he would let someone cut his hair and tame those unruly side-whiskers.

"Ah. Still getting ready, I see. Unfortunately, this is as good as I get, so I will head down, unless you prefer I wait for you?"

"I would like to go down with you," she said. "I am nearly ready. Right, Libby?"

"Last pin, ma'am. There you are."

Sophie rose and turned to him. "I hope I don't embarrass you."

"Impossible. You look . . . terrified."

A burst of nervous laughter escaped her. "Not very gallant of you."

He offered her his arm. His strong, steady arm. And she decided she appreciated that more than a dozen flowery words.

Drawing strength from his calm confidence, she walked beside him down the stairs and into the anteroom where his family gathered before dinner.

Mr. Overtree and Colonel Horton, also in dark evening attire, stood together near the hearth, heads bent in low conversation. Mrs. Overtree stood near the door, looking elegant in deep claret silk and a lovely ruby necklace. Her cool gaze swept Sophie head to toe.

The woman formed a vague little smile,

which left little doubt in Sophie's mind that she found her daughter-in-law's gown lacking. Or perhaps her daughter-in-law in general.

A young dark-haired woman rose from the sofa, eyes lighting up, a smile breaking over her dainty face.

"Stephen!" She hurried across the room and threw her arms around her much taller brother.

He stooped to receive her embrace with comfortable familiarity. "Hello, Kate. How are you? Allow me to introduce —"

Ignoring his formal opening, the young woman turned to her, all smiles. "And you must be Sophie. I am so happy to meet you! You can't imagine. Stephen has long professed himself a bachelor, but I knew better. And here you are!"

She pressed a kiss to Sophie's cheek, and Sophie was stunned to feel tears sting her eyes. Her warm greeting was sweet relief after the reserved reception from Stephen's parents.

"Welcome, welcome, a hundred times welcome. How jolly it will be to have another young lady about the place. Miss Blake comes often, of course, but . . . Oh, you don't know Miss Blake yet. I shall have to bring her round tomorrow."

"Give Sophie time to grow accustomed to the rest of us first, Kate," the captain said.

"We don't want to scare her away."

"Scare her away? As if we could, silly. She is your wife. And I can't wait to hear all about how you two met and your whirlwind court-ship."

"Kate, I don't think —"

The butler opened the dining room door and announced, "Dinner is served."

Relief. Saved by the butler.

The meal passed more smoothly than Ste-phen would have guessed. He'd been worried his mother would begin interrogating Sophie on her background and family connections before the fish course. Instead, the conversa-tion remained innocuous, with Kate monopo-lizing Sophie's attention, taking it upon herself to tell her all about the parish and their neighbors — whom they dined with and whom they did not, and the vicar, and the church, and so on. Stephen felt his heart surge with affection — and gratitude — for his much younger sister.

At one point, their mother reprimanded, "Katherine, do pause in your chatter long enough to eat your dinner."

"And to breathe . . ." their father added wryly.

Kate dutifully nibbled a bite and then dove right in again. Her cheerful chatter left Ste-phen free to converse with his father and grandfather, and to hear the parish news and what he had missed on the estate. Lambing was coming on soon, and they'd hired an extra few lads to keep watch over the flocks. Jenson was busy repairing the crumbled stone fence on the west boundary, and the farrier was concerned about Grandfather's old horse, Valiant.

He glanced across the table at Sophie, who ate absently while smiling in apparent pleasure at his sister, now and again asking a clarifying question or laughing softly at something the girl said.

Maybe this wouldn't be so difficult after all. . . .

Sophie breathed a sigh of relief as dinner drew to a close — too soon, she realized, when Mrs. Overtree asked her and Kate to join her in the white parlour while the men smoked and drank port.

Stephen partook of neither, she knew, except for his one lapse on their wedding night. And she found herself wishing he would excuse himself from the men and stay with her. She was surprised at her reticence to leave his company. Odd that the man who still intimidated her seemed safer than his mother. The old saying went through her mind, *Better the devil you know than the one you don't. . . .*

Kate plopped down onto the sofa beside her. "I want to hear every detail of his proposal, but I'll wait until he's here, so I can see him turn bright red."

"Does he blush? I would not have guessed it."

"You're right. He probably won't. Still, it will be amusing to see him squirm a bit."

Mrs. Overtree rubbed a finger over her brow. "Katherine, that is enough foolishness for now. You have monopolized Sophie's attention quite long enough. Now, please play something quiet and soothing and give my poor nerves a rest."

"Very well, Mamma." Kate rose. "But don't tell any secrets while I'm out of earshot." She dutifully went to the pianoforte and began playing a sweet, simple melody.

Mrs. Overtree sighed. "Much better. Now, Sophie, do tell me more about yourself. Your mother is . . . ?"

"She passed away. Seven . . . no, nearly eight years ago now. It's hard to believe it has been so long."

"And your father remarried? I heard you mention young sisters."

"Yes. My father married a widow with three children. I have a four-year-old stepbrother and two stepsisters, aged six and eight."

The woman's brows rose. "Such young children — at their ages?"

"Yes, well, my stepmother is some ten years younger than my father."

"I see. And your father is an artist. Would I

have seen any of his work?"

Interesting way to probe into his prominence. "I could not say, Mrs. Overtree. He has painted several distinguished people in London, Bath, and elsewhere. Sir Thomas Acland, for example. And he teaches and mentors younger painters, like your eldest son."

"Wesley is beyond needing teachers now. Quite a natural talent, that one. But yes, we paid for the best masters and academies in his youth. And now he journeys to Italy again, no doubt to increase his skill. He studied there, you know. Several years ago."

"Ah," Sophie said noncommittally, though Wesley had told her a great deal about his time there.

"Your father is successful, then?"

"I would say so. He isn't wealthy, but the commissions keep arriving and he even on occasion must turn down requests. So yes, he does as well as any painter without a court appointment can expect."

"I am surprised he thinks it wise to turn down commissions, if he is, as you say, not wealthy."

Sophie forced a smile. "He has taken on an assistant — a promising young painter, related to his wife. So he hopes to increase his capacity soon."

Mrs. Overtree nodded her understanding, then raised a dismissive hand. "Well, enough

149

of that. We don't want to talk about business, do we?"

She had been the one to bring it up, but Sophie did not remind her of that.

"Have you been to London?" Mrs. Overtree asked.

"With my father, yes. Several times." But not to participate in the season, Sophie thought, though she did not clarify. Instead she asked, "You have been there, I imagine?"

"Yes, but not in years. Mr. Overtree's health prohibits us."

"Ah. I am sorry to hear it."

She waved away Sophie's sympathy and continued her questions. "And who are your father's people — your family? Would I have heard of them?"

"Unlikely. His father was a printmaker who married a vicar's daughter. My mother's parents were from Holland, as I mentioned, but I don't know much more about them."

"Why not?"

"They died before I was born, but I gather they didn't approve of their daughter's marriage and severed all ties with her."

"I understand. Sometimes parents must take a hard line when children stray."

Yes, Janet Horton Overtree no doubt empathized with Sophie's disapproving ancestors. She hoped Stephen's relationship with his parents wouldn't suffer irreparable damage due to his marriage to her.

The men joined them, and Sophie's uncomfortable interview with Mrs. Overtree ended at last.

Captain Overtree sought her out and said quietly, "You look tired."

"I confess I am."

"You've had a long, trying day. Why don't you go up? I think I'll stay and talk a little while longer."

Sophie nodded gratefully. She truly was tired. But moreover, she had fretted about what it would be like if they both went upstairs at the same time. She thought of the crowded dressing room. Would the maid undress her in the bedchamber right in front of him? Or would he remain in his dressing room like a schoolboy covering his eyes? That didn't seem like Captain Overtree. Nor could she realistically ask it of him — though she wanted to.

Even her stolen moments with Wesley had not diminished her natural modesty. And he'd had to woo her and cajole every rare inch of skin bared.

Stop it! she scolded herself, cutting off that line of thought. *Stop it now.* Those were memories best forgotten, and the sooner the better.

Upstairs, she rang for Libby, who came and helped her change from her evening gown, stays, and shift into a long nightdress of lawn. She brushed Sophie's hair and braided it into a plait, tying off the end with a ribbon. "Would you like any paper curlers around your face, ma'am?"

"Oh, um. No thank you." Sophie quailed at the thought of appearing to such disadvantage to Captain Overtree.

The girl must have guessed her thoughts.

"Not on your honeymoon, hmm?"

Sophie's face heated, but she managed a weak grin. "Right."

"Then I shall curl your hair with hot irons in the morning — never you fear. We'll have you looking your best for your new husband, or my name's not Libby Lester."

"Thank you, Libby."

Finally, alone in the bedchamber, Sophie slipped on a dressing gown over her thin nightdress for good measure, stepped on the needle-worked footstool to climb into the high bed, and pulled the blankets over her chest. Why was she so nervous? It was not her first night as Captain Overtree's wife. But he had been foxed the first night, ill the next, and then the girls had been with them in Bath. Now they were here, in his home, in a big bed befitting a married couple. A newly wedded couple supposedly in their honeymoon period. She swallowed, and pulled the blankets up to her chin.

Was Captain Overtree an experienced man? Had he a lover? As a religious man, perhaps he had abstained. She had been an innocent until a few months ago, but she doubted a military man in his late twenties would count himself among the uninitiated.

She covered her face with her hands. How had she gotten herself into such a predicament? Why oh why had she given in to Wesley? Why could she not have resisted him? How naïve she had been to believe he was about to ask her to marry him. Once again she pecked at the memories, rehearsing every scene, every conversation. Had she only imagined he'd mentioned the word marriage? Or like so many foolish females before her, had she heard what she wanted to hear in a man's sweet nothings? Assumed he *meant* he loved her and would marry her, when all along he meant nothing of the kind?

And now here she was, carrying his child and married to his brother, of all people. A brother who showed little interest in becoming better acquainted with her — physically or otherwise. She should be grateful. She was, as a matter of fact. But even so, it left her with a ball of dread in the pit of her stomach. The captain must really believe he did not have long to live. Either that, or he found her repugnant. Or . . . Did his heart belong to another? Jenny? Miss Blake? Someone else?

Footsteps sounded through the wall. Was it Captain Overtree coming to bed? Her pulse quickened.

The footsteps paused. She closed her eyes,

listening, her damp hands fisting the bed-clothes. The footsteps continued but sounded as if they were coming not from the corridor beyond the bedchamber door, but from off to the side. Libby, perhaps, returning through the dressing room? Or maybe the footman who served as the captain's valet? A door creaked open somewhere nearby.

She called tentatively, "Libby . . . ?"

No reply.

A chill passed over her. How foolish. Now she almost wished the captain would come and end her waiting. Silence resumed, except for the ticking clock on the mantel. Would she have to fetch Captain Overtree up to their room as she had on their wedding night? How mortifying. *Please, God, let him not be drunk again.*

Unable to sleep with wondering and nerves, she pushed back the bedclothes and climbed from bed, forgetting how high it was and stumbling. Catching herself, she crossed to the door and listened. All was quiet. She let herself into the corridor and tiptoed to the stair railing. Voices drifted up to her.

Mrs. Overtree's clear voice rose. "Why her, Stephen? A girl of inferior birth. Little family. No connections?"

Stephen's low voice rumbled in reply, but Sophie could not make out his words.

"Her father may be an artist," his mother retorted. "But it sounds as if she helps him keep a sort of a shop in his studio, selling paints and brushes like a peddler. In trade!"

Her mother-in-law's words stung. But Sophie could not refute them. Perhaps she had her answer as to why Wesley had not asked for her hand. It made her all the more surprised his brother had done so.

"I suppose she brings no dowry," Mr. Overtree's mild voice added.

Again Stephen's rumble of reply was unintelligible, but she didn't need to hear him to know the answer. She had only a very modest dowry, set aside for her by her mother. Her father had added a small sum as well, probably believing Sophie's looks alone would not secure her an advantageous match. Sophie knew that some of his commissions paid quite well and he could have given her a larger dowry. She'd sometimes wondered if he preferred she not marry and remain his unpaid assistant.

Mrs. Overtree said, "If she were a great beauty, I might understand, but . . ."

Sophie slunk back to her bed, torn between offense and mortification to be the object of such scathing criticism.

A short while later, the outside door to the captain's dressing room opened and candle-light leaked under the door. Low male voices — attempting to whisper but failing — seeped through as well. Captain Overtree and his valet.

"I understand what my mother directed, but I am capable of undressing on my own," Captain Overtree grumbled, then sighed. "Oh very well."

A few minutes later, the door into the bedchamber creaked open.

Sophie froze, unsure whether to feign sleep or sit up and send him away. Had he not said he would sleep in the dressing room?

Although faint moonlight came in through the windows, Sophie lay half-hidden by shadows and bed-curtains. She peered at him from beneath her lashes.

Captain Overtree stepped silently into the room, wearing a dressing gown over his white nightshirt, his feet encased in soft slippers. He carried a candle lamp in one hand, and carefully closed the dressing room door behind himself, wincing as it clicked closed.

Her heart hammered. Did he mean to sneak up on her? Join her in bed?

For a moment he stayed where he was, his back against the door, his head cocked to one side, listening. She too heard the faint scuff of shoes and the scraping of drawers within.

Then he took a tentative step toward the bed. Then another. Sophie's pulse rate accelerated.

He stopped a few feet from the bed. "Are you awake?" he whispered. Or tried to.

Sophie swallowed. Tell the truth, or remain silent? "Yes," she whispered back, fully opening her eyes at last.

"Don't be alarmed," he said in a hushed voice. "I am only awaiting the valet's departure. It will start rumors belowstairs if it is obvious I am sleeping in the dressing room so soon after our wedding. To hear Father tell it, husbands usually avoid such punishment for a month at least."

"Oh . . ." she murmured.

He stood there a moment longer, looking down at her by the light of his candle. How must she appear, hands fisted on blankets pulled to her chin, eyes wide in the shadowy cave of the canopied bed.

He shook his head, mouth twisting. "Poor little rabbit."

He'd whispered it so softly she thought she had imagined it. He could whisper after all, she realized. When he truly wanted to.

A faint click of a shutting door reached them, and a few moments later Captain Overtree turned and disappeared — not into the dressing room, but rather out the main door. She wondered why. Where was he going at this hour, in his nightclothes?

Curiosity nipping at her, Sophie rose for the second time that night, climbed from bed without stumbling and tiptoed to the door. She inched it open and looked out into the corridor in time to see him creep quietly up the stairs. The furtive sight disheartened her somehow. Since she had not invited him into her bed, was he on his way to meet up with some willing housemaid? It was an uncharitable, baseless suspicion, and she cursed her scandalous imagination. Still, she hoped she was wrong.

CHAPTER 9

In the morning, Sophie found herself surrounded by unfamiliar bed-curtains and wondered where she was. Then she remembered — Overtree Hall. She rolled to her back and looked upward. Above her in the paneled oak canopy, she noticed a square opening to allow smoke to escape, and guessed Colonel Horton must smoke a pipe or cigar. She glanced to the side and saw morning sunlight filtering through sheer lace draperies, the window shutters opened by a stealthy Libby, she guessed. Her gaze quickly darted to the captain's dressing room, door slightly ajar and silent.

Libby entered through the other dressing room, and seeing her, Sophie sat up and pushed down the bedclothes.

"Is Captain Overtree . . . ?"

"Already gone downstairs, ma'am. Early riser, your husband."

Sophie climbed from bed, stepped to the washstand, and cleaned her face and teeth.

"What would you like to wear today?" the maid asked.

"I don't know. What do you think would be most appropriate? I suppose the Overtree ladies wear morning gowns and then change for dinner?"

"*You* are an Overtree lady now, ma'am, don't forget."

Libby pulled out the deep gown drawers in the dressing room one by one. "If you don't mind my saying, ma'am. New gowns might be in order. Please don't be angry!"

"I am not angry, Libby. Only embarrassed."

"No need, ma'am. They are not bad." She shook out an ivory muslin day dress. "This one would suit, I think. But you could use a few more. Especially if the elder Mrs. Overtree takes it into her head to invite neighbors in to meet you. Everyone will want to see the captain's new bride."

The neighbors might be curious, Sophie allowed, though she privately doubted Janet Overtree would be eager to show off her "inferior" new daughter-in-law.

Libby helped Sophie dress and fulfilled her promise with the hot iron, curling tight ringlets on either side of her face. Sophie hoped she did not look like one of Thomas Gainsborough's poodles — or as silly as she felt.

A short time later, Sophie was surprised and relieved to find herself alone at breakfast.

But that feeling soon seeped away, replaced by unease. Had she slept so terribly late? Had she broken some family rule?

"Excuse me, have the family all eaten?" she asked the attending footman.

"The mistress has her breakfast sent up on a tray, and the young miss is taking hers in the morning room." He added, "Captain and Mr. Overtree are meeting with Mr. Humphries, the estate manager, but I expect them shortly. And Colonel Horton ate earlier and has gone off riding."

"I thought his horse was unwell."

The young man nodded and brought her a toasted muffin. "He took one of the other horses, or so I heard the groom mention. Some errand that would not wait."

"I see."

Sophie was just finishing her solitary breakfast when Mr. Overtree came in, his hair windblown.

"Good morning, Sophie," he said. "I trust you slept well and the room is to your liking?"

"Yes, thank you." She regarded his ruddy cheeks and bright eyes. "You look well, I must say."

"Do I? It must be that I've gone for a brisk morning stroll. My first in weeks."

"I am glad you felt well enough to do so."

"Yes, I found myself equal to a short walk today." He grinned. "Especially as my wife

161

was not yet down to object."

Sophie returned his smile. She remained a few minutes longer, asking about the weather and his plans for the day, and then excused herself to seek out Kate.

She found the girl curled up on a sofa in the morning room, a cup of hot chocolate on the end table beside her, feet tucked under a lap rug and paper curlers peeping out from beneath her cap. She looked up and brightened upon seeing her in the doorway.

"There you are. My new sister. Come in and join me. Shall I ring for chocolate or coffee?"

"I've just had my breakfast, thank you."

"Sleepy head. Up late last night, I imagine?" Her dark eyes shone with too much mischief for a girl her age.

Sophie crossed the room. "I did not sleep well, no. Does everyone in your family rise early?"

"Yes, except for my brother, Wesley. Though Mamma takes forever to dress. We rarely see her before eleven."

Sophie glanced at the book in the girl's lap. "What are you reading?"

"A novel called *Sense and Sensibility.* Have you read it?"

"I have not. I don't read many novels."

"You should. They are so romantic. Amusing too." Kate patted the sofa next to her. "Come and sit. You promised to tell me all about how you and Stephen met and how he proposed to you."

Sophie sat down. "Did I?"

Kate nodded, paper curls bouncing against her brow, eyes alight. "Yes, I want to hear every romantic detail of your whirlwind courtship. Everyone in our family has them. Oh, and you should hear how Grandfather won over our grandmother. We have passionate natures, Grandfather says."

Her face looked so innocent and eager that Sophie hated to disappoint her.

Captain Overtree's voice startled her from the doorway. "Come now, Kate," he cautioned. "You know my taciturn disposition too well to think me a romantic cavalier."

"You are just being modest." Kate turned those hopeful eyes toward Sophie. "Is he not?"

He grimaced. "Kate, I am sorry to disappoint you, but the truth is . . ."

"Actually, you are perfectly right, Kate," Sophie interrupted. "It was quite . . . unforgettable."

"I knew it," Kate breathed. How did you meet?"

"I was standing atop a windy cliff at sunset . . ."

"Oh! How gothic!" the girl enthused.

"Yes. And I dropped . . . something."

"A handkerchief?"

"No. A letter, with sentimental value

163

from . . . an old friend. I tried to reach it myself, but your brother dashed up the path, called over the roaring wind for me to stay back, and insisted he would rescue it for me."

"Stephen!" Kate beamed at him. "I knew it would be something wonderful!"

"My wife exaggerates," he said, eyeing her speculatively. "In fact, she astounds me with her storytelling ability."

Sophie continued dramatically, "He brandished his sword —"

"Walking stick," he corrected.

"And reached the letter, dragging it unharmed to the path."

"More likely soiled and spoilt."

"A gust of wind nearly pushed me over the edge —"

"Only her bonnet."

"But he caught me just in time."

He huffed. "Now I really must protest."

"Was she truly in danger?" Kate asked eagerly. "Did you save her life?"

He hesitated. "I . . . did wonder when I first saw her if she meant to — if she was in danger there on the cliff, reaching over the edge as she was, foolish woman. But I don't think she really would have fallen."

"Quibble over details all you like, Captain," Sophie said softly. "But you rescued me in Lynmouth. You cannot deny it."

His stormy gaze met hers, caution, surprise, and something more flickering in his eyes. "I have no wish to deny it."

"And did he propose then and there?" Kate asked.

Sophie thought back. "Not that very night. But the next day, yes."

Kate turned to her older brother, all wide-eyed naiveté. "Was it love at first sight, Stephen?"

Sophie expected the captain to joke off the uncomfortable question, to ruffle his sister's hair and say, "Enough now. You've had your romantic tale."

Instead he slowly shifted his focus from his sister's earnest face to Sophie's and said solemnly, "Yes, it was."

Sophie's breath hitched. For a moment she held his gaze in surprise. Then she looked away first.

"I knew it," Kate repeated on a sigh, sinking back into the cushions with a wistful, faraway expression, a contented smile on her pixie-like face.

Sophie reminded herself the captain had probably fabricated his answer, or at least exaggerated, caught up as she had been in her rosy version of their meeting. Surely that was all.

Mrs. Overtree entered, looked from one to the other, then frowned at her daughter.

"Katherine, go and dress, my dear. We don't want Sophie to think proper young ladies lie about in their caps all day."

"Very well, Mamma." Kate set aside her book and rose.

Mrs. Overtree turned to her son. "I was thinking a tour of the manor and grounds might be in order for Sophie. Though with the wind whipping outside as it is, perhaps just the house for now."

"Excellent idea, Mamma. I would join you but Grandfather asked me to meet with the farrier for him. He had to leave on some errand that could not wait, apparently."

"Did he say what it was?"

"Not to me, no."

"Very well. I shall give Sophie the tour myself. Come along."

Sophie rose and followed Mrs. Overtree around the square-plan house, trying to imagine Wesley and his siblings growing up there. They went through the public rooms, a few of which Sophie had already seen: dining room, morning room, white parlour, billiards room, library, and hall.

Surveying the high echoing chamber once more, Sophie was again struck by its familiarity. Perhaps she had seen a hall just like it in one of the fine houses she had visited with her father. In the musicians' gallery above, she noticed a plaster mask on the wall that looked like a jester's face. She had certainly not seen it before. That, she would have remembered.

Mrs. Overtree led the way up the stairs. The

first floor up held primarily bedchambers. She pointed out Kate's, Stephen's old room — now the colonel's — and theirs. Mrs. Overtree pushed open the door to her and her husband's room, very similar in layout to the one Sophie now shared with the captain. Then Mrs. Overtree led her into her "boudoir," a large dressing room with sofa and chair as well as the requisite wardrobes and cupboards. She opened one of these and ran a hand through the fine fabrics within. "If you need any gowns now you are here, you need only say so. If fact, I think I shall ask my lady's maid to take in a few of mine to fit you."

Sophie wasn't sure whether to feel grateful or embarrassed.

Then they walked up another flight of stairs and through a long echoing gallery, and Sophie imagined the Overtree children riding hobby horses and chasing each other in games of tag and hide-and-seek when the weather kept them indoors. Mrs. Overtree pointed out Wesley's bedchamber as well as the room adjacent that served as his studio, and the guest rooms sometimes used by Mr. Keith or Miss Blake.

From there, Mrs. Overtree gestured up the stairwell leading to the highest floor. "Up there are the old nursery, schoolroom, and housemaids' bedchambers. I doubt you shall have any occasion to venture there."

Sophie doubted it as well. But she wondered again if Captain Overtree had ventured up there, and why.

On their way back downstairs, Mrs. Overtree paused to point out a portrait among the dozens they had passed unheralded. Sophie sucked in a breath and prayed her expression gave nothing away.

"And this is my eldest son, Wesley Overtree. Oh, perhaps you have met him?"

"Yes. In Devonshire."

"Ah. You are probably not well-acquainted, but is it not a fair likeness?"

"Yes . . ." Sophie dragged her gaze from the handsome visage to her new mother-in-law, noticing the similarities between them. "He looks a great deal like you, Mrs. Overtree."

"Thank you. He takes after me far more than either Stephen or Katherine. In looks and in artistic temperament."

"Oh? Do you paint as well?" Sophie asked.

"When I was young, I painted for my own enjoyment, though I was never trained. If I had ever learnt, I should have been a great proficient." She sighed. "But that was before the responsibilities of caring for my children, husband, and household took precedence. You will find out soon enough how becoming a wife and mother changes everything. For better and for worse."

Sophie forced a smile. *Oh yes, she would.*

And sooner than anyone might guess. If only she could joyfully anticipate the birth of her child like a happily married woman!

Mrs. Overtree nodded toward the next portrait. "And Wesley painted this one of Katherine when she was sixteen."

Sophie recognized Wesley's style but didn't judge it his best work. In the portrait, Kate appeared to be in the awkward throes of adolescence, her nose rather squat. And he had captured none of her vibrant personality.

"And of course you recognize Stephen." Mrs. Overtree gestured toward a portrait on the other side of Kate's.

Actually, Sophie had not recognized it. In fact, she might have walked right past without noticing. She stepped nearer, studying the image. How young he looked. How innocent. His eyes were clear and blue. So full of life and hope, with none of the guard and callous irony she saw now when she looked at him. And no scar marred his face. No overgrown hair and side-whiskers masked its planes.

"He looks so different," she breathed, an odd ache beneath her breastbone.

"Yes," Mrs. Overtree agreed. "He *was* different. He has lived several hard years since then. I hope the worst is behind him, and that marriage will do him good."

Sophie nodded. "So do I." But considering the nature of their marriage and his misgivings about his fate, she doubted it.

When they returned to the morning room where they'd begun, Sophie saw that Kate had dressed for the day. Another woman sat across from her.

Kate smiled. "Sophie, allow me to introduce my good friend and neighbor, Miss Angela Blake. Angela, my new sister, Sophie Overtree."

The woman winced as though a bright light shone in her eyes, but she managed a convincing smile.

Angela . . . Sophie's attention caught on the name. This, then, was not "Jenny."

Miss Blake was an elegant redhead with a long, aristocratic face, faint freckles warming china-white skin, and childlike lips, the top lip heavily bowed in the middle. Her thick ginger hair was swept back to the crown of her regal head, and from there lustrous curls tumbled down her neck. She wore an ivory gown with a fern green overdress, excellent for her coloring. She held herself in pristine posture, unlike Kate's casual ease. But then, Miss Blake looked to be in her midtwenties, whereas girlish Kate was only eighteen.

"I should not introduce Angela as my *particular* friend," Kate said, "as she has been chasing after my brothers since before I was born, growing up just over the garden wall as she has."

"Don't say 'chasing after,' " Miss Blake corrected with a self-conscious laugh. "As though I set my cap at them."

"Of course not! I only meant that you played together as children, running wild all over the parish, to hear Stephen tell it, and getting into mischief."

"That I cannot deny."

Kate turned back to Sophie. "The Blakes live in that pretty red brick manor house. Have you seen it? It's lovely. Perhaps you might give Sophie a tour one day soon, Angela?"

The woman dipped her head. "If she likes."

"I have just given her a tour of Overtree Hall," her mother-in-law said. "Let's not overwhelm her all at once."

"Sophie, tell Angela the story of how you and Stephen met," Kate urged.

Sophie demurred. "Oh, I don't think Miss Blake wants to hear all that."

A housemaid appeared, carrying a tea tray, and laid it on the table between them.

"Ah, saved by the tea," Miss Blake said. "Perfect. Do you want to pour, Kate, or shall I?"

"Please do, Angela," Mrs. Overtree said, taking her seat. "Katherine is forever spilling it."

Captain Overtree entered the room. "Ah, Angela. I see you've met my . . . Sophie."

"I have met *your Sophie,* yes. I must say I was surprised to learn you had married. I thought you were a confirmed bachelor."

A teasing grin played about the captain's mouth and his eyes shone. Seeing it, Sophie felt a stab of . . . What? Insecurity? Jealousy?

"Oh? And what about you?" he said. "You are —"

Something flashed in her eyes, and he abruptly changed tack, "You are the one who once told me you pitied the woman brave enough to marry me."

Miss Blake blinked up at him innocently. "Did I?" She turned to Sophie. "Should I pity you, do you think?"

Sophie hesitated. "I . . . wouldn't say so, no."

"Not very convincing."

Mrs. Overtree accepted a cup of tea and said politely, "I hear your brother has recently become engaged, Angela. Is that right?"

"Yes," Miss Blake replied, her smile barely forming before disappearing again. "And him only one and twenty. I am surrounded by happy couples. My joy knows no bounds."

Sophie wondered at her brittle, barely concealed sarcasm . . . or was it wistfulness? Did she fear herself a spinster? Miss Blake was no longer in the first blush of youth, but she was still an attractive woman, and still young enough to marry. Had she wished to marry Captain Overtree herself? Sophie hoped not.

She didn't know what to say. She didn't want to ask a hurtful question or say the wrong thing. Had Miss Blake ever been engaged? Had a suitor? Flirted with the Overtree brothers? Perhaps she would ask Kate sometime. She doubted she'd have the courage to ask Captain Overtree himself.

"I have not seen your marriage mentioned in the papers," Miss Blake said. "And you know some say the newspaper announcement is more important than the wedding itself, socially speaking, of course."

Mrs. Overtree interjected, "I intend to remedy that, never fear. I shall write to the *Times* and the *Courier* myself. Something simple, I think, like: 'Lately, Captain Stephen Overtree of the 28th North Gloucestershire Regiment, to Miss Sophie Dupont of Bath.' "

"Nothing about Sophie's family? Or the wedding itself?" Miss Blake asked.

"Sometimes less is more."

"So . . ." Miss Blake glanced at the captain, fingering the fringe on the sofa cushion. "I suppose your brother attended as witness? Or was it that friend of yours from the army, Keith something?"

"Neither, actually. Wesley has sailed for Italy again. And Lieutenant Keith was . . . indisposed. Though he did mention he would be coming here. In fact, I am surprised he isn't here already."

"Do you expect him soon?" Miss Blake asked.

"Yes, I do."

"Heaven help us all," Mrs. Overtree sighed. "I shall have to warn Cook to double her recipes."

CHAPTER 10

After the captain excused himself and Mrs. Overtree left to talk to the cook, Kate looked out the window and said, "Come, Sophie. The sun is out and the wind has died down. Let us go and take a turn around the grounds."

"Thank you. I would enjoy that."

She and Kate went to retrieve their wraps, bonnets, and gloves, while Miss Blake reclaimed hers from the footman. They went out a side door and through a stone archway into a walled garden beyond.

"In a month or so, there will be flowers everywhere," Kate said.

For the present, they enjoyed the circle of shaped hedges, the topiaries, vine-covered trellises, and fountain. They walked around the back of the house, past a lawn-bowling green and a pretty stream crossed by a small stone bridge. Then they continued around the side, near the stables.

There, Miss Blake pointed to a rooftop visible through the trees beyond the garden wall. "Windmere lies just there. See that door in the wall? I use it more than anyone, I think."

They continued their circle around the house until they approached the front. There Sophie admired a charming dovecote resembling a miniature cottage with a tiled roof.

As they reached the entrance gate, Kate pointed out the church on its other side.

"Have you met our vicar?" Miss Blake asked her.

"No, not yet," Sophie replied.

Sophie's gaze trailed over the stone wall separating the manor from the churchyard with its leaning cankered headstones and junipers dotted with frosty white and blue berries.

Kate began to explain something of the history of the church, but Sophie wasn't really listening. She was not fond of moldering old churches. And besides that, she was distracted by something. An awareness. A prickle of unease crept up her neck, as though someone was watching her. She looked at Miss Blake beside her, but the woman's gaze remained on the church. Sophie glanced over her shoulder at the manor and saw a curtain fall back into place in a top-story window. *Had* someone been watching them? A little shiver passed over her, even as she told herself she was being foolish. Probably only a curious housemaid. Hadn't Mrs. Overtree said their rooms were up there?

A thin young man with light reddish-blond hair stepped out of the church.

"There's Mr. Harrison," Kate said, abruptly ending her history lecture and breaking away from their trio, walking over to speak to the man over the low wall.

"The vicar is such a young man," Sophie observed.

"Oh no, that isn't the vicar," Miss Blake said, making no move to follow Kate. "That is his . . . well . . . son."

"Why do you say it like that?"

"Mr. Nelson and his wife took in David Harrison there when he was a lad of five or six. Raised him as their own."

"What happened to his parents?"

Miss Blake hesitated. "It is very sad, really. I don't normally speak of it, but as you are Kate's family now, I suppose it is all right to tell you." She lowered her voice. "Mr. Harrison's mother was not married. His father was supposedly a gentleman, but he could not be brought round to do his duty, apparently. It was a terrible scandal. Her parents were mortified. Her father lost his curacy over it, and refused to receive her or support her. Poor Mr. Harrison was born in a poorhouse — but don't tell Mrs. Overtree — I don't think she knows that detail, and it will not help his cause with Kate. Such as it is."

Sophie was filled with sorrow and empathy

for these people she'd never met. "What became of his mother?"

Miss Blake sighed. "She died of consumption eventually. Alone and in poverty. It breaks my heart to think of it."

Sophie was surprised to see tears brighten Miss Blake's eyes. Sophie felt tears sting her own eyes, and whispered, "Mine too."

When they returned to the house, Captain Overtree was just coming down the stairs. "There you are," he said to Sophie. "Good walk?" When she nodded and removed her bonnet, he said, "Would you mind coming with me? There is someone I would like you to meet."

"Of course."

"Let me guess," Kate said. "Miss Whitney."

"Yes." He turned to Sophie and added, "Our old nurse."

"Horrors." Miss Blake shuddered. "Don't let the old thing frighten you, Sophie. Or tell your fortune."

Kate playfully smacked her arm. "Angela, don't say such things. Winnie is an old dear, and you know it."

Miss Blake shook her head. "I beg to disagree. That's not how I recall her, especially when we were younger. Always seemed to know what we were up to, and caught us misbehaving, as if she could read our minds. . . ." She shivered theatrically.

"You exaggerate."

"I cannot believe your mother puts up with her."

"Hush. Don't give her any ideas. She wouldn't hesitate to put her out if Stephen were not so insistent."

"Why he is, I shall never understand."

"She still lives here in the house?" Sophie asked in surprise.

"Yes," Kate replied. "Tell her I shall be up to see her tomorrow."

"That makes one of us," Miss Blake said. "In fact, you may refrain from mentioning me altogether," she added, and bid them all good-day.

As Sophie and Captain Overtree crossed the hall together, Sophie said, "I am surprised she still lives here. Kate is too old for a governess, let alone a nurse."

"I know. But Kate and I have always been fond of Miss Whitney. We have kept her on as a retainer. She had nowhere else to go, and her age and . . . health . . . make finding another position unlikely. It took some doing to convince Mamma to let her remain in the house, but in the end, Kate and I prevailed."

Captain Overtree led her up one flight of stairs after another, toward the top floor. Sophie thought of the window curtain she had seen flutter closed. Might it have been this Miss Whitney? Was she the reason the captain went up these stairs last night, and not to visit a housemaid as she'd feared?

"Mamma rarely ventures up here," he said. "None of the family do, save Kate and me."

They reached the landing at the top of the stairs, and he knocked on the first door.

A female voice called from within, "Just a minute!"

"Winnie? It's me. Stephen."

With a reassuring smile at Sophie, he pushed open the door and gestured her inside.

A slight woman beside a wardrobe whirled toward them. "I said, just a minute!" She looked flushed and guilty, as if caught half-dressed or doing something wrong.

"Oh. It's you, Master Stephen." She pressed a hand to her chest. "You gave me a start."

She wore a blue gown with a white lace collar. Fair, silvery hair pulled back in a loose coil framed a well-shaped face and cornflower blue eyes. She had been handsome once, Sophie thought. And still was in her way.

The sitting room was larger and cheerier than Sophie would have expected. And through an open door, she spied an adjoining chamber with a single bed. More than twenty years of memorabilia decorated the walls: finger-painted flowers and childish drawings. A jar of daffodils and hand-lettered sentiments sat propped on her side table. One caught her eye: *To Winnie. Get better soon. Love, Stephen.*

The captain introduced her, and Sophie said, "How do you do, Miss Whitney. Captain Overtree speaks very highly of you."

The woman clucked her tongue, a twinkle in her eye. "So formal. I am Winnie, and he, as you very well know, is Stephen. Of course I realize many married women insist on calling their husbands by their surnames, but if one is to share a life and a bed and children I think one might justifiably use one's Christian name, don't you agree?"

"I . . . shall have to give that some thought."

Miss Whitney remained standing with her back to the wardrobe. From inside came the sound of muffled mewing.

She said, "I . . . was afraid it was your mother come to call. I know how she feels about . . ." She pressed her lips together and darted a glance at Sophie. Another meow of protest came from the cupboard. "And how does the new Mrs. Overtree feel about . . . pets in general?"

Sophie bit back a grin. "I have never had one. But I've always thought cats must be charming."

Miss Whitney expelled a sigh of relief and turned to open the cupboard door. An orange tabby immediately emerged, miffed and indignant, and quickly trotted over to investigate Captain Overtree's boots.

"Cats are delightful, indeed," Miss Whitney agreed. She sat gracefully on a worn but pretty chaise longue that reminded Sophie of the one in Mavis Thrupton's spare room. Sophie noticed an open magazine, spectacles, teacup, and plate of biscuits close at hand.

Sophie had imagined a staid old woman sitting bent over her knitting. But Stephen's former nurse was not a frail octogenarian, but rather a woman in her early sixties. She was slight but apparently spry. Captain Overtree had mentioned something about her health, but Sophie noticed no obvious ailment. She wondered what was wrong with her.

"It is a pleasure to meet you, my dear," the woman said earnestly. "Master Stephen is the first of my 'children,' as I think of them, to marry. Happy thought indeed."

Sophie smiled. But the woman did not return the gesture. Instead she studied Sophie's face with concern, a wrinkle between her brows. Voice low and gentle, she asked the captain, "What is she afraid of . . . ?"

Captain Overtree pulled a face. "Me, I guess."

"Can't blame her for that," Miss Whitney teased, then sobered again, looking at Sophie closely. "Poor girl. . . ." she murmured.

"Whatever do you mean?" Sophie asked, feeling discomfited under the woman's scrutiny.

"I see . . . sadness in your eyes. Heartache. You miss someone."

"I . . ." Sophie felt rattled. Awkward. Who did the woman mean? How did she know? "I miss my family, of course. But that is only natural."

The woman's eyes narrowed in thought. "Your mother, I think, most of all."

Sophie blinked in surprise. "Yes. But my mother is —"

"Passed on, yes. Poor child."

"How did you know that?" Sophie turned to Stephen. "You must have mentioned it to her."

"Not that I recall, though I may have done." The captain shrugged. "Winnie has always had a way of knowing things."

"Or perhaps Miss Katherine mentioned it," Winnie suggested. "She was just up to see me yesterday. Brought me these lovely daffodils."

She patted the empty spot next to her on the chaise, and Sophie dutifully sat down. The orange tabby leapt onto Winnie's lap. "Oh, Gulliver." Winnie shook her head and scratched the cat between the ears.

"As in *Gulliver's Travels*?" Sophie asked.

"Why, of course! Master Stephen's favorite book as a boy. Every night, he begged me to read one more chapter."

The captain crossed his arms and said fondly, "Most of the time, she gave in."

Sophie smiled, trying to imagine Captain

Overtree as a little boy, eager for an adventure story.

Winnie shifted the purring cat and grinned at Sophie with girlish dimples. "And what have they told you about me? That I am off in my attic? A danger to myself and others?" She tsked her tongue and shook her head. "The mistress would have put me out long before now, but thanks to Master Stephen here, I have a roof over my head."

"It is the least I could do, Winnie."

"You're a good boy."

Captain Overtree stepped to the window, frowning at the inordinate number of birds fluttering on the ledge outside. "Deuced things — they must be nesting in the eaves. I shall ask Jensen to send a man up . . ."

"Please don't, Master Stephen. I have taken to feeding the birds on that little ledge. I hope you don't mind. They give me such pleasure."

"Oh. Very well. If you don't mind the mess."

Winnie turned back to Sophie and patted her hand. "Well, Mrs. Overtree, you come and visit me whenever you like. But not at night, if you don't mind. I prefer . . . daytime visits."

"Of course." Recognizing her cue to leave, Sophie rose. "A pleasure to meet you."

The captain held the door for her, and together they made their way back down-stairs.

Sophie whispered, "Does she never come

downstairs?"

"Not often. She has become something of a hermit up there, sorry to say."

"But she isn't an invalid or anything. She appears quite fit, at least physically."

He nodded. "Now and again Kate cajoles her out into the garden. Or to church on Holy days. Otherwise she prefers to keep to herself. She always ate her meals in her room or the nursery — with us when we were children — and now on her own."

When they returned to their bedchamber, he said quietly, "I have known Miss Whitney all my life. She is kind and wise." He made a rueful face. "She is also the person who told me I would not live to see my thirtieth birthday. I don't credit it completely, of course. But she's been right about so many things over the years. . . ."

Sophie stared at him. "Then perhaps your mother is correct, and Miss Whitney's mind is slipping."

He shook his head. "I think she is perfectly lucid. Yes, she forgets things now and again, especially when she is tired or ill. But that is normal for her age. Probably doesn't help that she is alone so much."

"Has she no friends? Other women in her situation? Retired governesses, or nurses like herself?"

"Not that I know of. Most governesses and nurses are the poor spinster aunts to equally

struggling relations and end up in an alms-
house somewhere."

"How sad."

He nodded. "It is why I have made such an
effort to keep her here. I want her remaining
days to be as comfortable and secure as the
early days of my life were, thanks in great
part to her."

Sophie had never heard the quiet captain
speak so much or so warmly about anyone
else. She found his loyalty to his old nurse
touching and, in this instance, slightly trou-
bling.

"May I ask why you are so attached to
Winnie, while your mother and others clearly
are not?"

He nodded. "She and Mamma have often
butted heads over the years. Winnie thought
my parents preferred Wesley, so she in turn,
doted on me. Mamma always resented it, I
think. As did Wesley."

"But . . . she said you weren't going to live,
and you believe her?" Sophie hoped she
didn't sound as incredulous as she felt.

He shrugged. "I know it doesn't make
sense. But I have to allow for the possibility,
because I have never known Miss Whitney to
be wrong." His gaze lingered on her face.
"Though I hope that this time she might be."

Stephen's explanation had been true, if

186

generalized. He could recount many times in his youth when Miss Whitney had inexplicably known things. But as far as the enmity between Winnie and his mother, he would trace its roots to a specific occasion when he and Wesley were adolescents. The housekeeper had reported two medals missing from their grandfather's desk. Wesley lost no time in reporting that he had seen one in Stephen's room. Stephen denied stealing anything, but the major — his grandfather's rank at the time — had given Stephen one of his campaign medals in private, for his last birthday. But he was away on duty at the time and not there to defend him. Stephen had not mentioned the medal to his family before then, since the major had given one only to him, and not to Wesley.

Doubting her father would have given away one of his few prized medals, his mother had not believed Stephen's version of events. Finding the one medal in his possession was damning evidence in her eyes. She accused him of taking both it and the missing one as well. Stephen faced serious consequences for the theft — he would lose his beloved horse and receive a switching in the bargain. Mamma had even brought in the vicar and tried to force her son to confess. Stephen had rarely felt so powerless. His parents' trust — gone. His word — worthless.

But then Winnie got wind of what was going on, and stood up to his parents, telling them she knew for a fact Major Horton had given his grandson one of his medals, because Stephen had taken it upstairs to show her, so proud of it he was. His mother had not wanted to believe the nurse. Wesley went so far as to say Winnie had made it up to try to protect Stephen, her favorite. So it had been Winnie's word and Stephen's, against Mamma's and Wesley's.

Then Winnie delivered a final blow, and said she could *prove* Wesley had taken the other medal. She proceeded to tell Mamma exactly where to find it — beneath a tray of colored pencils in Wesley's drawing box. Though how she knew where it was, Stephen never learned. Wesley had tried to deny it, saying why would he *want* an army medal, and accusing Winnie of putting the medal there herself, to shift blame to him. Stephen doubted his accusation but had never asked Winnie about it. He wasn't certain he wanted to know. . . .

At all events, his parents had gone up to Wesley's room, and the missing medal was back on Grandfather's desk the next day. As far as Stephen knew, Wesley was never punished. Apparently their parents believed his claims of innocence, and the matter was dropped.

Later, his mother had apologized to the vicar for the "inconvenience." She had been misinformed, and the medal found. It had clearly galled her to admit she had been mistaken. She was embarrassed and vexed to be proven wrong by a subordinate. And Stephen knew his mother had never forgotten, and probably still resented it.

Stephen had never questioned Winnie's word on the subject, or any subject for that matter. But now . . . Sophie's incredulity about Winnie's mental state, and about her "prophecy," gave him pause. Unlike his mother, Sophie was an objective observer. Might there be reason to doubt Miss Whitney's mind . . . and her word?

CHAPTER 11

Later that afternoon, Captain Overtree left to attend a village council meeting. Alone and lonely, Sophie found herself thinking of Wesley. She supposed it was only natural, surrounded as she was by reminders of him — his paintings everywhere, his portrait, his family, his very home.

She remembered Mrs. Overtree pointing out the closed doors of Wesley's bedchamber and studio during her tour of the house, and was curious to see them. She was also curious to see if the full-size portrait he'd painted of her last year might be inside. Apparently it was not on display anywhere in the house, as no one had mentioned it, nor having seen her somewhere before. What had he done with it?

But she knew she probably shouldn't venture up there. What excuse could she give if caught?

Instead, she went and stood in front of the portrait of Wesley again, unable it seemed, to help herself. Gazing up at his likeness, she found her thoughts returning to the first year he'd come to Lynmouth. . . .

The week after she had first met Wesley Overtree, the two again stood on the summit of Castle Rock as the sun began to sink in the sky.

She sensed his gaze on her profile and felt self-conscious, knowing her nose was not flattered by a side view.

He said, "Ah. My first impression was correct — the sunset indeed becomes you. You are quite beautiful. But I suppose you know that, Miss Dupont?"

She shook her head, too stunned to speak.

"Surely you have been told that before?"

Again she shook her head.

"I assume many of your father's students and colleagues have asked to paint you. I don't want to be tiresomely redundant, but —"

"No one has asked."

"You must be joking." His eyes widened. "Incredible. Blind fools . . . Then may I be the first?"

The first . . .

She shook her head. "How self-conscious I would feel. Father says it is beneath me. You know the reputation painters' models have."

"I would never think that of you, Miss Dupont. You are clearly a modest young lady of excellent character as well as beauty and talent."

"You needn't offer to be kind. I know I am not the feminine ideal."

"No? Just leave that to me."

Eventually she agreed.

He began on a small scale, sketching her however she happened to be dressed or wearing her hair. First, he painted only her head and shoulders, testing different hues to bring out the many colors of her hair and eyes. Then, he painted her full-length but in miniature, situating her in different poses — all very modest — to best capture her features.

And he had been right. She had been surprised the first time she saw her likeness. If beauty was in the eye of the beholder, Wesley Overtree certainly saw her as beautiful. In his rendering, her eyes seemed larger, more soulful, more arresting. The long slope of her nose proportionate to her oval face. Her cheekbones high, shadowed by a delicate blush. Looking at those first sketches, the woman gazing back at Sophie seemed almost afraid. Those large eyes pensive. Worried. But gradually they warmed, softened. Believed themselves as beautiful as he said they were.

Finally, he hit upon the pose, the composition he wanted to commit to a large canvas. And after that she had had to sit in that pose for several more days — looking at him over her shoulder. How her neck had ached.

He gave her time to rest and treated her with gentlemanlike respect throughout those days. He did not try to touch her but patiently gained her trust as though taming a wild fawn, until he had her eating from the palm of his hand.

When he departed that first spring, he left her quite in love with him. How she hoped he would return the following year. Maurice told her she was making a cake of herself, saying a wealthy, pretty boy like Wesley Overtree would never take a respectable interest in her. He, on the other hand, would. But Sophie continued to rebuff the impertinent fellow as gently and soundly as she could. Her thoughts, her hopes, were pinned on Wesley Overtree. The first man to tell her she was beautiful.

Sophie returned to the present with a sigh. There was no doubt in her mind that Wesley Overtree had found her beautiful. How special, how desirable she had felt in his presence. But what, she wondered, did Captain Stephen Overtree see when he looked at her? Apparently nothing irresistible.

She retreated to her bedchamber, stunned anew to think she was sharing it with Wesley's brother. *God, have mercy on us all.*

That evening, Libby again helped her dress

for dinner. Sophie didn't know where the captain was, and the dressing room was silent, so she decided to go downstairs on her own. In the anteroom, she drew up short at the sight of a familiar figure slouched in an armchair, a newspaper spread on his lap, a glass of something in one hand, the other sleeve of his evening coat hanging limp. Carlton Keith.

He looked up at her, and a lazy smile lifted his face. "Ah, Miss Dupont. No, sorry. It's Mrs. Overtree now. How could I forget."

He set aside the paper and belatedly rose, performing a perfunctory bow and nearly spilling his brandy in the process.

Ignoring the slight, she curtsied in turn. "Mr. Keith. A pleasure to see you again. I had heard you might be joining us."

"So not an unwelcome surprise, then? I am glad to hear it. My presence irritates Mrs. O, I can tell you. But I once told Katherine the story of how I saved her brother's life, and she told her parents . . . and now I am an honored guest here at Overtree Hall whenever I like."

"And the captain does not correct your account of who rescued whom?" Sophie asked. "Remember you already told me the true story."

"Nah. He is content to let me be the hero. Not fond of fawning attention, our captain, if you haven't learned that yet. Unlike me." He grinned. "I drink it like broth from a bowl."

He gestured toward his evening clothes and cravat. "I clean up pretty well, don't I? Vexes the colonel's valet no end having to dress me, too." He chuckled. Then his green-eyed gaze swept her curled hair and satin gown. "You clean up well yourself."

"Thank you."

Mr. Keith stepped to the sideboard and refilled his glass. "Look at the pair of us. Both here in Overtree Hall, where we've both longed to be for some time, I imagine." He smirked. "Now don't look daggers at me like that. We each have our ways of getting what we want. I imagine you had been practicing writing a certain name in a hopeful hand long before you met the captain. *Mrs. Sophie Overtree. Mrs. Sophie Overtree . . .*" He drained his glass.

Captain Overtree entered, looking masculine and almost civilized in black evening attire and starched white cravat. Only his longish hair, overgrown side-whiskers, and his glare marred the image of a well-turned-out gentleman.

"Keith. What have you been saying to my wife that has her looking so ill?"

"I was simply congratulating her on her marriage, old man. And the same to you." Mr. Keith crossed the room, hand extended. "I wish you happy, Captain. I sincerely do."

Colonel Horton joined them late for dinner, saying little about the errand that had taken him away that day, except that he had paid a visit to an old friend. Sophie remained quiet throughout the meal as well, discomfited to find Mr. Keith's amused gaze watching her, and feeling even more self-conscious than she had before about sitting at the Overtree table as though she belonged there.

Afterward, when the ladies rose to withdraw to the parlour, Captain Overtree excused himself from the other men and walked out with them. He drew Sophie aside and led her into the empty great hall. "Are you all right?" he asked.

"Hmm?"

"You were awfully quiet at dinner. Are you worried about Lieutenant Keith?"

Sophie sighed. "A little, yes. I think he knows, or at least suspects, what went on between Wesley and me."

The captain nodded. "Likely. Come to think of it, he mentioned having to spend a great deal of time away from the cottage while Wesley painted you. The insinuation was definitely there, if not the absolute certainty."

She felt her face heat. "At first painting was truly all it was. I refused to pose with Mr. Keith there, lying on his pallet, head propped on his hand, smirking up at me. Especially when Wesley asked to paint me in Grecian robes, though I drew the line at one bare shoulder." She shook her head. "What a hypocrite you must think me. You no doubt scoff at the notion of my modesty."

"Not at all. I can see you are modest and ladylike by nature."

She blinked up at him timidly, afraid to find irony or sarcasm there. When he earnestly met her gaze, she sighed in relief. "Thank you. I am usually, yes."

"And it becomes you. Try not to worry about Keith. I will speak to him."

"And after you leave . . . ?"

A muffled sound caught her ear. A scuff or cough. She turned to look over her shoulder.

The captain frowned and looked around the hall as well, but there was no one there.

He lowered his voice, "I will make sure he knows there will be consequences if I hear of any disrespect or innuendo."

"Thank you."

Neither of them raised the unspoken question: But what if the captain didn't live to return, let alone to dish out the threatened consequences?

Later, after they'd spent a little time with the others in the parlour, Stephen suggested he and Sophie retire early, which caused knowing looks to be exchanged and Sophie's face to redden. He silently cursed his lack of tact.

As they climbed the stairs together, Sophie hissed, "Did you have to do that? Now they'll all wonder what we're doing . . ."

He gave her a sidelong glance. "We are supposedly on our honeymoon, Sophie. I don't think they'll wonder if we slip off alone now and again. In fact, they would wonder if we didn't. And as I am due to leave soon, I thought we should talk."

"Oh." She swallowed. "Of course."

When they reached their bedchamber, Stephen closed the door behind them, then closed the door to each dressing room as well.

He began, "I realize you have only been here a brief time. But I hope you are, in general, comfortable here? After being with you in Bath, I confess I detest the thought of you raising your child in the same house as your stepmother, not to mention her nephew. I would like you to stay here. Our physician will help you through the birth itself. And my family will take care of you afterwards. Of course, I cannot insist you stay here after I leave. But my mind would be easier knowing you were here." He looked at her closely. "What do you want to do?"

Sophie considered. "I am not eager to return to Bath either. Assuming your family is agreeable, I will stay, for now. Though I cannot promise for how long."

He nodded. "I have already spoken with my parents, and they quite naturally assumed you would live here. I thought it best not to mention the child any earlier than necessary to avoid raising questions, but I can, if you would prefer me to break the news."

"Let's wait." She bit her lip, then said, "And what about when Wesley returns one day . . . ?"

He crossed his arms. "That is up to you, I suppose. If I don't come back, I shan't be here to object either way."

She touched his sleeve. "Stop saying that. I did not mean that I . . . that I anticipate anything with Wesley if and when he returns. I just fear how he might react to me being here. In his house."

"In our house," Stephen insisted. "Don't forget. You are my wife. You have every right to be here whether he likes it or not."

"And if he reveals our . . . past?"

"Then I shall kill him. Or would, were I here." Stephen ran a frustrated hand over his face. "God willing, he has more sense and discretion than that."

"Do I have to tell him the child is his?"

"He may be an artist, but I think even he can count backwards and realize the truth. Unless the baby is long overdue. But hopefully Wes will keep his suspicions to himself."

Sophie nodded. "He'll probably be relieved you have claimed responsibility for me and the child."

"I can't pretend to guess how he will react.

If Wesley asks, it is up to you to decide whether or not to confirm the facts. I would prefer the baby to be known as mine, for my pride's sake, perhaps, but also for the child's, so he or she will not be viewed as illegitimate and grow up under the shadow of scandal."

"I agree."

Stephen was surprised she consented so readily. "Well, good."

She asked, "Do you have a preference about what I name the child, assuming I give birth while you are away?"

Stephen hesitated. Would it not be pre-sumptuous of him to suggest names for her child? His brother's child? All he knew was that he didn't want her to name the child after Wesley. He faltered, "My . . . grand-father's given name is George. But beyond that, I have no . . . preference." *Or rights.*

Again a faint sound reached Stephen's ears. A scuffing step. If one of the footmen was eavesdropping, so help him . . . He stalked to the door and jerked it open. The corridor was empty. He checked his dressing room, and taking his cue, she checked hers. No one in sight.

He sighed. "Sorry to be tense. I'm imagin-ing things, no doubt."

"If you are, then I am as well. Though I suppose an old house like this makes many odd noises."

"True. Well." He turned back to his dressing room. "I will excuse myself and allow you to change."

He closed himself into the dressing room, rang for the valet, put up with the man's meticulous help in folding his clothes, and washed and cleaned his teeth. All while thinking about Sophie and their conversation.

Then he knocked softly and entered the bedchamber to wait while the valet tidied up and went to dump the wash water. He was surprised to see Sophie sitting at the dressing table in her evening gown, hair down. His chest tightened, and he tried not to stare.

He swallowed. "Sorry. I thought I gave you enough time."

"Libby is apparently running late this evening. After all, we did retire earlier than usual."

His gaze ran over her golden hair, falling like a silky curtain around her face and shoulders.

"Your hair is beautiful," he said, before he could stop himself. "I have never seen it down like that before. It's lovely."

"Thank you." She dipped her head, clearly embarrassed. "I took it down straightway. The pins were giving me a headache tonight. Do you mind if I brush it while we wait?"

"Of course I don't mind."

But a minute or two later, he cleared his throat and turned to the door. "You know, I think I will go up and check on Winnie. Good night."

He left the room — and the tantalizing sight of Sophie brushing her hair — hoping to quell his desire. Time with his old nurse would certainly do that. But when he reached Winnie's door and knocked, no one answered. Filled with concern, he let himself in but found the room empty. He wondered where she was and hoped she was all right.

In the morning, Sophie awoke to murmuring voices. Libby and another housemaid were talking somewhere nearby, perhaps in her dressing room or out in the corridor.

"Hush, Flora," Libby said, a barb of irritation in her usually cheerful tone.

Sophie had seen the maid, Flora. She was a pretty, buxom brunette with a ready if crooked smile.

Flora said, "I'm only repeating what Edgar told me. The captain sleeps in the dressing room. He's almost sure of it."

"And I repeat — hush."

"All I'm saying is if she won't let him warm her bed, he can warm mine."

"Flora, if Mrs. Hill heard you say that, you'd be out on your ear."

"And who's going to tell her?"

"I will, if I hear you spreading this clap-trap . . ."

The voices moved on.

Sophie felt her ears burn quite literally to be the subject of such unflattering supposition. Kind Libby probably knew or at least suspected there was truth in what Flora and Edgar had said, but how loyal of her to try to curb the gossip.

She thought of Captain Overtree saying he was going to check on Winnie last night and heading up the attic stairs in his dressing gown. Had he really been going to see Winnie? Especially when the nurse had said she didn't want visitors at night?

If he *were* seeking another bed to warm, had Sophie any right to feel the resentment that curdled her stomach at the thought? She could not blame him if he pined for or desired someone else, not when she did that very thing. But she was not carrying on a physical relationship — nor a relationship of any kind — with another lover. Could he say the same? She did not really think Captain Overtree would have an illicit relationship with someone in his employ. At least she hoped not. She wanted to believe that Stephen Overtree was an honorable, moral, godly man.

But was he?

That afternoon, Stephen and his father interviewed two possible candidates to take Humphries' place as estate manager. One man was young but showed potential. The other had more experience but would probably follow Humphries into retirement in a few years. Stephen wondered if it was worth the trouble to train in a new man for such a short time. Then again, there was no guarantee a younger man would stay on longer. He might take the experience he earned with them to another post.

He and his father debated the merits and drawbacks of each but made no decision, his father wishing to think on it some more, perhaps wait and see if anyone else applied to their advertisement first. Stephen, however, had hoped to see the matter settled before he left.

Later, Stephen went upstairs again to check on Winnie, since she had not been in her room the night before. He found her contentedly feeding her birds, her cat watching and chattering from the windowsill. He idly wondered if she fed the birds for her own amusement or the cat's.

When he asked her where she had been last night, she paused to think. "Gracious, I don't know. What time? Oh, yes . . . I may have gone down for some warm milk around then." She winked at him. "Gulliver couldn't sleep."

"But you are well?"

"Oh yes, perfectly. Besides worried for you, of course."

"For me? Well, yes, I suppose you would

be." He assumed she referred to his imminent return to duty. "But no need to worry. I am prepared to meet my fate, whatever it may be."

"I believe you have already met your fate." Winnie grinned. "And her name is Sophie."

Confusion flickered through Stephen. Had she changed her mind about her prediction of his demise? Or was she losing her faculties as others suggested? Not that he'd ever admit the possibility, especially to his mother.

A housemaid entered, bringing in Miss Whitney's dinner tray, which reminded Stephen it was time to dress for his own dinner. He bid Winnie farewell and went downstairs, though his former nurse remained on his mind.

After dinner, the family attended Evensong together. Everyone except for his father, as the evening wind was too cold, his mother insisted, and would be bad for his chest.

The service of hymns, prayers, and a brief sermon was not Stephen's favorite. He wasn't fond of singing, and knew his low, craggy voice added nothing to the enjoyment of those near enough to hear him. Even so, it was good to be in a candlelit church with his mother, grandfather, and sister. And now his wife as well. How strangely pleasant to have her tucked beside him in the family box, to share a prayer book and hymnal. She sang quietly and tentatively, not familiar with the words or tunes. Still, her shy alto voice was like warm velvet in his ear, and he had to resist the urge to lean nearer.

After the service, he presented Sophie to the vicar and his wife. Several neighbors also sought them out for introductions. Even those neighbors and tenants too timid to come forward favored them with curious looks and smiles. Had things been different — were she his wife in more than name — he would have gladly overcome his unsocial disposition and proudly introduced her to one and all. But as things were, their reticence to intrude was welcome.

Later that night, they again went through their bedtime ritual. Stephen changing in his dressing room, then stepping into the bedchamber to wait for Edgar to tidy up and take his leave. Sophie sat at her dressing table, fully clothed. Libby was again late in coming up.

While they waited, he said, "After I leave, I would consider it a great favor if you would visit Winnie from time to time. Kate goes up fairly often, except when Miss Blake is here. Mrs. Hill sends up trays and a maid to help her, but she is busy with the household. Please check on her for me every few days, will you?"

"Of course. Happily."

"Thank you."

Libby rushed in, apologizing for her delay,

and moaning about polishing endless rounds of silver.

To keep up the pretense that he planned to spend the night with his wife, he remained in the room, instead of ducking back into the dressing room like the interloper he felt himself to be.

Sophie swiveled on the dressing stool to face Libby, and the maid flipped back the hem of her gown and began untying the ribbons holding her stockings above her knees.

Over the maid's bent head, Sophie sent him a shy, uncertain glance. What did she expect him to do? Turn his back like a stranger? A monk? Instead he went to stand at the window, even though he could see almost nothing of the dark gardens beyond.

But his rebellious gaze now and again shifted to the side, capturing a glimpse of bare ankle as the maid rolled down one stocking, then the other. Then a glimpse of upper arm, when she unlaced Sophie's gown and stays, and her shift slipped from one shoulder.

When the maid pulled the shift up and over her head, Stephen forced himself to avert his eyes, fisting his hands in a wad of drapery, every muscle tense. He forked his free hand through his hair in agitation. Another swish of white fabric and Sophie's nightdress was over her head, cascading over her body and rustling to the floor. Only then did Stephen release the ragged breath he'd been holding.

When the maid disappeared into the dressing room, he whispered, "Only one more night, little rabbit. Never fear."

Only one more night, Overtree, he added to himself. *Be strong. You can do this.* It was a good thing he was leaving the next day. He wasn't sure he could resist much longer.

CHAPTER 12

In the morning, Stephen trudged down the stairs toward the breakfast parlour. He had not slept well. Dashed sofa was a rock. His thoughts about the woman in the next room had not helped either, as usual. But he congratulated himself — he had made it. He was about to leave to rejoin his regiment with his dignity intact, and his vow to himself, and to Sophie, honored. As he had promised, he had not expected anything of her or pressured her. He had been a perfect gentleman, at least in outward behavior. His foul, irritable moods and sometimes his words? Not as gallant as they might have been. His inward thoughts? His desires? Probably not as pure as God would have liked. But then again, she was his wife . . .

Even so, he had kept his distance, at least physically, hoping that would make the coming separation less painful. Or would he second-guess himself every hour? Berate himself for not taking her in his arms while he could?

"May I walk with you?" Sophie's voice called from above.

He paused and waited for her on the half landing. "You're up early."

"I wanted to be. For your last day."

He nodded and they continued down the stairs together. In the breakfast parlour, he helped himself to a full plate, knowing it would be a long time before he ate this well again — if ever.

Sophie chose hot chocolate and a bread roll. She sipped daintily at one and picked at the other.

"I hope you eat better than that while I'm gone." He glanced toward the door to make sure they were alone. "You are eating for two now after all."

She nodded, and her chin quivered. Was she sad to see him go or relieved to be rid of him? Who knew? Women were strange, foreign creatures.

His grandfather entered the room, waving an open letter like a flag. His face was as jubilant as a child's on Christmas. "What a surprise I have in store for you, my boy. You shall never guess. Ah, good, Sophie is here as well."

"What is it?" Stephen felt himself tense. He despised surprises.

"We shall call it a late wedding present."

"Oh?"

"I rode over to see my old friend Forsythe a few days ago and just received confirmation. I negotiated another fortnight's leave for you. No bridegroom should have to run off to rejoin his regiment when there isn't a war on. Another two weeks of wedded bliss with your bride. Not a real wedding trip, I grant you. Your grandmother and I traveled the continent for the greater part of a year. But as this more than doubles your current honeymoon, I think it must suffice."

Stephen sat there, stunned. He turned toward Sophie, meeting her startled look. Without removing his gaze from hers, he said, "I . . . don't know what to say. You shouldn't have, sir."

"Of course I should. No use reaching this rank if I can't be of some use now. It is a great pleasure to do something good for my grandson and his wife."

"But I am all packed. Sophie and I have discussed everything related to my absence and have said our good-byes."

"Well, then, now you may say hello and good-bye all over again. Though I daresay you shall enjoy the former more than the latter." The colonel's eyes twinkled.

"It is very thoughtful, sir. But I don't think I ought to remain here any longer. My commander expects me."

"Forsythe will take care of all that. He said to tell you not to give it another thought. It's all arranged. He did mention something about naming your firstborn child after him, but I never cared for the name Ethelbert myself, so I made no promises." He winked.

The colonel looked from one to the other, and his boyish smile faded. "I begin to think you do not like my gift, though I cannot fathom the reason. Are my feelings to be hurt? And no doubt your wife's in the bargain?"

Sophie spoke up at last, "It is very kind of you, Colonel. Truly. We are only taken aback. We dared not think of such a possibility, when we have been steeling ourselves for the . . . inevitable."

Colonel Horton patted her hand. "There, there. What a good soldier you are, my dear. You chose wisely, my boy — I can see that already. Now let me do this small thing for you. All right?"

Stephen met her gaze again, and she gave a slight nod. "Then indeed I shall stay, sir," he said. "And bless you for it."

"Yes, Colonel," Sophie added. "We are very grateful."

"Now that is more like it," the older man said. "And I have thought of some diversions for the two of you while you're here. You ought to take a picnic to Norcombe Wood. Very romantic, picnics are. And I shall speak to Janet on the subject. No doubt she will have some ideas as well. She was once a new bride herself after all."

"Well" — the colonel rattled the letter in the air once more — "time to go and share the good news with the rest of the family."

After he left, Stephen and Sophie remained where they were, both facing the door but not speaking.

The long-case clock ticked, ticked, ticked. Finally he said quietly, "I'm sorry."

He felt her gaze fly to his profile. "Why should you be sorry? It wasn't your doing. That is . . . I am not in such a hurry to be rid of you."

He sent her a wry glance. "No? I am glad to hear it." He drew himself up. "So . . . a picnic, hmm? That doesn't sound like such hard duty. Do you think we can manage it?"

She nodded. "I do. Shall we invite your sister to join us?"

His pleasure dimmed. "If you like. Miss Blake and even Keith might enjoy such an outing. And the free food, of course." He forced a grin.

She must have seen through him. "If you'd rather it be just the two of us, I don't mind. I simply thought . . . so much food and preparation for only one couple . . ."

"Yes, I agree. There is safety in numbers, after all."

"I didn't mean —"

"It's all right, little rabbit. I understand."

At dinner that evening, Mr. Overtree beamed at them both. "I hear we are to have the pleasure of your company for longer than expected, Stephen. What happy news. And no doubt you rejoice as well, Sophie."

"I . . . Yes, of course. I am all astonishment."

Mrs. Overtree watched her reaction, then turned to her son. "Your grandfather mentioned a picnic, among other things. Just name the day and I shall have Mrs. Hill make arrangements with Cook and the servants."

"A picnic, my dear?" Mr. Overtree's eyes brightened. "Perhaps we should go along. Heavens, when was the last time you and I went on a picnic?"

"I'm sure Stephen doesn't want his parents chaperoning their outing."

"You would be very welcome," Sophie said. "In fact we were thinking of asking Kate and Miss Blake. And perhaps Mr. Keith might like to come along."

"I adore picnics," Kate enthused. "And I'm sure Angela would like to join us. What about you, Mr. Keith?"

"I think a basket of Mrs. John's pies beneath a tree sounds just the thing. A bottle of claret wouldn't go amiss either."

"A picnic is all very well." Mrs. Overtree nodded and drew back her shoulders. "But I have decided that since we have another fortnight before Stephen rejoins his regiment, we shall also host a dinner, in place of the neglected wedding breakfast, to congratulate the newly married couple."

"Thank you, Mamma. But that is not necessary," Captain Overtree said. "You know I am not keen on large parties, and Sophie would be quite overwhelmed. It is kind of you to offer, but I see no need to go to all the expense and trouble to pull off such an event in a couple weeks' time. No Mamma. Thank you, but no."

Her eyes sparked. "I was not asking your permission, Stephen. In fact, the wheels are already in motion. You needn't make a speech if you don't like, but you cannot deny our friends and neighbors the opportunity to meet your wife, and to wish you well before you leave us again for who knows how long. You are the first of our offspring to marry though, Lord willing, not the last. You must allow us to acknowledge the event. Do you want everyone to think we are not proud and happy about your marriage?"

He held his mother's challenging gaze a moment, and Sophie feared he might continue to argue. Beneath the table, Sophie reached over and gave his arm a gentle squeeze.

He cleared his throat. "Well, I . . . suppose a dinner would be harmless."

"Can we have dancing, Mamma?" Kate asked eagerly. "I've had all those lessons and have never been to a real ball. Please, Mamma, can we?"

"Now, Kate. No one said anything about a ball," Captain Overtree protested.

Kate turned to her. "You do like to dance, Sophie. Say you do?"

"Well, I . . ." She glanced at Captain Overtree's scowl, then away. "I don't dislike it."

"Have you never been to a ball either?"

"Oh, I have danced in the Bath assembly rooms several times."

"The Bath assembly rooms . . ." Kate breathed. "Is it as marvelous as they say? Crystal chandeliers, fashionable ladies and gentlemen by the score, presided over by a dour master of ceremonies?"

"Yes, all of that. But such a crush it is difficult to move, let alone dance. Especially at the height of the Bath season."

"Please, Mamma, we must have dancing," Kate said. "For Sophie."

Sophie shot another nervous glance at her husband. "It isn't up to me, Kate. I would be more than content with whatever your mother thinks best."

"Well, there's no harm in a few dances after dinner," Mrs. Overtree decided. "Those who wish to dance may, and those that don't may sit down to tea and coffee, or cards."

"Shall we have musicians, Mamma? We have that dusty old gallery that no one ever uses."

"I don't know that we need to hire musicians for a few country dances, Katherine. Perhaps you girls might take turns at the pianoforte."

"No, Mamma, please. Then we shan't be able to dance."

"I am afraid I don't play," Sophie quietly admitted.

"No? What a pity."

"And we must have more gentlemen, Mamma," Kate said. "I don't want to dance with my father all night. Pray do not be offended, Papa."

"Indeed I am not."

"I don't know that your father shall feel equal to dancing in any case," Mrs. Overtree said.

"I'm not dead yet," Mr. Overtree retorted. "I think I can manage a sedate dance or two, though I shall leave the reels to the younger men."

Kate turned to Sophie and explained, "Unfortunately our neighborhood has a dearth of young gentlemen and an overabundance of young ladies."

Carlton Keith, Sophie noticed, had remained silent through the talk of dancing. And little wonder, she supposed, with his disability.

"Angela's brother might come," Kate suggested. "Though now that he is engaged to marry, I suppose we would have to invite his intended as well, so that wouldn't help our numbers." She asked her brother, "Have you no friends in the area, Stephen?"

"I am afraid my friends are primarily military men like myself and are away from home, as I should be." He rectified, "Were it not for Grandfather's kind influence, that is."

Kate looked at her mother. "You will invite Mr. Harrison, I trust?"

Mrs. Overtree opened her mouth to reply, then pressed her thin lips together, thinking the better of whatever she'd been about to say. "We shall discuss the invitation list later, Katherine. Let's leave it for now."

Mr. Keith set down his glass with a sardonic grin. "And what am I, Miss Katherine? Yesterday's rubbish? No doubt all the ladies will be clamoring to dance with me, the one-armed wonder. To grasp this empty sleeve."

Everyone froze, forks or glasses midway to mouths. Kate's face reddened, and Sophie felt embarrassed for Mr. Keith's sake and for all of them. Had they discounted him so thoroughly as a man, or had they sought not to mention him out of polite sensitivity? Sophie wasn't sure, but awkward unease hung heavy in the dining room, as glances shifted one to another.

Kate grew uncharacteristically grave. "I am sorry, Mr. Keith. I did not stop to consider your feelings."

Keith waved away her apology with his

good arm. "No harm done, Miss Katherine. That was done by the French. Besides, losing this arm has had its advantages, I assure you. Ah, the pity of pretty females and the hospitality of a fine family." He lifted his glass in salute. "Thank you, Boney. You changed my life."

The former lieutenant was clearly somewhat drunk, and feeling a little brazen. But his bravado and ironic humor didn't quite cover the pain in his eyes.

"I know," Captain Overtree quipped. "We shall engage a fiddler to play Irish jigs all night. We'd all have to keep our arms at our sides for that dance."

Mr. Keith grinned at him. "Excellent notion, Captain. Hear, hear."

Around the room, people exhaled, relieved the tense moment had passed.

The next morning, Mrs. Overtree gave the cook a few days notice to ready the picnic, and scheduled the dinner for Stephen's final night to give the servants the most time to prepare. Soon, invitations were ordered and the dressmaker summoned. Mrs. Overtree insisted that both Sophie and Kate have new gowns for the occasion. The dressmaker, Mrs. Pannet, arrived, followed by her thin, workworn assistant bearing a sample case and portfolio.

After surveying her subjects' coloring and

taking their measurements, the dressmaker pulled forth fabric swatches and drawings of fashionable but relatively simple gowns, considering how quickly they were needed. Mrs. Pannet and Mrs. Overtree conferred together and settled on their choices. Sophie deferred to her mother-in-law, who was far more decisive and who, after all, would be paying the dressmaker's bill. Kate's gown would be pale pink satin with a crossover bodice, while Sophie would have a gown of blue net over white, with a broad neckline front and back and a high waist. Sophie was especially glad for the high waist.

On Sunday, Stephen's mother announced, "Your father will not be joining us for church today. Not with this damp weather. It is not good for his chest."

"I feel perfectly well, my dear," his father protested.

"Now, yes. And I should like to keep it that way. But the old church with its chilly draughts and sniffling children? Very catching. Especially in your weakened state. No, you stay here, quiet and warm. Better yet, in bed. Don't forget Dr. Matthews comes tomorrow with a new elixir from London. I won't have him thinking I've grown lax in my duty." She pulled on her gloves. "We shall pray for you."

Poor Papa, Stephen thought. It must be

hard at times, being married to a woman raised by a take-charge army commander.

They put on their coats and hats, and made ready to leave. The footman handed around umbrellas, just in case. The ladies accepted, but the colonel waved away the offered implement and made do with turning up the collar of his greatcoat. Stephen did the same.

As they walked to church, the damp mist turned to steady rain. Around him, three umbrellas opened like mushrooms. A flash of orange caught Stephen's eye. He glanced over and saw Gulliver dash through the wet grass and behind the church. *Uh oh.*

"Where is that cat going?" His mother wrinkled her nose. "Mangy creatures. A stray, no doubt. Better in the churchyard than Overtree Hall."

Stephen exchanged concerned looks with Kate. Then he tried to catch Sophie's eye, but her gaze remained on the fleeing feline. He hoped she wouldn't give away Winnie's secret. He sifted through his sluggish mind, trying in vain to think of something to say to distract them both.

"Do you . . . never miss church, Mrs. Overtree?" Sophie asked his mother, sending him a subtle, knowing look.

Stephen exhaled in relief.

"Never. I attend every divine service, and give alms to charity, and pray without ceasing. Who knows what would happen if I failed to do so?"

"Mamma . . ." Stephen gently protested. "It isn't all on your shoulders. It's on God's. Do you really think that if you were to miss one service, or forget to pray, or even heaven forbid, do something wrong, that God would take Papa from you as punishment? Or say, allow me to die, when I otherwise would have lived?"

"Of course He might."

"Mamma. . . . I don't think God works that way. Yes, He wants us to pray, read the Scriptures, and fellowship with other believers, but it isn't as though marking off duties on a list is a guaranteed cure-all."

She sniffed. "I don't know that I agree with you. In any case, it is better to be safe than sorry."

"But it sounds almost like a superstition for you. And how taxing to believe you hold Papa's fate, not to mention that of your entire family, on your own shoulders. Do you never grow weary?"

"Always. But it is my lot in life."

"Your mother is a paragon, Stephen," his grandfather spoke up. "The vicar respects her highly and holds her up as a model for his other parishioners. We should all be half as diligent."

Stephen nodded, but he thought that his mother secretly enjoyed all the attention she received as the long-suffering, dutiful wife of sickly Mr. Overtree. He wished she relied a little more on God and a little less on her own good deeds and religious observances.

They entered the church as the bells rang. Around them, the congregation filled the boxes and pews.

The parish clerk called the service to order as the vicar, Mr. Nelson, climbed into the pulpit. For a moment, Stephen tried to imagine himself in those black forms and white collar, instead of his usual uniform — visiting the sick, helping the poor, and making sermons. Perhaps his grandfather had been right to steer him away from the church. He enjoyed being active and outdoors more than studying, though reading the Scriptures certainly satisfied his soul. Whatever the case, Stephen wouldn't "put his hand to the plough and look back." He wanted to serve God, his country, and his family wherever he was. And if he could do some good to friends or neighbors along the way, so much the better.

The topic of Mr. Nelson's sermon that day was God's merciful redemption of the world, through Christ's sacrificial death. He read from Psalm 32, "Blessed is he whose transgression is forgiven, whose sin is covered." And he ended with Galatians 1, "Grace be to you and peace from God the Father, and from our Lord Jesus Christ, who gave himself for our sins, that he might deliver us from this present evil world, according to the will of God and our Father: To whom be glory for ever and ever. Amen."

Sophie, he noticed, listened intently through it all. Did she know the matchless peace that came from God's merciful grace — sending His Son to die to pay the price for mankind's sins, so all might live with Him, forgiven, forever?

He hoped and prayed she did.

Chapter 13

The day of the picnic arrived, and Stephen found himself both anticipating and dreading it at the same time. He doubted he had the courtly manners to eat dainties on his lap without spilling and help ladies with their parasols over rough ground, all the while keeping up a pleasant flow of polite conversation. His ideal day out-of-doors would be spent fishing or hunting, stopping to drink water from a stream when he was thirsty, and when he felt hungry, to eat a pie wrapped in waxed paper begged from Mrs. John's kitchen. Stephen sighed, dressed himself in trousers and tweed, and decided to make the best of it.

The weather was fine and the wood not far off, so the party gathered in the hall to walk to Norcombe Wood together. Stephen looked forward to the exercise, which would no doubt rouse their appetites. Mrs. Hill, however, arranged for a horse and wagon to carry the hampers of food and drink, and a footman to serve it.

Together, the five of them walked beneath the entrance gate and strolled down the lane into the open countryside. Daffodils bloomed among the trees, and birdsong punctuated the peaceful silence. Newborn lambs cavorted in the meadows while bored-looking ewes chewed and bleated. Stephen relished every sight. Perhaps no artist would be eager to paint this landscape, but to him it was a beautiful scene. It was home. He was proud to think his family owned a great deal of the land stretching in all directions.

He hoped Sophie liked what she saw as well, that she would come to love this place as he did. He glanced at her, noticing she wore an elegant lilac dress and white spencer, her gloved hands clasped behind her back. Honeyed strands of hair escaped her bonnet and gleamed in the sunlight. He swallowed, and shifted his gaze.

Angela Blake also looked stylish in a green and buff dress and bonnet, her parasol wavering in the spring breeze. He saw scant vestiges of the reedy girl with red plaits who had shadowed him and Wesley growing up, sometimes beating them at their own races and games. Lieutenant Keith, Stephen noticed, remained near her side.

After about a mile, they crossed a stone bridge and turned into Norcombe Wood. They halted at the edge of a clearing bordered

by a stream — one of his favorite spots to
fish. In fact, there was a man on the bank
now, casting a line into the water. The figure
turned, and Stephen recognized young Mr.
Harrison.

"How delightful!" Kate beamed and called
a greeting. Mr. Harrison waved in reply.

Miss Blake sent Stephen a sidelong glance,
eyes innocently wide. "What a fortunate coincidence."

Stephen doubted it.

Kate hurried ahead, and Angela called after
her, "You must invite him to join us, Kate!"

Stephen did not miss the mischievous slant
of her smile.

"Are you acquainted with Mr. Harrison?"
Sophie asked, looking from him to Miss
Blake and back again.

Stephen nodded, eyes narrowed. He knew
Mr. Harrison, of course, but not well. With
his mother's disapproval in mind, he did not
wish to encourage the man where his sister
was concerned.

Sophie's hand on his arm surprised him.
She whispered, "You're not going to send him
away, are you?"

Stephen met her hesitant gaze with a wry
grin. "I am not so ill-mannered, I assure you."

"Good."

She dropped her hand, the feathery warmth
of her fingers disappearing. He should have
reacted more quickly — laid his hand over

hers — but it was too late.

The groom helped carry over the hampers and spread the picnic blankets, then returned to the horse and wagon while the footman remained behind to serve.

Keith offered to hold Miss Blake's parasol while she sat down and arranged her skirts. Then he dispatched a trespassing insect from the blanket as though a sworn enemy. Stephen studied Angela's reaction, trying to gauge if she minded the man's attentions. His former lieutenant could be overbearing at times, especially when drinking, but it was early in the day and he had yet to start. Angela's expression remained benign as she regarded Keith, apparently tolerating his attentions as one tolerates warm licks from an overeager pup.

Stephen sat near Sophie, feeling awkward, unsure what to do with his long legs. Sophie tucked hers beneath herself with enviable ease. Mr. Harrison looked awkward himself, standing there with his fishing rod and empty pail.

"No luck, Mr. Harrison?" Miss Blake asked with a smile.

He shook his head. "Not today."

"He'd finally hooked one," Kate apologized, "but it got away when we interrupted him."

Mr. Harrison shrugged. "A small sacrifice for the pleasure of your company."

Miss Blake patted a spot on the blanket

between herself and Kate. "Do sit down."

With a questioning look at Stephen, Mr. Harrison set aside his gear and complied. "Thank you for inviting me to join you."

Kate motioned to the feast before them. "We have plenty to share."

"As long as he sticks to the lemonade," Mr. Keith muttered.

Their cook, Mrs. John, had outdone herself. There was enough food for a party twice their size: a joint of cold ham, roast chickens, veal and pigeon pies, and preserved fruit. There were also cheeses, bread, butter, lemonade, and the promised bottle of claret, which Carlton Keith helped himself to, though not as liberally as Stephen might have expected.

Looking at the overabundance of food before him, Stephen felt a stab of guilt. He ought to be with his men, drilling, living in stark conditions with them, not in the lap of luxury while they ate poorly and slept in crude tents.

The footman brought out raspberry jam tarts and ginger biscuits for dessert. He noticed Sophie wrap two biscuits in a linen table napkin, and surreptitiously slip them into her reticule. For her later enjoyment, he supposed. He had heard women in her condition were prone to food cravings at all hours.

Noticing his attention, she mouthed, "For Winnie."

"Ah." His heart warmed at her thoughtfulness.

Miss Blake asked, "And what are your plans for the future, Mr. Harrison? Will you follow your father into the church?"

"I don't think so, no. I aspire to be a writer."

"Oh? A novelist?" Kate asked.

"I'm afraid not. I am primarily interested in history."

"Oh. Well, history is good too, I suppose."

Mr. Harrison asked Kate about her favorite book, and Kate eagerly complied with an enthusiastic and detailed description of *Sense and Sensibility.*

After they had eaten their fill, Mr. Harrison thanked them and rose. "Well. If you will excuse me, I had better head home."

Kate's expression dimmed. "Must you go already?"

"I'm afraid so. I'll need to stop at the fishmonger's on the way." He smiled sheepishly. "Mamma has her heart set on perch for dinner. Hopefully, my skill in buying fish exceeds my skill in catching them."

Kate returned his smile. Then Mr. Harrison bowed in farewell and took his leave.

After their guest departed, Stephen relaxed. The ladies sat primly on one end of the blanket in the shade, Miss Blake and his sister talking and laughing while Sophie listened. He and Keith sprawled nearby at their leisure with legs outstretched, lulled by warm air, peaceful birdsong, and the murmuring stream.

Keith groaned with satisfaction. "I could not eat another bite — or move."

Kate passed him the biscuit tin, and with a shrug he popped one into his mouth, earning himself a headshake from Miss Blake and an amused swat from Kate.

Keith refilled his glass of claret and offered to pour Stephen a glass. He declined, as usual.

Kate and Angela prattled on like eager schoolgirls, making Keith the frequent recipient of their good-natured teasing, which the man clearly enjoyed. Stephen, however, grew restless and rose to stretch his legs, and to put some distance between himself and the incessant chatter.

As he walked away from the group, Sophie called after him. "Captain?"

She had risen to her feet but paused to accept the parasol Miss Blake thrust toward her.

"If you must walk about in the sunshine, I insist you use this. Think of your fair complexion!"

Stephen waited where he was.

Unfurling the parasol, Sophie approached him. "May I walk with you?"

"Of course. I only wanted to stretch my legs — and rest my ears."

She grinned up at him, and he returned the

gesture, feeling his heart lighten.

They walked along the stream in silence for several moments. Then she must have felt his gaze resting on her profile, for she glanced over at him.

"I feel like an imposter," she admitted, twirling her parasol for emphasis. "Or an actress playing a role. This dress isn't mine, nor even this bonnet. It's like a costume."

"You look charming in it."

"Thank you. But all this —" She gestured back toward the blanket and spread of food, the sweep of her arm encompassing the idyllic spring day. "It's like a stage. Or a painting."

He nodded. "You ought to have brought your easel."

"I wish I had," she agreed on a sigh. "Though I would feel too self-conscious to paint in company."

As her words sank in, Stephen squinted up at the sun shining through the canopy of tree branches above them. He said, "And you find the role of my wife a difficult one to play, I gather?"

She sent him a worried look. "You know what I mean. Pretending that we are a normal, newly married couple."

"What is normal? A lot of marriages begin less than romantically. Look at my parents . . . On second thought, perhaps not. Mamma was handsome and Papa a wealthy heir. They may not be the ideal to aspire to."

He stopped walking and looked at her sharply. "Not that you are not handsome. I did not mean that. You know I think you are lovely. But I am certainly not a wealthy heir pursued by beautiful women for his money." What an idiot he was. He should know better than to open his mouth around women — especially one he found attractive. Especially his wife.

Sophie ducked her head, and a becoming blush stained her cheeks. "Thank you for clarifying."

Perhaps he had not botched things so badly after all.

She looked up and said, "May I ask, Captain, if you have ever been in love, or considered marriage before? Perhaps with . . . Jenny?"

Shock squeezed Stephen's chest. He felt his mouth part. "Where on earth did you hear that name?"

"You . . . em, said it in your sleep on our wedding night."

He winced. "I would prefer not to talk about that, if you don't mind." Especially not when Sophie was just beginning to warm to him, to change her earlier assessment of his "black" character. Abruptly, he said, "Shall we rejoin the others?"

She looked away and forced a smile. "Of course."

They turned and strolled back toward the picnic blanket.

There, Miss Blake was talking to his former lieutenant. "Keith . . . Is that a Scottish surname?" she asked.

Carlton nodded. "In my case, yes. Though my family has lived in England for several generations."

"Angela has been to Scotland," Kate interjected.

Keith looked at Miss Blake with interest. "Oh? What took you there?"

Angela sketched a little shrug. "I traveled there with my aunt once. She had always wanted to see the Highlands."

"When was this?"

"Five years ago."

Kate added, "She was gone for months."

"Well, we saw more than Scotland," Angela explained. "The north of England, the Peak, and then on to the Highlands. A bit of a grand tour, but here in old and relatively safe Britain, rather than abroad as young gentlemen do."

"Or soldiers shipped to foreign parts. Scotland sounds better than the battlefields of Spain, ay, Captain?" Keith winked at Stephen, then returned his gaze to Miss Blake. "Did you enjoy the trip?"

Miss Blake shook her head, eyes distant. "I can't say that I did."

"I am sorry to hear it."

"Then why did you stay away so long?" Kate pouted. "I missed you terribly."

Warm eyes focused on Miss Blake, Keith said quietly, "Yes, I can understand that. . . ."

Stephen noticed the way Keith's gaze lingered on Angela, and felt uneasy. A woman like Angela Blake — an accomplished young lady from a leading family of gentry — was not likely to return the affections of a disabled former lieutenant with no fortune and few prospects.

Finding Mr. Keith looking at her, Angela ducked her head self-consciously. Also strange, for Angela was never shy or retiring.

She shifted and changed the subject. "And you, Mr. Keith? Did you enjoy being an officer and all it entailed?"

Keith screwed up his face. "Not in the least. I never wanted to be a soldier — wasn't cut out for military life. I had about as much right to wield a gun as Marsh has to wield a paintbrush. Really, it was ridiculous."

"I don't agree," Stephen grumbled. "I am quite effective with a paintbrush. Painted the barracks singlehandedly one year."

Keith replied, "Only because Major Wilson wanted to put you in your place."

But Angela ignored their little exchange, her eyes fastened on Keith. "Then . . . why choose that profession?"

"Because when my father died, every farthing of his fortune was gone, gambled away, except for the commission he'd purchased for me. He left me no choice."

Stephen could relate. He'd been given little choice in his career either.

Keith glanced over and saw Kate and Miss Blake hanging on his words. Something flashed in his eyes as he continued.

"I know you ladies like the notion of a brave soldier. But if a woman was tempted to look at me that way — to idealize me, or romanticize this —" He lifted his empty sleeve. "Then she is certain to be disappointed. Isn't me. Never has been, and never will be."

Miss Blake watched him closely. "Then what will you do with your life? You have been honorably discharged, and your father isn't here any longer to force you to do anything. Can you not choose what sort of man you want to be?"

Keith held her gaze. "I'm afraid the man I want to be seems far from reach, Miss Blake." He poured another glass.

Sophie watched the volley of words between Mr. Keith and Miss Blake like a spectator at a shuttlecock match. So much reverberated beneath the words — those said, and those not said. Sophie had never before felt sorry for Carlton Keith, but seeing the bleak longing in his eyes when he looked at Angela Blake, she thought she just might.

Mr. Keith rose and ambled somewhat

unsteadily toward the wagon.

Miss Blake watched him go — part wistful, part irritated. "My father warned me about him," she said in a low voice. "He was some acquainted with the elder Mr. Keith — a heavy drinker and gambler. Like father like son, I suppose."

Sophie glanced at the captain, wondering if he would contradict her, but he did not. Probably could not.

A few minutes later, Keith walked back, two fishing rods in hand. The men had packed gear in the wagon along with the hampers.

"Care to fish, Captain?"

"In a minute. You go ahead."

Keith yanked off his boots and stockings, baring his calves, and then stepped into the shallows in knee-length pantaloons. "Hang me, that's cold!" He lifted his knees in a little jig as he cast his line into the current.

Kate and Angela discreetly rolled off their own stockings beneath their long skirts and tucked them into their shoes at the side of the blanket. Together they giggled and walked across the stream on a series of rocks spaced apart almost like a path. Sophie could imagine them as younger girls doing the same, against the warnings of their mammas or governesses.

"Sophie, come and join us!" Kate called, arms outstretched like a tightrope walker.

She waved at them. "I shall find it more diverting to watch you two."

"Hear, hear," Keith agreed.

"Come on. Don't be a spoilsport," Kate cajoled.

Sophie turned to Captain Overtree on the blanket nearby. "Is it deep?"

"Only about three or four feet, depending on recent rains."

She glanced down at the dress she wore. "Your mother had this dress altered for me. I wouldn't want to spoil it."

"Sophie!" Kate called again.

"Oh, very well." Sophie set aside the parasol and pulled off her gloves. "Just a moment!"

"Be careful," he warned. "The rocks can be slippery."

Remembering her shoes and stockings, Sophie hesitated.

Noticing the direction of her gaze, he patted the blanket beside him. "Come closer. I'll help."

Her face heated. "Thank you, but I can do it myself."

He said in a low voice, "No one is near. And we are playing roles, remember?"

He slid nearer, grasped her half boot, and — laying one ankle onto his own outstretched leg — began untying and loosening the laces.

Embarrassed, Sophie protested, "That's quite all right, Captain. I am perfectly capable of —"

"Shh." He made quick work of removing one half boot, then shifted to the second. Her face burned at the thought of him reaching up her skirt to roll down her stockings. No. That would not do. Not here. Not . . . anywhere. When he set aside the second boot, she scrambled to her feet.

"Th-thank you, Captain."

She stepped behind a stout evergreen for privacy and removed her stockings herself. Avoiding his gaze, she discreetly tucked them into her boot tops before turning toward the bank. The captain, she noticed, had yanked off his own boots as well.

By now, Kate and Angela had reached the other side of the stream and were waving her over.

Sophie stepped carefully onto the first rock, then to the next with ease. But the farther out she went, the farther apart the rocks were spaced, something she had not realized from shore. She hopped from one rock to the next, and wavered, stretching out her arms as Kate had done to balance herself. She judged the distance to the next rock — it was even farther away. How had Kate and Angela made it look so easy? She felt suddenly dizzy and off-balance. She would go back. But when she tried to turn on her narrow perch, she teetered, almost losing her balance. The rock she had just come from suddenly seemed too far away. What was wrong with her?

Perspiration itched along her brow, and she tasted bile.

Splash, splash, splash. Footsteps slapped through water and suddenly Captain Overtree was there, hands on her elbows, steadying her, heedless of the water darkening his buff trousers.

"Steady. I've got you."

"Oh no, your clothes. I'm sorry. I have lost my balance and my nerve. Foolish of me, I know. It's only water."

"Are you all right?"

"Of course. I . . . ." Her skin prickled, and spots dotted her vision like a lace curtain. She felt herself sway.

A moment later she found herself lifted in his arms. She uttered a little cry of protest and, fearing she might fall, wrapped her hands around his neck. His arms supported her knees and back, her side pressed to his abdomen. She was in Captain Overtree's arms — her husband's arms, she reminded herself — and felt off-balance for an entirely different reason.

"What's wrong?" Kate called. "Is she all right?"

Sophie faltered, "I am well, just —"

"Just a ploy to get me to take her in my arms," the captain called back in teasing tones.

Sophie looked at him askance, but inwardly applauded his tact in easing Kate's anxiety, and her own.

Well played, Captain. Well played.

The picnic ended soon after that. The footman and groom packed up, and Mr. Keith returned to shore empty-handed, not managing a single catch — fish or female.

CHAPTER 14

The next afternoon, the girls had another dress fitting to endure. As Sophie left her bedchamber for the appointment, she noticed Captain Overtree climbing the stairs to the attic and assumed, or at least hoped, he was going to visit Miss Whitney.

Mrs. Pannet and her assistant returned with the tacked-up dresses, which, in her estimation, were coming along nicely. Kate's gown had remained simple, as planned, but the dressmaker had decided to embellish Sophie's, since the new Mrs. Overtree would be an honored guest for the party. She had added chenille embroidery, and ribbon trimming at the shoulder for height and elegance. Blue rosettes adorned the bodice, and the white skirt was shot through with the same blue threads. She also planned to add a flounced hem of the same blue, if madame approved.

Both Mrs. Overtrees heartily did so.

When her fitting ended some twenty or

thirty minutes later, Sophie went up to Miss Whitney's room. She assumed Captain Overtree would still be there and decided to join them, taking the ginger biscuits she'd saved from the picnic the day before.

When she entered, Miss Whitney turned from the window. "Oh, hello, Mrs. Overtree."

Sophie glanced around the room. "Where is the captain? I thought he would be here with you."

"No, he hasn't been up to see me today. But I saw him. He rode off a quarter of an hour ago."

"Did he?" That surprised Sophie.

"Mm-hmm," the woman said, her gaze returning to the window. "I've just been bird watching."

Sophie crossed the room to see what had captured the woman's devoted attention. Besides a very fat pigeon, she saw no birds at present. But down below across the drive she did see Kate and young Mr. Harrison talking over the churchyard wall again. *Bird watching, indeed.*

She decided not to comment. Instead, she held out the biscuits on the linen napkin like the friendship offering it was.

Miss Whitney's eyes brightened. "Thank you, my dear. I adore biscuits."

Sophie noticed an overflowing glass dish of wrapped sweets on the table. "And you like sweets, apparently."

Miss Whitney shook her head. "Not particularly. But they are a sweet victory."

"How so?" Sophie asked, confused.

Miss Whitney chewed her lip. "Don't tell Stephen, but I rarely eat them. They stick to my teeth. But he's been giving them to me for years on my birthday and at Christmas, and I hate to hurt his feelings."

"Perhaps I might think of a tactful way to suggest another gift?"

"Oh, I don't mind. I find uses for them."

"What else do you like, Miss Whitney? I shall keep a lookout for your favorites."

"I like fruit, especially berries. But it's a bit early in the year. Otherwise, I'm not particular. The only foods I cannot tolerate are turnips and shellfish. Cook knows that and sends them up often." Winnie made a funny face and sighed. "At least my cat enjoys the fish. I have yet to find a taker for the turnips."

Sophie grinned. "Surely Mrs. John doesn't send fish and turnips every night."

"No. But she is stingy, that one. Sends up the smallest portions — leavings by the looks of it. A crust of bread, a chicken leg, a dollop of pudding. I may be thin, but I need to keep up my strength. Probably thinks I sit about all day and night and don't need to eat. But it's not true. And what I *do* get, I have to share with Gulliver and the birds. She refuses to send up anything especially for them. I dare not complain to the mistress. I don't want to give her any reason to send me packing."

"Surely the captain and Kate wouldn't let that happen."

"I don't worry when the captain is in residence, but after he leaves . . . ? And as far as Kate, I am fond of the girl, but I think if her mother or Miss Blake made a big enough fuss, she would go along with plans to put me out."

Winnie sat down, took a bite of her biscuit, and asked eagerly, "Now. How goes married life?"

"Well, I . . . I don't know," Sophie faltered. "There are many adjustments to make when one finds oneself bound to a man she barely knows."

"And not the man you thought you'd marry."

Sophie reared her head back in surprise. "Excuse me?"

"I . . . only meant that the person we first meet is not often the person we come to know on longer acquaintance."

"Ah. That may be. But Captain Overtree is a good man. I see that."

"He is indeed. The best of men. I'm glad you recognize that. So many seem to prefer Master Wesley, even though Stephen is kinder than his handsome brother. To me at least."

Sophie thought it wisest not to delve into the subject of Wesley and which brother she might prefer.

Instead she asked the woman, "Did you never think of marrying?" Sophie thought again of having blurted out this same question to Captain Overtree. She'd been unsettled by his refusal to answer.

"I thought about it often," Winnie replied. "There was a shoemaker I considered marrying once. Perhaps I should have. I didn't love him, but he would have provided for me. I wouldn't find myself living alone, all but forgotten in the only home I've known for the past thirty years."

"Do you never go outside, or into society? You must become bored at times."

Miss Whitney gave her a knowing look. "Are you bored, when you're alone with your paints?"

Sophie blinked at her. "How did you know I paint?"

"Oh. Perhaps it's second sight." She winked. "Or perhaps the fact that you have paint beneath your fingernails. . . ."

Sophie looked down to check, though she'd not painted in weeks.

"Made you look!" The old woman giggled like a schoolgirl. "Sorry, my dear. I was only teasing you. Stephen told me."

"Oh." Sophie forced a polite little chuckle, though she was discomfited by the changeable woman. She asked, "But don't you miss being among other people? You must get lonely up here."

"Lonely, I can't deny. But not bored. I like to read, although nowadays my mind wanders along with my eyes. I still like reading short stories, and news articles. Magazines are my favorite. Kate brings up hers when she has finished with them. Do you subscribe to any?"

"I'm afraid not."

"That's a shame." Winnie sighed. "Kate said she would ask Miss Blake to lend me her copies of *Ackermann's Repository,* but so far she hasn't been willing to part with them. At least not to me. She's on Mrs. Overtree's side where I'm concerned. The elder Mrs. Overtree, I mean."

"I knew who you meant."

Miss Whitney cocked her head to one side and mused, "And what about the younger Mrs. Overtree? Which side will she end up on, I wonder?" She watched Sophie, her blue eyes alight with interest and perhaps a trace of worry. "Do you mind sharing a few morsels of your husband's time with me?"

"Not at all." *Better you than flirtatious Flora,* Sophie thought, but she didn't say so.

"Good. I lived in a poorhouse once, as a girl." Winnie shuddered. "And it's an experience I hope never to repeat."

That evening, as they walked down to dinner together, Sophie asked the captain where he

247

had gone while she had been busy with the dressmaker and later with Winnie.

An odd look filled his eyes — surprise, secrecy, guilt? "I . . . am not at liberty to tell you just yet. But it's nothing to fear, I assure you."

Sophie hoped that was true.

That night, the captain was late coming up for bed. Libby had come and gone and still he had not appeared, nor did she hear anything from his dressing room. Sophie climbed into bed with the first volume of *Sense and Sensibility,* which Kate had lent her, and tried to read.

Sometime later, Sophie paused and looked up. What had she heard? A thump and a scrape as though someone had tripped behind the bed. If there were mice in the walls, they were awfully big. She closed her eyes to listen, and heard the drone of a voice coming from somewhere nearby. From her dressing room? Her pulse accelerated at the thought.

Breathlessly, she whispered, "Who's there?"

But silence was the only reply. She laid aside the novel, climbed from bed, and tiptoed to her dressing room. Moonlit and empty.

She returned to her book.

A short while later, she heard footsteps and muffled male voices, and again rose to investigate. Quietly opening her door, she saw the captain and Edgar carrying a crate between them, up the stairs. The corner hit the stair rail and nearly dropped. The captain let out a mild epithet. Then the men repositioned their grips and continued upward.

Sophie's stomach clenched. Was that the crate that held Wesley's paintings of her — those they had packed up in Lynmouth? Was he carrying them up surreptitiously, to avoid his parents asking to see them?

She tiptoed across the corridor and partway up the stairs, curious to know if they were taking the crate to Wesley's room. She assumed they were. But the men continued up the next flight of stairs toward the top floor. *Why?* Was he hoping to hide them, to keep them from being discovered even after he'd gone? Was he so ashamed of them? Of her?

Or did the crate not hold paintings at all? Was it something for Winnie, or . . . someone else? She wanted to ask, but considering his evasive answer about his earlier errand, and about "Jenny," she decided against it.

The next day, after Captain Overtree left to meet with a tenant, Sophie grew restless. She thought about that crate she had seen him and Edgar carrying. She thought about the paintings Wesley had done of her this year. She was also still curious to discover if the large painting she had posed for last year was up in his room or studio. Otherwise, what had he done with it? She knew it was risky —

249

emotionally and otherwise — but she wanted to take a peek. Dare she? Especially now with Mr. Keith in residence?

Feeling self-conscious, Sophie walked up one flight of stairs. First, she strolled through the gallery, her heels clicking and echoing down the long room. She ran a hand over the hobbyhorse. Studied the old family portraits. And stood at the window overlooking the gardens and beyond, Miss Blake's home, Windmere, which she could see quite clearly from there. She glimpsed Captain Overtree talking to a man in brown coat and flat cap beside a low stone wall. A female in green cloak and bonnet came by — Miss Blake, she guessed, though she could not make out her features. The man in brown tipped his hat and returned to his work on the wall, but the woman remained to talk with Stephen. Sophie wondered what the two had to talk about, and reminded herself they were childhood friends.

Gathering her courage, Sophie walked out into the corridor and paused at the door to Wesley's studio. Venturing in there would be easier to explain than being found in his bedchamber, she decided, though she was curious to see that as well. Listening for anyone nearby and hearing no one, Sophie inched open the door and slipped inside, closing it quietly behind her.

For a moment she simply took it all in.

Dust motes floated in shafts of sunlight from tall windows. A shrouded easel. Jumbled supplies, scattered papers and rags. The faint smell of paint and turpentine.

Then she saw a crate in the corner.

Heart thumping, she crossed to it on tiptoe, not sure whose room was below this one and not wanting to announce her presence. She scanned the direction and recognized Maurice's handwriting. Here, after all, were the paintings she and the captain had packed away. Then what was in the crate she had seen Stephen and Edgar carrying up to the attic?

She bent to look closer and noticed with relief that this crate was still nailed shut. She assumed — hoped — Wesley's parents wouldn't open it without him present.

Sophie moved on and fingered through his brushes, remembering the long, capable fingers that had held them. Held her . . . Then she looked through the canvases propped against the walls. She recognized several Lynmouth landscapes — the harbor, the Valley of Rocks, the village itself. But nothing of her. She was relieved, yet still wondered what became of that large portrait.

She stepped to the easel to assure herself the canvas it held was not the one of her. She lifted the cloth and recognized the painting with a little jolt, though she was not its subject. Now she understood why the hall in this house had seemed familiar when she first arrived. She had seen this colorful scene before, during Wesley's first winter in Lynmouth. . . .

One day Sophie had stopped by the hillside cottage, bringing Mr. Overtree a batch of almond biscuits. While he painted, she looked through the canvases propped against the wall, stopping to admire his painting of a masquerade ball — masked and costumed figures milling and dancing by the glow of a hundred candles.

"This is unusual for you," Sophie observed. "So many people. You usually paint single subjects."

"True. But it's an image I've wanted to re-create for years."

"I have never attended a masquerade ball," Sophie confessed, moving on to the next canvas.

"Nor have I," he said.

Sophie turned to him in surprise. "But . . . how did you paint this, then? You told me you prefer realism to mere fancy."

"Right again. I have never attended a masquerade, but I did witness one. When I was a boy, my parents hosted a ball at Overtree Hall. I was supposed to be in bed. Instead, I sneaked behind the musicians' gallery and looked down into the great hall from the squint there. Our old nurse caught me and whacked my backside. There went my biscuits for a week." He popped one of her biscuits into his mouth with a grin.

Sophie chuckled to imagine the mischievous boy he had been, then looked at the painting again. "It was worth it, I assure you. Though how challenging this must have been. All these figures . . ."

"Yes, though at least most of the faces were covered in masks, so I didn't have to paint every pair of eyes."

"The hardest part, according to my father."

His gaze shifted from the canvas before him to her face. "*Your* eyes are definitely challenging. Comprised of a dozen shades of blue, as well as green and grey and yellow. And don't get me started on your gorgeous hair!"

She bit back a smile and felt her face heat.

He studied her closely. "Nor can I adequately capture the elegant turn of your head, the long curve of your neck, or the sweet blush that blooms on those high cheekbones of yours whenever I tell you how beautiful you are. . . . Ah, you see? There it is again."

Sophie returned to the present, remembering with a little ache what it felt like to be admired. To be in love. Then she stepped to the open, adjoining door and looked into Wesley's bedchamber — masculine and tidy, under the housemaids' care in his absence.

No portrait of her hung on his wall. No miniature on his side table. She considered going in to look closer but remained in the threshold. She didn't want to cross the line into his bedchamber. She knew from experience the trouble that could cause.

She looked back over her shoulder at the disorderly supplies and scattered papers. The studio was clearly off limits to the housemaids. Crossing the cluttered room again, she idly bent to pick up a crumbled wad of paper in the corner — probably tossed at the hearth but had missed its mark. Hoping it wasn't a discarded sketch of her, she flattened it, and instead found a cryptic note.

We have to talk. — J.B.

Who was J.B.?

Behind her the door creaked open, and Sophie whirled in alarm. There stood Mrs. Overtree.

"Oh!" Sophie pressed a hand to her chest. "You startled me."

Her mother-in-law's eyes widened to see her there, then abruptly narrowed. "Sophie . . . ? I thought I heard someone skulking about in here. My boudoir is directly below this room."

Sophie winced. *Of course it is.*

"I thought one of the housemaids was trespassing."

"No. Just me. I was . . . only curious. Don't worry, I haven't touched anything." She guiltily curled her fingers around the wadded paper.

Mrs. Overtree's gaze swept the room, hesitating on the crate in the corner. Sophie's pulse quickened. Did Mrs. Overtree know about the crate? Would she suggest opening it then and there?

Sophie swallowed and walked toward the door, hoping her swaying skirts blocked the woman's view of the crate. "Your son is really quite talented, but I shouldn't have intruded. I suppose he would not like . . . anyone . . . looking at his work without him?"

"Quite right. This room is off limits."

"To the housemaids, or to family as well?" Sophie didn't like having to remind the woman she was a relative now, but neither did she like being lumped in with the staff.

Mrs. Overtree glanced around the studio once more, then backed from the doorway. "Well, I don't think he likes anyone in here. He's very particular." She held the door open. "After you."

Sophie complied and forced a smile, hoping to chase away the suspicion lingering in the woman's eyes.

CHAPTER 15

Early the next morning, Captain Overtree knocked on the dressing room door while Sophie was still in her nightclothes.

"Just a minute!" she called. She slipped her dressing gown around her, then went to the door.

When she opened it, she saw he was already dressed in her favorite of his coats. A dark Spanish blue that brought out the color of his eyes.

He asked, "What would you say to an outing today, just you and me?"

"An outing?"

"Yes, a little respite from watchful eyes, family obligations, and . . . playacting." A corner of his mouth quirked.

"Sounds lovely."

"Good. Dress in something fine. We'll go in the landau — it's a beautiful day." He turned back with a little smirk. "Bring that parasol you are so fond of."

"Another picnic?" she asked.

"No. Something more . . . refined. No need to remove half boots and no rock climbing. I promise."

"Very well."

When Libby entered, Sophie explained the day's plan. She chose a blue carriage dress, buff leather slippers with blue tassels, and a bonnet trimmed in lace and a tinted silk hydrangea.

"You look beautiful, madam," Libby said, fussing with the curls peeking out from beneath the brim.

"Thank you, Libby."

An "outing for just the two of them" was not exactly accurate, for a coachman took the reins and a groom rode on the rear of the landau.

They started off in the same direction they had taken for the picnic but continued straight for several miles once they crossed the stone bridge. The air smelled faintly of hyacinths and new grass, and birds flitted among the hedgerows. The sky above reminded her of one of her favorite pigments: a light wash of Prussian blue, and the wispy clouds like lace in shades of grey-toned lead white.

"Where are we going?" she asked, not really caring.

"We are going to Langton. Famous for its art collection. Have you heard of it?"

Her heart gave a little leap. "Yes! Is the

estate nearby?"

"Not far. I am some acquainted with Lord Thorp. I wrote to him and he has graciously offered us a private tour of his collection."

She stared at him, afraid to believe it. "You are teasing me."

"I am not. What — are you telling me you've already seen it?"

"Heavens no! And I can think of very few things I would enjoy more."

He smiled. "Then I am glad I went to the trouble."

Anticipation singing through her, Sophie sat back to enjoy the ride and the beautiful spring day.

Sometime later, they turned up a long gravel drive and through an iron gate. Clearing a border of oak trees, a classical red brick manor came into view, situated before a reflecting lake and flanked by large topiary houses.

Footmen in powdered wigs came out to greet their arrival and take charge of the carriage. Captain Overtree and Sophie alighted and approached the imposing pillared entrance. At the door, they were met by a black-suited butler who took Captain Overtree's card, announced, "His lordship is expecting you," and led them into a nearby library to wait.

"He's very proud of his collection of books," the captain noted. "Nearly as much as his art collection. It is why, I think, he receives visitors in this particular room."

A few moments later, a second door opened and an impeccably dressed silver-haired man of about sixty years entered.

"Hello, Overtree. Good to see you, my boy."

"My lord, thank you for receiving us. May I present my wife, Mrs. Sophia Overtree. Sophie, Lord Thorp."

The nobleman bent over her hand. "A sincere pleasure, Mrs. Overtree. Welcome. I do hope your husband has not exaggerated your interest in seeing my collection?"

She smiled. "I doubt that possible, my lord."

He beamed and gestured for her to precede him from the room. "Right this way . . ."

The Langton picture gallery stretched for a hundred feet of the ground floor. Stephen admired the original old oak woodwork, while Sophie gaped at the walls lined with portraits three high in some places, set in extravagant baroque gilded frames. "That's a van Dyck . . ." she murmured. "And a John de Critz."

She paused before a portrait of Charles the Second.

"Do you like this one?" Lord Thorp asked.

She grinned. "I like that it was painted by a woman."

His eyes twinkled. "You're right. Mary Beale."

They continued on. Many pieces in the collection were religious paintings — depictions of the crucifixion and resurrection, or of angels ministering to the broken body of Jesus. Others were portraits of family members by Thomas Gainsborough, Joshua Reynolds, and George Romney.

Sophie admired the gracefulness and life in the figures, and a strength of coloring that struck her from one end of that gallery to the other. The collection — and its effect — were beyond anything she had ever experienced. She felt at the same time transported and quite at home.

Craning her neck to better view two portraits high on the wall, Sophie whispered, "Sir Peter Lely and Sir Godfrey Kneller . . ."

Lord Thorp reared his head back in surprise. "You have married a gem, Overtree. Rarely have I met a lady so knowledgeable about artists. You remind me of my grandmother, my dear. Not in age or looks, of course. But she devoted her life to art, and I have collected since I was a young man because of her."

"Have you anything by Claude Dupont?" Stephen asked.

"Dupont? That name does not ring a bell." He lifted an index finger. "But I do have one from another name you might recognize. Follow me." He led them through the door and out into a narrower passage. "I am nearly out

260

of wall space, I fear. So I have resorted to hanging two of my recent acquisitions here. You may have heard of the artist, Wesley Overtree?" He grinned at Stephen. "I bought these from your brother last spring."

Captain Overtree drew up short and stood rigidly still.

Sophie's heart beat dully and her stomach cramped. One was a Lynton landscape. The other was the large portrait of her — looking over her shoulder, hair pinned in a round cushion at the back of her head, eyes somber, expression torn between embarrassment and a smile.

Sophie stood there, mouth dry, wishing she could disappear. She felt Lord Thorp's focus swivel from the painting to her, hesitate, than look again.

"I say, this woman bears a remarkable resemblance to your wife, Overtree."

For a moment, Captain Overtree said nothing. Then he said with apparent nonchalance. "Do you think so?"

The man returned his gaze to the paintings. "The landscape was painted in Devonshire, I remember Wesley telling me. His favorite escape from winters here. I have never been to that part of the country, but now I almost feel that I have been. As far as the woman, I don't remember what he said about her, so much as how she struck me. Her expression, her modesty, her shyness. As though on the cusp of trusting. Of smiling. I confess it reminds me just slightly of Da Vinci's *Mona Lisa,* though in my view this woman is far more attractive."

Sophie licked dry lips. Thank goodness this was the portrait Wesley had painted last winter, before he had talked her into Grecian robes and exposed shoulders.

"I . . . did have the opportunity to *meet* the captain's brother in Devonshire," Sophie admitted. "My father enjoys retreating there during the cold months as well."

The captain added, "I suppose Wesley may have been inspired by meeting Sophie on one of his trips there. That is where I had the good fortune of meeting her as well. She is, as I am happily aware, a beautiful woman."

"Yes, of course," Lord Thorp agreed politely, a little frown line lingering between his brows. Then he drew himself up and smiled at them both. "Well, I am doubly glad to own it now. I shall have to ask him about his inspiration when next I see him. When is he due home?"

"We don't know exactly. He's gone off to Italy again."

Lord Thorp rubbed his palms together. "More work to anticipate! There is no place like Italy for artists. Do tell him to call when he returns."

"Indeed we shall," Captain Overtree agreed. "Though I will have returned to my regiment by then. But my wife can ask Wesley to call. Can you not, my dear?"

"Of course."

They completed their tour. Sophie asked about a few more paintings she was unfamiliar with, and Lord Thorp in turn obliged her by showing her his favorite pieces in the collection.

He offered to ring for tea, but the captain politely declined, mentioning the hour and the return journey ahead. Sophie thanked their host warmly, and he in turn pressed her hand.

"You are a balm, my dear. An absolute delight. I don't suppose you have a much older sister?"

She smiled. "I am afraid not."

"Ah well, such is my luck. Come back and visit anytime you like. My door shall always be open to you."

In the landau on the ride home, Stephen glanced at Sophie and said soberly, "I am sorry. I had no idea." He'd been as stunned as she was. And had instantly recognized the painting as a larger, more detailed version of the one he carried.

"That's all right," she said, gloved hands clasped in her lap. "It's not your fault. But how shocking to see it there."

"Yes. To my knowledge, those are the first pieces of Wesley's Lord Thorp has ever acquired. I am surprised Wes did not trumpet the news to one and all."

Sophie nodded vaguely, and Stephen inwardly chided himself for speaking ill of his brother to her, when he'd been striving to avoid that petty temptation.

He added, "If Lord Thorp bought it, it must be quite good. He's something of an expert, they say. You ought to show him some of your work."

Sophie shook her head. "Heavens, no. Mine are for my eyes only."

He challenged lightly, "And what would you say if Lord Thorp kept his collection for his eyes only?"

She shook her head again. "That argument won't work. His august collection deserves to be displayed and admired. My little scratches are not in the same class."

"How do you know?"

"I know. Believe me, this is not false modesty. I am a painter's daughter. I have been surrounded by art and artists my entire life. And that's all right with me. I don't paint for praise or fame." She chuckled. "And certainly not for money."

She shifted on the seat and changed the subject. "Do many people tour his collection?"

He nodded. "I gather Langton is a popular destination, and the housekeeper often leads tours. As far as I know, Lord Thorp only personally shows his collection to friends."

She gave him a shy smile. "Then how fortunate for me he counts you as a friend."

He enjoyed the warmth of her smile, then asked, "Are you worried my parents or someone else of our acquaintance might see it?"

"The thought did cross my mind."

"It's nothing to be ashamed of," he said to reassure her, but inwardly he dreaded the prospect as well.

"It certainly raises the question of how long I have known your brother and in what capacity. Which reminds me. I had been thinking about the paintings you sent back from Lynmouth. I confess, when I saw you and Edgar carrying a crate upstairs, I thought you intended to hide them in the attic. But then I —"

"No," he hurried to assure her. "I had that crate hauled up to Wesley's workroom, unopened." He was surprised to learn she'd seen him and Edgar that night. He'd thought his secret was safe.

"Yes. Well, thank you," she said. "Do you think your parents might open it in Wesley's absence?"

"I don't know. And I can't ask them not to, not without raising questions."

She nodded thoughtfully. "Is there anyone else locally who might have bought one of Wesley's earlier paintings?"

"Not that I know of." He was relieved she had not pressed him about the crate he'd had carried up to the top floor. Not yet.

"Good," she said on a sigh. "Hopefully Lord Thorp has the only one of me on display."

Stephen thought again of the miniature painting he carried with him. Considered showing it to her. Explaining . . . But the words wouldn't come. Instead he thought back to the day he had found it last year. . . .

He had let himself into the room adjacent to Wesley's bedchamber that his brother used as a workroom. Stephen was looking for the deed to a cottage they had recently purchased to accommodate a tenant farmer with a large family. The deed wasn't in Humphries' office, though Wesley had promised to deliver it there. Stephen guessed Wesley might have mislaid it among his personal papers and sketchbooks. Probably drawn something on it in the bargain.

Stephen fingered through the papers on his desk, and then those scattered around his easel. He found another haphazard pile near the hearth, apparently rough sketches rejected and being used as kindling. *If Wes inadvertently burnt that deed, so help him . . .*

Stephen sank to his haunches and sorted through the pile. And then he'd found her . . . Those soulful eyes. That golden hair. That long graceful neck. Why was this small portrait among Wesley's castoffs? Stephen had wondered. And he'd kept it, without one ounce of guilt.

His brother had discarded it, after all. But Stephen had saved it from the flames.

The next afternoon, inspired by all the art she had seen at Langton, Sophie slipped her drawing pad from her dressing table drawer, where she'd kept it out of sight until now. She did not presume to think she might be able to draw or paint anything fractionally as good as the masterworks she'd seen in Lord Thorp's gallery, but still her fingers itched to hold a drawing pencil or paintbrush again. Painting was difficult to do discreetly, requiring a palette and easel. So for the present she would attempt to satisfy her craving with drawing.

She began in her own bedchamber for privacy, but when Flora came in with her housemaid's box and carpet broom, Sophie gathered her supplies and left the room. She went quietly downstairs and slipped from the side door into the garden. There she sat on a bench with her pad, pencils, and a set of Conté drawing crayons her father had given her for Christmas. She began by sketching the ivy on the garden wall, and the daffodils and another flower she was unfamiliar with — but then a plop of rain landed on her paper, quickly followed by another. She picked up her things and hurried back inside. She went into the morning room, which was rarely used in the afternoons, when Mrs. Overtree entertained callers in the white parlour.

Without flowers as a convenient subject, Sophie fell to sketching a face without any definite plan about whose face it was to be. She took a soft pencil, gave it a broad point, and began working away. Soon she had traced on paper a rectangular face with a broad forehead and a square jaw with a decided cleft down the middle of it. The contours pleased her, and her fingers continued to fill the outline with features: dark, strongly defined eyebrows, a long nose with a straight ridge and full nostrils, and a broad mouth with pleasingly shaped lips downturned in stern lines. She tufted in thick, bristling side-whiskers and black hair falling over the forehead. She left the eyes for last, because eyes were always a challenge and required the most careful working. And because to render them would render futile her willful denial of whose face it was. Finally, she drew prominent eyes and shaped them with a somber slant at the outer edges. She lightly shaded the irises and framed them in dark lashes.

She held the drawing pad away from her and regarded the whole. Something was missing. She darkened the shading, so that the resulting highlights flashed more brilliantly. Yes, he had a decided glint in his eye, though whether of anger or frustration or something else she was never certain.

She held it away once more. Much better. But still there was something missing. Dared she? Why not. The drawing was simply for her own amusement. An exercise for her languishing skills. No one but her would see it.

She took up her pencil again and added in the scar, snaking out from the bristly side-whiskers and across his cheek, the skin there darker, and pulling slightly at the side of his mouth, giving one corner an ironic lift.

There. She had Captain Overtree's face under her gaze; at least a decent likeness. She knew she could do better with a model and in paint, but she was content with her first attempt.

So absorbed was she, that she did not hear anyone enter the room until a voice nearby broke the stillness like a cymbal. She jumped.

"Sophie? What are you doing?" Kate asked, a little frown of surprise creasing her face. Carlton Keith stepped in behind her, a drink in hand, though early in the afternoon.

Sophie quickly closed the sketchbook. "Oh, just . . . passing the time."

"Why are you hiding in here all alone?"

"I'm not hiding. I just wanted . . ." It would

be rude to say she had wanted to be left alone. Instead she said, "Some quiet place to wait while the maid is working in my . . . our room."

"What are we drawing?" Mr. Keith snatched the sketchbook from her hand, and opened it to — thankfully — a page of flowers.

She pulled the book away from him. "Just some flowers and ivy I saw in the garden, before it began to rain."

"Very pretty," he drawled.

She detected a patronizing tone in his voice and wasn't surprised. She knew Mr. Keith had idealized Wesley and stood in awe of his talent.

"May I see?" Kate asked.

Knowing it would only raise suspicions if she refused, she angled the page of flowers for Kate to see before once more closing the sketchbook and tucking it under her arm.

"Lovely," Kate breathed. "I wish I could draw like that."

"That's right . . ." Keith mused, a speculative glint in his eye reminding her of Captain Overtree. "You are a budding artist yourself. Not surprising, I suppose, given you are a painter's daughter. Wesley claims to have tutored you." He lowered his voice and leaned nearer. "But I confess I doubt that's what you two were doing alone together all those hours."

"What?" Kate asked. "What are you talking about? Wesley and Sophie were friends? I did not realize."

Sophie ignored her burning cheeks and said as nonchalantly as she could, "Oh yes, I met your brother last year in Lynmouth. My father keeps a studio there and I often accompanied him. I have met several artists there. Poets, too."

Keith gave her an indulgent grin.

She coolly held his gaze. "In fact, I met Mr. Keith there as well. Though at the time I did not know about his love of mischief. In fact, I didn't even know he had been a lieutenant in the army, until Captain Overtree referred to him by that title."

"And how did you think I lost this arm?" Keith smirked. "Cut myself shaving?"

The captain passed by the morning room door, stopped abruptly, and backed up a step, his broad shoulders filling the doorway. His eyes shifted from Kate and Sophie to Keith in wary concern. "And what are you three on about?" he asked. "Is Keith scorching your ears with tales of his exploits in Spain?"

Keith said, "Hardly. We have discovered your wife's secret."

Captain Overtree stiffened. "Oh?"

"Don't be so gothic, Mr. Keith," Kate chided, then explained to her brother, "We came upon Sophie with her sketchbook, making the loveliest drawings, which she clearly prefers to keep to herself. That's all."

"Ah." Captain Overtree nodded. "Then why not be courteous and grant her the privacy she obviously wishes?" He sent his former lieutenant a challenging look.

"Right," Keith drew himself up and stepped past him through the door, a sheepish Kate behind.

"Thank you, Captain," Sophie said quietly. "But it's all right. The morning room is not my private domain."

His eyes flashed, and he opened his mouth to say something. Instead he turned on his heel and strode away without another word.

The next day, Sophie and Kate walked into the village together, admiring the bonnets in the milliner's window and the cakes in the baker's. At the newsagents, Sophie bought Winnie the latest edition of *Ackermann's Repository,* the periodical she'd mentioned wanting to read.

Later, when they returned to Overtree Hall, Sophie thanked Kate for the outing and the two parted ways in the library. Sophie went directly upstairs, eager to give Miss Whitney the longed-for magazine.

But when she reached the top of the stairs, voices gave her pause. She peeked around the corner and was stunned to see Captain Overtree coming out of a room next to Winnie's, and the maid Flora coming out after him!

Her heart sank. The two spoke in low tones, and the captain shut the door quietly but firmly behind them. Then he pressed a coin into the housemaid's hand.

Flora smiled and slipped it into her apron pocket. "Don't be telling Mrs. Hill, now, or she'll be docking my pay."

"Mum's the word," he agreed.

Feeling nauseated, Sophie turned and hurried back down the stairs as quickly and quietly as she could. Her morning sickness had passed, but she felt she might be sick even so. She told herself not to jump to conclusions. There could be — must be — another explanation. But what was it?

In their bedchamber, she laid aside the periodical, removed her gloves and bonnet with unsteady hands, and plopped down on a chair to think.

A short while later, she heard the door to her dressing room open, and Libby speaking to someone.

"What were you and the captain doing up there alone together?"

Flora answered in a suggestive singsong voice, "I'll never tell . . ."

Bile rose at the back of Sophie's throat. She reminded herself that she did not love Stephen Overtree. Theirs was a marriage in name only. If either of them should feel betrayed it should be Captain Overtree, who knew his wife loved his brother. Is this how it felt? Queasy dread, insecurity, and vulnerability all rolled into the pit of one's stomach and pinching one's heart? If so, poor man . . .

But she was no doubt flattering herself. He probably felt little more for her than she did for him.

Sophie avoided the captain the rest of that day and spoke little to him that evening. He looked at her in curious concern but said nothing.

The next morning, she took the magazine up to Winnie, earning a warm smile and thanks. "Your kindness shall be rewarded, my dear. Mark my words."

Sophie then went for a solitary walk. In the afternoon, she again attempted to sketch in the privacy of the dim morning room. Captain Overtree found her there a few hours later.

"There you are," he began. "I think it's time I shared a secret with you."

Sophie instantly stiffened. What secret?

"Better yet," he said. "Come upstairs with me and I'll show you."

Sophie's pulse accelerated. Good heavens. What was he going to show her?

He led her up the stairs. She thought again of seeing him climb these stairs at odd hours and wondering what drew him there. Had it really been to see his old nurse, or had there been some other, clandestine reason? What *had* he and Flora been doing up there alone together? And what about that crate she had seen him and Edgar sneaking upstairs?

She asked, "Are we going to visit Miss Whitney again?"

"Not this time."

Her heart beat a little harder than it should have for the exertion of the climb. She told herself she was foolish to worry. Foolish to care. She was only a duty to him, was she not? An unwanted responsibility.

"When you see, I think you will understand the reason for my secrecy."

That didn't bode well.

He led her past Winnie's door and instead stopped at the next — the one she had seen him and Flora exit together.

She drew up short, bumping in to him. "Pardon me."

He lightly touched her arm, as though to steady her, but his hand lingered.

"I tried to keep it quiet, but my valet knows, and at least one of the housemaids. Hopefully no one from the family . . ."

Worse and worse.

"I hope you don't think it presumptuous of me. I no doubt chose poorly, but not having your experience, and not wishing to ask and reveal my secret . . ."

Her ears roared. "You know what. I don't need to know. I will just go back downstairs and you can keep your secret — whatever it is — to yourself."

His expression fell. "No! Just look . . . I am making a muddle of this. I hope you will like it. But if you don't, you needn't pretend."

Now she was well and truly confused.

He opened the door gingerly, looking both ways down the passage as if to assure himself there were no witnesses. "It's the old schoolroom," he said. "It was the most private place I could think of. No one comes here anymore."

He gestured her inside and quietly closed the door behind them.

It took her mind a few moments to realize what she was seeing. Although shelves of forgotten schoolbooks lined one wall and an old desk stacked with slates and globes had been pushed against another, the items in the center of the room were new: an easel positioned near large windows. A high three-legged stool. A drawing box, and a set of paintbrushes arranged in a ceramic pot as though a potted plant in bloom.

Her heart pounded. "For . . . me?" she asked, voice tight.

"Yes, of course. I paid one of the housemaids to do a little cleaning in here after hours, but it may need more." He ran a finger over a dusty shelf, murmuring, "A lot more."

She stared at him. Stunned, stupid, remorseful.

"I am so sorry!" she blurted.

He frowned. "Sorry for what? Don't you like it? Did I get the wrong things? I can return them and —"

"No!" She shook head vigorously. "I didn't mean that. I . . ." How could she explain what she suspected, and foolishly feared?

Instead she walked forward and began fingering through the brushes, admiring the fine bristles, the varying thicknesses, the quality handles. "They're wonderful."

"Good. I asked the dealer to suggest the best, but he could have sold me a child's playset and I doubt I'd have been the wiser. I decided against going to the shop Wesley frequented. I didn't want a receipt to find its way into Father's hand and raise questions, since I know you are keen to keep your work hidden from view."

"I don't mean to be secretive . . ." Sophie murmured. "I am just self-conscious. I have no wish to give your family reason to compare my amateur attempts to Wesley's — or anyone else's."

"I think you underestimate yourself."

"And I think you are biased."

He looked at her squarely. "Yes. I am."

She looked away from his intense gaze, unsettled, then continued her perusal of the papers, canvases, cakes of watercolor paints, and an array of oil-paint pigments. "Goodness! You must think I am going to be here for a long while. I could fill Langton's portrait gallery all over again, figuratively speaking, of course. I shall make them last, I assure you."

"Don't. Use whatever you like. I have set up an account in your name. Here is the dealer's card. Write to him and tell him what you need and he will send it. The new manager will settle the bills discreetly in my absence."

She shook her head.

"No?" he asked.

"I cannot understand why you are so good to me."

"Can you not?"

She shook her head once more, his warm look filling her with prickles of anticipation.

He opened his mouth to reply, closed it, and began again. "I understand my family can sometimes be a trial, and I hope this gives you a retreat, a place to spend some pleasant hours during the days ahead."

Had that been what he'd meant to say? She didn't think so.

"Indeed it shall," she assured him. "I shall spend many happy hours here. It was very thoughtful of you, Captain. I don't know how to thank you." Impulsively, she held out her hand to him.

A spark lit his blue eyes, and he took her hand in his. Bending near, he raised her hand. He hesitated a moment, his warm breath tickling her knuckles. Then she felt the firm pressure of his lips against her fingers. Her heart fluttered. Why should it? After all, she had offered her hand — any gentleman knew what the gesture meant and how to respond. But it felt more significant somehow.

Her husband had kissed her. And even if it had only been her hand, she felt the sweet pleasure of it through her entire being.

CHAPTER 16

Sophie visited her new studio in the old schoolroom the very next morning, carrying with her the sketchbook, drawing pencils, and crayons she had brought with her from Bath. She had never had a studio of her own — always sharing a small corner of her father's, or drawing out of doors. Now she felt almost frozen by the freedom, and the wealth of possibilities before her.

She placed one of the new canvases on the easel, as well as a maulstick with its soft leather head to support her hand while she painted. Then she turned to the paints. Such expense was represented here. How daunting to open these pristine new vials of pigment, mix them with oil, and scrape a full palette for . . . what? A few homely flowers from the Overtree gardens? Even watercolors would require her to unwrap all the cakes of paint, so charming in their new packages. She felt she needed something worthy to justify the expense. She stood there for several minutes thinking, but the canvas — that big expanse of nothingness — remained blank. She needed to start with something more modest, and not spoil a whole canvas while she was so out of practice. For the time being, she made do with preparing a canvas for later, and set it aside.

Then she pulled a chair nearer the window to take advantage of the sunlight and opened her sketchbook again. Pulling out her set of crayons, she added dimension and detail to the flowers she had already sketched. It was satisfying to see the flowers become more and more vibrant and realistic. With a satisfied sigh, she turned the page and regarded her pencil sketch of Captain Overtree's face. What would it be like to paint him with the full depth and color variations presented by oil paint and canvas?

Except for the wonderful room, Sophie had not yet used anything the captain had given her. But she would. And she would think of him every time she did.

That afternoon, after sitting through Mrs. Overtree's litany of details for the upcoming dinner party — menu, seating arrangements, and a tedious discussion of precedence among the guests — Sophie excused herself, claiming the need of fresh air and a turn around the garden. Entering through its archway a few moments later, she saw the gardener coming out of the hothouse and asked if it would be all right if she cut a few flowers.

"Of course, madam. Though the real beauties won't show their faces for another month yet." He provided shears, a flat-bottomed basket, and a tip of his hat.

She picked one showy daffodil, yellow-and-white primroses, several bright orange tulips, a branch of pink camellias, and green fronds and ferns. These she took indoors with her and up the stairs. In the schoolroom, she found an old sunny yellow vase. A crack marred one side, but if she turned it away, it would work well for the composition she had in mind.

As she set the prepared canvas on the easel, the old rhythm returned to her, and peace like a long-lost friend descended. She'd missed this.

She slipped a blue apron over her head to protect her pale yellow frock. Then she mixed the paints with the new palette knife in a wheel pattern around the wooden disk. Choosing a brush, she turned to study the still life before her. Something was missing. It was too ordinary. Too perfect. True, flowers and fruits were the accepted domain of ladies who dabbled in painting. Still lifes were deemed safe for the gentle sex, along with the occasional portrait and genre scene. But Sophie liked to give her paintings something unique. A thought or theme to express in even the simplest subject.

Then she realized what she wanted. She rose and turned the vase so that the crack faced her and rearranged the flowers once more to their best advantage. Yes, better.

First, she gave the prepared surface a dark yellow underpainting. Then she began establishing the composition. Using ochre and umber, she outlined the flowers, and quickly blocked the vase and table in thinned paint, capturing the most important shapes and dominant values. Satisfied, she left the paint to dry and went downstairs to dress for dinner.

She returned the next day and began by building up layers of color to form shadows, applying paint in thicker brushstrokes, and adding white highlights where light hit the vase. In some areas, she left the underpainting untouched, creating the illusion of depth. Then she chose a slender brush to paint the fine details of the petals and foliage. She added more Naples yellow directly to the canvas for the petals of the daffodil, knowing each time she mixed the paint, the tone would be slightly different, adding more richness to the canvas. She continued to add and blend the colors until the flowers came to life.

The door creaked open behind her and

Sophie whirled, paintbrush suspended mid-air.

Kate stood there, peering in. Gulliver darted past her feet and trotted into the room.

Sophie released a breath. "Kate, you scared me."

"Winnie told me flowers were blooming in the old schoolroom. I had to come and see what on earth she was talking about." Her eyes settled on the painting — too big, too out in the open for Sophie to hide. "I thought she'd really lost her mind this time," Kate said. "But apparently not."

Surely Winnie's sixth sense, or whatever it was, hadn't picked up on something as ordinary as a humble painting of garden flowers. Perhaps Winnie had simply peeked into the schoolroom looking for Gulliver, who even now lay curled in a patch of sunshine near the window.

Sophie explained, "Your brother ordered the supplies and set all this up for me, knowing I am private about my work, or rather, pastime. So kind of him."

"It's clearly more than a pastime. You're very good, Sophie. I may not be an expert, but I did grow up in the same house as Wesley, so I'm not completely ignorant."

"Of course not. And . . . thank you. But I grew up in the same house as Claude Dupont, so I know not to esteem my little skill."

"I think your father was too hard on you,"

Captain Overtree said from the doorway.

Kate turned and greeted her brother. "Hello, Stephen. How romantic of you to set up a studio for Sophie!"

"It was nothing, Kate. Please don't mention it to others."

"Very well."

The captain returned his gaze to Sophie. "Perhaps your father didn't want you to become vain. Or wanted to push you to keep improving your skills."

"Or perhaps he is simply a realist," she said. "Amateur drawing and watercolors may be admired in accomplished young ladies, but art as a profession is not."

Kate said, "But I've heard of several professional female artists."

"Yes, but those women are the exceptions. In general, it is frowned upon."

"Why?" Kate asked.

"It is thought to divert women from their prescribed roles as wives and mothers."

Captain Overtree's eyes glinted like glass. "Is that how you see it? Do you regret you've taken on the prescribed role of wife and someday mother?"

She stared at him, taken aback by his hard expression. "No. I never said that. I . . . have always hoped I would one day marry and have children." She instinctively laid a hand over her apron-covered midsection.

Kate looked from one to the other, a

wrinkle of confusion between her brows at the tension between them. She said in forced brightness, "Then all is as it should be. You are blessed, indeed. For you have a husband who supports your interest in art."

Sophie replied to Kate, but kept her focus on the captain as she did so. "I am blessed, yes. You are perfectly right, Kate."

He held her gaze, and his expression softened.

"Will you give me lessons, Sophie?" Kate asked. "We can have them up here, if you like. I can understand not wanting Mamma peering over your shoulder. I wouldn't want her peering over mine either. At least not until I have improved the rudimentary skills my poor governess tried to teach me. Wesley has offered, but he's never here long enough."

"I don't know, Kate," Sophie said. "I have never taught anyone before. I am sure if your parents knew you wished to learn, they would hire a qualified instructor for you."

"But I would be far more comfortable with you. And it would give us an excuse to spend time together and become better acquainted."

The girl's sweet dark eyes widened and it was difficult to refuse her appeal.

"I shall teach you if we have a suitable model to paint." Sophie turned to Stephen. "If you, Captain, will sit for us. How fortunate that I have a husband who supports my interest in art." She slanted him a challenging look.

He raised his hands. "Oh no. No one need paint this battered mug. Not when more pleasant alternatives abound." He gestured toward the vase of flowers, then hesitated, looking again at the cracked vase with a frown. "I'm sure we could find you a better vase."

"No, thank you. I like that one."

He turned back and for a moment studied her face.

Kate implored, "Oh, please, Stephen? I painted plenty of flowers while Miss Flynn was here. But I've never tried a portrait. Please?"

He ran a hand through his hair. "Tell you what — practice on flowers or what have you for now, and maybe later . . . We'll see."

"But you leave soon, Stephen."

"Kate's right," Sophie said. "I would normally agree with you that it would be better to start with something easier than —"

"Than this face?"

"— than a portrait of anyone. But considering how few days you have left . . . Here, I mean. We had better start soon."

Still he hesitated.

Then Sophie added softly, "I would like to have a portrait of you, before you leave."

He looked at her again, emotions flashing behind his eyes. Then he waved the notion away. "There is one hanging downstairs."

"But it is several years out of date, painted when you were young."

He smirked. "And I am ancient now, am I?"

"No, but you were only, what, twenty at the time?"

He nodded. "Father hired an artist to paint Wesley when he came of age. Had me sit for him at the same time, since the man came from a distance."

"It is time for a new one."

"I prefer the way my face looks in the old one," he grumbled. "Remember me that way."

"How can I, when I never knew that Stephen?"

She rarely used his Christian name, and he swiftly lifted his head at the sound.

"More's the pity," he said, then heaved a sigh. "Oh, very well. I give in. I should have known I never stood a chance with the two of you joining forces against me." He sent Kate a mock scowl. "But not today. I have a meeting with the new estate manager, Mr. Boyle."

"Tomorrow, then," Kate said. "And while you're at it, meet with your barber as well. You could use a haircut."

"Thank you, Kate. You do wonders for my pride."

"Have him trim your side-whiskers too,"

Sophie suggested. "We want to see your face."

"No you don't."

"Yes," she insisted gently. "We do."

At the appointed hour the next day, Captain Stephen Overtree took a deep breath and entered the schoolroom.

Sophie turned, her gaze sweeping over him and her mouth parted.

"Kate insisted I wear my dress uniform, but if you prefer, I can change."

"No, it's . . ." She hesitated. "I have never seen you in uniform. You look very handsome in it. And I like your hair shorter like that. Your side-whiskers too."

His uniform was of fine scarlet with stand-up collar, gold epaulets, and yellow facings over light trousers and Hessian boots. He carried an ornamental dress sword in one hand, and a tall black hat with a plume under his arm.

"Please. Be seated." She gestured toward a chair positioned in front of the easel.

Stephen sat. "Miss Blake came to call, so Kate is detained. She said to proceed and she will join us as soon as she is able."

"Very well."

She stood beside her tall stool near the easel for a moment, just looking at him. Uncomfortable under her intense scrutiny, he shifted.

"Turn your head, Captain. No, the other way."

"But this is my good side," he said. He'd obliged them by getting his hair and side-whiskers trimmed, but now his scar was more noticeable.

She shook her head. "Look at me straight on. I want to paint your face, not just your profile."

He wished he could turn away, hide that part of him in the shadows. Instead she had him sit near the window, sunlight spilling over him, revealing every inch of his scar in grotesque detail, or so he feared.

"If I am to have my likeness rendered, I should not like the focus to be on my scar."

"Is this portrait for you, or for me?" Sophie asked. "Will you be looking at it while you're away, or shall I?"

"No one shall, if I have anything to say about it."

She tilted her head, expression thoughtful. "Think of it this way, Captain. A portrait is like an ornamental headstone. It is not for the subject, but for those who look upon it. For those who want to remember."

"Interesting analogy, Mrs. Overtree," he said dryly. "Though yes, this is a grim occasion in my view, so an apt comparison." He lifted his sword. "I salute you."

She gave him a rueful smile. Then she tilted her head the other way, peering at him. Had he cut himself shaving? Had he food in his teeth? Or . . . ?

She rose and walked toward him. Unsure of her intention, he watched her approach, forgetting to breathe.

She lifted a hand toward him. "May I?"

He managed a nod.

She raised splayed fingers and tentatively rearranged the hair falling over his brow, brushing the stubborn lock into submission.

He tried not to enjoy the feeling of her fingers in his hair. Not to reach out and capture her hand. Or put his arms around her and draw her near for a kiss on her maddening mouth.

She stunned him by lowering to her knees before his chair, taking his free hand in both of hers, and looking up at him — earnestly. Beseechingly. She could have asked for anything at that moment and he would have been powerless to refuse her.

"I know this is difficult for you. But please believe me when I tell you that I like what I see when I look at you. Your scar is much bigger in your eyes than in mine or probably in anyone else's. It's a small part of a big man. It only serves to make you look more . . . masculine. Now, will you please trust me?"

His chest tightened, and his heart beat hard. "I do trust you, Sophie." *Probably more than I should for my heart's sake,* he thought.

She squeezed his hand, and smiled gently into his face.

To blazes with resolve, he thought, and

291

leaned down to kiss her. Her eyes widened in surprise as he neared, but she did not pull away.

"Here I am!" Kate announced, bolting breathless into the room. "Thought she'd never go. And of course I could not tell her why I wanted her to —" She drew up short, looking from Stephen's posture to Sophie on her knees. "Oh, you newly married couples!" she protested. "Shall I leave you alone? And after I have all but pushed Angela out the door so I might watch Sophie paint you!"

"Not at all, Kate." Sophie blushed. "We were just, em . . ."

Stephen straightened. "As you can see from Sophie's posture, she was simply begging me to go along with this little scheme of yours," he teased. "And I have agreed, out of the goodness of my heart."

Sophie painted for nearly an hour, quietly explaining to Kate what she was doing as she went. Then she checked her watch pin and announced they had better end for the day — the dressmaker was due soon. The captain rose in relief and made his escape.

Kate remained to help Sophie clean her brushes, and then the two women left together. They paused at Winnie's door to greet her, but she was not there. They continued downstairs and parted ways toward their respective rooms to wash hands before the fitting. As Sophie approached her bedchamber, she was surprised to see a brown-paper-wrapped package propped against her door. She picked it up and opened it. Inside she found an old book, and angled it to look at the title: *The Rearing and Management of Children.*

Her breath hitched and she looked around, relieved to not see anyone nearby. Sophie went inside and closed the door behind herself, breathing a little too hard. Surely Captain Overtree would not leave such a thing out in the corridor. But who else knew she was expecting? She quickly flipped through the yellowing pages, and saw they were dog-eared and underlined.

Winnie . . . Who besides a nurse who'd had the charge and care of children for decades would possess such a well-used book? Did Winnie know she was with child? Or was she simply looking ahead to a likely eventuality? In either case, Sophie rewrapped the book and tucked it deep into her bedside table drawer for the present. She didn't want anyone else to see it and deduce the truth. Not yet.

Mrs. Pannet arrived on schedule for the final fittings on the dresses for the dinner party. Mrs. Overtree called the girls into her boudoir, where she could sit in comfort and oversee and approve. The dressmaker's assistant helped Kate into her pink satin gown, and did up the fastenings, while Mrs. Pannet surveyed the girl from all angles. "Well, madame?"

"Perfect," Mrs. Overtree declared.

Then it was Sophie's turn. The blue-and-white gown settled into place, and the assistant laced up the back, pulling tighter, and struggling to fasten the little decorative buttons at the back of the bodice.

The dressmaker frowned. "Have you put on weight since I first measured you?"

Sophie felt her face heat, flashed a look at Mrs. Overtree and faltered, "I'm afraid I may have . . ."

Mrs. Overtree said, "We eat well here at Overtree Hall. Don't we, Sophie?"

"Yes," Sophie agreed. "I confess I am not accustomed to sweets and puddings with every meal. I shall be plump in no time at this rate."

"Yes, a young lady must take care with her figure. Even when newly married. Unless . . ." Mrs. Overtree let the phrase dangle, unfinished. Her eyes surveyed Sophie head to toe and lingered on her middle.

"I shall have to alter this," the dressmaker said, long-suffering and officious. "But I will have it finished in time for the big day — never fear."

The dressmaker and her assistant gathered their things and took their leave, while the Overtree ladies remained on the comfortable sofa and armchair in Mrs. Overtree's boudoir. Libby brought the ladies tea, and they sat sipping and talking.

Mrs. Overtree said, "Only a few days from now and still so much to do."

"Mamma, you did invite Mr. Harrison, did you not?" Kate asked.

"No, I did not. Not specifically. Though of course I had to invite Mr. and Mrs. Nelson and they will probably bring him along."

Kate nodded. "He is their son, after all."

"No, he is not. They have only raised him out of the goodness of their hearts. Which I do admire — don't mistake me. But why must they try to pass him off as a gentleman? I know they are fond of him, but really. It isn't fair to put the rest of us in such an awkward position socially."

Sophie recalled what Angela Blake had told her in confidence about the circumstances of the young man's birth. She asked tentatively. "Is his background so bad?"

"Yes. His mother was unmarried. His father, we know not who. Our vicar and his wife, never having children of their own, took the boy in as a lad and raised him after the poor girl died. Very Christian of them, I am sure. And were he to come here seeking a post or collecting donations for the poor fund, I would look on him kindly enough. But to come here as our equal? To dress and act the gentleman and turn our Katherine's head with his good looks and toothy grins? I think not."

"Mamma!" Kate protested. "You are unfair. He is educated and gentlemanlike in his manner and, yes, extremely good-looking." Kate's dimples appeared as she said the final phrase.

"You may train and dress a man to play the part, but a gentleman is born and bred."

Kate pouted. "Mamma, I like Mr. Harrison. And he, I think, admires me. I —"

"Of course he does, Katherine. I give him credit for taste at least. But you are above his station. He ought to know his place and keep it."

"Mamma. You sound the shrew."

"And you the impractical romantic. This is the real world, Katherine. You may think me shrewish all you like, but that does not change the facts. If you married him, many doors would be closed to you. Your father and I could not approve of a match between you. Not to be cruel, but because we want what is best for you. So you would do well to put it from your mind."

She began to pass Sophie the plate of biscuits, thought the better of it, and handed the plate to Kate instead. "You should be pleased to know we have invited Sefton Darby-Wells. A very handsome man, you cannot deny."

"I don't deny it, but he has never shown a whit of interest in me."

"He is well connected and from a good family. And his Mamma wrote to me to hint that he would welcome an invitation to Overtree Hall."

"Really? I am surprised to hear it. I thought he seemed interested in Miss Parkland."

"Apparently not. Just promise me you will give him a chance, Katherine. Don't let your fancy for young Mr. Harrison cause you to overlook a man ten times his consequence."

"Very well, Mamma. At least Miss Blake and I shall have another partner. I do recall Mr. Darby-Wells being an excellent dancer." She sniffed and murmured into her teacup. "But I still hope Mr. Harrison comes as well."

CHAPTER 17

That evening, dinner was quieter than usual. Kate was uncharacteristically subdued, probably thinking of Mr. Harrison, and Mr. Keith was not there to add his droll quips and amusing stories. He had been invited to Windmere for the evening by Angela Blake's brother, who was at home for a few days.

Later, when Sophie and Captain Overtree walked upstairs together, she asked, "What do you think, Captain? Are the circumstances surrounding young Mr. Harrison's birth insurmountable? Do they truly render him unsuitable for your sister or any other young lady?"

"In the eyes of my parents? Yes. They do."

"That doesn't seem fair. He cannot help that the *gentleman* who fathered him refused to marry his poor mother. He is innocent of wrongdoing."

"I don't say it is fair. But it is reality."

"Can you not talk to them on his behalf? For Kate's sake? Persuade them?"

"I have nothing against the young man personally. But do I want him to marry my sister . . . ?" He shook his head. "No."

She stared at him, disappointed. "I did not expect you of all people to share that view. After all, you married beneath your station. And a person shadowed by scandal."

"Do you not see the differences? They would be poor and excluded from polite society. Most of my parents' friends among them."

"But they would be happy."

"Would they? I doubt it. Not with so many factors against them."

"The vicar and his wife are not ostracized. Why would their son be?"

"Mr. Nelson is granted a certain latitude on account of his calling. People admire that he took the boy in. That doesn't mean they want Mr. Harrison to marry their daughters."

"Then your parents and their friends are . . ." She bit back the word *pompous*.

He sighed. "They are not perfect. But my parents care about their daughter and want her to be happy. Not just for a few months, but for the rest of her life. And they are thinking not only of her but of her future children as well."

"It still isn't fair."

He pressed her hand. "I know. Listen, I know what you want me to say. I realize you feel this very personally, because of your own . . . recent . . . situation. But your child will not grow up under a cloud of scandal as Mr. Harrison has. Your child will be legitimate in the eyes of society and the law. He or she will be an Overtree, with all the protection and privileges that name confers."

Sophie made no reply.

They parted ways at the dressing room door. And in a pique as she was, she turned her back on him without saying good-night.

Captain Overtree did not return to her bed-chamber to await the valet's departure as usual, forgoing the pretense that he meant to share her room.

Changed and in bed a short while later, Sophie had difficulty falling asleep. She kept reviewing her conversation, or rather her argument, with Captain Overtree. And what would give her no peace was not Mr. Harrison's situation or even Kate's daunted hopes, but the realization of all she and her child had been spared because Captain Overtree had married her. He'd not only protected her from shame — he'd also rescued her child from a life of scandal and exclusion. Not to mention possible poverty and deprivation.

She thought of something the vicar had said in church, about how Christ took on our sin and shame on the cross, giving his life to save his people eternally. Oh, she knew humble and human Stephen Overtree would deny any similarities between what Christ had done and what he had done for her, but at the moment the realization burned in her chest like a hot coal. And how had she repaid his great kindness? By remaining aloof. By neglecting him. By idolizing another. She had done the same to both God and Stephen Overtree. *Oh, Lord, forgive me . . .*

Unable to lie there any longer, she rose from bed, and walked carefully across the room, hands stretched before her and hoping not to stumble into anything in the dark. She reached the dressing room and found the door latch. Dare she? She didn't know exactly what she meant to do, but she wanted to at least apologize for their argument. And maybe thank him again. And maybe . . . kiss him. And maybe . . . more.

She quietly unlatched the door and inched it open, hearing only silence in reply. Within, Captain Overtree lay on his makeshift bed, a book open over his chest, eyes closed. Nearby on a ledge a candle guttered, its flame struggling to stay alight in a puddle of wax. She tiptoed inside, knelt beside the sofa, and watched him sleep. How would he react to wake and find her in his room? What would he do? Might he take her in his arms and kiss her? She longed to be held, body and soul. But by Stephen Overtree?

Yes.

Remembering the feeling of his hair beneath her fingers in the studio, she reached out and gently touched his head.

He lurched upright, grabbed her wrist painfully tight, and uttered a strangled yell.

She sucked in a startled breath. "It's all right, Captain. It's me. Sophie."

His eyes were open but unseeing. A haze of violent emotion faded from them and he blinked awake. "Dreaming . . . thought you were the enemy."

"No. Your wife."

He loosened his grip and straightened. "I'm sorry. Did I hurt you?"

"No. I'm all right."

"I scared you, didn't I."

"A bit."

"Sorry, little rabbit." He tilted his head to better see her face. "Was I talking in my sleep? Did I wake you?"

She shook her head.

Mild confusion crossed his face. "Then . . . Did you want something?"

Did she?

"I . . . just wanted to make sure you were all right."

For a moment he said nothing. Then, "I am, thank you. Are you?"

"I . . . am sorry for our argument earlier."

"Think nothing of it. I am sorry as well."

She rose. "Well, good night, then, Captain."

"Good night."

Courage and flame sputtered and died, replaced by darkness and regret.

■ ■ ■ ■

In the morning, Stephen sat on the edge of the sofa, hanging his head. What began as his usual morning prayers devolved into speculation and remorse. He'd been in a stupor last night. The vestiges of a dream — the French attacking, battle, charging — still very real in his mind, overpowering other thoughts until it was too late and he had frightened her away. Why had she come to him in the dressing room? He tried to recall their brief conversation. He'd asked her if he'd talked in his sleep and woken her, but she'd said no. But in the same breath she'd said she'd wanted to make sure he was all right. That didn't make sense to him, though perhaps he was misremembering. She'd said something about their argument. Apologized. He should have made room for her on the sofa, and offered to talk with her about it. And relished her nearness in the bargain. He chastised himself for not thinking of it at the time. Surely she had not come for anything more . . . romantic . . . in nature? He was a fool to even think it.

Rising in frustration, Stephen washed in cold water, dressed, and went downstairs. He had several last-minute details to discuss with the estate manager before his departure in a few days. How quickly this fortnight was flying by. Too quickly.

Afterward, he donned his uniform and went upstairs to sit for Sophie again. He arrived before Kate, and instantly felt the tension in the air between them.

He said, "I'm sorry about last night. Grabbing your arm like that. I did not intend to scare you off. You are, uh, . . . more than welcome in my dressing room any time." He pressed his eyes closed. He sounded like an idiot. A desperate idiot making a desperate offer.

She ducked her head, embarrassed. "That's all right. You didn't do anything wrong."

"I didn't do anything right either."

"I should not have intruded."

"You didn't intrude. Sophie, you know I —"

Kate knocked and poked her head in with a mischievous look. "All clear?"

"Of course, come in," Sophie said, clearly relieved to see her.

Inwardly he sighed, feeling as if he had made things worse.

He resumed his pose, and Sophie began painting. Kate looked on, peppering her with questions.

Finally, to stem the flow, Stephen posed a question of his own. "And where is Angela, your shadow? I saw her stalk by the house this morning on her way somewhere. Did she not stop in?"

"No. She is in a pique, apparently," Kate said. "Wants to avoid us, or at least our houseguest."

"Oh no. What has Keith done now?"

"Horace is home and invited Mr. Keith to dine with them at Windmere last night."

"So I heard. Angela did not approve?"

"Actually she seemed pleased by the prospect. But apparently Mr. Keith and her brother did more drinking and gambling than dining. My maid said he arrived back here very late and very foxed. James and Edgar had to all but carry him up to his room. And now the laundry-maid has the unhappy task of scrubbing sick from his evening coat."

"Thunder and turf . . ." Stephen breathed.

"Sit still and stop scowling," Sophie instructed.

After one final scowl, he complied.

That afternoon, Stephen sat reading his Bible in a wing-back chair in the library, when Angela Blake strode into the room, Carlton Keith on her heels.

"Miss Blake. Wait."

Before Stephen could react or announce his presence, she whirled on Keith. "Why do you insist on playing the part of the drunken fool? Gambling away what little money you still have. Gambling away your chance, your life . . ."

"My chance? My chance at what?"

She turned away, freckles receding beneath her blush.

He grasped her arm and turned her toward him. "Are you saying I have a chance with you? Or did have, before I acted so stupidly?"

She averted her face, refusing to answer.

Stephen sat there, taken aback to find himself an unwilling witness to the scene. Partway through he had decided it would be too mortifying for them all to make his presence known.

Keith shook his head in wonder. "I had no idea. Never guessed you would even consider a man like me. I know I am not good enough for you. But God help me, if I have any chance at all, I will try to be worthy of you."

"I don't know if that is possible," she said. "Now even my brother thinks the worst of you. Pull yourself together, Mr. Keith. For your own sake, not mine." She jerked her arm from his grasp and fled the room.

Keith remained where he was, watching her go.

Stephen waited a moment, then cleared his throat. Keith turned.

"Sorry. I didn't know whether to say anything or not."

Keith walked over and flopped down in the chair across from him. "Doesn't matter. I've ruined everything. And didn't even know there was anything to ruin."

"What happened?"

"Besides my constant drunkenness, impudence, and crass ways?"

"Yes."

"Her brother invited me over to Windmere for dinner and cards last night. I drank too much and wagered too much. I lost my money and my supper. I doubt I shall be asked back."

Stephen winced on behalf of his former lieutenant. "Not one of your more clever maneuvers."

"Tell me something I don't know." Keith sighed. "I can curb the gambling. It's fairly easy to resist when I'm broke. But the drinking . . ." He shook his head. "It's so dashed hard. It's served at every meal, except breakfast. Everyone drinks."

"Not everyone."

"You used to."

"True."

"Why don't you drink anymore, Captain?"

Stephen shrugged. "I saw what it did to me. I didn't like the man I became and what he was capable of."

"You, Captain? And what have you ever done that's so bad? Besides work the devil out of us men and earn the name Captain Black? But that's no sin."

"Oh, I have sinned, all right. It's not something I like to remember, let alone talk about. I . . . once took advantage of a woman and left her alone to face the consequences,

307

whatever they might be." Stephen cringed at the thought of Jenny, as he always did. "Remember the silversmith's daughter, in Dublin?"

"Ah . . ." Keith lifted his chin in acknowledgement.

"I tried to find her later, when I had sobered up and realized what I'd done. But her father's business had collapsed like so many in those years and no one could tell me where they'd gone. So I could not make amends. But I promised myself I would never do the same again."

"You did more than most men would have."

Stephen shifted uneasily. "I hope that isn't true. Whatever the case, I vowed to abstain from hard drink after that. It wasn't easy. Especially after a particularly gruesome battle or the death of a friend. When I wanted to forget. . . ."

He grimaced at the memory. "Sometimes I gave in. Sometimes I managed to resist, with fervent prayer and staying clear of the mess tent or the sergeant with the ready bottle. And the more I resisted, the easier it became to resist again."

He sighed, weary to recall the struggle. "You see me now. I drink spring water or ask for coffee, tea, or ginger beer. I limit myself to one glass of wine with dinner. I enjoy it, but no more. But when I first stopped, I couldn't allow myself even that. For one glass made it too easy to say yes to another, then three, then four."

Stephen shook his head in self-deprecation. "I have only been foxed once in the last five years. Care to hazard a guess when? Not after a particularly horrible battle. Not after someone died. But after my own wedding."

Keith's brows rose nearly to his hairline. Then he chuckled, shaking his own head. "Poor Marsh. Not the wedding night either of you dreamed of, ay?"

"That's putting it mildly." Stephen rubbed his neck. "I hated her seeing me like that. I promised her I would never do so again, and I shan't with God's help."

Stephen tilted his head and regarded Keith. "Why *do* you drink so much? Does the arm still pain you? Or are you trying to forget the war, or . . . ?"

"No. I don't know. I suppose it helps me act the jolly fool, all bluster and bravado. Angling for a laugh. Doing anything to keep women, or at least a particular woman, from feeling pity for me." He snorted. "Stupid, I know. And apparently I've been successful. Miss Blake doesn't feel sorry for me. She feels disgust." Keith shook his dark head. "That strategy may have won a battle but cost me the war. But I will try. For her sake, I shall give it up."

"You'll need help."

"No, Captain. You'll be off fighting, or drilling your men. You don't have time to play nursemaid to me."

"I wasn't thinking of me. Ask God to help you. Every day. Every hour. Every time you're tempted."

"I haven't your faith."

"That may be part of the problem." Stephen raised a hand. "No, I don't say it's the cure. All men struggle with some temptation or another, but God will help you. It would also be wise to have someone keep you accountable. My grandfather, perhaps."

"The old colonel frightens the wits out of me," Keith admitted. "But I'll try."

"Good." Stephen rose, then turned back. "And Carlton? You heard Angela. Don't do it for her — do it because it's the right thing to do. Because life is precious and you don't want to waste it. Otherwise, if she chooses another man in the end, you'll go right back to your old ways. Or if she does marry you, you might be tempted to think, 'I have her now, what can a few drinks hurt?' Then you will end up finding out just how much you can hurt your wife and your children."

"Like my own father did."

"Right."

He pressed Keith's shoulder in a rare display of affection. "You can do it, Lieutenant. It's all uphill from here."

Keith gave a rueful grin. "That's what I was afraid of."

CHAPTER 18

A few days later, Mr. Keith and Colonel Horton rode off together on some mission, but no one seemed to know where they went or how soon they would return. Mrs. Overtree muttered aloud that it must be nice to go gadding about at one's leisure while others had a thousand things to do to prepare for a party.

Sophie offered to help but was politely refused. As one of the guests of honor, she should not have to lift a finger, her mother-in-law insisted. Personally, Sophie thought Mrs. Overtree liked being in total control, preferred to manage the staff and details like a general commanding her troops and dictating battle plans. She was welcome to it.

Sophie devised her own small battle plan to prepare for the party. She was looking forward to it more than she would have guessed and wanted to look her best for Captain Overtree's final night at home.

■ ■ ■ ■

The day of the dinner, Sophie began getting ready hours ahead of time. Libby, with the help of a footman, carried up a tub, screen, and several large cans of hot water so Sophie could have a real bath in her room, instead of the sponge or hip baths she usually relied upon. She soaked in the warm scented water and relished the pleasure of Libby washing her hair.

The captain bathed after her, while the tub was set up behind the screen near the fire. She assured him she did not mind. With all the extra work the servants were already doing, there was no need to ask for the tub to be moved into the dressing room — even if it would fit, which was questionable.

Sophie sat at the dressing table, towel drying, then combing out her long hair to help it dry faster and remove the tangles. She angled her back and faced away from the tub. The screen had been set up to block the view from the door, should anyone enter. It partially blocked her view as well. But now and again, she sneaked a glimpse of him in her mirror: muscular shoulders and arms, scarred chest, flat abdomen, damp dark hair, skin glistening . . .

Sophie swallowed. He glanced over and caught her looking. She quickly feigned interest in a tangle and worked to remove it with her comb.

When the captain had dried off, covered himself in a dressing gown, and left the room, Sophie released a long breath.

Libby bustled in to help her dress. She tied silk stockings over Sophie's knees and cinched long bone stays over her shift. She had to loosen the laces but made no comment. She then helped Sophie on with her new gown, doing up the lacings and tiny pearl buttons at the back of the bodice. The new evening dress was not quite as formal as a ball gown but nearly so, and Sophie felt like a princess in it. Especially now that it had been altered to fit her expanding figure.

Libby brushed Sophie's hair until it shone gold, then pinned it high on her head, with two braids looped like garlands at the back. With hot irons she curled spiraling tendrils at each temple.

The maid touched the faintest tint of rouge to her lips and cheeks, and powdered her nose. Then around Sophie's neck she fastened a simple strand of glass beads that Kate had lent her, insisting it would look perfect with her blue-and-white dress.

Finally Libby stood back and admired her work. "There. You look beautiful, madam. If I do say so myself."

"Thank you, Libby. You are a real artist."

Libby winked. "Takes one to know one."

313

Sophie rose and turned to regard her reflection in the long cheval mirror.

The maid shook her head, dimples showing, "Just you wait until the captain sees you. My, my."

Sophie glanced at the closed dressing room door, assuming Captain Overtree had finished dressing and gone downstairs. She longed to hear him say she looked all right. And hopefully not too showy.

Sophie gave her reflection a final inspection. She *was* pretty, she thought. No matter what her father said about her being too plain to model. For a flash of a moment she wished Wesley were there to see her. To see how lovely she was and regret leaving her. She willed away the foolish, disloyal thought. Tonight was about Captain Overtree. And her. And their marriage, such as it was.

She pulled on long white gloves and made her way downstairs.

From the half landing, she saw Captain Overtree standing at the bottom of the stairs in full evening dress. He looked serious — jaw set, shoulders wide and squared — and wonderfully masculine in black tailcoat, brocade waistcoat, and linen cravat. Knee breeches and white stockings emphasized his muscular legs.

He glanced up, and then again, mouth parting. "Sophie . . ." he breathed.

She paused to relish the look on his face.

The low timbre of the single word more powerful than any long speech could have been.

She continued down the stairs, her stomach tingling.

As she tentatively approached him, he held out both hands. Surprised but happy to do so, she slipped her gloved hands into his.

His warm eyes traced her hair, her face. "So beautiful . . ."

"Thank you."

He slowly shook his head, drawing in a long breath. "Hang me. I shan't be able to stop staring long enough to eat a bite or remember a single dance step."

She smiled. The captain's black hair, for once brushed back from his brow, showed the strong contours of his face. She had never seen him look more handsome.

Kate appeared, *ooh*ing and *ahh*ing over Sophie's dress and hair. The younger woman was a picture of loveliness in the pale pink gown, pearls, and gloves, and her brother was quick to compliment her. Then he excused himself to greet one of the guests.

When he'd stepped away, Kate leaned near and whispered, "You'll never guess who just arrived."

"Mr. Harrison?"

"Why, yes!" Kate's dark eyes sparkled. "I encouraged him to come — assured him we were expecting him."

"I'm happy for you." Sophie hesitated, then asked, "How did your mother react?"

Kate wrinkled her nose. "Oh! That reminds me. Mamma wants us to welcome Mr. Darby-Wells. So pleased with himself. Though I suppose Mamma is right and I should try to like him. He is handsome, I own. Tell me what you think."

Kate took Sophie's arm and led her across the hall. In the anteroom, they first encountered the vicar, his wife, and son. Kate drew up short, pulling Sophie to a halt beside her.

"Mr. and Mrs. Nelson. Mr. Harrison!" Kate enthused. "I am so glad you came." She turned. "Sophie, you remember the Nelsons and Mr. Harrison, I trust? You met in church, I believe."

"Yes." Sophie greeted them warmly. She felt a tug of empathy for Mr. Harrison, who looked uncomfortable in formal evening attire and stiff cravat.

"Did you know Mr. Harrison is writing a book?" Kate beamed.

"Is he indeed?" Sophie smiled at the young man.

"It's quite true." The vicar's chest puffed with pride. "A history of the county."

"Papa . . ." Mr. Harrison self-consciously ducked his head. "Mrs. Overtree doesn't want to hear about that."

"On the contrary. I think it wonderful."

"He was going to stay home tonight and

work on it," Mrs. Nelson added. "But I assured him it was no doubt an oversight that his name was not included on the invitation. He thought it would be impolite to presume. Then I reminded him, had not Miss Overtree personally told him her family was expecting him?"

"Indeed I did, Mrs. Nelson," Kate said. "You are all very welcome."

Sophie knew that wasn't wholly true but nodded her agreement.

Across the room, Captain Overtree and his parents approached an elegant blond gentleman. Mrs. Overtree glanced their way and tried to catch her daughter's eye.

Noticing, Kate's smile faltered. "Well, if you will excuse us, I see Mamma beckoning. Someone else she wishes Sophie to meet, no doubt. I will look forward to talking with you more later. In the meantime, do enjoy yourselves."

"I am sure we shall," the vicar assured her. "Thank you, Miss Overtree."

His son seemed less convinced.

Heedless, Kate smiled at Mr. Harrison and might have kept standing there had not Sophie gently taken her arm and led her through the milling crowd.

As she and Kate approached the others, Sophie heard Mr. Darby-Wells offer the captain hearty congratulations on his marriage. Then he turned and congratulated Mr.

and Mrs. Overtree as well.

When he spied Kate, he smiled at her. "Miss Overtree. What a pleasure to see you again. You are lovelier than ever."

With a glance at her mother, Kate returned his smile. "Thank you."

Poor Mr. Harrison, Sophie thought. Mr. Darby-Wells was well-spoken and indeed handsome, with fine features and confident bearing. But when the young dandy bent over her hand, Sophie caught an oily gleam in his eye as his gaze lingered on her bosom — fuller now than it had ever been, though still, she hoped, modest.

Mr. Darby-Wells returned his attention to Kate, asking to dance with her after dinner. She sweetly agreed.

While the two young people talked, Mrs. Overtree stepped between Sophie and Stephen and whispered, "A charming young man, don't you think?"

"Apparently," Stephen agreed.

Sophie held her tongue.

At that moment, her attention was captured by Carlton Keith, elegant in evening clothes. There was something different about him. . . . Then she realized. Both of his sleeves were filled, and a gloved hand protruded from each.

Astonished, Sophie walked over to him. "Mr. Keith! How well you look."

He grinned at her. "Limbs suit me, don't

you think? Two arms are all the crack these days, so I thought I'd give it a go."

She returned his grin, then asked, "But how did you manage it?"

"Colonel Horton took me to see a Scottish bladesmith he knows who makes these contrivances. Not bad, ay?"

"It's very realistic."

"Made of metal, actually." He tapped it against a nearby door latch, producing a muffled clank.

The hand was skillfully shaped — and encased in a glove, as it was now, the illusion was convincing.

"Does it . . . function?" she asked as he stood there, arms at his sides.

"Afraid not. But I wager it's better than a hook, or an empty sleeve."

His grin faded as something over her shoulder caught his eye. She turned to look and saw Angela Blake, resplendent in green silk, and a man Sophie assumed must be her brother, with similar red hair.

Seeing her, Angela approached and said, "Mrs. Overtree, may I introduce my brother, Horace Blake. Horace, Mrs. Overtree, Stephen's wife."

She curtsied, and he bowed. "A pleasure."

Angela's eyes turned frosty when they settled on Sophie's companion. "Mr. Keith," she acknowledged with cool civility but quickly turned to greet someone else, her brother swept along in her wake.

When the butler announced dinner was served, they all entered the dining room in order of precedence, though Sophie still didn't understand all the particulars. She waited until Stephen offered his arm and was grateful for his nearness and relative familiarity amid the sea of strangers.

The dining room was awash in candlelight from candelabra and wall sconces. The table had been extended to its full length to accommodate their many guests and laid with fine linens, the family china, and decorative arrangements of fruits and hothouse flowers. Place cards directed her and Stephen to one end of the table near Angela Blake, Mr. Keith, and Mr. Darby-Wells. Kate sat on his other side, while Mr. Harrison and his parents were seated at the opposite end.

During dinner, Mr. Keith waved away refills of wine, Sophie noticed. Taking his cue from the captain, he nursed a single glass, while sipping on spring water.

Mr. Darby-Wells leaned toward Mr. Keith. "Haven't seen you in months, Keith. Been to White's lately?"

"No, not in ages. I've been in Devonshire with Wesley Overtree."

"Ah. Devonshire." The handsome man nodded sagely. "Spend any time with the Exmoor ponies while you were there . . . ?" His tone dripped with innuendo.

A euphemism for betting on horse races, Sophie guessed.

"Afraid not," Mr. Keith replied.

"Care for a friendly game after dinner?" the man asked.

"No, thanks. I've given it up."

"Have you indeed? That's a shame."

Keith's eyes glinted. "No. It's a shame when you lose your family's estate and have to marry for money." He gave the young man a pointed look.

"Do you say that from personal experience?" the dandy retorted.

"Yes, but I was not thinking of myself or my father in this instance." Keith's eyes held the other man's steadily. Knowingly.

Darby-Wells gave a casual shrug, but Sophie noticed him shift in his chair.

"Bah. You know how rumors spread . . ." The young man smirked and leaned closer, lowering his voice. "I may have lost a fortune, but at least I still have all my appendages."

Sophie sucked in a little gasp and looked at Stephen and Kate, but they hadn't heard. Miss Blake had, however. So had Mr. Keith, and the bravado faded from his eyes. He lowered his artificial hand into his lap.

After dinner, Kate begged for dancing, and soon the men set aside their port and pipe, and the women their gossip, to oblige her.

Together the party moved toward the great

321

hall. In anticipation of the dancing, servants had rolled up the carpets and laid a fire in the massive hearth to chase away the chill in the cavernous room. Mr. Overtree had surprised his daughter by hiring musicians after all, who even now sat at the ready in the raised gallery above. As the company entered they began playing a jaunty tune with fiddle, flute, and pipe.

Kate and Mr. Darby-Wells claimed the position of head couple and called for a Scottish reel. Its militant pace put Sophie in mind of soldiers marching into battle. At the thought, her heart fell, knowing Captain Overtree might soon do just that.

The tune reminded Stephen of his regiment's bandsmen. He blinked away an unwanted image of a drummer boy who looked no older than twelve, lying dead in a Spanish wheat field. This was not the time or place for such remembrances. If only he could wipe them from his mind forever.

As other couples joined in, Stephen touched Sophie's elbow. "May I have this dance?"

She blinked up at him in surprise. "I did not think you cared enough for dancing to wish to begin so early."

"I don't. But I refuse to waste a moment with you."

She bit her lip. "Would you mind terribly if we waited until the next? I don't think I'm equal to a reel after that large meal."

"I don't mind at all, as long as you stay near."

She smiled shyly up at him. "I shall."

They stood beside one another, watching the dance. Stephen grinned at Kate's enthusiastic, energetic steps compared to her partner's smooth, polished style.

"They may not be well matched in dancing, but no great matter," he said. "A dance is fleeting, but marriage is forever." Where had that come from — was he a philosopher now? Stephen inwardly cringed. What a thing to say when their marriage could very well be short-lived.

"I don't think they are well matched for marriage either," Sophie said mildly.

Stephen didn't challenge her and was relieved when she didn't expound on her reply. He hoped to avoid another argument, this night of all nights.

The first set ended, and the gentlemen escorted their partners from the dance floor. Then the musicians began another tune.

Stephen watched in surprise as Mr. Harrison led Kate on to the floor, her face flushed and radiant as she smiled up at him. He wondered how his mother felt about Mr. Harrison's presence.

A few feet away from them, Keith leaned near Miss Blake and said earnestly. "I beg your forgiveness for my behavior at Windmere. Upon my honor, it shall not happen again."

"I forgive you."

Keith reared his head back in surprise at how readily his apology was accepted. A moment later, he asked glibly, "I don't suppose you'd care to dance with a one-armed pauper?"

Stephen knew the man's teasing tone hid his fear, or perhaps even his assumption, that she would refuse him.

"I would indeed," Angela replied, as though he'd referred to himself as a titled lord.

Stephen's fondness for his childhood friend deepened then and there.

"I recognize this music," Sophie spoke up. "A favorite in Bath. It's called 'Our Mutual Love.' "

"Well, then," Stephen replied. "We had better dance to it."

They shared a private smile and joined the other couples forming two lines down the center of the long hall. As they moved through the patterns, Stephen observed Mr. Harrison as he danced with Kate, noticing the young man's respectful distance and correct, if faltering, steps.

Soon, he and Sophie found themselves at the top of the line with Miss Blake and Mr. Keith. Stephen was glad Angela and Sophie would be the two ladies taking his lifeless hand.

He and Keith stepped around their partners, then turned them with both hands —
or in Keith's case, one hand. Then the ladies
did the same. The two couples changed
places, right hands across, left hands back,
moving down through the line. Stephen
relished Sophie's nearness and the feeling of
her hands in his. It only made him want to
hold her closer. *God give me strength.*

He watched Sophie with unabashed admiration. When Mr. Keith could not reach or
turn, she continued on fluidly with enough
grace and ease that only those watching
closely would know Mr. Keith did not per-
form his role perfectly. Miss Blake was a little
less serene looking, as though concentrating
very hard on the steps and hoping not to
make a fool of herself. Or perhaps hoping
others were not scoffing at her partner. And
he had to admire Keith's bravery as well.
Dancing in such august company, with many
eyes on him, took a great deal of bravery.
Nearly as much as facing a line of French
infantry.

When Stephen and Sophie reached the bottom of the set, they stood out for a round as
the dance dictated. This left another couple
at the top of the line to dance the steps and
repeat the pattern. As they waited to rejoin
the dance, they were free to converse. To flirt.
It was the time that young men, whether
courting or simply admiring a fair partner,

looked forward to most of all. A time to have a lady's undivided attention away from the listening ears of chaperones. To talk, or tease, or whisper sweet words of flattery. Instead, standing there with his wife, Stephen found himself tongue-tied.

He faltered, "Your dress is . . . well, you *in* that dress, I should say. You take my breath away."

"Thank you, Captain." She looked down, embarrassed, and he thought, or at least hoped, pleased at his praise. She said, "I am glad your mother had it made for me."

"So am I. And here I am in ordinary evening attire like every other man in the room. Perhaps I ought to have worn my dress uniform, but as it is my last night as a civilian . . ."

"You look very handsome as you are."

His body warmed at the shy admiring glance she gave him from beneath her lashes.

"Why, Mrs. Overtree, are you flirting with me?" he teased.

"And . . . if I am?"

He took her hand in his. "You, my wife, may flirt with me any time you like. The way you are looking at me now, I almost think you mean it."

She met and held his gaze. "I do."

His heart beat hard, and he swallowed in vain to dislodge the lump in his throat. He said in a voice low and hoarse, "Careful,

Sophie, or I may begin believing you. And then you had better lock the adjoining room door."

She looked at him quickly, then away, the veil of her golden-brown lashes falling over her eyes once more. What had he seen there? Hope? Fear? Uncertainty?

Before he could decipher her look, the music rose and another round began. Keith and Miss Blake looked at them expectantly. It was time to rejoin the dance. But, dash it, Stephen doubted he would be able to concentrate on the steps. Dancing was not what he had in mind.

As soon as Mr. Harrison escorted Kate off the dance floor, Mr. Darby-Wells downed his drink, swept to her side, and claimed her again. Sophie noticed Mr. Harrison's gaze follow the two as they danced, his expression tinted with sadness . . . or perhaps, resignation.

She and the captain danced another set, and then Sophie begged off to rest. Between her constricting stays and added weight, she found herself becoming out of breath easily. Meanwhile, Captain Overtree danced dutifully with Miss Blake and then his sister.

Mr. Overtree asked his wife to dance, but she shook her head. "I don't want you to overexert yourself. And really, dancing is the province of the young."

Earlier, Sophie had seen Colonel Horton talking with several couples nearer his own age. But now he sat alone. It sent a blade of sorrow through her heart, to see his solitary figure amid all the happily paired people, no doubt missing his wife.

Sophie went and joined the older man, noticing he rolled a wrapped sweet between his fingers. "May I sit with you?"

"Of course. Catching your breath, are you?"

"Yes. Unless . . . would you care to dance, Colonel?"

"Thank you, no. My dancing days are over. Mrs. Horton was an excellent dancer." He looked up at his daughter's approach. "Was she not, Janet?"

Mrs. Overtree sat on the colonel's other side. "She was indeed, Papa."

"Well, my dear, is it a victory?" he asked. "Have the rank and file carried out your orders and plans as you'd hoped?"

Mrs. Overtree released a long breath. "I think so, yes."

He looked at his daughter in fond amusement. "This is the longest I've seen you sit still in a week."

She gave him a rueful smile of acknowledgement, then said, "I confess I am a *little* weary."

"I should say so."

A peal of laughter sounded — Kate's — drawing their attention to the line of dancers.

The colonel lifted a knobby hand toward

his grandchildren. "Look at Stephen and Katherine." He shook his head, then smiled at Sophie. "Should have seen that boy when his little sister came along so late. Him already ten years old. Holding that wee bundle with such pride. Such affection."

"Yes," Mr. Overtree nodded, eyes distant in memory. "They were always close. I think she shall miss him more than anyone when he leaves." Mrs. Overtree shot Sophie a look, amending, "Besides you, of course, Sophie."

Oh yes, she would miss him indeed.

Next, Mr. Harrison guided Kate onto the dance floor a second time.

Mrs. Overtree huffed. "Is he still here?"

The colonel said, "Oh, let Kate enjoy herself. She is young. It's only right she should have several suitors vying for her attention."

Mrs. Overtree's lips thinned. "I do not consider David Harrison a proper suitor for our Katherine."

The colonel patted her hand. "There, there, my dear. Don't fret. It's only a dance."

Sophie watched the gentle way Mr. Harrison held Kate's hand and gazed into her eyes, and knew it was more than a dance. Her heart ached for them both.

Later, when the number of couples dwindled, Sophie and Captain Overtree left the hall by

unspoken agreement before the final bou-
langer.

"Tired?" he asked.

"My feet are tired. But otherwise I am well.
Though I have definitely had enough of dancing. Have you?"

"An hour ago."

They shared a smile and slowly climbed
the stairs together.

"Is there no one you need to say good-bye
to?" she asked.

"The whole night was about saying good-
bye to me and hello to you. I won't subject
either of us to another dozen farewell
speeches." He added, "And I still have tomorrow to bid my family good-bye, so they won't
mind us retiring early."

Us . . .

They arrived at their bedchamber door, and
Sophie's hands trembled as she fumbled for
the latch. He reached out to open the door
for her at the same time, and his hand closed
over hers. Sophie's chest tightened at his
touch.

He followed her into the bedchamber as
usual but did not cross to the dressing room
door.

Her nerves quivered.

With all the servants needed belowstairs for
the party, no fire had yet been lit in the room,
no candles burned, and the shutters were still
open. Moonlight shone in through the tall

windows. Distracted, Sophie moved toward their light and stood gazing vaguely outside. The moon shone brightly in a clear sky, illuminating the garden and shaped topiaries below. But her attention was far more focused on the man behind her.

She heard the soft creak of floorboards, sensed his nearness, the air crackling with tension between them.

His large hands descended softly over her shoulders like a cape, instantly warming her. They lowered, cupping her upper arms. She felt him lean down and rest his forehead on the back of her head.

For several moments they both stood still, their bodies not touching, not moving. Hardly breathing. Now and again the distant sounds of carriages drawing up or departing reached her, but she barely took notice.

She tilted her head to one side and tentatively leaned back. He moved forward, closing the gap between them. Resting her head on his shoulder, she allowed herself to relax against him — well, as relaxed as she could be considering the tension thrumming between them. Sophie felt the solid warmth of him against her, supporting her. Protecting her. Yet again.

He laid his cheek against her hair, one hand moving down her arm, then around her waist, drawing her more fully against him. How good it felt to be held.

He bent lower, and she felt his warm breath against her ear. He pressed a gentle kiss to her cheek, and she closed her eyes to relish the sweet sensation. With his free hand, he brushed tendrils of hair from her neck and pressed a feathery kiss to the bare skin of her shoulder, then another on her neck. Shivery pleasure ran through her. Then both of his arms were around her, holding her close.

They did not speak. Sophie felt to do so would be to raise questions she wasn't ready to answer. Break the spell. Cause him to retreat. And maybe he feared the same in her, for he said nothing either. The silence was like a tight violin string between them, binding them from her center to his. Growing more taut with each tick of the mantel clock.

He slowly trailed kisses up the length of her neck. Her jawline. Her earlobe.

Then he moved sideways and turned her to face him as deftly as a dance step. Their eyes met and locked.

His hands slid upward from her cap sleeves, over her shoulders to her neck, and then he framed her face with his palms. She drew a ragged breath. How wide the blacks of his eyes were in the moonlight. Intense with longing, yet uncertain.

He slowly lowered his head, gaze flicking over her face, her eyes, her lips. She didn't move. Barely even blinked. He touched his lips to hers, softly, tentatively. A rush of sweet, heady pleasure flowed through her.

When she did not object, he wrapped his arms around her, gathering her near, and kissed her again.

Slowly, firmly, deliciously, his mouth caressed hers. He traced one corner of her lips, then the other, before lingering on the soft center. He lifted his head to look into her eyes, to gauge her reaction, her willingness, before descending again.

She reached up, cupping his jaw with her hand, her thumb stroking upward from his chin to his cheek, already bristly with new whiskers. Sliding her other hand around his neck, she threaded her fingers into the thick hair at its nape, splaying her hand against the back of his head and drawing him closer yet.

"Sophie . . ." he breathed.

He lifted his head and looked into her eyes, his expression almost fierce. "I vowed to keep my distance, but I can't. Send me to the dressing room now or never."

In reply, she stood on tiptoe and kissed him again.

She ran her hands over his shoulders and down the ropey muscles of his arms before sliding to his chest. Even the layers of evening clothes could not conceal the hard muscle beneath.

He angled his head, deepening the kiss, and pulled her tight against him.

The room around them faded. A voice

sounded from the garden below, two voices. But Sophie barely heard them, her attention focused on him, on his kiss, on his hands warm and sure on her waist. Not wandering, not pressuring, content for the moment to hold her. To slowly kiss her, pleasure and passion building.

If she had known kissing him would be like this . . . Oh why had they waited so long — and how would she ever let him go?

Suddenly Stephen stiffened and wrenched his mouth from hers. He turned toward the window, releasing her to lean near the glass and peer outside.

"What is it?" she whispered, shaken by his sudden withdrawal.

"That's Kate," he breathed, frowning in disbelief and confusion.

She followed the direction of his gaze. Two figures stood in the garden below. A man and women as evidenced by their outlines and dress, although their features were shadowed.

The man grasped the slight woman by the shoulders and pressed his face to hers, but the woman was clearly pulling back, trying to turn her face away. A cloud shifted, and moonlight shone on his blond hair and her distressed face. It was Kate. With Mr. Darby-Wells.

Sophie drew in a sharp breath. Beside her Stephen tensed and seemed to expand, his shoulders squared, his nostrils flared, and his jaw clenched. He turned and bolted from the room.

"Stephen . . ." she called after him, worried for Kate, but also worried about what he might do to that presumptuous dandy. *Oh, God, don't let him kill the man.* At least he had not diverted into his dressing room for either sword or gun. Then again, judging from the murderous look on his face, bare hands would be more than sufficient weapon.

Stephen thundered down the stairs. He was vaguely aware that Sophie had called him by his given name, but at the moment he could not stop to savor it. Fury and a savage protectiveness flashed through him like wildfire, consuming the tender passions of only moments before. *If he hurts Kate, so help me . . .*

Hands fisted, Stephen ran through the house, ignoring startled looks from his parents, who were bidding farewell to a final few guests, and charged out the side door toward the garden.

"Let me go," Kate cried.

"Come on, little miss. Don't play the innocent. You know your mamma has been trying to foist you on me all night."

Stephen's blood boiled. And the moonlight gave everything — garden wall, Kate's dress, and the man's blond hair — a red cast.

He launched himself through the garden

archway, grasped Darby-Wells by the shoulders, jerked him away from his sister, and sent him flying to the ground.

He said, in a voice deadly calm, "Apparently you did not hear the lady. She said to let her go."

Sprawled on the ground, the young man scowled up at him. "Dash it, Overtree, you've spoilt my coat."

"To the devil with your coat. This from a man who would ruin a young lady but care more for his worsted wool."

The man rose, dusting off his tails and torn lapel. "Cost a fortune. I shall send you the bill from my —"

"I'll pay it now." Stephen coiled his arm. Somewhere in the recesses of his mind, he calculated the dandy's fine bones and slight weight and restrained his force — a little — as he delivered a stunning blow to the man's face. *Smack.* Down he went again.

Kate gasped and pressed her hands to her mouth.

Stephen turned to her. "Are you all right, Kate?"

She nodded, tears filling her eyes. Hopefully not because he'd hit the handsome lecher.

His fears were laid aside when his sister leaned in to him, sobbing. Stephen draped one big arm over her shaking shoulder like a black wing.

From the house came several people who had followed Stephen outside in alarm. His father, his mother, the young footman, and the butler, carrying a lamp. And there, running out behind them, breathless and anxious, was Sophie. She looked from Kate, to the fallen man, to him, her mouth drooping open, her eyes downturned. Apparently, she did not see anything heroic in his actions, but rather barbaric. It reminded him of how she'd reacted when he'd fought off the young thieves in Plymouth. He had allowed himself to think her opinion of him had changed since then. Evidently he was wrong.

In the aftermath of raised voices and explanations and getting the fallen gentleman to his feet, Sophie retreated. In more ways than one.

Their father took Kate into his comforting arms.

Their mother, however, hissed, "I wanted you to encourage a proposal of marriage, not a tryst in the garden." Then she turned her disapproving face toward Stephen. "Could you not have simply ordered him to cease like a civilized person without resorting to violence?"

With brittle politeness, she offered to send for a cloth and ice for the man's swelling eye.

Mr. Darby-Wells angrily waved away her offer, face contorted in disgust. "Can you not control your offspring, Mrs. Overtree? First your daughter leads me a merry dance and then your behemoth son attacks me from behind. Really. I don't know what sort of people you are. This is the nineteenth century, if you were not aware. I think it a good thing Captain Black is returning to his regiment. The sooner the better. He's a danger to society."

"We . . . apologize if your actions were misunderstood," his mother said, lips tight.

"Don't apologize to that snake, Mamma," Stephen growled. "For all his airs and graces, he is no gentleman." Sophie had been right about the man.

Teary-eyed, Kate said, "I'm sorry, Mamma. I didn't mean to make him think I was that sort of girl. Truly I didn't. He said he needed some air and asked if I would show him the garden. I thought he liked me. I never imagined he would not take no for an answer."

"Oh, come, Miss Overtree." Darby-Wells rolled his eyes. "I hardly dragged you out here against your will. Save the dramatics. You were not crying like a missish schoolgirl five minutes ago — no need to play one for your parents now."

Stephen fisted his hands again.

Noticing, his father said, "Young man, you had better leave, and quickly, if you don't want your left eye to match your right."

By the time Kate had been calmed, reassured, and settled, Mr. Darby-Wells sent home, resentful and livid in his barouche, and possible repercussions discussed and dissected with his parents, another hour or more had passed.

Finally, Stephen trudged back up the stairs with none of the hopeful fire he'd felt going up with Sophie hours before. He sighed a deep, weary sigh and let himself into his dressing room using the servants' entrance. Through the door, slightly ajar, he peered into the moonlit bedchamber. Sophie lay in bed on her side. Her back to him. Again.

He didn't bother calling for his valet, considering the hour, but undressed himself and dropped to his hard sofa. He hoped his wife slept well. He, for one, would not.

CHAPTER 19

The next morning, Sophie awoke feeling uneasy. She had not meant to fall asleep before Stephen returned last night. But when an hour had passed and he'd still not returned, her eyes refused to remain open. She didn't know what time he'd come up, but he had not woken her. She hoped Kate was all right. A small part of Sophie wondered if Kate had — well, not deserved it, of course — but had encouraged the man's advances by going out there with him in the first place, dazzled by his looks and charm.

It reminded her of her own foolish reaction to Wesley's attention. It had gone to her head and made her lose her better sense. Perhaps the same thing had happened to Kate. She would seek her out later and see how she fared. But her first priority was finding Stephen. She wanted to apologize for falling asleep — assure him it had not been a pretense to avoid him. She wanted to tell him how she felt. That although they were not long acquainted, the more time they spent together, the more she admired him, and the more her hope for the future grew.

He wasn't in his dressing room, where she assumed he'd slept last night. Oh, it should have been in that big bed, with her. Remorse filled her. Thank heavens they had the rest of the day together.

Libby entered in response to her bell, all eagerness to talk about the evening before.

"What a night, ay, madam? Such goings-on as this old house hasn't seen in ages."

Sophie formed a vague smile, but her heart wasn't engaged in the idle chatter. It was already missing Captain Overtree. The only "goings-on" she cared about at the moment were those that had happened in this very room. And those that had not.

"Young James got into the open champagne. He's as green as a gherkin this morning, poor fool. And we're all agog about your husband giving that Darby-Wells fellow the setdown he deserved. Miss Katherine isn't the first female he's tried to have his way with, not according to Flora. Had it coming, she says."

Sophie felt a prick of remorse for having briefly entertained the notion that Kate might have been at least in part to blame. Now she was glad Stephen had knocked him down — and hopefully knocked some sense into him, though she doubted it would be the last time he refused to take no for an answer.

"Have you seen the captain this morning?" Sophie asked. "He . . . rose before I awoke."

"Oh yes. He's had his breakfast, and last I heard he was closed up in the library with some men from his regiment who showed up bright and early. I don't know what it's about. But lots of exclamations and dark looks from what Edgar said."

"That sounds ominous."

The maid shrugged. "Who knows with men? Always ready to declare war over some trifle or another. Now, the blue day dress or the ivory?"

When Sophie was dressed, she asked Libby to let her know as soon as the captain finished his meeting and the callers left. In the meantime, she went to the breakfast room, selected a few things for Winnie, and carried them upstairs. She felt bad that the old retainer had been left out of all the "goings-on" the night before.

When the old nurse replied to her knock, Sophie entered. Inside, Miss Whitney was wearing her customary blue dress with white lace collar, and a smile.

"Good morning, Winnie. I've brought you some breakfast. . . . But, my goodness, it looks as if someone has already brought you a feast!"

"Yes." The woman smiled somewhat sheepishly at the tray overflowing with plates of roasted meats, salads, slices of cake, and an entire tower of fruit. On the floor nearby, Gulliver lapped smoked salmon from a china dish.

"Don't tell me Mrs. John sent up all of that?" Sophie asked in disbelief.

"No. But I can't tell you who did."

That piqued Sophie's curiosity, but she didn't press her. "Well, you deserve every morsel, having to stay up here alone and miss the party last night."

"Who said I missed it?" Winnie asked, a twinkle in her eye.

Had the woman sneaked downstairs to watch? She thought of the squint Wesley had once used to view that long-ago masquerade ball. Might the nurse know about it as well?

"I don't miss much," Winnie added. "In fact, I saw men in uniform arrive a few hours ago. Trouble's brewing. Mark my word."

Her words reminded Sophie about Captain Overtree's doubts about his future. "Miss Whitney, Captain Overtree confided in me about your . . . well, prediction. Do you really believe it? Surely you might be mistaken, right?"

"Hmm?" the old woman asked distractedly, nibbling on a sugared date. "What prediction?"

"Did you not tell him he would die?"

Winnie paused, brow furrowing. "What do

you mean, die? We shall all die one day, Sophie."

"I know, but . . . did you not tell Stephen you didn't think he would return home this time?"

She frowned. "I don't recall saying that."

"Don't recall? Something about he wouldn't live to see his thirtieth year?"

The woman shook her silvery-white head. "Good heavens. What a tragedy. For you, for me, for the entire family. Except for Wesley, perhaps."

"What?" Sophie asked, flummoxed.

Winnie's face puckered in confusion. "I'm sorry, my dear. I don't recall saying he would die. He must be mistaken."

The woman rose in agitation and stepped to her window. "Have you seen my new hatchlings?"

Sophie ignored the question. "But . . . Winnie. Don't you . . . hear voices and predict things? Stephen told me he's never known you to be wrong."

"Dear boy. How kind of him." She picked up a bread roll and opened the latch. "Yes, I hear things, but I am no prophet, however biased the dear boy might be. I have been wrong once or twice. What a gentle memory he has." She crumbled the roll and sprinkled the crumbs on the ledge.

Then she closed the window and turned back, eyes alight. "Oh! Now I think on it, I may have said he wouldn't live to see his inheritance. . . ."

"Inheritance?" Sophie asked. "But he's a second son."

"Yes, but he has an inheritance from his grandfather, held in trust until his thirtieth birthday." Winnie inhaled and drew herself up. "And that's more than a year from now."

Sophie felt befuddled. Did it not amount to the same thing? Or had Winnie changed her story for some reason? Perhaps Stephen *had* misunderstood her. Or were Mrs. Overtree and Miss Blake right and the old nurse was off in her attic?

Miss Whitney went on, "Of course my memory isn't anything to boast about these days." She tapped her temple. "I remember things I did twenty years ago better than I recall what I ate for supper last night. Don't get old, Sophie. Not if you can help it."

"I don't think I like the alternative."

"True. We all must die. It's only a question of when, how, and where we're going afterwards." Winnie sighed. "I pray I shall not end in the poorhouse or a pauper's grave yet."

Sophie forced herself to reassure her yet again, even though she was irritated with the woman and confused in the bargain. "I am sure Captain Overtree won't let that happen."

Winnie shook her head. "But he is off to fight the French soon. He cannot control everything. Only God can do that."

"The French? But Napoleon has been exiled. The war is over."

"No, my dear. I don't believe it is. I hear Napoleon has raised his bold head again like a serpent refusing to lay low."

"How would you hear that? Did a voice tell you that?"

"Oh yes," the old nurse said, eyes strangely distant. "I hear voices almost every day."

Not sure what to think, Sophie started down the stairs, determined to find Stephen. She stopped first in their bedchamber, saw the dressing room had been disturbed but was otherwise empty, and then continued downstairs. In the hall, she was stunned to see Captain Overtree in full uniform, hat under his arm and bag in hand. Her heart lurched. *No!* They were supposed to have more time.

She hurried forward.

At the sound of her footsteps, he turned. "Sophie, thank heaven. I couldn't find you."

"I was upstairs with Winnie. What is going on? Tell me you're not leaving already."

"I'm afraid so. Napoleon has escaped exile and is back in France. Two others from my regiment are here. We are traveling together. I have to go."

"But we . . . I thought we had all day. If I had known, I would have come down sooner."

"No matter."

"But it does matter. How could you even think of leaving without saying good-bye?"

"I sent a footman and housemaid to find you, but —"

"Never mind that now." She reached out and grasped his arm. "I asked Winnie about the prediction. She said she doesn't remember saying you would die. Perhaps you misunderstood her."

His brow furrowed and his eyes narrowed. "She denied it?"

"Well, she didn't deny it completely. She remembers saying something about your inheritance, but surely if she'd meant anything so dire she would remember."

He tilted his head to one side and gazed at her fondly. "Are you sure you are not saying this to . . . boost my confidence? To try and trick destiny?" He said it in a light, teasing tone, but she remained serious.

"I wouldn't lie about something like this."

He sobered. "No, of course not. But neither would I. Winnie's memory may be faulty, but mine is mercilessly clear. Don't forget, I changed the course of my life — and yours — at least in small part because I believed her declaration possible."

"Are you sorry you did so?"

"You know better than that."

"Well, I don't believe Winnie has your future in her hands. Nor does Napoleon Bonaparte. Only God."

He squeezed her hand. "I believe that too."

He turned toward the door, but she held fast to his arm. "Don't go."

"I have to. But Lord help me, I wish I could stay . . ."

Her eyes heated. "Then you have to promise to come back."

"I promise to try."

"Good." She smiled, causing a hot tear to spill forth and trail down her cheek. "Don't forget me."

He pulled a miniature portrait from his pocket and showed it to her. "Never."

She was stunned to see it was one of the early likenesses Wesley had done of her. "You have that?"

"Yes. You go with me wherever I go." He tucked her hand beneath his arm, and they walked outside together.

She glanced around at the family waiting to say their good-byes, the coachman and groom, and fellow officers in the carriage. She murmured, "If there were not so many people, I would —"

He pulled her into her arms and murmured in her ear, "What other people?" He kissed her temple, then the tear from her cheek. She raised her face, and he pressed his mouth to hers in a fierce, possessive kiss. She wrapped her arms around his neck and kissed him back, and he drew her closer still.

One of the officers hooted from the carriage and the other whistled.

"Come on, Overtree. We'll miss our ship at this rate."

"Aww, let him kiss his missus. Still on their honeymoon, after all."

The captain broke the kiss at last, resting his cheek atop her head. He said in a gravelly whisper, "*If* I do come back, that will be the end of separate beds. Understand?"

"Yes," she breathed, heart beating hard. "I should hope so."

His eyes met hers, serious. Measuring. "You're killing me, woman. You know that, don't you? I didn't realize you were on Boney's side."

"I am not. I want you to live."

He kissed her palm, then pressed it to his heart. "Live or die my heart is yours, Sophie Dupont."

Tears filled her eyes. "Sophie Overtree, and don't forget it." She tried to grin, but it wobbled away.

Oh, God, don't let it be too late for us. Bring him home to me. Give us another chance.

Stephen reluctantly released her and bent to pick up his kit.

His family, who had waited some distance away in patient, perhaps stunned, silence — no doubt taken aback by their public display of affection — now hurried forward to say their final farewells.

His kissed his mother's cheek, hugged Kate, and shook his father's hand.

His grandfather slapped his shoulder with a fond grin. "What did I tell you, my boy? A few weeks with your bride were just what you needed, ay? Want me to see if I can eke out another few days?"

"Thank you, sir. But no. Duty calls." Hearing of Bonaparte's return to France had struck him like a death knell that morning.

"Not having second thoughts, I hope?" the colonel asked. "Remember your thirtieth birthday will be here before you know it. You've done well, my boy. Just persevere for king and country a little longer. Make me proud."

Stephen inwardly chafed at the platitudes. At his grandfather's plans for his life. If Boney was back, it could be years before the war ended and he could return. If ever.

Mr. Keith came forward, looking both sheepish and resolved. The two men shook hands.

"Any marching orders, sir?" his former lieutenant asked.

"Keep a civil tongue in your head, Keith. And the cork in the bottle."

"Aye, aye, Captain."

"Be respectful of my wife. Do you hear me? And help her keep an eye on Winnie for me."

"Of course, sir."

Stephen climbed into the carriage, his heart

and body rebelling at the thought of leaving Sophie.

Keith leaned in the open window. "And shall I watch over Wesley again should he return? Keep him safe?"

Stephen scowled. "Devil take Wesley. Protect my wife."

Thoughts of Wesley cast a pall over his departure and threw cold water on his hopes for the future. He swallowed bile, and stoically lifted a hand to his family and winked at Kate. But as the carriage moved away from Overtree Hall and passed through the gate, he was filled with a sense of doom.

Sophie retreated from the others, slowly walking toward the churchyard. She thought she might have a good cry in the quiet church and pray for Stephen's return. Seeing the warm light in his eyes had given her hope that he believed he would be coming home again. That he would survive the war, and return to her. That there might be a future for them after all.

Movement from above caught her eye, and she glanced up. There in a top-story window stood Miss Whitney, looking down and watching as Stephen's carriage drove away. The old woman was now dressed head to toe in black — from veiled hat to bombazine gown. There was no sign of her usual white collar, and even her silvery white hair was covered. Her face was somber, her eyes squinted to watch the carriage as it disappeared. She was seemingly unaware of Sophie, or anyone else for that matter. Winnie pressed a hand to her black breast, then solemnly raised it, palm forward, and pressed it to the glass.

Sophie's heart began to thud in a heavy, dread-filled beat to look upon the sight. And to wonder what it meant.

CHAPTER 20

Unable to sleep that night after Stephen's departure, Sophie sat up late, reading in bed by candlelight. After a time, she laid aside her novel, and pulled *The Rearing and Management of Children* from its hiding place. She flipped through the pages and ran a finger down the table of contents: Infant Care, Feeding, Washing, Health, Digestion, Teething . . . She would read it all, she decided. She had little experience with infants and wanted to take excellent care of her baby. Be the best mother she could be. No matter who had given it to her, the book would be useful. And she could use all the help she could get.

She read through the introduction, then abruptly stopped. Something thudded hard in the corridor beyond her room, followed by the sound of breaking glass. She heard no call for help, no padding feet of a summoned servant.

Sophie reminded herself that Overtree Hall

housed many servants who kept busy about the place at all hours, answering bells, lighting fires, bringing water. Perhaps one of them had simply dropped something. It didn't necessarily mean that anything was amiss.

She turned the page.

Then a high-pitched cry, like a cornered cat or a woman in pain, reverberated through the wall and sent shivers up Sophie's spine.

She lay frozen, book in hand, telling herself not to be silly. There was undoubtedly a simple explanation for the sound. Perhaps Gulliver had sneaked down and become trapped somewhere on this floor. If so, she hoped Winnie found the cat before Mrs. Overtree did.

Sophie lay still a moment longer, listening.

"Now you've gone and done it," came a mournful moan. "That'll be the end of you. He's gone, and you're next."

Sophie laid aside her book, threw back the bedclothes, and rose. She tied her dressing gown around herself, picked up her candle lamp, and carried it to the door. Inching it open, she peered into the dim corridor.

From a distance, came the faint sound of someone playing the pianoforte downstairs. But from much nearer by, a muffled groan reached her.

Pulse pounding, Sophie crept forward, candle high to light her way. She rounded the corner and was stunned to see Miss Whitney crumpled on the floor.

Sophie gasped in alarm. "Winnie! What's happened? Are you hurt?"

"He's gone," she wailed. "And I'm next. I know it."

Is that why the woman had dressed in black? To mourn Stephen's departure — her defender at Overtree Hall? "Hush," Sophie gently urged, kneeling beside the woman. It was clear from her slurred speech and bleary eyes that she was intoxicated. Sophie glanced at the broken drinking glass beside her, and smelled brandy.

Miss Whitney followed her gaze and her look of sorrow deepened. "Oh, now look what you've gone and done, Winnie old girl." She leaned over and began sweeping at the shards of glass with bare fingers.

Sophie grasped her hands to stop her. "No, Winnie. Leave it. You'll cut yourself. I'll take care of it. Let's get you to your room before Mrs. Overtree sees you like this."

Sophie tried to help Winnie up, but in her current limp and uncooperative state, she couldn't manage it alone. "Winnie, stay here and be quiet. I'll get help and be back directly, all right?"

"Not coming back . . ." she moaned again. "What if he doesn't come back . . . ?"

"He will. And so will I. Give me two minutes."

Sophie hurried down the stairs, the sound

of the pianoforte growing louder as she neared the white parlour. Mr. Keith, she guessed. He had played as a younger man and had recently begun trying to learn how to do so with one hand. She opened the door. There sat Mr. Keith, up late, quietly plunking away at the pianoforte to amuse himself, or perhaps to keep his hand too busy to pour a drink.

"Mr. Keith, can you help me?"

He stopped playing and looked up at her in concern.

"It's Winnie," she explained quietly. "She's fallen and I need help getting her to her room."

He rose. "Is she badly hurt?"

"No, but she is somewhat . . . incapacitated."

His brows rose, but he didn't press for details. "Take me to her."

He followed her back upstairs. There, Winnie's tart breath, swaying form, and slurred muttering rendered her condition obvious.

Keith looked from her to Sophie, brow puckered. "Sink me. Is that what I'm like when I'm foxed?"

"Worse," Sophie said, then softened her reply with a grin.

"Very funny, Mrs. Overtree. You are beginning to sound like your husband."

Together they helped Winnie to her feet and

half-dragged her, half-carried her to the bottom of the stairs. "Now what?" Sophie asked.

Keith looked up the daunting flight. "Easier if I could carry her, but I'm not exactly sweeping women off their feet these days. Wait a minute . . ." He paused to think, then said, "Support her upright a moment."

Sophie did so, and he bent and hefted the old woman over one shoulder like a sack of cabbages.

"Wooee . . ." Winnie squealed. "The world's gone topsy-turvy. Ohhh . . ." she murmured. "I don't feel well . . ."

"Don't be sick on my shoes. Hear me, Winnie? They're my only decent pair. Nor down my back." He looked at Sophie and made a face. "Probably serve me right if she did."

A wrapped sweet fell from Winnie's inverted pocket, and Sophie bent and picked it up. Again Sophie hoped that no one would come upon them and see Winnie in this state — or in her current position! What a sight they must make.

Finally they reached the attic, Keith huffing and puffing. Sophie opened the door to Winnie's room and helped Mr. Keith gently slide the elderly woman from his shoulder to her bed.

Keith bent over, resting his hand on his knee. "Hang me, I'm lathered. That scrawny old bird weighs more than a drunken gunner."

Sophie smiled gratefully at the man. "Thank you, Mr. Keith. Captain Overtree would be pleased to know you helped."

"I know he would. He asked me to look out for you and the old girl. And I plan to do my duty."

"How good of you both. Now you go to bed and I'll finish cleaning up. You've done more than your fair share of work tonight."

"Carried my share of the load, I think you mean." He rotated his shoulder and stretched his neck. "I'll be sore in the morning — that's for da . . . dashed sure. Sorry. Night."

Sophie removed Winnie's shoes, spread a blanket over her, and then went back downstairs. While she was cleaning up the glass, the colonel stepped from his room into the corridor, fully dressed. "Is everything all right?"

"Oh . . . um, yes, Colonel. Everything is fine. Dropped something, that's all, and didn't want to wake a housemaid at this hour. Nothing to worry about."

"Well, good. I thought I heard something . . . else."

"What?"

"Never mind. Well, if you're sure you're all right. Good night, my dear."

"Good night, Colonel."

In the parlour the next evening, Mr. Overtree held up a crystal decanter — nearly empty — and eyed it in disgust.

He glared across the room at Mr. Keith. "Good heavens, man. Must you drink all my brandy? I know for a fact Thurman refilled this decanter yesterday."

"I didn't ha —" Mr. Keith broke off with a swift glance at Sophie. "That is, I . . . don't know what to say, sir."

Sophie came to his defense. "Mr. Keith has been abstaining lately. I don't think it could have been him."

"Oh, come now," Mrs. Overtree scoffed. "Who else in this house drinks so much of that awful stuff?"

"Thank you, Mrs. Overtree." Keith's eyes were on Sophie as he said it. "But perhaps I did and merely . . . forgot."

"Forgot? Well, if you drank all this, I imagine you did." Mr. Overtree scowled. "Probably have a thick head today as well."

Colonel Horton winced and spoke up. "Don't be angry with the lieutenant, Alan. Truth be told, I drank quite a bit of brandy myself last night. Rough day with Stephen leaving. Maybe Keith isn't the only one who wanted to dull the pain."

Keith stared at the colonel, stunned speechless.

Sophie watched the elderly man with confusion, curiosity, and growing realization. If he

359

offered her a sweet, she would not be surprised.

To distract herself from loneliness, Sophie invited Kate up to the studio the following day, and together the two young women spent several pleasant hours — Sophie instructing while Kate attempted a still life of flowers and fruit. For the time being the partially finished portrait of Captain Overtree stood shrouded against the wall, too poignant to look at.

Miss Blake had gone to Oxford the day after the party to visit her future sister-in-law, so Sophie had Kate's undivided attention. Except, perhaps, for Gulliver, who lounged nearby.

Mr. Keith, Sophie knew, was restless with Miss Blake gone, sure the new sister-in-law must have six strapping brothers who would all vie for her regard. Through the window, they heard *crack* over and over again as he hit cricket balls singlehandedly across the lawn, only to fetch them and begin again.

Finally silence reigned and Kate and Sophie looked at each other in relief. But after a few minutes passed, the sound of the pianoforte being banged in a discordant racket wound its way up the stairwell. Sophie winced, and Kate shook her head as she continued to paint. Sophie was amazed the girl could concentrate.

Some time later, carriage wheels crunched on the drive below, and Sophie stepped to the window. "Miss Blake is here. I thought she meant to stay in Oxford longer. Shall we go down?"

"Oh . . ." Kate dabbed paint to a flower petal. "Let Mr. Keith have her to himself for a while."

The two women shared knowing grins.

Then Sophie sobered. "Have you . . . talked to Mr. Harrison since the party?"

Kate sighed. "I tried to. But he says we must respect my parents' wishes and not further our acquaintance. He says it's all for the best, as he needs to focus on the book he is writing."

"Kate, we haven't discussed what happened with Mr. Darby-Wells. Are you all right? Anything you want to talk about?"

Kate shrugged. "I'm all right. Embarrassed that I put myself in that compromising position in the first place. I confess I thought he *might* try to kiss me, but I never guessed he would push for more like that. I don't like that I've disappointed Mamma's hopes for the future now that I've run him off."

"You didn't 'run him off.' He is the one who behaved badly. You were only trying to protect yourself."

"Well, thankfully Stephen was there to stop him — even if Mamma didn't approve of his methods." Kate shrugged again. "Considering everything, it could have been worse."

"Yes," Sophie agreed. Much worse, as she knew too well.

The following week passed uneventfully, and Sophie settled in to a pleasant routine at Overtree Hall: painting, reading, spending time with Kate and Winnie. She wrote to her father and stepsisters, prayed for Captain Overtree, and for the most part, managed not to think about his brother.

Then Sophie received a letter from Mavis Thrupton — a thick letter. Mavis must miss her. Sophie certainly missed the dear woman, and took the letter into the morning room to read at her leisure. She sat in a comfortable chair and broke the seal. As she unfolded it, a second note fell into her lap. She read Mavis's letter first:

My Dear Sophie,

I hope this letter finds you in good health and faring well in your new home. Has Captain Overtree returned to his regiment? I will pray for him and for you. Do write when you can and let me know how you do.

I am enclosing a letter for you that was sent to your father's studio. I confess I hesitate to forward it on at all. As you will see, it was posted several weeks ago. I discovered it recently when I stopped by the studio in search of a missing payment a lodger assured me he'd sent. I found the place in complete disorder and searched for the payment amid an overflowing stack of bills and correspondence on the desk. And what did I find at the very bottom, half hidden beneath the blotter? A letter addressed to you in a hand I think you will recognize.

Maurice came in and demanded to know what I was doing. I berated him for the state of the studio and asked why he had not forwarded your post. He shrugged and said he must have mislaid it. I didn't believe him. He wanted the letter back, saying he would take it with him to Bath, but I told him you were no longer there. I insisted I had your new address and would send it to you myself. (I didn't want the letter to end up in Mrs. Dupont's hands.) Even so, I had to all but wrest it from him. The seal, as you will see, has been broken. I fear he may have read it. The young man seems quite bitter towards you. It is well that you are away from here — and even Bath — where he would have lived under the same roof with you.

Hopefully old hurts and rumors will fade in time, my dear. In the meanwhile, remember what I told you, and make the best of your new life.

As for me, I have engaged a new woman (Mildred Dooley) to clean the cottages. Bitty has gone off with her sailor. I continue in good health, but my mother continues ill. I have left the cottages in Mildred's care and spend all the time I can with my mum while I have that privilege. I know you, dear girl, will understand how I dread the loss to come.

All my love,
Mavis

Tears pricked Sophie's eyes, both from the remembrances of her own mother sparked by the words, and in nostalgia for the dear woman she missed almost as much as her beloved mamma.

She wiped them away, then picked up the second letter. With a thudding heart, she recognized the loopy artistic handwriting — both from the letter of farewell he'd scratched on the back of her portrait, and from the bold way he signed his paintings.

Miss Sophie Dupont
Dupont Studio
Lynmouth, Devon

It had been posted from Plymouth only a few days before she, Mavis, and Stephen had traveled there. With trembling fingers she opened the folded sheet and read the lines written in that familiar, admired hand.

Dear mia Sophia,

I am imagining your lovely face as I write this. Your deep, sorrowful eyes. More sorrowful now, I fear, because of my thoughtlessness. How sorry I am that I did not say good-bye to you in person — that I left you that way. That I left you at all. I regret to think of that hasty and heartless parting note. I allowed the prospect of a trip to my beloved Italy to overwhelm my better judgment.

I hope and pray that everything is all right with you. But I know it cannot be, really. (You may remember me mentioning my younger sister. And if a man trifled with her in such a manner, I would horsewhip him.) You deserve better than that. I know I have disappointed you. The truth is, I have disappointed myself.

I did not lie to you. The feelings I expressed were true. But I confess I allowed fear a foothold when I realized you held my heart in your hands. A vulnerable, frightening prospect for this independent man, I can tell you. So when the unexpected invitation came, I acted out of self-interest and accepted it. You know I created some of my best work in Italy. And you have heard me recount (too many times, no doubt) my unforgettable experiences there several years ago. Therefore I hope you understand, at least in part, my desire to go back.

*How often is an artist granted such an op-
portunity? I justified that it would be foolish
to let the opportunity pass me by.*

*So I made my choice, and we departed.
But my spirit has been troubled ever since.*

*We sailed here to Plymouth and from its
port will shortly board a merchant ship
bound for Naples. The voyage is paid for,
the plans made. But my heart is not in them.
I am tempted to return to you even now. To
forego the ocean journey altogether and
return to L & L overland. Would you welcome me back? Forgive me? I believe you
would, dear loving woman that you are. With
that hope, may I ask you to wait for me? I
don't know how long you plan to remain in
Lynmouth before returning to Bath. But I will
come and find you as soon as I can. Will
you be patient a little while longer, mia
Sophia? I pray you will be, and will be there
waiting for me, when I return.*

Yours ardently,
W.D.O.

Sophie's breath hitched. Her stomach knotted. Could it be true? Had Wesley realized
his true feelings and regretted leaving her
even before he'd departed England's shores?
Already planning to return to her? *Oh no. . . .*

For several minutes, Sophie stared unseeing at the letter before her, written only a few

short days before she married his brother. How dare Maurice read it?

Drawing a shaky breath, Sophie refolded the letter again and again, smaller and smaller.

She had thought she had mastered her thoughts. Once she had become his brother's wife, she had not let her mind dwell on Wesley nor remember intimate moments with him. But now, spurred by this letter, by these words she had longed to hear, she allowed the memories to come . . .

Not long after Wesley Overtree returned to Lynmouth the second year, he and Sophie stood side by side with their easels atop Castle Rock, dressed warmly against the cold. She painted the landscape, while he painted her.

The winter days were still short and the sun began setting late in the afternoon. They watched it together, she now and again feeling his gaze on her profile.

She glanced at him as well, admiring his fine features, full lower lip, and perfect nose slightly pink from the chilly wind. She could have looked upon his face for hours.

When the sun faded into the horizon, they packed up their things and began the brisk walk back.

As they navigated the rocky path, he said, "You are unique, Sophie. Any other woman would become bored within a quarter of an hour and begged to be taken shopping or to the theatre, but you and I can paint together in companionable silence for hours."

He slid his supplies under one arm and took her hand in his. "You make me happy, Sophie. I hope you know that."

Her heart thumped, and she smiled shyly at him. "That is quite a coincidence. For I have never been happier in my life."

They returned to the rented cottage and set aside their things, pulling off their gloves, mufflers, and winter coats. There was no sign of Carlton Keith.

"Sit for me, will you?" Wesley asked.

She shook her head. "You must be growing tired of painting me. Let's do something else."

"Not at all! You are *la mia musa*. Besides, I have an idea for a new portrait." He rubbed his hands together. "I am thinking of calling it *mai stata baciata*."

Sophie's mind instantly translated, *Never been kissed*. She ducked her head, feeling her cheeks heat. "However accurate, I don't know that I want that fact captured in oil."

He took her hands and warmed them between his own. "Then perhaps I shall call it *il primo bacio*."

The first kiss. Her gaze flew to his. Was he teasing her?

His golden-brown eyes warm on her face,

he said in a low voice, "I know you have never been kissed, mia Sophia. But I mean to change that."

She blinked, faltering, "I . . . I don't know that we should."

He lit several lamps and positioned the chair where he wanted it. "Don't worry. You don't need to do anything, sweet girl. Just sit here and look as appealing as you are. I want to see your reaction. Try to capture it."

Should she allow him to kiss her? Could she resist?

Heart pounding, she asked timidly, "Just . . . kiss?"

His watchful eyes grazed hers. He said softly, "If that's what you want . . ."

"I want to be able to trust you."

"I want that too. You know I would never hurt you, Sophie. That I care for you? Adore you?"

"I do know that."

"Then close your eyes and focus on your mouth."

She obeyed, closing her eyes, her pulse beginning to trip a little faster with every second of waiting.

Finally she felt his sweet breath on her cheek, her lips. Cinnamon and tea . . .

"Mia Sophia, ti adoro," he whispered, and the warm breathy words sent shivers up her neck.

She felt the faintest whisper on her lips.

"Shhh . . . Don't move. . . ."

She kept her eyes closed, overwhelmed by his nearness, the heady smell of his shaving tonic, the aching inches between them.

His mouth gently rested on hers, feather-light. "What do you feel, *amore mio*?"

She managed to breathe, "You . . ."

His lips moved softly, slowly against hers, dampening, gently pressing.

Suddenly he pulled away, and her eyes flew open in surprise. Disappointment.

"Don't move," he repeated, and stepped quickly to his easel, picking up palette and brush, staring at her face, her eyes, her mouth. . . .

By the end of that evening, her lips were tender, and her hair a mess. And he had long ago quit trying to capture her expression. Instead he had captured her body and soul.

Sophie knew she should resist. Wait until they were married. But she wasn't overly worried. Wesley Overtree was a gentleman and he cared for her. He would protect her as well. And God would forgive them, she justified, once they were married. At least she hoped He would.

As the weeks together passed, she imagined a bright future for them. Creating side by side. Traveling with him. Living with him as his wife. A longed-for escape from her stepmother's home and father's studio. A life of being cherished by the man she loved.

He hasn't actually said he loves you, or plans to marry you, a quiet voice whispered in the back of her mind. *If he did, he would wait.*

If only she had heeded it.

But he *had* called her *amore mio* — my love — and so many other endearments in both English and Italian. And she had come to trust him, to believe he would stay with her. Marry her.

She could not blame Wesley alone. She was naïve but not completely ignorant. She had known the risk she was taking, and had taken it anyway. Certain he would catch her if she fell.

Now she realized that perhaps he would have, after all. She folded his letter even smaller. Had she misjudged him? Had Stephen? Even if she had received Wesley's letter soon after he'd posted it, it would have been too late. She had already eloped with his brother.

Sitting there in the Overtree Hall morning room, Sophie held her head in her hands. She had realized it would be difficult when Wesley returned home at some future point after his travels and met his new sister-in-law — the woman he had left behind to search for a new *la musa*. She had known it would be awkward. Embarrassing. But she'd thought if Wesley had not wanted her himself, how could he complain if his brother had decided to marry her? The awkwardness would pass soon enough, she'd told herself. She'd hoped.

But if Wesley still had feelings for her, longed for — even expected — to continue their relationship where they had left off, only to find she had married another? And worse yet, his brother? She shook her head, and a groan escaped her.

Fortunately, Wesley was not expected back from Italy any time soon. Perhaps he would have found his new muse by then. Maybe he had already met a dark and vivacious Mona Lisa and was even now regretting having written this apology — this olive branch — to a quiet and pale painter's daughter. There was a chance that had happened. A hope.

Though the thought brought little comfort.

CHAPTER 21

Wesley Overtree asked the driver to let him off at the end of the lane. He would walk from there. He wanted to stretch his legs and see the old place from a distance. When the horse and gig stopped, Wesley gave the man a half crown and thanked him for the ride from the coaching inn. It was a relief to walk on solid, familiar ground after the tedious sea voyage followed by hours on the dusty, pitted road.

The whole long journey had been a waste of time. He had not even stepped foot on Italian soil. Storms had plagued them, followed by a dead calm that delayed their progress. And then the ship had turned back at the island of Sardinia. The captain heard reports of Napoleon's escape and imminent return and insisted on turning around before war broke out and made the sailing route dangerous or impassable. Of all the bad luck . . . Or perhaps it had not been luck at all, but a sign. Or a punishment. God telling him to quit running and go home.

A part of him had been oddly relieved. He would see Sophie even sooner than he thought. He hoped she had received the letter he'd posted, and had accepted his apology.

Reaching Plymouth about a month and a half after he'd left it, Wesley traveled overland to Lynmouth by stage coach, rehearsing what he would say to her. Imagining, anticipating her smile. Her shy lovely eyes shining with surprise and happiness to see him back so much sooner than anticipated.

When he'd alighted at the Lynmouth coaching inn at last, he claimed his bags and strode along the harbor, a spring in his step. How he'd missed her. He could not wait to take her in his arms.

He drew up short. The Duponts' place was dark and empty. A *Closed* notice sat propped in the lower window, printed with Mr. Dupont's Bath direction, for those who wished to contact him there. Wesley frowned and squinted through the glass. He knew Dupont had returned to Bath. But where were Sophie and that sniveling Maurice? He knocked, in case the lazy young man was sleeping midday.

No answer.

Wesley shifted his increasingly heavy luggage and walked up the steep hill to Mrs. Thrupton's place, remembering Sophie had been sleeping in the woman's spare room to avoid being alone at night with her father's assistant. He knocked, but no one answered there either. Strange.

He went to the cottage he'd rented and where he'd left his recent paintings and the supplies he'd not taken with him on the trip. The door was locked, as it should be. He had left his key under the planter, not knowing when he'd be back, but it was not there now. He finally found a maid he did not recognize cleaning one of the other cottages and asked her where everyone was. Mrs. Thrupton was gone to sit with her ailing mother, she told him. And no, she was not acquainted with the Duponts nor knew where they were. Only that they had gone, and she and Mrs. Thrupton were tending their cottages for them until they returned. There was nothing in number one, she told him, but he did not believe her. His pleading smile and a coin had persuaded her to unlock the door.

"I told you, sir. I cleaned it myself. There was nothing personal in here save some rubbish and one old stocking. You may have it if you like."

He had been astounded and unhappy. Surely Sophie had not thrown away or burned all his belongings as some sort of revenge. He hoped she had crated them up and stored them somewhere, probably in their studio. No, the maid did not have a key to the

Duponts' studio and wouldn't be opening it for a stranger even if she did. He could wait for Mrs. Thrupton to return, if he liked, but there was no telling how long she'd be, illness adhering to no schedule.

Wesley had mustered his manners and thanked the woman. From there he had decided to head back to Overtree Hall. Not knowing what sort of reception he might receive — especially from Sophie's father — he was not eager to show up in Bath unannounced. And he was running dangerously low on funds, not to mention clean clothes. He was also distracted and concerned about the fate of his missing paintings and wanted to discover if the Duponts had sent them to Overtree Hall. That would have been kind of them. And they were kind people. Once that possibility had occurred to him, he decided he would find Sophie as soon as he'd assured himself his paintings were safe.

He assumed Carlton Keith would have made his way to Overtree Hall by now, probably shorter on funds than he was and in need of a place to stay. Not to mention access to a wine cellar. He had left Keith behind in Lynmouth, so hopefully the man would know if Sophie had received his letter, where she was now, and the whereabouts of his paintings. Perhaps Keith had taken it upon himself to have them sent home, though he doubted the man would take his role as nursemaid that far.

Whatever the case, Wesley made up his mind to spend a few days at home, wash the travel dust from himself and his clothes, and then seek out Sophie.

Wesley now passed through the Overtree Hall gate and looked up at the house, admiring its grave lines and pleasing symmetry.

When he reached the door and let himself in, the butler stepped out from his nearby pantry, disapproval etched on his face until he saw who it was.

Wesley nodded to him. "Hello, Thurman."

"Sir. Welcome home." The old retainer took his coat and hat. "I believe your parents are in the white parlour. Would you like me to announce you?"

"No need. I'll just —"

"Wesley!" Here came his mother, arms outstretched and a smile brightening her thin, weary face.

"Hello, Mamma. Miss me?"

"You know I did, impertinent boy. What a question! Worried about you too. Sailing all that way on your own. And you're as thin as a rail, did they not feed you? I thought the Italians were known for their food."

"I did not reach Italy, Mamma. With Napoleon back in France, the captain insisted on returning to England before war broke out again, so —"

"Wesley, my boy!" his father boomed across

the hall. "How good to see you whole and hale. We didn't expect you."

"Hello, Papa. How are you? In good health, I trust?"

"I am well, thank you. And —"

"He is not well," Mamma interrupted. "It's his heart. That's why we sent Stephen to find you and bring you home."

Wesley frowned. "Stephen? I never saw him."

"Yes, we know that now. He returned from Devonshire empty-handed."

His father tucked his chin. "Not quite empty-handed, my dear. Don't forget whom he brought with him."

Wesley nodded. "I knew Keith would have turned up by now."

"Yes, but that's not who I meant."

Perhaps hearing his name, Carlton Keith appeared in the threshold of the billiards room, stick in his hand, leaning on the doorframe. "Well, well. Hello, Wesley. Didn't expect to see you for months."

Wesley turned and narrowed his eyes at his friend. "Are you the presumptuous person I have to thank for emptying my cottage? I couldn't believe my paintings and things were not there. Worse yet, neither was Miss Du—"

"Yes, well, things change," Keith interrupted. "The captain had your things crated up and sent back here since you made no arrangements to do so."

"I would have done. I wasn't planning to stay away forever."

"You haven't heard the news, then?" Keith asked.

"What news?"

"Your brother is married. Went looking for you, and came home with a bride instead."

"What?" Incredulity washed over Wesley. "Captain Black found some poor wretch willing to marry his sour self? I don't believe it. What sort of woman would marry Marsh? Did no one warn her?"

"I tried to."

"Yes, it's quite true," his father said. "Your younger brother beat you to the altar."

"Please remember he is serving his country, Wesley," his mother scolded mildly. "And in his absence we must all make every effort to accept his new wife and make her feel at home here. In fact, I think you may have met."

Wesley smirked. "That bad, is she?"

"Wes, um . . ." Keith jerked his head to the side. "Perhaps you and I could step away and have a word, before —"

His father looked toward the staircase. "Here she is now."

From the corner of his eye, Wesley had noticed motion on the stairs. A slender figure in white floating gracefully down. He had taken in only the vaguest impressions — female. White dress. Fair hair. For some

379

reason, he would have expected a woman as dark and broad as Marsh himself.

Carlton Keith hissed something urgently under his breath, but Wesley didn't make out the words. He turned and gaped.

The female on the stairs stopped abruptly on the half landing, staring down at him with mouth ajar, her expression mirroring his own no doubt.

Twin waves of emotion struck him at once. Sophie was here! Sophie was . . . *here*? A trickle of foreboding snaked up his spine. Had she come to take him to task for his abrupt departure? He could not blame her but was astounded at her boldness.

His sister came down the stairs. She paused to glance at the statued Sophie, then looked down to see what had arrested her attention. "Wesley!" Kate's face split into a toothy smile, and she ran down the stairs and flung herself into his arms.

"Hello, poppet," he said, embracing her. "Don't break me."

"What a lovely surprise! Oh, and you must meet Sophie!"

She turned and gestured to the stairs with a wave of her hand.

As eyes turned toward her, Sophie began moving again, slowly descending the remaining stairs, looking nearly as pale as her frock.

"Sophie, come and meet my other brother."

"Hello, W . . . Mr. Overtree," she said

woodenly.

Wesley searched her face in confusion. "Sophie, what are you doing here?"

Mr. Keith elbowed him in the side. Wesley scowled at him, feeling befuddled, and then returned his raised-brow gaze to Sophie.

She hesitated. "I . . ."

His sister's gaze swiveled from one to the other. "Oh! That's right. You two know each other from Devonshire."

Sophie faltered, "Um, yes."

Kate turned to him. "Stephen went there to find you and instead found Sophie! What luck!"

Wesley could fashion no suitable reply. He only stood there like a fish tossed up on shore, gaping in disbelief.

"Oh!" Kate grasped Sophie's arm. "Tell Wesley how you and Stephen met and your whirlwind courtship. I love that story!"

"I'm sure he cannot wait to hear it," Keith said dryly, coming to his rescue. "But another time, perhaps, Miss Katherine. Your brother has just arrived and is no doubt exhausted."

Wesley's mind whirled. Sophie — his Sophie — fell in love with Marsh? Married him? Slept with him? The news struck him like a kick in the gut.

"But . . . I don't understand." Wesley winced in thought, trying to make sense of it. "When did all this happen?"

"It was all very sudden," Sophie replied,

fingers primly clasped. "We met the day you left for Italy."

Wesley fisted his hands. "I can't believe it. He lost no time, did he."

"Em, Wes, old man, let's have a drink, shall we? Catch up a bit, ay?"

His mother protested, "Really, Mr. Keith. My son has just arrived home after months away. I believe we have priority —"

"I know, Mrs. O," Keith persisted. "But just . . . trust me. I need a little time with him. I promise I will see him cleaned up and dressed and all yours in time for dinner."

"Dinner?" She frowned across the hall at the long-case clock. "Good heavens. It is time I went up and changed. Oh, very well, Mr. Keith, but I expect to have Wesley's undivided attention then. I cannot wait to hear about his latest work."

"I'll go up as well," his father added, with an uncertain look from Wesley to Keith.

His parents were barely up the stairs when Wesley wheeled on Sophie.

"What in the world were you thinking?"

Keith hooked his arm through one of Wesley's. "Come on." He pulled him toward the billiards room. "A stiff drink is what you need. Even if I can't join you."

"Mr. Keith?" Sophie spoke up. "Only give him one, if you please?" Worry pinched her face.

"Ah. Right you are, Mrs. Overtree. Best to

382

avoid loose lips. He might rant and storm in his cups."

In the billiards room, Wesley jerked his arm from Carlton Keith's grasp. "Thunder and turf, CK. I leave her for less than six weeks and this is what happens?"

The former officer went to the sideboard and unstopped the decanter.

"What were *you* doing at the time?" Wesley went on. "Having a great laugh at my expense? Or were you struck mute? You might have said something to Marsh. Warned him off."

Keith turned to him, not appearing at all sheepish or repentant as he would have guessed. "Why are you so angry? You left without word — left her to go off and find a new muse."

"I left to paint in Italy. And I didn't leave without a word. I left her a note."

"A note. How touching. Any promises in that note? Any declarations?"

"I am not likely to dash off such important sentiments in a note, am I?"

"Did you *ever* make her any promises? Promise to return for her? Or to marry her?"

A pinch of guilt cramped Wesley's gut. He had said plenty of warm words. He didn't like to think of all he'd said in the flush of passion. "Not . . . initially. But I did send a second letter from Plymouth. Apologizing.

Asking her to wait for me."

"That's an important message to leave to chance. Or the post." Keith handed him a small glass.

Wesley gulped it down, hoping the burn in his throat would ease the pain in his heart. Did Keith know he'd been intimate with Miss Dupont? The man couldn't know for sure, but they'd given him plenty of reason to suspect — the locked cottage door, his affectionate attention, her blushes. And all those paintings. . . . Wesley chose his words carefully. "Did Marsh know that she and I had spent a good deal of time together?"

"I believe I mentioned it. But he doesn't exactly ask me for permission before he acts, does he?"

Wesley pounded the table. "How dare he? I'll kill him."

"You'll have to get in line behind Boney's men for that. Doubt you'll have a chance."

Wesley ran a hand over his face. "What do I do now?"

"Nothing, my good fellow. Not one blessed thing. Like it or not, she is Miss Dupont no longer. She is Mrs. Overtree."

Wesley grimaced to hear her referred to by that name — especially when he was not the man who'd given it to her.

"If you care for her at all — even a little — don't say or do anything," Keith urged. "Why ruin her life? You cannot go back and change things, or undo the marriage. Why would you expose her in front of your family? They hardly approve of the captain's choice of bride as it is. If you were to cast doubt on her character, as well as her situation in life, that would be cruel. And avail nothing but heartache for her. You cannot be that selfish. At least I hope you are not."

Wesley stared at the man, taken aback. He'd been prepared to overcome his parents' objections to Sophie's family and station in life but was stunned to hear Keith defend her so earnestly.

"What's got into you, CK?" he asked. "You were my 'live and let live' good-time companion. Now you sound like a moralist. Or like Captain Black himself. You're taking his side."

Mr. Keith shrugged, but his eyes glinted. "I am not taking anyone's side. I'm on my own side — and that's whichever one is enjoying themselves more."

Wesley didn't believe his bravado. He studied him through narrowed eyes. "Did you know ahead of time? Did she say anything to you?"

"She never mentioned she was thinking of *marrying* the man, only wondered what I could tell her of his character. Like you, I was stunned to learn they were engaged to marry."

Wesley slumped into an armchair, shaking his head. He wondered if she had married his brother to spite him. More likely Marsh had done so, getting his revenge at last.

An hour later, anxiety needled Sophie's stomach as the seven of them took their seats in the dining room. Wesley's parents sat at head and foot as usual. The colonel at Mr. Overtree's right. Kate beside Wesley. His friend Mr. Keith beside her. There Sophie sat in the middle as Stephen Overtree's wife — with her lover directly across from her. How unreal. How unsettling. When she lifted her glass, her hands were not quite steady.

They began the first course of ox-tail soup. Sophie took three sips she barely tasted before she found the courage to look up from her bowl. Wesley was even more handsome than she remembered. The portrait in the corridor did not do him justice.

His golden brown eyes held hers over the table, even as his voice was intentionally casual. "And how long have you been in residence, *Mrs.* Overtree?"

She licked dry lips. "We arrived in March."

"You came here directly after your . . . marriage? No wedding trip?"

"We visited my family in Bath, of course, and then came here. Captain Overtree did not have much time before he needed to rejoin his regiment."

"Or so he thought," Kate interrupted, a sparkle in her eyes. "But Grandfather ar-

386

ranged for Stephen to have another fortnight of leave so they could spend more time together."

"Did he?" Wesley looked at his grandfather, irony in his voice. "How good of you, Colonel. But then you always had a soft spot for Stephen. The star in your eyes — and among your collection of medals."

Colonel Horton gave him a knowing look. "I care equally for all my grandchildren, Wesley. But yes, I take great satisfaction in the fact that one of them followed me into the army."

"Destroying one's fellow man is more estimable in your view than creating something of lasting beauty. I know. You needn't remind me."

The colonel frowned. "No honorable man likes the inevitable bloodshed. It's about serving and protecting one's country."

"We shall never agree, Grandfather. So perhaps we ought to let the matter drop."

"Hear, hear," echoed Mr. Overtree.

"Come, Lieutenant Keith," the colonel said. "You agree with me, surely?"

Keith shook his head. "Oh no. You'll not draw me into this debate, Colonel. How do you think I survived this long? It's knowing when to duck and when to retreat." He lifted his glass of water in salute.

Sophie noticed Wesley narrow his eyes at Keith's glass. He'd probably never seen the man drink water in his life.

Wesley directed his gaze and his next question to her. "And where were you married?"

Sophie felt her face heat, knowing the subject embarrassed her in-laws. "We hadn't time to post the banns. Or rather, we didn't think we did — not knowing the colonel would so kindly arrange additional leave. So we married on the Island of Guernsey, in a lovely church there. Mrs. Thrupton chaperoned our trip."

"Did she indeed?" Wesley murmured in surprise.

"How considerate of her to concern herself," Mr. Keith said, "I don't recall her being so fastidious before."

Sophie felt her mouth droop open and her eyes sting.

A *whack* sounded from beneath the table, and Mr. Keith's face contorted in pain.

"Devil take it!" He glared at Wesley. "You needn't have kicked me."

"Did I? Sorry. Just stretching my legs."

Mr. Keith recanted, "I only meant that Mrs. Thrupton was always so busy overseeing her neighbor's business as well as her own. I am surprised she could get away."

Sophie pretended interest in the next course of boiled tongue and croquettes of chicken, avoiding everyone's eyes. "It was very kind of her, yes."

Wesley sawed at his piece of tongue. "An

elopement, hmm? I am surprised monkish Marsh would countenance a scandal."

"Wesley," his mother admonished, "please have some consideration for your father's poor nerves."

"My nerves are perfectly well," Mr. Overtree spoke up. "But elopement isn't something we wish to dwell upon or share with our neighbors — for obvious reasons. Please endeavor to remember that in company, Wesley."

Wesley nodded, chewed a bite, and then set down his fork. "I know!" he exclaimed, beaming first at his parents, then settling his smile on Sophie. "Perhaps I ought to paint a bridal portrait of my new sister."

Sophie coughed into her goblet, then cleared her throat. "Thank you, but no. That isn't necessary."

"Sophie is right, Wesley," Mrs. Overtree agreed. "If Stephen had wanted such a portrait, he would have commissioned one."

"I doubt he had the time or even thought of it. Art is not exactly at the top of his priority list, is it?"

Mrs. Overtree looked from her son to Sophie and back again. "Well *if* we decide to pursue the idea, I am sure Mr. Benedict would be grateful for the commission and do a . . . commendable job."

"Benedict? He's a hack. I wouldn't let him paint my pony." Wesley spread his hands as though a great benefactor. "Come now, I insist. A wedding present. A portrait of Sophie in all her wedding finery." He glanced at her, one brow raised. "You *did* wear something fine?"

She lifted her chin. "Not especially, no. What with the limited time and the sea journey and all." She did not think Mrs. Thrupton's silk shawl and cap would qualify as "fine" in the Overtrees' minds.

"Ah. Well. Perhaps we might rectify that now."

"No." Mrs. Overtree adamantly shook her head. "Wesley, I don't think Sophie wishes to spend hours in the company of a man she barely knows. It wouldn't be . . . quite . . . right."

"Oh, come my dear," Mr. Overtree protested. "What would be improper about Wesley painting a portrait of his new sister? Why, he painted one of Kate, what, two years ago."

"This is quite different."

Did Mrs. Overtree suspect? Sophie wondered. Or did she simply want to discourage talk among the servants?

"Yes, but I detest that painting," Kate pouted. "He gave me such a big nose."

Wesley leaned toward his sister, a teasing light in his eye. "I didn't give it to you, Kate. God did. Or perhaps Papa."

Kate swatted his arm. "Then paint another of me, Wesley. More flattering. In fact," she added with a mischievous air, "make me heart-stoppingly beautiful. We shall have prints made and send them to all the eligible bachelors in the land, and then I shall have my pick of handsome husbands."

Sophie knew the girl was only joking, but Wesley shook his head.

"That is beyond my ability."

Kate blinked, her smile falling.

Mrs. Overtree admonished, "Wesley!"

"What?" He looked in confusion from face to face. Comprehension dawned. "I simply meant I only paint realism — ask Sophie." He looked around the table. "Oh, come now — you know I think Katie the most charming creature on earth. The most likeable poppet I've ever had the privilege of tickling to tears, or hiding a jar of noisy crickets beneath her bed."

"I knew that was you!" Kate exclaimed. "You tried to blame Stephen, but I always knew."

"I am certain your brother didn't mean that as it sounded, Kate," Sophie said, her heart going out to the girl. "Artists can be overly critical of any slight imperfection, which we all have, of course."

Mrs. Overtree frowned. "I am sure Wesley meant no such criticism of his own sister, Sophie. You just don't know him well enough to understand his teasing."

"I meant no censure, Mrs. Overtree."

Wesley smiled fondly at his sister. "I realize Katie was only jesting, but she wouldn't want me to paint an idealized or alluring portrait of her. She might gain the wrong sort of attention from the wrong sort of man."

"Yes, she might . . ." Mr. Keith murmured, slanting a look at Sophie.

Sophie's cheeks burned.

"Why do we not change the subject?" Mr. Overtree suggested. "I for one feel indigestion coming on, and we haven't even had our pudding yet."

"Oh, my dear!" Mrs. Overtree exclaimed. "Is it your heart?"

"No, my love. It is not my heart. It is my stomach. Too much sour talk and rich food."

Mrs. Overtree asked Wesley about his travels, and for several minutes the topic moved to more neutral ground. But then Mrs. Overtree asked to see his latest paintings from his winter in Lynmouth — the ones still crated up in his room.

What would his parents think to see their new daughter-in-law in such poses? Sophie wondered. The notion filled her with dread.

Wesley opened his mouth to reply, then with a swift glance at her, closed it again.

He said, "Perhaps later, Mamma. Now, acquaint me with all the parish news . . ."

Sophie released a tense breath. She prayed Wesley would leave the lid on that crate nailed shut. And the lid on their past too.

After dinner, Sophie excused herself to retire early. Mr. Keith rose and stepped to the door to open it for her, taking the opportunity to whisper an apology for his earlier rude comments.

Wesley watched them with a frown, brows raised in question, but she turned without acknowledging him. She feared he might follow her, but Mr. Keith, she noticed, clamped a hand on his arm.

Sophie had difficulty falling asleep that night, rolling one way, then the other. Sweet, lovely memories returned to torment her. Wesley's affection. His praise of her talent and beauty. Then sour memories — his leaving, that dismissive note — wrestled with the sweet, until she felt quite nauseated.

She heard a floorboard creak and stilled. Then she heard slow, surreptitious footsteps somewhere nearby. Was it Wesley coming to her door? Would he dare enter her room? Surely not. Perhaps she should have locked it, and let the servants wonder what they may. Or perhaps she should rise and open it. . . .

With a groan, she pulled the blankets over her head and willed sleep to come. And temptation to stay away.

CHAPTER 22

Sophie did her best to avoid Wesley the next day, having her breakfast sent up on a tray and retreating to the privacy of her attic studio. The portrait she had begun of Captain Overtree was still covered in cloth, but she thought she might begin working on it again. Doing so would remind herself of the man she was married to, and keep his image always before her. She retrieved the canvas from where it waited, silent and shrouded against the wall, and carried it back to the easel in the center of the room, where the sunlight could shine on it once again.

The door opened behind her, and Sophie spun toward it.

Wesley stood in the threshold of her studio — her sanctuary, Stephen's gift to her.

Pulse tripping, she asked, "What are you doing up here?"

He stepped inside and began to close the door behind him.

"Leave it open."

He hesitated. "Do you think that wise?"

"I think it a wise precaution, yes."

He met her gaze. "Are you sure you want the servants to hear what I might say to you?"

She swallowed and bit her lip, making no further protest.

He slowly closed the door with a click.

He began, "Katie mentioned your little studio up here. You cannot hide from me forever, you know. We need to talk."

"Nothing you say will change anything," she cautioned. "But I will listen if you want to talk."

"I disagree," he said, then his voice gentled. "I'm hurt, Sophie. I can't believe you turned around and married someone else right after I left. After us. Did I mean nothing to you?"

He'd meant everything to her. But now irritation flared. "Don't lash out at me. You are the one who left without saying good-bye. If you were so interested in talking to me, you might have done so then. But instead you left only that cool, dismissive note." Her voice rose. *"Thank you for a beautiful season. I shall always remember you fondly . . . ?"*

He winced. "That was wrong of me. I did send a letter of apology as soon as I reached Plymouth. Asking you to wait for me. Did you receive it?"

"Only recently. Mrs. Thrupton forwarded it here. Maurice had mislaid it — perhaps intentionally."

Wesley ran an agitated hand through his hair. "Dash it."

"It wouldn't have mattered," she said. "By the time it reached the studio, I was already bound for the coast with your brother."

"Why? Is this my punishment? For traveling to Italy to further my career?"

"No."

"I should have spoken with you, I know. Explained myself. I tried to find you, but when I asked O'Dell where you were, he said you had gone to Barnstaple for the day."

"Barnstaple? I went nowhere except the cottage and Castle Rock."

He huffed in disgust. "I should have guessed he lied."

Her throat tight, she managed a raspy, "You couldn't wait for me? Or look for me?"

"The captain refused to wait. The ship was leaving with the tide. I had little time to decide, so I took my chance while I could." He stepped nearer and lowered his voice. "But you have read my letter now? You know how I feel?"

Sophie nodded, tears burning her eyes. The words she'd longed for — too late!

"I was wrong to leave. I regretted it immediately and knew I had to come back to you. And here I am. Only to find you married."

He shook his head in disbelief. "Of all the men in the world, why would you marry an ogre like Marsh? I can't bear the thought of him touching you."

She did not correct him — did not admit they had not consummated their marriage. It made no difference, legally or otherwise. Instead she lifted her chin and challenged, "Why do you insist he is loathsome? He is not."

Without intending to, she glanced at the shrouded portrait on the easel. He followed the direction of her gaze. With a furrowed brow, he stepped forward and yanked off the cover in one jerk.

"Don't!" She felt as exposed as if a stranger had ripped the clothes from her body. "How dare you come in here and —"

"How dare I?" He gaped at the partially completed portrait, then at her, frowning darkly. "You are painting *him*?"

"Yes," she said defensively. "Kate asked me to teach her. And we both thought a new portrait of Captain Overtree, before he left for war, would be a good idea."

"If Katie wants to learn to paint, why did she not ask me?"

"Apparently she has, but you have yet to find the time."

He made no reply, scowling at the painting.

She went on nervously, "You are welcome to teach her. I don't pretend to match your skill." She grew increasingly uncomfortable as he stared at her work in progress.

She lifted her chin. "How would you feel if I barged into your studio and uncovered one of your paintings in its early, vulnerable stages?"

"I invited you into my cottage studio in Lynmouth. Into my life. And this" — he gestured toward the painting — "is my reward."

She shook her head. "It's not for you or about you."

"How you've idealized him. You've made him better looking than he actually is. It isn't realistic."

She told herself his criticism had more to do with the shock of discovering her marriage than about her actual skill, but the harsh words still hurt.

He glowered at it. "Your perspective is off. The hands look flat, wooden, lifeless. The colors lack value."

"Have you finished?"

He turned to her. "No. I haven't even begun." Stepping close, he grasped her arms.

"Let go of me."

"Not until you tell me why. Why could you not have waited? Why did you have to marry him? Why, Sophie? Why?"

Looking at the portrait, she echoed Wesley's own words back at him, "His ship was leaving. I had little time to decide, so I took my chance while I could."

A double knock sounded at the door, and

Wesley's grip loosened. Sophie quickly pulled away, putting several feet of space between them.

Carlton Keith opened the door and stuck his head in. "Hello? Anybody home?"

"Oh, Mr. Keith. You are just in time. Come in."

Wesley glared at him. "Go away, CK."

"Nonsense," Sophie said, "You are just in time to settle an argument." When he hesitated, she added, "Please, Mr. Keith. I insist."

"Very well." He stepped into the room, looking from one to the other. "Can't deny the request of a lady, can I, Wes?"

"Only if you don't value your teeth."

"I do, yes. But surely you wouldn't hit a one-armed man."

"I am giving it serious consideration."

For a moment, Wesley's stern demeanor reminded her of Stephen, and it unsettled her further. Perhaps the brothers were more alike than she'd realized.

She said, "Mr. Overtree criticizes this portrait of Captain Overtree. I would appreciate your honest opinion." She didn't really care what Mr. Keith thought — she simply wanted to keep him there between them.

Keith nodded. "That's Marsh, all right. Well done, Mrs. Overtree."

Wesley scowled again. "Oh, come on. Marsh never looked so good in his life. This is a romanticized ideal of the honorable captain. His chin isn't half so determined. And his scar twice so."

Mr. Keith asked her gently, "Is this how you see him, Mrs. Overtree?"

She looked at the portrait. "Yes. I don't claim my work is flawless, but I believe I have captured his appearance."

"Balderdash," Wesley protested. "It's too flattering by half."

Keith looked at him. "I seem to recall you, Wesley, painting a certain dowager countess with gratuitously flattering lines."

"Yes, I admit I took certain liberties to make sure the lady was pleased with her portrait — she paid a hefty commission for the privilege. But this . . . ?"

"I like it," Mr. Keith said.

"And I would like you to leave."

"Actually, I promised Mrs. Overtree I would play for her this afternoon, did I not?" Mr. Keith said, raising his brows at her.

Had he? "Oh . . . yes. I nearly forgot."

"Play?" Wesley asked. "Play what?"

"You are looking at Gloucestershire's renowned one-armed *pianiste,*" Keith said with self-deprecating humor. "Care to hear me play — no charge?"

Wesley crossed his arms. "Later."

"Oh, but the light is just right now for reading sheet music. I do so hate trying to squint by candlelight to read those reeling notes."

He offered Sophie his arm. "Mrs. Over-tree."

"Thank you, Mr. Keith." She squeezed his arm. "And I mean that sincerely."

During dinner that night, Wesley could not keep his gaze from sliding across the table to Sophie, admiring her like a favorite painting. She was even more beautiful than he recalled. Her cheeks were rounder and pink with the blush of health. Her figure more womanly than he remembered. Had the flush of happiness, of wedded bliss, put those roses in her cheeks? Wesley doubted marriage to his stern, dour brother could have done so. Whatever the case, the more he looked at her, the more he regretted letting her go.

As they enjoyed Mrs. John's sponge cake and orange jelly, Kate said, "I came looking for you today, Wesley, but I could not find you. Where did you go?"

Sophie flashed him a concerned look, clearly worried he would tell them.

"Careful . . ." Keith warned under his breath.

Beneath the table, Wesley shifted his leg away from Keith's chair, just in case Keith was tempted to kick him in return.

"Well, Kate. You happened to mention Sophie's little studio in the attic, so I thought I would pay a call. See what all the fuss is about."

"Studio?" the colonel asked. "In the attic? What are you on about?"

"Oh yes, it's quite true," Kate said, all smiles. "Stephen secretly set up and supplied an art studio for Sophie in the old school-room, knowing how much she likes to paint. Such a romantic gesture."

Marsh — romantic? Wesley lost his appetite.

"I don't understand," his mother said, a little frown line between her brows. "Why all the way up there? Sophie, you might have done your little watercolors or what have you in the morning room or the garden like most young ladies."

Sophie hesitated. "I . . ."

"She is modest, Mamma," Kate defended, "and prefers to paint in private."

"Then why did Wesley think it necessary to intrude?"

He felt his mother's pointed look on his profile, but ignored it. He said easily, "Simply to see it, and to judge whether or not it might be a good setting in which to paint Sophie's bridal portrait."

"That again. You have always painted in the room adjacent to your own."

"Yes, but there is surprisingly good light up there. Wish I had thought of it sooner."

With a glance at Keith, Sophie said evenly, "I have been thinking. If you insist on paint-ing my portrait, Wesley, perhaps Kate might like to sit with us while you do so. She has expressed interest in learning to paint and might find the experience valuable."

"Oh yes. That's an excellent notion," Kate agreed.

Sophie added with a sheepish little laugh, "I might even try to paint her while you paint me."

"What?" his mother asked, brows high.

"Mamma, Sophie is an accomplished painter," Kate said. "You should see her portrait of Stephen — though it isn't finished yet."

"I don't pretend that my skills are on par with your son's," Sophie said quickly. "Nor would I expect my efforts to ever hang on any wall. I just thought it might prove a pleasant diversion to break up the long monotony of sitting."

"A portrait of someone painting a portrait?" Wesley asked with a smile. "What a novel idea." Was she remembering when they had done the same at Castle Rock?

She nodded. "I saw an artist attempt it once."

"Oh?" he asked. "And how did it turn out?"

She met his gaze. "Not well."

"It might be an interesting exercise," Mr. Overtree allowed.

"Sounds amusing," Kate agreed.

"Sounds dangerous," Keith added, although thankfully too low for everyone else to hear.

"Well," his mother said, a wry glint in her

403

eye. "I don't want either of you to be disappointed, but I shan't go removing Katherine's current portrait from the wall just yet."

No doubt relieved to shift the attention from herself, Sophie asked, "What will you wear, Kate?"

"Oh! Good question. What do you think, Mamma?"

"Whatever you like, my dear. Though I have always liked you in blue." His mother turned to him. "In the meantime, when may we see your Lynmouth paintings?"

Wesley hesitated, then put her off once more, knowing his parents would not be pleased to see their new daughter-in-law in such poses. He knew he couldn't evade them forever. But seeing the look of fear cross Sophie's lovely face, he decided he would leave that crate nailed shut for now.

The three of them — Kate, Sophie, and Wesley — set a time to meet in the attic studio the following day. Sophie had worked the night before, preparing her canvas and doing some preliminary sketches. Sophie wore a simple muslin day dress for the sitting, but instead of her usual workaday apron, she wore a pretty lace apron instead. It wasn't as fine as Mrs. Thrupton's shawl, but she would not risk getting paint on that. Then she smoothed her hair, telling herself not to worry about her appearance for Wesley's sake.

At the appointed hour, she left her bedchamber and headed for the stairs. There, she drew up short. Wesley leaned against the newel post, strikingly handsome in green frock coat and buff trousers. Seeing him waiting for her, her palms grew instantly damp.

Kate's door opened, and she popped her head out, "I'm not ready yet. Libby is curling my hair. I want to look a picture!"

Sophie hesitated, nervous to be alone with Wesley any longer than necessary. "All right. But don't be too long."

"Take your time," Wesley drawled. "We'll get started without you."

Kate wrinkled her face. "How will you do that?"

"Oh, I have a few ideas . . ."

Sophie said officiously, "By mixing paints and preparing our palettes, of course."

"Ah. Right. Be up soon."

As Sophie and Wesley ascended the stairs, she said, "I have already primed my canvas. Have you?"

"No. Thankfully I had one in my studio. I suppose it's second nature for you. You primed your father's canvases and painted his backgrounds for years. I am surprised he is managing without you."

"Oh, I am sure he does well enough. After all, he has Maurice to help him."

"That ambitious young man will steal half of your father's commissions by year's end if

I don't miss my guess."

"I hope you are wrong."

They entered the studio and began preparing, Sophie opening the shutters and moving aside the portrait of the captain to make room for the freshly primed canvas.

She noticed Wesley's resentful gaze resting on his brother's image. "Marsh has finally had his revenge." He shook his head, eyes glimmering in memory.

"What do you mean?"

"There was another woman of our mutual acquaintance. She and Marsh had known one another for years, but there was no specific understanding between them, nor any promises between our families. Stephen may have expected her to marry him eventually. Assumed it a *fait accomplit,* I don't know. But somewhere along the way, this young woman began to prefer me. I could not help it if she developed feelings for me. I did not steal her away, whatever Marsh might think. A woman is not like a fine watch in a shop that might be put in one's pocket and carried away."

Was this the "Jenny" Captain Overtree preferred not to talk about, Sophie wondered, or someone else?

Wesley positioned his own easel, avoiding her eyes. "Whatever the case, apparently he's never forgiven me, but bided his time. I suppose he convinced you I wouldn't return? Cast doubt on my character?" He shook his head, a bitter twist to his lips. "Now his revenge is complete."

Had Captain Overtree married her out of revenge? Sophie didn't think so. She surely hoped he had not. She thought again of the captain's proposal of marriage. He had said he didn't think Wesley would return for her. He also told her he had reason to suspect he might die while away on duty and leave her a widow. Might he have fabricated both for his own ends, so she wouldn't question his motives for marrying her in the first place? So she would accept him? She hated to even contemplate the possibility.

Kate came in, curled and powdered and pretty in a frosty blue gown, white ribbon waist and gloves, with delicate blue and white silk flowers in her hair. She beamed in anticipation of their reaction, and Sophie was quick to oblige her. "You are beautiful, Kate."

Wesley stared at her, wide-eyed. "When did my little sister become a young woman?" he breathed.

"While you were off traveling somewhere, no doubt," Kate said. "Or had your nose stuck in a canvas."

Was Sophie imagining it, or did his eyes mist over? He certainly looked remorseful.

He smiled fondly at Kate and tweaked her chin. "Sophie is perfectly right, Kate. You are beautiful. If I don't miss my guess, you shall soon have your pick of gentlemen, flattering portrait or not."

The following week, Sophie received a brief letter from Captain Overtree, posted from Dublin, where his regiment had been garrisoned.

> *Dear Sophie,*
> *Only have a moment to write. Everyone rushing to prepare for departure. We embark soon for Belgium to join Wellington. Know that the warmth of our parting remains near, and gives me great encouragement. My thoughts and prayers are with you always.*
>
> *Yours,*
> *Stephen*

Her heart welled with a sweet pain, followed by guilt for her lingering memories of Wesley. Letters like these would certainly help in that regard.

She wrote back to the captain but refrained from mentioning his brother. She didn't want to worry him.

Over the next few weeks, life continued without incident at Overtree Hall. Every afternoon, the colonel and Mr. Overtree read the newspapers and reported on recent developments. First, those in authority debated over whether or not to reenter the war. Then came reports of Wellington's struggles to amass sufficient troops. The colonel exchanged letters and visited friends with connections to both Wellington and parliament and shared news as he could with the family.

With all the correspondence arriving, Sophie hoped for another letter from Captain Overtree, but nothing else came for her. She reminded herself that Stephen might not have even reached Belgium yet. And once there, he would probably be too busy to write letters.

But she continued to check the post anyway, just in case. And to tread carefully in Wesley's presence in the meantime.

Early one morning, Wesley suggested Carlton Keith join him for a ride. The man struggled to mount without his left hand and was mortified to require the groom's help, but once in the saddle he managed to ride fairly well. After a few miles, they paused at a stream to allow their horses to drink.

As they waited, Wesley looked over at Keith. "It's strange how the tables have turned. In the past, Marsh sent you along to protect me. But now you're trying to protect Sophie *from* me."

Keith said, "Look, I have sympathy for your cause, Wes. But I promised the captain . . ."

"Once the underling, always the underling, ay, Lieutenant?" Wesley muttered.

Keith gave him a humorless smile in reply,

but Wesley knew the man well enough to see his comment had stung and regretted it. "Sorry, old man," he said. "Don't mean to take out my anger on you."

"I understand. I know what it's like to pine for a woman who's out of reach."

Wesley wondered whom he referred to but didn't pursue the topic.

They remounted and began trotting toward home. "If you don't mind, I'll ride ahead," Wesley said. "Meet you back at the stables, all right?"

Keith nodded.

Wesley spurred his horse to a gallop on the straightaway, needing to vent his frustration and put some distance between himself and Keith before he said anything else he would regret.

Afterward, as the two men walked from the stables toward the house, they came upon Miss Blake and Kate playing battledore and shuttlecock in the garden. Sophie, he noticed, sat nearby on a garden bench, a large-brimmed bonnet shielding her face.

It was the first he'd seen of their neighbor since arriving home. He inwardly groaned. And in Sophie's company yet. He hoped Angela would behave herself and play fair.

Kate glanced up. "There's Wesley. He'll play."

Miss Blake turned her ginger head in his direction, her green eyes watchful and wary as he approached. They had known one another so long, he could read every expression on her long, freckled face, every quirk of her mouth with its heavily bowed upper lip. It saddened him that they'd lost their former camaraderie and knew he was partly to blame. But there was nothing he could do about it now.

"Ah . . . the prodigal son returns," she said with a little smirk. "Hello, Wesley."

"Angela." He acknowledged her with a dip of his head, determined to be polite.

Kate bent to pick up two spare racquets and thrust one toward him. "Do say you'll play, Wesley."

"How about a game of doubles?" Miss Blake suggested.

Kate regarded Mr. Keith and bit her lip. "That is . . . if you think you can — might want to play?"

Keith grinned. "Thank you, Miss Katherine. I believe I am equal to the task." He accepted the second racquet and looked at Miss Blake. "Shall we join forces, Miss Blake? Though I suppose you'd rather have Wesley as your partner . . ."

"Not at all, Mr. Keith. I have seen Wesley play."

Wesley gave her a sour smile. "Be forewarned, Keith. Angela's a crack shot and will knock you down to reach the shuttlecock before you."

"I'll take my chances."

Wesley wondered how the man would serve with one hand, but he needn't have worried. Keith gripped the handle with three fingers, and pinched the shuttlecock feathers between index finger and thumb. He released the shuttlecock with a little loft, repositioned his hand fully around the racquet and whacked the shuttlecock in a high arc to Kate.

"Well done, Mr. Keith," Miss Blake praised.

Kate swung hard, sending the shuttlecock high. Too high. The wind caught it and carried it behind her. "Sorry!"

While Kate hurried off to retrieve it, Wesley asked Miss Blake, "How's the family?"

"Oh, Father is his usual absent self. And if you have not heard, Horace is engaged to be married."

"Horsey . . . engaged? He can't be, what, eighteen or nineteen . . . ?

"One and twenty."

"Good night. I feel quite ancient."

Kate returned and prepared to serve. Miss Blake adopted a ready stance, bouncing lightly from foot to foot. She looked just as she had when she was twelve years old.

He asked her, "Who's the lucky girl? Would I know her?"

"Probably, knowing you." She returned Kate's serve with a hard smack that bulleted the shuttlecock right at Wesley's face.

Wesley leapt back to get his racquet under

it, but the feathers fell to the ground.

Kate said, "I don't think Wesley ever met the Fullerton family. Horace met them when they were here on Boxing Day, but Wesley had already left for Devonshire."

"Yes, it seems Wesley is always leaving."

"Not always." He served again, hoping Sophie wasn't listening to their exchange.

The shuttlecock flew, and Keith ran forward and tapped it lightly to Kate. She hit it back, hard, and Keith had to quickly run backward. Wesley thought he might miss it, but the man had an impressive wingspan — even if only one wing. He reached back, back, and whacked it high overhead.

"Excellent arm, Mr. Keith," said Angela approvingly.

"Why, thank you, fair lady."

Miss Blake addressed Wesley across from her once again. "And how long are we to have the pleasure of your company this time?"

"I have not yet decided." He tapped the shuttlecock, then glanced at Sophie. When he returned his gaze to Angela, he was chagrined to realize she had noticed the look.

Angela stepped backward, raised her racquet, and . . . missed. She never missed.

"Sorry." She gave her partner an embarrassed half smile.

"No problem," Mr. Keith assured her.

Angela picked up the fallen shuttlecock and served to Wesley again. "And were you as surprised as the rest of us to meet Stephen's wife?"

"More so, I imagine."

Kate spoke up. "And here I thought both my brothers were confirmed old bachelors."

"Speaking of which, any word from Stephen?" Angela turned toward spectator-Sophie as she said it.

"Not lately," Sophie replied.

Angela added kindly, "We all pray for a quick end to this renewed threat, and his safe return."

Sophie nodded. "Thank you."

Miss Blake sent Wesley a sidelong glance. "We do *all* pray for Stephen's safe return, do we not?"

"Hmm?" Wesley murmured, taken aback. He noticed Keith and Sophie both watching them, and said, "Oh, yes, of course."

Unfortunately, Angela could read him as accurately as he could read her. He hoped her good breeding would guard her tongue.

CHAPTER 23

They rested on Sunday, but the following week Sophie and Wesley returned to the studio to work on the portraits — his of her and hers of Kate.

Sophie had already captured the general outline of the girl's pose, hair, hands, and dress, and now worked to add detail to her features. Soon Kate grew tired of sitting still, and Sophie released her to go for a walk with Miss Blake into the village. Sophie could continue on for a time without her model.

Wesley continued as well, now and again asking her to stop painting so he could focus on some detail of her face or hair.

"Lovelier than ever, mia Sophia."

"Stop calling me that. I am not yours."

"Maybe not now. But don't you remember what we had between us?"

"No, I don't."

"Don't, or won't?"

She refused to answer. The truth was, she was trying hard *not* to remember what had passed between them, how she had felt about him, and sometimes still did. After all, she had only been married to Stephen for two months, but she had been in love with Wesley for more than a year.

He set aside his palette and rose, stepping behind her stool and leaning down to whisper in her ear. "You can deny it all you like, but we both know there was a time you were mine — heart, soul, mind, and body. . . ."

She lurched to her feet to put distance between them, pretending the need to adjust the light coming into the room. She stepped to the window and stretched up to reach the top shutter, her gown flattening, straining against her body as she did so.

She glanced over at him and realized he was staring at her — not at her face but at her midsection.

He frowned, strode over to her, and before she could protest or flee, clasped her around the waist, his exploring hands far more measuring than romantic.

She squirmed in his hold. "What are you doing? Release me."

"Thunder and turf, Sophie. Are you with child?"

Her mouth parted. "What? I . . ."

"You are. I can tell. I knew something was different about you, but I didn't think . . . Not so soon."

"Please lower your voice, Mr. Overtree. I
—"

"Are you going to deny this too? Don't
bother. Don't forget, I once knew your body
as well as my own. Every curve. Every dip.
Every inch."

Her neck heated. "Hush."

His jaw slackened. "That's why you married Marsh! What an imbecile I am. I knew
there must be some other reason. I cannot
believe I didn't guess immediately."

Sophie raised a hand. "Stop it. Stop it right
now. *If* I were with child. And if I *have* a
child, he or she will be the captain's —
Stephen's."

He shook his head, eyes alight. "No. It's
mine, isn't it?"

She held her tongue, refusing to confirm or
deny his guess.

He gripped her shoulders. "Did you know
before I left Lynmouth? Why didn't you tell
me?"

Sophie struggled inwardly. Might it not be
better for everyone — the child, and Stephen,
and the family — if she admitted nothing but
kept up the pretense? The words she held
back escaped as silent tears running down
her cheeks.

Wesley's beautiful eyes filled with tears as
well. "You are carrying my child, and you
married my brother? How could you? Why
didn't you wait?"

The dam broke. "Because you left me with no other choice!" She jerked away from him and fled, hurrying from the room.

Sophie retreated to her bedchamber, shaking and breathless. Now she had done it. What would Wesley do? Would he tell everyone? Heaven help them all.

She didn't go down to dinner that night, sending Libby to let Mrs. Overtree know she didn't feel well and wouldn't be joining them. It was certainly true. Libby brought soup and tea on a tray to her room, and afterward Sophie went to bed early.

She was about to drift to sleep when a soft knock nudged her alert.

"Sophie? It's me."

Wesley's voice. Afraid he would enter if she did not respond, Sophie snatched up her dressing gown and hurried to the door, opening it only a few inches.

"What are you doing?" she whispered. "Go away."

"I might have stayed away. Or at least tried. But now that I know you are carrying my child . . ."

"I never said that!" she hissed. "It's Stephen's. *I* am Stephen's. Now go away before a servant or your parents find you at my door. Would you ruin my life all over again?"

Looking stricken, he turned away, and she regretted her sharp words. She closed the latch and rested her back against the door.

418

Overwhelmed with worry and regret, she slid down to the floor, leaned her head back against the wood, and let the tears come.

Finding out Sophie carried his child clarified the situation in Wesley's mind. He had been angry and disappointed with her, but now he understood why she had married so abruptly. He shook his head in wonder. He and Sophie had created a child — the ultimate masterpiece. The realization filled him with love and awe. Suddenly the prospect of losing Sophie and their child frightened him. But what other choice did he have?

Several days passed with he and Sophie tiptoeing around one another — she avoiding him, or greeting him with cool civility whenever their paths inevitably crossed. Him being as kind to her as she would allow.

Kate returned to pose again, and then remained to watch and learn from Wesley as he painted Sophie.

"Why do you add the red first?" Kate asked. "That is not the color I would have chosen . . . Do you think umber might be better . . . ?"

"Kate, please be quiet for two minutes together," Wesley replied. "I have answered your last thirty-seven questions with the utmost patience, you must allow. But I cannot concentrate with all your chattering."

"Very well." Kate shrugged and sat back

down on the stool near his — but not too near — to watch him work.

Silence reigned for several minutes. Blissful silence, broken only by the occasional coo of a mourning dove in the eaves beyond the window. The melancholy sound apparently matched Sophie's mood. He had rarely seen her expression so forlorn.

He said, "Now I am going to paint your eyes, so if I could ask you to look at me, Sophie. . . ."

She blinked, clearly struggling to hold his gaze.

"The eyes, the eyes," he murmured. "Oh, the tales they tell."

"Hers tell a sad tale indeed," chirped a voice at his elbow.

Wesley jerked around. Sophie started as well.

Nurse Whitney had silently entered the room behind him and now stood there, peering over his shoulder. Irritation flashed through him. It was the first time he'd laid eyes on her in several months, which suited him perfectly. He'd never liked the meddlesome woman.

"Dash it, Winnie. Don't skulk about and sneak up on people."

"Me, the one to skulk and sneak? That's the pot calling the kettle black. You wouldn't be so skittish, if you didn't have something to hide. But then, you do, don't you?"

"Rubbish." He jabbed his brush into the paint. "Save your mummery for someone who believes it."

"Wesley . . ." Kate admonished. Then she turned and said sweetly, "Winnie, we were just going to ring for tea, if you'd like to stay and join us."

Wesley pushed back his stool with a whining protest and rose abruptly. "If you ladies will excuse me, that's my cue to go and find something stronger." He stalked from the room.

Miss Whitney had always brought out the worst in him, Wesley realized. He knew she'd do anything to protect her darling Master Stephen — and now apparently his new wife as well.

Sophie watched Wesley go, wondering at his overreaction to his former nurse, then turned back to the other two ladies.

Winnie said, "Thank you, Miss Katherine. But I shan't stay long. I only wanted to see how Mrs. Overtree fares today."

"I am well, Winnie. Thank you," Sophie replied.

"And why shouldn't she be well?" Kate asked with a little frown of concern. "Sophie, have you a cold or something you've not mentioned?"

"No."

"Never said she had a cold, Miss Katherine," Winnie corrected. "But she has a child on the way, and had better take care of herself."

"A child?" Kate swiveled to look at Sophie, mouth ajar. "Have you? Has Winnie divined a secret?"

For a moment, Sophie sat there as stunned as Kate. But then she thought of the child-rearing book she'd received more than a month ago. Apparently, Winnie *had* learned her secret one way or another. She felt herself grow warm and self-conscious under their dual gazes. "Um . . . yes. I am expecting. But how did you — ?"

"Oh, Sophie, that's wonderful!" Kate beamed, throwing her arms around her where she sat. "Does Stephen know?"

"Yes, the father knows," Winnie answered for her. "Only recently found out."

Sophie looked up at the elderly woman, startled anew. What did she mean? Did she suspect Wesley was the father?

"Do Mamma and Papa know?" Kate asked.

"I don't believe so," Sophie said. *Not unless Wesley told them,* she added to herself.

"Another little Overtree on the way!" Winnie rubbed her hands together. "How marvelous."

Kate smiled. "I am so happy for you. When is it to be?"

Sophie hesitated. "I am not certain . . . exactly. Late this autumn, I imagine."

"Excellent! Then I shall not be the youngest Overtree for long! What a welcome-home gift for Stephen that will be."

Sophie managed a smile, hoping Stephen's parents were as accepting as his sister was.

"When will you announce the news?" Kate asked.

"Well, it isn't something one generally blurts out in mixed company."

"May we tell Mamma at least? She will be so happy."

"Will she?" Sophie asked softly, stomach twisting. Something told her Mrs. Overtree would ask far more questions than innocent young Kate.

That evening after dinner, the men remained behind over port, and the women withdrew to the white parlour to wait for them as usual. Mrs. Overtree seemed little given to conversation that night, worried as she was about Stephen. News had reached them that Wellington was preparing for battle in Belgium. Sophie didn't blame the woman. She was worried too.

To distract herself, Sophie asked Kate to play a game of draughts while they waited, but for once Kate, who adored the game, demurred. Silence fell on the parlour, punctuated by the spring rain specking against the windows.

Finally Kate burst out, "Oh, do tell her,

423

Sophie. Before the men come in and mix our company."

Mrs. Overtree looked up. "Mix our . . . ? What are you talking about, Katherine? Tell me what?"

Kate looked at her for approval, and Sophie gave a little nod.

Kate turned to her mother, all suppressed glee and dimples ready to burst. "Mamma, Sophie is going to have a baby! Isn't that wonderful news?"

Mrs. Overtree directed a raised-brow gaze toward Sophie. "Is she indeed?"

Again, Sophie nodded.

"Well then. We must ask Dr. Matthews to call."

"Sophie expects the child in late autumn," Kate added.

Mrs. Overtree's brows rose even higher. "So soon?"

Sophie felt her cheeks heat but told herself to remain calm. Squirming and blushing and looking ashamed would only make things worse. She reminded herself that she was a married woman after all.

She forced herself to hold her mother-in-law's gaze, but her disobedient cheeks heated all the more. She could think of nothing to say beyond, "We've known or at least suspected for some time."

"Stephen knows?" she asked.

"Yes."

"I am surprised he did not tell us. You should be seen by a doctor as soon as may be."

"Doctor? Who needs a doctor?" Mr. Overtree asked as he stepped into the room, the colonel and Wesley following behind.

"My dear, Sophie is expecting a child," Mrs. Overtree said. "I am sorry to raise the feminine subject, but as you've overheard . . ."

He waved a dismissive hand. "Never mind your proprieties, my dear. I'm to be a grandfather! That's excellent news. Though I must say I feel altogether too young to be married to a grandmother." He winked at Sophie.

"And what about me? I shall be a great-grandfather." The colonel turned to Wesley. "Is that not good news, my boy?"

"I am all astonishment," Wesley said flatly.

"You're to be an uncle. What do you think of that?"

"I think it . . . extremely ironic."

"What — that Stephen beat you to it? Your fault for dragging your feet and avoiding all attempts to lure you into matrimony." The colonel smiled at Sophie. "When's the great day to be?"

The estimate was repeated.

"Good heavens! Someone wasted no time!"

A moment of awkward silence passed in which Sophie imagined each of them was counting the months backward. She twisted her hands and looked at Wesley. He gazed back at her, brown eyes wide and beseeching.

"There, there, my dear." The colonel patted her hand. "No need to be embarrassed. Not the first to put the cart before the horse. That's the passionate family nature for you. Can't blame the boy."

Cheeks burning, she stole another glance at Wesley. He was looking heavenward as if for self-control, hands fisted at his sides.

Mrs. Overtree's gaze flickered from him to Sophie, taking in his fists and her red face. Her eyes narrowed. Did she suspect Stephen was not the "boy" to blame?

Sophie forced a smile. Oh, how she wished Stephen was at her side.

The family physician was sent for and arrived the following afternoon. Mrs. Overtree offered to stay with her since she was unfamiliar with the man, but Sophie assured her mother-in-law she would be all right on her own.

The kind, elderly doctor examined her in her bedchamber. He confirmed Sophie's condition, her good health, and an approximate due date even earlier than Sophie had expected.

Flushing from the examination itself and unable to meet the man's eyes, Sophie said quietly, "I've told the family late autumn. Captain Overtree and I were only married in March."

"Ah," Dr. Matthews said with a nod of understanding. "Well, don't worry. These predictions of mine are not exact science. Late autumn it is. Children often come ahead of schedule." He smiled. "Especially a child born in the first year of a marriage."

A few days later, Miss Blake joined them for an early dinner after church, and afterward lingered over a game of draughts with Kate, while Mr. Keith played the pianoforte. Although he primarily played only the melody, he had become remarkably adept with one hand. It was a pleasure to hear him. Sophie sat nearby with her sketchbook and attempted to draw his profile.

Wesley absented himself from their little party. He had invited Sophie to go with him to pay a call on Lord Thorp. She thanked him, but explained she had already been to Langton.

"When was this?" he asked in surprise.

"The captain took me to meet him. He thought I would enjoy seeing his collection."

"How jolly thoughtful of him," he grumbled.

"Lord Thorp showed us the two pieces of yours he has on display. We . . . did not, em, explain your . . . connection with the subject of the portrait."

"Ah." Wesley nodded in understanding. Then he excused himself to pay a call on

Lord Thorp alone.

After he left, Sophie tried to concentrate on her drawing but felt distracted, managing little more than shapes and idle sketches. She wished she knew how to knit. That would give her hands something to do, and help her prepare for the child to come. But she hesitated to attempt it in front of Wesley. She did not wish to pour salt on his wound.

Kate moved one of her pieces, then asked, "Angela. Have you heard our news? Sophie is to have a child."

The woman stilled, white knight midair, and turned to look at Sophie, a strange, bleak light in her eyes. She exhaled on a sigh. "Of course she is."

Kate looked at her in confusion. Seeing it, Miss Blake summoned a smile and added, "She is married to an Overtree and will now bear an Overtree child to the praise and happiness of the entire family. How perfect for her. Why, we will have no end of celebrations and christenings and the knitting of little booties. . . ."

Sophie glanced at Mr. Keith. Seeing him apparently absorbed in his playing and paying their conversation no heed, she asked softly, "Do you not like children, Miss Blake?"

"Like them? Everyone likes them. Welcomes them with open arms. That is, if they come at the correct time. To properly married people."

Sophie stared at the woman, stunned. Did she know Sophie's secret? Had she guessed?

Kate's eyes widened. "I am sorry, Angela. I did not intend to raise a sad subject."

"Why should it be a sad subject?" Miss Blake's eyes flashed, but Sophie thought she saw tears there too.

Kate added gently, "I know you wish you might have married before now and had a child of your own."

Miss Blake scoffed. "I entertain no such wish, I assure you."

"But why?" Sophie blurted. "You are beautiful and accomplished and from a well-connected family. You might marry any man you like."

Angela turned and narrowed her eyes at Sophie, perhaps weighing the sincerity of her words. "Not everyone gets to marry the man of their dreams, Mrs. Overtree. As you should know."

Sophie blinked back at the woman, afraid to ask what she meant. Not certain she wanted Kate to hear the answer she feared she might receive. Instead, Sophie asked, "Do you mean because of your age? You cannot be much more than five and twenty."

Lieutenant Keith stopped playing, Sophie noticed, and soberly awaited the woman's answer.

Miss Blake fidgeted and crossed her arms. "No, that is not what I mean. But let's leave the tiresome subject. I have no intention of marrying anyone."

"But you told me you once thought you would," Kate said plaintively.

"That was in the past, Kate. There was someone I once hoped to marry, but it amounted to nothing. And that's an end of it. Now." She rose in agitation. "Who wishes to challenge me in another game of battledore and shuttlecock — or perhaps archery? I need to shoot something."

Wesley rode back from Langton, feeling both gratified and frustrated. Gratified to see his work valued and displayed among the greats. Frustrated to look upon the image of Sophie, to have all the memories the painting evoked come rushing back, and not be able to acknowledge what she meant to him. What they'd had together.

His mind remembered. His body remembered. And it was dashed difficult to look at her as a sister. To treat her as his brother's wife. Especially when she carried his child.

Did that not trump everything?

He did not wish to cause a scene or create a scandal, to shame her or his parents. But to sit by and do nothing while she presented *his* child to the world as his brother's? Intolerable. It was beyond his strength. How would he manage it? Especially since Marsh had not even given him the chance to object to

430

their marriage, or to do the right thing himself. Anger surged through him at the thought. He longed to confront Captain Black in person — give him a piece of his mind. But since he wasn't there, Wesley decided he would write a letter to that effect.

When Wesley got home, he did so. Then he went looking for Sophie, steering clear of the parlour where he heard Kate and Miss Blake chatting within. He slipped up the stairs and gave a cursory look through her bedchamber door. Empty. He continued up to the old schoolroom, where he'd guessed she'd be. Sure enough, she sat at her easel working on that dashed portrait of Captain Black in uniform. Her palette held shades of red with black and white for light and shadow.

"Sophie."

She turned and looked at him over her shoulder. She must have seen in his expression some of what he was feeling, because she rose and turned to face him, setting her jaw.

He made up his mind — he was going to kiss her. And if he ended up with a slap for his trouble, so be it. He shut the door and strode toward her.

She held up her paintbrush like a sword to warn him away, but he put his arms around her and gathered her close, unheeding, capturing her hands between their bodies, brush and all.

"Don't!" She cried, struggling in his arms. "The paintbrush —"

"Hang the brush." He reached between them, jerked it from her grip, and sent it flying across the room. Then he pulled her close and lowered his mouth.

She turned her face away, and his lips caressed her cheek, her ear, her neck.

"Sophie. Please."

"No. I can't," she choked out. "Don't you unders—"

He found her lips, covering her protest with his mouth. How he had missed this. Missed her. Victory flared in his heart, but then she wrenched her mouth away.

"Stop it!" she cried. "Please . . . stop . . ."

The door banged open, and Wesley turned with a snarl, ready to send Keith or a housemaid or whoever it was packing. Instead Miss Whitney stepped inside, broom raised high.

"Let her go, Master Wesley."

Sophie ducked her head in mortification and pulled from his arms.

He stared down at the irksome old woman. "Mind your own business, Winnie. It isn't what it seems."

"It is exactly what it seems. And you have the mark to show for it."

She pointed to his chest, and he tucked his chin to look at his shirtfront. At the blood-red smear over his heart.

Behind them, Sophie let out a gasp. He

looked over in alarm, and saw her press her hands over her mouth, staring at something across the room. Wesley followed her gaze, and his gut twisted. When he'd whipped the brush away in frustration, he'd sent a spray of paint over her portrait of Stephen. A drop of red ran down the captain's face like blood. Like an omen.

Sophie ran from the room.

Wesley squeezed his eyes closed and released an irritated sigh. Angry with himself and with the woman before him. He braced his hands on his hips and faced her.

"You think you know so much, old woman. But do you know I love her?"

She lowered the broom. "I know you think you do, and will say anything to get what you want."

"It isn't like that. We have history together. We belong together."

"You say you love her. But would you be true to her?"

"Of course I would."

She shook her head. "I think it quite likely you will be tempted to betray her this very night, before the jester sings and the cock crows."

He scowled. "What a bag of moonshine. Does Marsh believe all your superstitious tricks? I don't." He turned toward the portrait, considering how best to repair it. He would probably only vex Sophie more if he dared touch her precious Captain Black. Instead he stepped around Miss Whitney and crossed the room.

At the door he turned back. "You keep your mouth closed about what you think you saw here today, and I won't mention your skulking about to my mother, who would not think twice about dismissing you."

"Stephen won't let her."

"Stephen isn't here."

He saw fear flash in the woman's eyes and regretted his idle threat. He meant the old nurse no harm, but he'd dashed well had enough of her interruptions and prophetic nonsense.

Wesley returned to Sophie's room that night. He felt terrible about the scene in the schoolroom and wanted to apologize for damaging her portrait. And for allowing his frustration to get the better of him. He'd never in his life forced a kiss on a woman before today. Never had to. He knew he'd behaved badly and hoped she would forgive him. He also hoped that, without Miss Whitney there to interrupt them, Sophie might even admit her feelings for him.

He softly knocked, and when no answer came, tried the latch. Locked.

Dash it.

He rested his forehead on the cool wood, but it did nothing to cool his frustration. He was not such an idiot to break down the door and wake the whole house. He didn't want to incur the wrath of his entire family.

"May I help you, sir . . . ?" came a tentative voice.

He turned in alarm, but it was only a housemaid on her way up the attic stairs.

"No. I had something I wished to ask my . . . sister. But she is already asleep and I don't want to wake her. I shall ask her in the morning."

He waited until the maid had ascended out of sight, then started up toward his own room. Realizing he would not sleep for hours, he retrieved a candle lamp and continued up the next set of stairs. He might as well go to the schoolroom and work on Sophie's portrait, since it appeared that was as close as he would get to her that night.

The maid Flora paused at the landing and looked back down at him. "Is there something I can do for you, sir?"

"Hmm? Oh, no. I am just heading up to the schoolroom."

"Are you now? For a moment I thought you might be following me. Not that I would mind if you were. . . ."

She waited at the railing while he slowly mounted the remaining stairs. He had noticed the girl before, though she was relatively new, he believed. She was a pretty, buxom girl with dark curls peeping out from beneath her cap.

If not for her crooked teeth, she might be worth painting. Or . . .

For a moment he considered what she might be offering. She was clearly flirting with him, and her room was probably just around the corner. He was frustrated — in more ways than one. He felt as if Sophie had betrayed him by marrying Stephen. She should be *his* wife, sharing *his* bed.

He paused at the top of the stairs and stood looking at the girl, the hills and valleys of her face and figure showing to good advantage by candlelight.

A slow smile lifted her mouth. "A handsome man like you ought not spend his nights alone . . ."

For a moment, he was tempted to accept the maid's offer, but then Winnie's words came back to him. *"You will be tempted to betray her this very night, before the jester sings and the cock crows."*

Wesley pressed his eyes closed, blocking out the vision of the plump figure before him, fighting for the self-control to subjugate the urge for temporary pleasure beneath his future happiness. He didn't want to be the man Miss Whitney clearly thought he was. He didn't want to ruin things with Sophie, if there was any chance at all. . . .

Over the girl's shoulder a decorative plaster mask on the wall caught his eye. He stilled, peering at it. It was a jester's face — one of several masks throughout the manor. This one's mouth was wide open in an O, as if singing. Wesley knew of two similar masks in the house that disguised squints. Might this one as well? Might there be someone watching him at that very moment? He shivered, even as he told himself he was being foolish. No one had used those squints in years.

Wesley cleared his throat. "I am just going into the schoolroom to paint. Alone. And you had better get some sleep. I know Mrs. Hill makes the staff rise before the cock crows."

He stopped in his tracks, his own words echoing through his mind.

Seeing him hesitate, the girl tried again. "You sure? A body gets awful lonely in an empty bed. . . ."

Yes, he does.

Flora tried once more. "I saw you outside Mrs. Overtree's door, but you're wasting your time there. A cold one, she is. I have it on good authority the captain slept in his dressing room."

Wesley reared his head back in surprise. "You're joking. . . . Really?"

She nodded eagerly.

Would Captain Black have put up with that? Wesley wanted to believe the girl and exalted at the thought that maybe Sophie had refused Marsh for his sake. If so, was it possible they had never consummated the marriage . . . ? It seemed too good to be true.

Even though non-consummation alone was not grounds for annulment in England, the thought gave him hope.

He drew himself up. "Good night, Flora. There's a good girl. Work hard and don't gossip and you'll no doubt have a long and successful career here at Overtree Hall."

Her smile fell. Her confidence with it. "Yes, sir. Thank you, sir."

As the girl disappeared around the corner, Wesley stood staring at the mask of the singing jester.

Then, thinking the better of tempting fate — or remaining in tempting proximity to a flirtatious housemaid, Wesley changed his mind about painting and went downstairs, retreating into his own room.

He had no specific plan, but he saw his retreat as a minor victory. A first step in becoming a better man. To earning Sophie's trust all over again.

In the morning after breakfast, he went back upstairs, ready to deliver a setdown to his old, critical foe.

He tapped on Winnie's door, and when she called "Yes?" he opened the latch and stepped inside the dreaded room. Bad memories of noses in corners and scoldings surrounded him.

Miss Whitney looked up at him from her breakfast tray, dressed in one of the same blue dresses with a white collar she'd worn as long as he could remember.

"You were wrong, Winnie," he announced.

"Was I?" she mused. "I said you would be *tempted* to betray her and you were. Beyond that, I am glad to be wrong."

His triumph deflated. How had she guessed?

She tilted her head, giving him that knowing look that had so often struck irritation — or fear of consequences — in his young heart.

"Well, Master Wesley, perhaps you are growing up at last."

After that, Wesley began meeting with the new estate manager, Mr. Boyle, and their tenants and estate workers, doing his best to fill Marsh's big boots. He was heir to Overtree Hall, after all, so perhaps it was time to assume the duties that role entailed. It would prove to his family and to Sophie that he was responsible. And hopefully he would prove it to himself as well.

He also began planning a painting of *The Last Supper* to be placed over the chancel archway, at the church warden's request. Though he found out soon enough that his mother had instigated the idea and was acting as his patron, probably hoping to keep him busy. And perhaps away from his new sister-in-law.

Chapter 24

News of Napoleon Bonaparte's return from exile had caused an urgent recall of the 28th North Gloucestershire regiment. Stephen had rejoined his men in Ireland where they were garrisoned. As soon as the men assembled, they'd boarded transports and sailed for Ostend, Belgium, to join Wellington's troops and fight Napoleon's rebuilt army. Stephen had dashed off a few lines to Sophie before embarking, but there had not been time to write again. Their warm parting had given him hope for the future, but for now he needed to focus on the task at hand.

The Duke of Wellington decided to try to stop the French advance at a crossroads called Quatre Bras — four arms — some twenty-five miles south of Brussels. If Boney's men succeeded in taking the crossroads, the path of the Prussians would be cut off. The allies would then be unable to join forces against Napoleon, who was doing all he could to divide and conquer.

Wellington was determined to defend that crossroads and defeat Napoleon.

To that end, the 28th marched south in company with the 1st Royal Scots, only stopping to sleep for a few hours before starting again.

On June the 15th, Stephen forced himself awake at dawn. Around him men slept on, snored, or grumbled, a few already at work at small fires and cooking pots. Very soon, all would rise in a bustle of activity. They would march within the hour.

Taking advantage of the few quiet moments, Stephen read from his worn copy of the New Testament and drank a cup of bitter smouch — a cheap tea rumored to be made from ash leaves steeped in sheep's dung. It tasted even worse than it sounded, but any warm liquid was welcome on that damp morning.

Ensign Hornsby came and sat by him, asking bluntly, "Are you a Methodist, sir?"

Stephen chuckled, guessing who had put him up to the question. "No."

"Then why are you always reading that Bible of yours? The sergeant says only chaplains and dashed Methodists do so, outside of Sundays."

With a wry grin, Stephen shook his head. "He's wrong about that. The sergeant's a crusty old bird, but he says his prayers every morning just as I do, make no mistake." Stephen shifted to face the young man, whom he had known through several campaigns now. He supposed Hornsby wasn't so young any longer. But his auburn hair and freckles made him look young, and reminded him of Angela Blake.

Stephen said, "We are marching into battle, Hornsby. And while I have every confidence in the 28th, and in Wellington, and our eventual victory, not all of us will live to see it." He didn't mention his lingering doubts about surviving this campaign. He didn't want to worry him. "Whatever happens, I'll be all right, because my soul is square with God."

"How do you know, sir? If you'll excuse my asking. It's not that I don't think you're a good man, but . . ."

"I am not a good man, not by any measure," Stephen replied. "And thank God I don't have to rely on my own merit. I'd never be good enough to deserve to live forever with a holy God. But Christ is, and He already died to cover my sins. He sacrificed His earthly life for my eternal one. And for yours, and for everyone willing to accept Him."

"Like when you jumped in front of me in Talavera?" Hornsby asked eagerly. "And the French saber meant for me struck you instead?"

Stephen looked at the young officer in surprise. "I . . . don't recall many details of

442

that battle. But a good analogy, yes."

"You're just being modest, sir. It's clear as day to me, and always shall be. Every time I see that scar of yours, I know it should be mine — or more likely my death — had you not shoved me out of the way." Hornsby's gaze shifted to his cheek. "I hope you don't mind it, sir."

"I wasn't much to look at before I got this, Hornsby, so don't give it a second thought. I don't." *Or I won't,* Stephen resolved. *Not anymore.*

That afternoon, they reached the crossroads and joined the others who had arrived before them. Sir Thomas Picton, commander of the fifth division, rode over to greet him. He informed Stephen that the battle had begun slowly that morning with a few skirmishes but was now rapidly escalating. He was glad to receive some reinforcements, though they still awaited the Prussians.

Stephen and his men took up position on a knoll covered by tall stalks of rye. The overgrown fields made it hard to see and provided hiding places for approaching enemy scouts, spies, and sharpshooters.

Smoke from cannon fire wafted ominously across the battlefield, obscuring the enemies' position in the distance. An occasional mortar round landed among the troops, and the men instinctively spread out to make themselves a

443

more difficult target for the French artillery. Some men dropped to one knee, as if the slender blades of grain would somehow stop an eight-pound shot.

Around him, Stephen heard the sounds of fighting — gunfire, commands, grunts — as other regiments engaged in battle. It was only a matter of time before it was their turn. Their turn to kill or be killed. Their turn to fight the overpowering impulse to run. An infantryman's job was to stand there and shoot in the face of oncoming slaughter and probable death. The worst part was the waiting.

While many other regiments had to make do with inexperienced recruits, most of the men who served beside Stephen had been through all this before. They were veterans of the Peninsula War and the Egypt campaign that had brought the 28th its greatest glory. Even so, he knew the fate of his men was directly related to his ability to make decisions quickly in the heat of battle, while the very men he knew and loved were dropping dead beside him. There would be no time to shed a tear or even to flinch. And afterward he would have to live with the consequences.

Sir Thomas Picton rode his horse past the men. "You'll be all right, lads. Just remember, kill their officers first, aim at the bellies of the infantry and at the horses of the cavalry."

He left them with the rallying cry, "28th,

remember Egypt!"

The men cheered and the bandsmen began to play.

Stephen, however, remained somber. Using his spyglass, he stared toward the river that marked enemy lines, straining to catch any glimpse of the French through the growing smoke. Off to the left he thought he saw movement. He blinked and looked again and there it was, the unmistakable outline of a horse in full gallop some five hundred yards away. The smoke cleared just enough to reveal more horses galloping toward them. A cavalry charge.

"To the square, to the square!" Stephen shouted at the top of his lungs. Every second was crucial. He had to get his men into the defensive formation that would allow them to withstand the attack.

But over the gunfire and competing shouts, many did not hear. Or stood frozen in terror.

"Hornsby! To the square! Wilson — move!" Stephen grabbed several younger men and started shoving them into position. His old sergeant joined him, barking orders like a mastiff. If they didn't move, they'd be slaughtered.

"Left flank here, right flank over there!"

The experienced men of the 28th sprang into action, their incessant drilling and training paying off.

A square was made up of hundreds of men,

four ranks deep, with room at the center for supplies, aides, and the wounded. The outside line of infantry dropped to one knee and planted the butts of their muskets on the ground. They extended their bayonets upward to form a hedge of steel the cavalry horses would be reluctant to breach. Behind them soldiers knelt with their bayonets pointing outward to form another line of defense. The two remaining ranks were comprised of standing men with "Brown Bess" muskets, firing and then reloading in turn.

Stephen shouted orders, directing soldiers into vital positions in the square. "Lane, fill the gap. Stanley, raise that bayonet."

The flag bearer carried the regiment's colors safely inside, followed by the bandsmen and several pieces of field artillery. Any cannons left outside the square would be attacked and quickly disabled.

Glancing to his right, Stephen was disheartened to see several battalions in disarray. Other officers had been slow to recognize the threat and their lesser-trained troops were scattering in confusion. Some officers retreated, or remained well behind their troops in relative safety. But Stephen felt responsible for his men, some of them younger than Kate. He could not stand back.

Climbing atop one of the cannons for a better vantage point, Stephen saw that the fierce French cavalry were now within two hundred yards of their position, the red plumes above their helmets streaming behind them. In seconds they would be upon them.

"Prepare to fire on my command!" Stephen bellowed.

The men braced themselves and raised their guns to their shoulders. The exact timing of firing was critical. Too soon and the volley would be ineffective. Too late and the mortally wounded horses and riders would come crashing into the square.

His men stood firm, but Stephen could see the fear in the eyes of all but the most hardened veterans. Fear was a luxury he had rarely allowed himself. But love for Sophie made him feel vulnerable. Made him want to live as never before, which would only make his death more likely. Fear stole focus. Courage. Hadn't his grandfather reminded him of that over and over again?

Stephen could feel the vibrations from the thundering horses about to engulf them like a swarm of locusts. The French riders raised their long curved sabers high above their heads as trumpets sounded the attack.

Here they came, crushing rye in their wake. Sixty yards, fifty yards, forty. In bloodcurdling accents, the French shouted, *"Vive l'Empereur!"*

And Stephen yelled, "Fire!"

The sharp crack of a hundred guns deafened, creating a wall of smoke in front of the square. Almost instantly the French riders emerged from the smoke atop their striving mounts, lashing with their sabers and thrusting their lances. The well-trained horses stopped just short of the row of bayonets while others swept around the square like a rushing current around a rock in the middle of a river.

As the smoke cleared, Stephen saw that many French had been killed by the initial volley and several horses galloped riderless back toward enemy lines.

"Cease fire! Reload!" Stephen and his sergeant called to their men. The front line of musketeers stepped back to reload as the second line stepped forward.

The French took the opportunity to wreak havoc from high atop their war-horses. The front ranks of the 28th used their bayonets to try to keep them at bay, but their razor-sharp blades found their mark time and time again. A steady stream of wounded fell back into the center of the square.

The remaining men struggled through the painstaking steps to reload, while foul-smelling smoke made it nearly impossible to see.

Stephen shouted, "Ready. Fire!"

Again smoke and thunder erupted and more French met the ground.

The first wave of cavalry retreated, and his men sent up a shout, but Stephen knew they had precious little time before the French charged again. He rushed to the front of the square that had taken the greatest punishment, and helped the wounded. As he dragged one man back to the center, cannons sounded in the distance. He paused to look toward the enemy lines in time to see puffs of smoke emitted from their batteries. Before he could react, dozens of explosions erupted as cannonballs slammed into the earth all around them, the French gunners taking advantage of their tight formation.

Men screamed in agony as flying shards of metal tore into their bodies. Off to his right, Stephen saw the British cannons answering the barrage, and he prayed their shots would hit their mark.

The number of wounded in the center of the square was growing. Stephen moved along the ranks of men still forming the square, searching for weaknesses in the lines and directing reserves into the gaps.

Stephen once again climbed atop the cannon to survey the situation with his spyglass. The French cavalry massed near the river were separating into groups — waiting for the devastating effects of the cannons to take their toll before they attacked again.

Suddenly an explosion knocked him from his perch. A French cannon ball had hit one corner of the square. A dozen of his troops had been felled by a single shot and a huge gap blown open in their formation. Many of the men were killed instantly, but others were left to suffer in agony.

Stephen regained his footing and rushed toward the carnage. As he reached the gap, a trumpet blast in the distance signaled the next cavalry charge. He called for several men to move forward and reposition themselves in the critical corner of their defense. The men hurried to obey, but the enemy was almost upon them.

Stephen commanded, "Prepare to fire!" Once again the pounding of the horses' hooves made the ground shake all around them. He counted the distance and at thirty yards yelled, "Fire!" Then he grabbed a musket from a fallen soldier and joined the reinforcements filling the decimated line. A rider came barreling toward him, so close Stephen could see every detail of his blue uniform with red lapels, his body armor gleaming in the sunlight. The Frenchman's chest plate would deflect the point of a bayonet but could not stop a musket ball from this close range.

The rider brandished a saber in one hand and a pistol in the other, the reins gripped tightly in his teeth. A sharp pain ripped through Stephen's shoulder as a blade sliced into his flesh in a sickening blow. He slumped to one knee and blood ran down his arm. He looked up and saw the rider aim his pistol at

Hornsby nearby. As he fired, Stephen pulled the young officer down, cutting his hand on the man's blade. The bullet missed its target.

Hornsby helped Stephen to his feet as the battle raged around them. The soldiers sent another volley of lead into the attackers. His left arm now useless, Stephen could merely shout orders and fill the gap with his body, but he was able to offer little resistance.

To Stephen's horror, another group of cavalry charged just behind the first group. This group was larger and galloping straight for the weakened corner of their square. Right where he stood. Their only hope was to stop them before they crashed through the gap and slaughtered his vaunted regiment from within.

Stephen yelled, "Fire!"

The remaining infantrymen discharged their guns in a desperate attempt to stop the attackers. A large black stallion in full gallop was hit by the barrage. The brave animal stumbled and came crashing into their square, widening the gap in their protective ranks. The dead rider was thrown from the horse and landed at Stephen's feet, pistol still in hand. Stephen grabbed it.

In an instant another French cavalryman saw the opportunity and urged his mount toward the gap. If they did not thwart this intrusion all would be lost. Stephen aimed and fired. The shot hit home and the rider fell. The horse reared, hooves flashing, its front hoof delivering a blow to the side of Stephen's head. Stunned, he dropped to his knees.

"Captain, behind you!"

Another shattering collision of steel on flesh and bone, like lightning felling a tree.

Stephen fell face-first into the rye. The dying black stallion rolled and trapped him beneath it, knocking the remaining breath from his lungs. Around him the sounds of fighting and shouts and cries continued, but faded, growing more and more distant.

I am going to die, he thought calmly. Sadly. *Your will be done, Lord. Please comfort my family. And bless Sophie and her . . . our . . . child.*

His eyes were open, and his small patch of vision — his own bloody hand, Belgian soil, broken stalks, and torn earthworm — came into sharp focus, then narrowed. A dark ring framed his vision like a spyglass, the darkness spreading, his vision shrinking to a tiny point of light and then . . . blackness.

CHAPTER 25

An old friend of Colonel Horton's had been on hand in London when a dispatch from Wellington arrived. As a favor to the colonel, he'd sent a messenger to Overtree Hall directly.

The colonel summoned the family and Mr. Keith into the parlour and shared the grave report. "Sobering news, I am afraid. There's been a horrendous battle in Belgium — at a crossroads Wellington was determined to defend called Quatre Bras."

He read a brief excerpt.

"On 16th June, the 28th in company with the 1st Royal Scots marched to the support of the hard-pressed 42nd and 44th, forming square and standing firm to continuous attacks from French cavalry. The British line, supported by guns and cavalry, gallantly beat back their assailants, and the ground the French had taken during the afternoon was regained. The French fought back but could not hold and were eventually forced to retreat. In the end, Quatre Bras was held and the road to the Prussians still open, but at a high cost. Casualties among the Highlanders were especially severe, but many were killed or injured among the 28th as well. No specific numbers or names yet reported."

Sophie's heart fisted. *Please, God, no . . .*

The colonel refolded the message and removed his spectacles. "Not the resounding victory we hoped for. And the battle continues to rage elsewhere. The survivors of the 28th are moving north with the rest of the 5th Division in hopes of defeating Boney there."

Sophie's fear must have shown on her face, because the colonel patted her hand. "Chin up, my girl. The captain has lived through worse."

But Sophie feared the worst — especially knowing about Winnie's prediction. Because whether the old nurse remembered it clearly or not, Stephen did, and that might affect the outcome. She prayed again for God's protection, and for Stephen to come home.

Mr. Keith rose, saying he would walk over to Windmere and share the report with Miss Blake. Sophie hoped his visit would not be rebuffed. They had not seen much of Angela since the tense conversation about her marriage prospects. But Sophie guessed that all their neighbors and friends would rally around the Overtree family as this news spread.

Wesley watched Sophie's face as his grandfather read the report. Seeing her concern for Marsh stilled him, worried him, convicted him, even as he admired her for it. At first, he had suspected her attachment to Marsh was a performance for his family's sake, but he was shaken to discover her affection for his brother had not been an act. At least not in the end. Her loyalty, however misplaced, was genuine and touching.

He'd also been surprised at CK's eagerness to take the news to Miss Blake at Windmere. Wesley had noticed Angela had been making herself scarce lately and wondered if she was avoiding Overtree Hall on his account. He decided to be kinder to her in hopes of smoothing things over.

In the afternoon, he continued his painting of *The Last Supper* over the chancel archway. And when he entered the church, he stopped to pray, as he had rarely done before. For Marsh. For Sophie and the child. For patience.

It had been one thing when Wesley thought Marsh was lounging about in a Dublin barracks, ordering men about as he liked to do, and sharing a comfortable mess with fellow officers. But now that Wesley knew his brother was well and truly enmeshed in battle — his life at serious risk — Wesley decided to retreat from Sophie. Give her time and space.

He had offered to help her repair the portrait of Stephen, but she said she preferred to do it herself. It was clear she wanted to be alone — or at least, not alone with him. So that evening Wesley removed his easel and supplies from the old schoolroom and carried them back to his own small studio adjacent to his bedchamber. There he continued to work on his new portrait of Sophie. Now and again, he glanced at the crate in the corner. The crate that represented and concealed his past in Lynmouth. And his love for Sophie Dupont Overtree.

In the white parlour the next day, Sophie and Kate sat reading novels, Kate on the sofa and Sophie in an armchair nearby. Mr. Keith and Miss Blake played the pianoforte together — Angela serving as his second hand. They sat close to one another on the bench, playing and laughing and flirting. Sophie didn't know what Mr. Keith had said to Angela to bring about the change in her demeanor, or if something else had restored her spirits. Perhaps she simply wanted to be a comforting presence for the Overtree family during an uncertain time. Whatever the case, Angela was once again spending time in Overtree

Hall — and at Mr. Keith's side.

The sight of the two of them together struck Sophie as bittersweet. Sophie was happy for them, but sad for herself. She had never enjoyed a sweet, proper, public courtship. She and Wesley had spent most of their time alone on remote Castle Rock, or hidden away in his cottage. She should have held out for better. Valued herself more highly.

Still the pair were amusing, and Sophie looked from them to Kate with a smile. But the girl did not return the gesture. She turned the page of her novel with little of her usual enthusiasm.

Guessing the reason, Sophie said, "I have not seen Mr. Harrison lately."

"No. He's gone to London for the week."

"Oh?"

"Yes. Mr. Nelson told me he's visiting his old friend, Sir Theodore Terry. He has offered to use his connections to help him find a publisher for his book."

Sophie studied the girl's wan expression. "But . . . is that not good news?" she asked.

Kate shrugged. "If he is successful, I fear he will remain in London for some time."

"Yes, but if he is successful, will that not go a long way in winning your parents' approval?"

Kate looked up at her hopefully. "Do you think it might?"

Sophie nodded, and was gratified to see the

girl's customary smile return.

Wesley appeared, hesitating in the doorway. His gaze swung from Sophie and Kate, to Miss Blake and Mr. Keith at the pianoforte.

Kate patted the sofa cushion beside her. "Hello, Wesley. How was your meeting with Mr. Boyle?"

He shrugged and sat down. "All right. Old codger certainly knows how to make a short story long. His daughter has just made him a grandfather twice over — twins named Rachel and Rebekah, of all things."

"How charming." Kate turned to Sophie. "That reminds me. Have you given any thought to what you will name your baby?"

Sophie noticed Wesley send her a wary look. "I . . . have not yet decided."

Angela spoke up from behind the piano. "I suppose if it is a girl, you shall name her after yourself? It is traditional in many families."

"No. I think that would be too confusing," Sophie replied.

"Yes, it can be. As I know from personal experience."

Kate asked, "What did Stephen suggest?"

Sophie recalled that the topic had made the captain visibly uncomfortable. At the moment, it was making her uncomfortable as well. "He did not say much on the subject," she said. "Though he did mention the colonel's given name is George."

Angela offered, "Stephen's second name is

Marshall, as you probably know. And Wesley's is Dalton. Both fine old family names." She smiled sweetly from her to Wesley and back again.

Sophie swallowed. "I don't think so, no."

"Better not choose Marsh," Wesley muttered.

Mr. Keith stood abruptly. "What do you say to a game of billiards, Wes. Leave this sort of talk to the ladies?"

"Excellent idea. Thank you, CK." Wesley rose and led the way.

Sophie was grateful as well.

On the afternoon of June the 23rd, Sophie and Kate were again sitting in the white parlour together, when galloping horse hooves and scattering pea gravel drew their attention out the front windows. Young Mr. Harrison came riding in and all but leapt from the saddle, leaving the reins dangling before the groom even jogged out to take his horse.

"I thought he was in London," Sophie murmured.

"He was." Kate's brow knit. "I hope nothing is wrong."

Sophie inhaled a shaky breath. "I hope he doesn't bring bad news."

The two women hurried into the hall.

A moment later, the young man burst through the door, ignoring the footman's attempt to forestall him or take his coat. Mr. Harrison brandished a copy of the *London Gazette Extraordinary,* folded so that the headline in huge capitals caught Sophie's eye:

GLORIOUS VICTORY

"Victory!" he called. "We have triumphed over Bonaparte!"

Outside, the church bells began ringing on cue. Mr. Harrison smiled and nodded. "I rode past Papa on the way in and shouted the good news."

Mr. Harrison breathlessly explained that he had ridden all night from London as soon as he heard the report.

Word spread throughout the house, and the family and servants gathered as though to hear a town crier.

When all had assembled, Mr. Harrison read aloud of the victory obtained by the Duke of Wellington over Bonaparte at Waterloo on the previous Sunday, the 18th of June.

Cheers arose and echoed throughout Overtree Hall.

Mr. Harrison beamed at them all, clearly enjoying his role as bearer of glad tidings.

"What a celebration in London — the Tower guns fired, trumpets sounded, church bells rung. The mail coaches dressed in laurels and flowers, ready to carry the great news to the rest of England. Thousands of us filled the streets, cheering and shaking hands. I shall never forget it."

Around the room, God was praised and smiles exchanged. Backs were slapped and embraces shared. Only the two Mrs. Overtrees remained somber.

"What does it say of casualties?" Mrs. Overtree asked, eyes on the newspaper.

"Not much," Mr. Harrison replied. "No doubt more particulars will follow shortly."

And follow they did.

Every day after that, Sophie gathered with the family as they read the *Gazette* and other papers and discussed the latest news. Wellington had won, but at a staggering cost of human life.

Lists of the wounded and slain were printed as information reached London. The Overtrees read the lists with morbid dread, knowing they were among thousands of worried families doing the same.

Those early feelings of triumph curdled into sickening dismay, as the lists of regimental losses mounted, and now and again they recognized the name of a friend or acquaintance who had fallen.

The horrendous lists continued and were added to for days. Weeks. And every time they were read, Sophie sat silently praying and holding her breath.

Captain Stephen Overtree's name was not

on those early lists and the family began to hope, even believe he had survived. A tender sprout of hope began to grow in Sophie's heart as well.

The colonel patted her hand and tried to reassure her, saying they would no doubt receive a letter from him soon.

They did receive a letter. But it was not from Stephen. It was from someone named Ensign Hornsby. Sophie was sitting in the parlour with Mr. Overtree when it arrived. He asked Thurman to summon the family. Sophie stole surreptitious glances at her father-in-law's tense, pale face as they waited. His expression did not bode well.

Soon family members and Mr. Keith gathered in the parlour, clustered on sofas and chairs. Mr. Overtree stood beside his wife's chair, holding the letter in one hand, his other gripping her shoulder.

He read the words aloud in a quavering voice that grew painfully thin several times. He had to stop and start more than once to get through it.

"Dear Mr. and Mrs. Overtree and family,
I am sorry to be the bearer of bad news. Deeply sorry. But Sergeant Wallace urged me to write, saying the not knowing is probably worse yet.
As of this writing, your son, Captain Stephen Overtree, is missing and pre-

sumed dead. The bandsmen who swept the farmhouses and fields after the awful battle at Quatre Bras did not find him among the dead. I wish I could offer hope that he might yet be found among the living, but I saw him fall myself, struck by a French cavalryman. You know their reputation too well to doubt their merciless skill with saber. If not, Colonel Horton could tell you. I write this not to give you needless pain, but to assure you that he would not have suffered long.

I continue the grim task of searching among the bodies being interred, and among the wounded here in Brussels, where the entire city suddenly seems a vast military hospital, and will send word if I learn more.

I will close by telling you one thing I know for certain in these uncertain days. Your son saved my life, and the lives of many of my fellow soldiers. While other officers fell back safely behind the lines, Captain Overtree remained among his men, valiant and brave. He sacrificed his life for ours. And that sacrifice will never be forgotten.

May God grant you comfort as you grieve.

Ensign Brian Hornsby"

Sophie pressed a handkerchief to her

mouth, stifling the cry that longed to escape. Tears filled her eyes and coursed down her cheeks.

She felt someone's gaze on her profile and glanced over to find Mrs. Overtree looking at her, tears in her eyes as well. She laid her hand over her husband's in a rare display of affection.

Sophie felt more than saw Wesley's presence in the room behind her but did not look over. She did not want to see him at that moment. Afraid of what she might see — or not see — reflected in his eyes.

Then her fleeting thoughts of Wesley vanished, and all she saw was Stephen's face, Stephen's eyes. Unbidden, the scene as described in the letter flickered through her mind, and she winced, trying in vain not to see the strike, not to see the shock and pain that must have shown on his face, followed, she guessed, by resignation. Oh, she hoped the pain had not been unendurable. That this young officer was right and he had not suffered long. Poor, dear Stephen!

Pain and grief for him and for herself filled and wracked her chest, and she bent over in pain. Wesley's hand squeezed her shoulder, and she stiffened.

In a moment Kate was there. Dear Kate. She knelt and wrapped her arms around Sophie. Sophie leaned into her and cried as silently as she could, shoulders shaking.

"Now, now, my dears. We know nothing for certain," the colonel said.

"True," Mr. Keith spoke up. "Why, I once knew of a sergeant so badly injured that he was left for dead and buried in a shallow grave, only to revive later and crawl back to camp to rejoin his regiment."

"Cheery thought, CK," Wesley said dryly.

"All I am saying is, don't give up on the captain yet."

The colonel rose. "I will send a messenger to my old friend Forsythe and see what he can find out for us. In the meantime, Lieutenant Keith is right. Let's not lose heart."

Wesley found Sophie in the old schoolroom, slumped on the stool before the ruined portrait, tears flowing down her face. She glanced over when he entered, then dully turned away, as if he were no more than a midge coming in through the window.

He approached slowly, but she didn't seem to notice, her wet eyes fastened on the image of his brother's face.

His heart filled with compassion, for once drowning out his jealousy. He stepped around and knelt before her, looking up at her seated on her artist's stool like a mourning dove on its lonely perch.

"You really cared for him, didn't you," he asked quietly, no censure in his voice or his heart.

She nodded. Another wave of tears filled her lovely grief-filled eyes and coursed down her cheeks. Tears filled his own eyes in reply.

He whispered, "You might not believe it, Sophie, but I did too."

She blinked but did not look down at him.

He added, "I resented him, vied with him, grew irritated with him. But I always loved him. He was my brother, after all."

Her glance flickered down and met his, apparently measuring his sincerity.

"I even admired him, though I rarely admitted it. Though I knew he thought little of me."

"That's not true," she whispered. "He thought you were talented, and admired your ease with people. Your confidence. Though yes, he thought you irresponsible at times."

"Most of the time, I'd wager. And he was probably right. But that was then. And this is now."

"Oh? And what has changed?" She asked it mildly, with a slight humorless laugh that cut him, as though she already doubted whatever answer he would give.

"*I* have changed. Because now there is a woman I love, who needs me. A child I love. Our child. Who will need me too. I know I've made mistakes. Many mistakes . . ." He thought about the angry letter he had written to Marsh. Now, he regretted sending it. "But I want to make it right. I am not happy my brother is dead —"

"We don't know that for certain," she insisted, mouth tight, eyes drifting away again.

He gingerly took her hand in his. "You're right. There is still hope. And we will pray for his safe return. Yet even if he does not, I am not without hope. Because a part of me thinks this might be my second chance. A chance to put your well-being and happiness above my own."

"It would be quite a sacrifice to do so — is that what you are saying?"

"Of course not. Don't put words in my mouth," he said gently. "I know you are grieving right now. And so am I. But I think I may glimpse God's hand in all of this."

"I did not realize you were on close terms with God."

"I haven't been in the past. But these last weeks have driven me to my knees time and time again."

"Me too," she admitted.

Her eyes drifted back to the portrait. Her thoughts still of his brother and not of him. But she did not pull her hand from his grasp. And that was something.

After Wesley left her, Sophie blindly pushed her way into Winnie's sitting room, not bothering to knock. The woman turned, startled, quickly shutting her bedchamber door behind her as though hiding something, but Sophie had noticed nothing embarrassing through her tears. Her throat tight and burning she said, "A letter came. It said —"

"Stephen is dead," Winnie finished for her. "Yes, I know."

Surprise flashed through Sophie. "But how . . . ? Did Kate or someone come up to tell you?"

Miss Whitney shook her head, faded blue eyes troubled and distant. "No, you're the first."

"You see? You know things, Winnie. Stephen says you're always right. Is he really dead? Is he?"

"I don't know." The elderly woman shook her head again, eyes filled with worry and tears of her own. "I can't hear his voice. I listen and listen and I can't hear his voice."

"You have heard Stephen's voice in the past?" Sophie asked, incredulous and hopeful at once.

"Of course I have. He lived here, after all. I don't expect to hear his voice when he's gone. I meant God's voice. I asked for Stephen's life. I prayed. But no answer comes. I listen and listen, and I can't hear His voice."

CHAPTER 26

On Sunday, the family attended church together. It was comforting to hear Mr. Nelson pray for Captain Overtree and other men from the parish whose fate was uncertain, or who had been injured or killed in the war. It was touching to receive the hopeful condolences and promises of prayer from many neighbors, tenants, and their servants.

Then followed another tense week of waiting. Mrs. Overtree went to the chapel every day to pray. Miss Blake came over often, to keep Kate company and offer what comfort and diversion she could. Mr. Keith often played the pianoforte for them, or joined them for a walk or game to pass the slowly crawling hours.

Sophie became more aware of a quickening within her body and savored those moments, those small assurances that her child was alive and well. She asked Mrs. Overtree to teach her to knit and she agreed. Mrs. Overtree confessed she did not particularly enjoy needlework but did a great deal of it as charity work. "After all," she said, " 'it is more blessed to give than to receive.' "

The colonel retreated into himself, spending more time alone in his room, and began to look older than his years. Sophie noticed a slight bend in his back that had not been there before.

Sophie, determined to be true to her promise to watch over Winnie during the captain's absence, visited often, and brought her dainties saved from her own meals.

One afternoon, she cut flowers in the garden for Winnie, arranged them in a glass vase, and carried them upstairs. However, when she reached Winnie's room, she found it empty. She'd been told the woman rarely ventured from the top floor. Sophie had seen her downstairs only once — the night Stephen left — though she suspected Winnie had come down at least one more time to leave that book for her. Where was she now? Sophie had seen no sign of her in any of the public rooms she'd passed, nor in the gardens.

Flora came down the passage, and Sophie asked her if she had seen Miss Whitney.

The housemaid shrugged, lips pursed. "No, ma'am. Not since I brought up her breakfast tray this mornin'. The kitchen maid's job, but she has the day off on account of her father dyin'."

"Oh. Thank you, Flora."

Dying . . . Sophie did not like that word. She reminded herself that Stephen held an unflagging belief in eternal life. Since becoming better acquainted with Captain Overtree, and with God, Sophie hoped for heaven someday too. But that didn't mean she was ready to part with Stephen yet.

The following week, two letters arrived. An official-looking one for the colonel, and another for the Overtree family from Ensign Hornsby.

When the family had gathered, the colonel unfolded the letters. Kate gripped Sophie's hand. Wesley stood near Carlton Keith, while Mr. and Mrs. Overtree sat together on the sofa, faces drawn.

The terse reply from the colonel's friend, Forsythe, offered no new information.

"Checked up and down the chain of command — official and unofficial sources. Afraid answer is the same. Captain Stephen Marshall Overtree of the 28th is missing and presumed dead. My deep condolences."

The colonel went on to read aloud Hornsby's second letter on the family's behalf. The ensign began by saying he had visited all the hospital wards and surgery tents and found no sign of Captain Overtree. He added the following postscript:

471

"I don't say it's a proud military tradition, but tradition it is: the auctioning off of items pillaged from dead officers. So many were killed by the French that the prices were quite low. I recognized one specific watch among those piled alongside signet rings and dress swords awaiting auction. The watch is engraved with the inscription: To Stephen, on his 21st birthday, followed by the date. I was able to buy it for six shillings. Not for myself, of course, but for you. It is too risky to send by post, but I will find a way to return it to you when I return to England. Small consolation though I know it is."

The words struck Sophie like a fist. Mrs. Overtree let out a keening wail at the description of the watch.

Colonel Horton crumpled the letter in his gnarled hand. His face crumpled as well. "I shall never forgive myself. It's my fault. I pushed him. Prodded him. Thunder and turf, I even made his inheritance contingent on serving! So determined to have one of my grandsons follow in my footsteps. A way to relive my glory days, I suppose. Someone to brag about to my cronies. Someone to listen to my exploits, when no one else in the family cared. Selfish. Vain and stupid and selfish."

He turned and walked shakily out the door.

Around the room, other family members cried and embraced one another. Kate collapsed in Sophie's arms, and over the girl's head she was touched to see tears streaming down Wesley's face as well, while Mr. Keith clasped his shoulder. When Kate released her to fall sobbing into Wesley's arms instead, Sophie slipped away to find the colonel.

She found him sitting, elbows on knees, on a padded bench in the upstairs corridor, looking at the old portrait of Stephen. He glanced over as Sophie approached, and the tears in the stoic grandfather's eyes tore at her heart.

"He wanted to go into the church. Did you know that?" He laughed bitterly and shook his head. "I talked him out of it. Said he'd be wasted in some country parish, delivering sermons to sleeping parishioners and praying over the sick and dying instead of living life! Now look — he is the one dead. Cut down in his prime. Barely married. Never to see the face of his child. To hold him or her. Never to see you again, my dear. I am so sorry."

Sophie sat next to the elderly man. Though what comfort she could offer she didn't know. Not when Miss Whitney's prediction had been correct after all.

She took his hand in hers. "It isn't your fault, Colonel. It isn't. Stephen knew he might die in battle, and he accepted that. He was ready to meet his maker."

"Was he?"

"Yes."

He shook his head again. "He should never have given in to doubt. Fearing death invites death. How many times have I told him . . ." The old man's shoulders began to shake. Sophie wrapped her arms around his hunched figure as best she could.

"It's all right," she soothed. "It's all right." She repeated the phrase, trying to soothe herself as well.

When he'd calmed, she added gently, "If there *were* anything to be forgiven, you know Stephen already forgave you long ago. He loved you. Very much."

He nodded. "He loved you too, Sophie." He yanked a handkerchief from his pocket and wiped his eyes. "I gather yours was not a . . . love match. At least at first. But he did love you. Never doubt it."

"Thank you," she whispered. Had Stephen loved her? She wanted to believe it. But now she would never know for sure.

Before stepping outside a few days later, Sophie fastened a pelisse over her dress — chagrined to find it quite snug — and tied a bonnet under her chin. The weather was cloudy with intermittent rain. For a time the sun would shine, only for clouds to gather and release another grey drizzle. Like Sophie herself these days, never knowing when another wave of grief would wash over her.

Taking an umbrella for good measure, she crossed the drive and passed through the gate into the adjacent churchyard. She opened the creaking church door and left it open behind her to allow in more light and fresh air into the musty, lovely place.

She made her way up the aisle of the narrow nave to the front pew, sliding over to sit in a weak shaft of sunlight filtering bravely through the stained-glass windows. That's how she felt. Weak. Wanting to be brave. She looked up and studied the stained glass more closely. A triumphant Jesus stood in the center panel — red robe, halo, staff — flanked by golden angels with wings of blue and green.

The light shone through the image of Jesus and onto her. Warmed her. Made the dreary stone chapel beautiful. He was, after all, the light of the world.

She laid a kneeling pad on the cold floor — its needlepoint cover made by Mrs. Overtree herself. Sophie knelt, forearms on the wooden rail in front of her. She clasped her hands, bowed her head, and closed her eyes.

"Almighty God. All powerful, knowing Father. Nothing is too difficult for you. Can you work a miracle? Bring Stephen back to us? Not just for my sake, but for his parents', and Kate's, and the colonel's, and Winnie's. . . . But if that is not your will, help me. Help us all to accept, and heal, and live. And show me what I should do without him. . . ." Warm tears slipped from beneath her closed eyelids and trailed down her cool cheeks. She let them flow unchecked.

A few sounds penetrated her prayer. The rumble of distant thunder. The caw of a crow. A scuff of shoe leather. The creak of the wooden pew beside her.

Sophie looked up through blurry eyes and found Mrs. Overtree laying her own kneeling pad on the floor.

"May I join you?" she asked.

"Of course."

Her mother-in-law's gaze flickered over her face and Sophie ducked her head, sure she must be a mess of streaks and leaks. Mrs. Overtree withdrew a handkerchief from her reticule and offered it to her. "Here."

"But you might need it."

"Indeed I shall. I go through a dozen a day it seems." She managed a watery smile, pulled another handkerchief from her sleeve, and dabbed her nose.

Sophie wasn't sure whether the woman wanted to talk or pray, but considering their surroundings, she again closed her eyes and bowed her head.

"Sophie?"

"Hmm?" She looked up at her mother-in-law once more.

"I misjudged you. And I'm sorry." She

reached over and laid her gloved hand on Sophie's, giving it a gentle squeeze.

Somehow the comforting act sent a fresh flood of tears to Sophie's eyes. She shook her head, struggling to speak over her tight throat. "No," she managed, chin quivering. "You were right about me. I didn't deserve him."

Answering tears filled Mrs. Overtree's eyes. "Oh, my dear girl. You really did — do — love him, don't you?"

Sophie nodded. If only she had realized it sooner.

During the following week, Sophie avoided the studio — where Wesley might find her alone, where the ruined portrait of Stephen stood like a pitiful memorial. She would have to scrape off the portions of his face streaked with dried paint and do her best to repair the portrait — no doubt giving him another "scar" in the process. Or paint several new layers of paint over all to cover the red marks, but that would be almost like starting his face all over again. And already, she couldn't recall the details as clearly anymore. At all events, it seemed a daunting project, beyond her current energies and her skills.

Instead she spent time with Kate, Angela, and Mrs. Overtree, far more at ease with her mother-in-law than she had been before. She drew comfort from the female companionship and found the gentle stream of conversation — from trivial topics to deep insights as only women can do — soothing. Healing. She had spent so little time with women growing up, after her mother had died. She found she enjoyed their company — so different from that of men.

The four of them spent hours together in the morning room, knitting and doing netting work. Sophie took pleasure in creating in this whole new way. Together the women talked while their needles worked, making a baby blanket, a little woolen waistcoat, booties and caps. Her child would be well shod and clothed come winter. She wondered yet again if it would be a boy or a girl, especially now that he or she was making its presence felt with frequent movements. Sophie liked the name George for a boy, especially since Stephen had indirectly suggested it. But she still had not settled on a name for a girl.

Now and again, Sophie visited Winnie, taking a lopsided cap or bootie to show the woman her efforts, and a scone or a bowl of strawberries. Usually, she found Winnie feeding the birds to her cat's amusement, or reading on the settee, Gulliver purring on her lap. But one day, Sophie entered to find Winnie standing at the window alone.

"It's strange," Winnie said, turning to face her. "I haven't seen Gulliver for a few days. I don't suppose he's crossed your path?"

"I'm sorry, no," Sophie replied, holding forth a wrapped lemon scone.

"Ah, well. I'm sure he's just roaming about the neighborhood, naughty boy. In fact, I saw him from the window last week, courting another cat in the churchyard."

Winnie accepted the offered scone and took a crumbly bite. "You haven't been to the schoolroom lately," she observed.

"No." Sophie ducked her head, embarrassed to remember the scene the woman had witnessed between her and Wesley there more than a month ago.

Winnie set aside her plate and gripped Sophie's hand. "All is not lost, my girl. What is ruined is not ruined forever."

Sophie blinked at the woman. Was she referring to the fact that Sophie had been ruined, or what? Her cheeks heated with shame.

"Go on." Winnie tipped her head toward the wall shared with the schoolroom. "Go and see."

Sophie heard a shuffling noise from the next room. She whispered, "Is Wesley in there?"

"I should imagine so. But how would I know? I may have eyes in the back of my head, but I can't see through walls. Usually." She winked.

Sophie shook her head. "I'll wait 'til he leaves."

"Oh, go on. I think you'll be safe enough. Just shout if he tries anything and my trusty broom and I will be there in two shakes."

Sophie tentatively pushed open the old schoolroom door. Inside, things looked much as she had last seen them. Portrait on easel. Wesley standing, hands on hips. But the scene had a stillness. A peacefulness that the last encounter between them had lacked. He stood, not glaring down at anything, but with his back to her, staring out the window.

He slowly turned as she entered, his expression guarded. He glanced toward the portrait, then back at her, waiting, wary. Did he think she would rage at him for spoiling it?

She steeled herself and glanced over, telling herself to remain calm. It was only a painting. Only one of hers. She could bear one look.

Instead she turned and stared. Walked closer and studied the painting. Sunlight from the window shone gently upon Captain Overtree's face.

His perfect face.

"You repaired it," she breathed.

"I hope you aren't angry. I know you told me not to, but I had to do something. I had to try. . . . If you don't like it, you can paint over it. You would have had to anyway. I did my best to remain true to your style and brush work, and —"

"It's perfect." He had not only repaired the painting but improved it. Subtly, carefully. In a way that did not leave her feeling violated or discouraged. He had not commandeered her work or made it his. He had cleaned it up, polished it, removed extraneous or distracting bits, highlighted its strengths, and downplayed its weaknesses. It was masterfully done.

"Thank you," she managed, her heart full.

He came and stood beside her. Close, but not touching. Not presuming.

"I'm sorry, Sophie," he began. "About the portrait. About Stephen. About leaving you in the first place. Truly, I am, and I hope you will forgive me."

Sophie hesitated. Was she ready to forgive him? For all the upheaval, all the heartache, all the uncertainty?

When she did not reply, hurt and resignation crossed his handsome face, but he continued gently, "I love you, but I won't pressure you. If there is anything I can do, you need only ask."

She managed a wobbly nod, knowing she would cry again if she tried to speak.

Wesley stood memorizing every cherished feature, longing to take her in his arms but mustering the self-control to resist. Sophie looked so fragile standing there. So vulnerable with her thin hands, her wan damp face, her rounded middle — a portrait of loss and life.

"I will miss him too, Sophie. Don't think I won't. For all my complaints about Marsh, I depended on him. Loved him." Tears blurred his vision.

Looking up at him, Sophie's eyes downturned all the more, and she held out her hand to him.

He took it, and slowly drew her close. He gently, chastely, put his arms around her. She stood rigid a moment, then melted into his embrace, laying her cheek against his shoulder.

He held her trembling body, the swell of their growing child between them.

But, they had more than a child between them. They had history. Shared loss. And shared hope for the future. And he very much hoped, shared love as well. It would take time, he knew, and he would have to allow her to grieve.

He wondered again if what the maid Flora had told him was true — that Sophie and Stephen had not slept in the same bed — had perhaps not even consummated their marriage. Even if it wasn't grounds for an annulment in England, in several other countries it would be. . . .

But Wesley decided against raising the topic. With Marsh dead, it was a moot point. And whatever the case, Sophie's grief was real. And he needed to, and would, respect that. But he believed — hoped — that somewhere deep beneath her grief and disappointment, she still nurtured feelings for him. Yes, he would have to be cautious. Tread carefully and not chase her away. She had loved him once, he knew, and he would earn her love again, if it was the last thing he did.

CHAPTER 27

Sophie had avoided writing to her father, hoping she wouldn't have to. Finally, she sent a letter with the sad news, assuring him she was well, and he needn't worry about her.

It was mostly true. The throbbing ache of grief continued to hollow out her heart, weigh her down, sap her strength. Yet she could not deny that a part of her had warmed to Wesley. She appreciated his retreat, his quiet support and consideration, his affection for his parents and sister, his willingness to talk about Stephen in nostalgic tones, both proud and humorous in turns. She loved when he recounted journeys they had taken as a family, or boyhood exploits — riding and jumping the wall the colonel had told them to stay clear of, fishing when they were supposed to be studying, and pulling harmless pranks on Miss Blake, Kate, or even Winnie.

Mrs. Overtree's eyes brightened with tears or took on a dreamy remembrance whenever he spoke of the past. But she smiled now and again, too, chuckled, or shook her head in maternal exasperation to learn of some boyhood mischief she'd not known about.

Sophie found this Wesley — repentant and respectful — far more appealing than resentful, passionate Wesley. And she tucked away in her injured heart that he had finally said he loved her — outright and in person.

She also took comfort in the fact that Wesley had asked her to forgive him for leaving her. Seeing him soothe and comfort his grieving parents and grandfather, how could she withhold forgiveness from him any longer?

One evening, as they walked downstairs and through the hall together on their way to dinner, Sophie said, "You asked me to forgive you, and I do. I sincerely appreciate your kindness and your change of heart."

He quietly replied, "Thank you. It doesn't mean I have given up hope, Sophie. I believe we are meant to be together, but I am willing to wait as long as it takes."

"For how long?" she asked lightly. "Until England changes its laws? The law doesn't allow a brother and sister-in-law to marry, Wesley, even had we proof Stephen is truly . . . gone."

Wesley waved her objection away with an expressive hand. "It's not an insurmountable obstacle. We will wait a respectful amount of time, then sail to Italy — or France once it's safe. They don't have such laws there."

Napoleon was being exiled again, this time to distant St. Helena off the coast of Africa. The authorities were taking no chances this time. If all went as planned, it would soon be safe to travel to France once again.

Even so, Sophie shook her head. "No, Wesley. I've had my fill of scandal, thank you. And your family has barely recovered from one elopement. I'm sorry, but no."

They joined the others gathered in the anteroom, awaiting the butler's signal.

Kate glanced at the long-case clock with a little frown. "Angela is late. I expected her by now."

"Oh, is she joining us tonight?" Sophie asked.

"Yes. At least I thought so. Mamma invited her, since her father and brother are away again."

Thurman appeared and announced dinner was served. They filed into the dining room, took their usual places, and picked up their table napkins.

Miss Blake hurried into the room, then slowed her pace, smiling around the table. "I'm sorry to be late. Do forgive me."

"Where have you been?" Mr. Keith asked. "I thought I saw you come through the garden door an hour ago."

Kate turned to look at her as well. "Did you?"

Angela hesitated. "Oh, I . . . ran upstairs to

chat with Winnie, and lost track of the time."

"That was kind of you," Sophie said.

"If surprising," Wesley added.

"It was nothing. Now, don't let me hold up the meal."

The green-pea soup was served, and with it crimped perch with a Dutch sauce. "For Sophie," Mrs. Overtree said with a little smile.

Kate laid down her spoon and leaned nearer, peering at Miss Blake's head.

"What's wrong?" Angela whispered. "Hair out of place?"

"Looks like a cobweb. . . ." Kate reached over and extracted it for her.

Miss Blake self-consciously ran a hand over her hair. "Thank you. Probably from the attic. Always a hazard when venturing up there. Don't you agree, Sophie?"

"Hmm? Oh, I hadn't really noticed. But I'm sure you're right." Sophie smiled vaguely at the woman.

Angela went on to recount some of her brother's plans for his wedding trip, but Sophie wasn't really listening. Her thoughts were soon drawn back to Wesley and his unflagging belief that they were meant to be together.

Conflicting emotions needled her. She had come to admire and love Stephen, and mourned his loss. Wesley had his flaws, she knew, but he was the father of her child, and had said he loved her. Something his brother

487

had not done. Although Stephen *had* said, *"Live or die, my heart is yours . . ."* So, perhaps the colonel was right and Stephen did love her, or might have, had he lived.

Sophie felt Miss Blake's gaze return to her several times during the meal, and began to wonder if she had something in her own hair.

If Stephen was dead, must Sophie remain alone all her days, and her child fatherless? Would it dishonor the captain's memory to someday entertain Wesley's proposal? It would certainly scandalize his family.

Oh, Lord, Sophie prayed. *Help me guard my tongue. My heart. My honor. Help me do what's right.* Sophie's faith had grown over the months of attending services with the Overtrees, and praying and reading on her own. One of the proverbs she'd learned echoed through her mind at that moment: *"In all thy ways acknowledge him, and he shall direct thy paths."* She sincerely hoped God would guide her. For on her own, she did not know what to do.

The next day, Kate stayed in bed nursing a headache, so Sophie was alone in the morning room when Miss Blake arrived for her usual morning call.

Sophie looked up from her knitting. "Hello, Angela. I am afraid it's just me today. Kate is in bed with a headache. Mrs. Overtree may join us later, but Mr. Overtree has a trifling sniffle, so for now she won't leave his bedside."

Miss Blake peeled off her gloves. "That's all right. This will give you and I a chance to become better acquainted."

Why did that notion make Sophie nervous?

"Would you like to read one of Kate's magazines," Sophie offered halfheartedly, "or perhaps play a game of draughts?"

"I think not, thank you. Were it not such a dreary day I would suggest a turn about the grounds." Her green eyes lit. "I know. I will take you on a tour of the house."

"That is very kind," Sophie replied. "But Mrs. Overtree has already given me the complete tour and named every ancestor in every portrait, I assure you."

"Oh, I doubt she has shown you everything." Again the woman's green eyes glinted in her narrow, freckled face. "Come. I think you will enjoy it."

Sophie set aside her needles and yarn, and rose. "Very well. I would like to stretch my legs in any case."

Miss Blake led the way across the hall, pointing out the jester mask high on the wall in the musicians' gallery. "Have you noticed that before?"

"Yes, why?"

"You'll see." Together they climbed the stairs, Angela pausing to pick up a candle lamp on the landing.

Sophie asked, "Where are you taking me?"

"It's a secret. You like secrets, don't you?"

"Not especially."

"Well you certainly have some." Angela lowered her voice. "And so do I. . . ."

Miss Blake walked past the family bedchambers and around the corner. The corridor ended in a small alcove with a window seat overlooking the hedge maze below. There, as in most of the house, the paneled wainscoting rose over six feet tall, half the height of the rooms.

Miss Blake turned to her left, to a wall that looked like every other, slid her fingers behind a carved filigree, and pulled. A three-foot-by-five-foot section of wainscoting swung toward her like a small door, revealing a narrow chamber within.

Sophie inhaled a breath of surprise.

"This is an old priest hole," Angela said. "Many old houses have a secret room or passage, to allow someone to hide if he were, say, a priest during the reign of Elizabeth the First, or someone who found himself on the wrong side between Charles the Second and Cromwell."

Angela stepped in, gestured for Sophie to follow, and then pulled the paneled door closed behind them. Inside the room, there was no paneling, but rather exposed timbers on the walls and beams on the ceiling above.

One small window high on the exterior wall added to the candle's light, illuminating a single bed, tiny table, and a cross on the wall.

"Wesley and I used to hide in here as children and pretend his nurse was one of Cromwell's roundheads, come to kill us."

Sophie looked around the dim, stark room, trying to imagine hiding there for any length of time. "My goodness. That's rather . . . frightening."

Miss Blake nodded her agreement. "Yes, deliciously so."

Sophie traced her fingers over one of the timbers. "Look. Someone's carved their initials here. *W.D.O. + J.A.B.*"

"Very observant."

"Wesley plus . . . Who's J?" Sophie asked, the name "Jenny" going through her mind once again.

"Jane, I believe. One of the girls he used to admire. But never mind that now. That's not what I brought you here to see." Miss Blake stepped to another of the broad timbers running vertically along the interior wall. "There used to be a back passageway and stairs for the servants to use, to slip in and out of the family bedchambers without being seen," she explained. "But the house has been altered over the years, so access became difficult and they fell out of use. But you can still get to them through here."

She bent, grasped a nail near the bottom,

and pulled. The entire long beam lifted from the floor on a hidden pivot, revealing a narrow passage about fifteen or sixteen inches wide.

"If the house was being searched, a man could escape from this room either into the corridor we came from or through this passage, depending on which direction his pursuers were coming from."

Miss Blake eyed Sophie's middle dubiously. "Perhaps I should have given you this tour earlier. I hope you shall fit."

"And I hope I don't get stuck," Sophie mumbled, feeling uneasy. She wondered what had prompted Angela to bring her here now.

Slender Miss Blake easily slipped through the opening, and Sophie followed suit, sucking in her midsection and making herself as small as possible. In another few weeks she doubted she would have managed it.

"Watch your head," Miss Blake warned.

Candle lamp held high, they walked for several yards. "Shh," Miss Blake warned. "We're behind the family bedchambers now."

A passage ran behind her bedchamber? Did that explain the muffled footsteps and voices she sometimes heard? Who had it been? And if she could hear them, did that mean they could hear her and Stephen talking inside? A chill went over her at the thought.

"This is the first squint, placed here so one might see who was coming up the stairs, I imagine."

Miss Blake gestured toward two small holes, spaced apart, like eyes.

Sophie leaned close and peered out. It took her a moment to recognize the scene before her. There was the newel post at the top of the stairs, and there the Gainsborough landscape. And there came Flora carrying an armful of linens.

"Let's keep going." Miss Blake walked on, and Sophie hurried to catch up, not wanting to lose the light . . . or her guide. An eerie feeling crept up her neck at the thought of figures tiptoeing behind the rooms of this old house like mice crawling behind the walls, or like men fleeing for their lives.

Miss Blake whispered, "Tread quietly; we are near Mrs. Overtree's boudoir."

Sophie complied, dreading to be caught skulking around her mother-in-law's private apartment.

The passage ended at a T. They turned left and walked on until Miss Blake paused before another set of holes. "And this is my favorite. The squint in the musicians' gallery, overlooking the great hall."

Sophie bent to position her eyes in the holes, and this time felt a dizzy sense of unreality. It was as if she'd opened her eyes and found herself inside a familiar landscape she'd painted herself. She recognized the view. The vantage point. The way the great hall looked from this perspective — its windows high on the walls, the coat of arms over the immense hearth, the paneled screen dividing the great room from the entry doors. Although when she'd last seen it from this particular angle the room had not been empty and silent as it was now. But filled with brightly costumed people, dancing in Wesley's painting of a masquerade ball — a ball he'd watched as a boy from this very spot.

Miss Blake said, "The Overtrees hosted a ball once, and the children were supposed to remain in the schoolroom with Nurse Whitney. But instead, Wesley and I sneaked down here to watch. *He* got caught."

Wesley had not mentioned anyone had been with him when he'd watched the masquerade ball. Sophie wondered why.

Miss Blake added, "Sound carries very well from the hall."

A bad feeling began worming its way through Sophie's stomach. She glanced up at her companion, and the strange, expectant look in Miss Blake's eyes only increased her sense of foreboding.

With a jolt, she remembered. She and Stephen had talked in the hall one day and thought they'd heard something . . . or someone nearby. And last night she and Wesley had talked as they passed through the hall together. Thinking they were all alone. Safe from listening ears.

Had Miss Blake overheard her conversation with Stephen that day? Had she been in the manor visiting Kate and slipped away to eavesdrop? Had she been here last night when she said she'd been visiting Winnie? Is this where she'd gotten the cobweb in her hair? If so, she might know the truth about her and Stephen and Wesley. Is that what she was telling her by giving her this little "tour" and showing her the squints?

Sophie was afraid to ask. Instead she whispered, "Do others know about these passages?"

"Do you mean besides Wesley and me?" Angela shrugged, "I suppose Mr. Overtree might, growing up here as he did. Though I can't imagine him wandering about in all this dust. We didn't tell Stephen. We liked to hide from him, as well as Winnie, when there were lessons to be done or lectures to be heard."

Sophie asked, "What about Kate?"

Angela shook her head. "I did try to show her once, but I picked a poor time to do so — a stormy night. We'd gone no farther than the drafty priest hole when my candle blew out and she ran shrieking back out. Surprised everyone in the house did not learn about the passages then. She refused to go in after that, and I did not force her. I confess I liked having a secret with Wesley. Knowing something his own brother and sister did not."

"Are there passages on the other floors?"

Sophie asked.

Angela nodded. "The passage leads on to the old servants' stairs I mentioned. So you can go upstairs or down. The stairs lead all the way to a hidden door in the scullery. I don't know if there are exits on the upper floors or if they have been blocked. At least Wesley and I never found any others."

Miss Blake's foot kicked something and sent it skimming over the floor. She bent and picked it up, frowning at it by candle light. "That's strange . . ."

"What is it?"

"Half a biscuit." She handed Sophie the candle and broke it in two. "Still fresh. Someone else has been in here recently. Unless you hid a biscuit in that pocket of yours . . . ?"

"No."

Angela looked closer. Sniffed. "Almond. Wesley's favorite."

But the discovery made Sophie think of another person who loved biscuits, though she decided not to mention it.

Sophie regarded Miss Blake's profile by candlelight. Such fair skin spotted with freckles a shade lighter than her hair. Such delicate beauty. Such . . . unhappiness. Sophie wasn't sure what had happened to her in the past, but knew the woman was troubled.

"Miss Blake, are you all right?" she asked.

"Hmm? Of course. Why should I not be all right?"

"If there is anything I can do. To help. Please let me know."

The woman's bow lip twisted bitterly. "How could you help me, Mrs. Overtree?"

"You're right. There's probably nothing I can do. But God can. So I will pray for you, if you don't mind."

"God? Ha! He abandoned me years ago. Five years ago, to be precise."

"How did He?"

"He made me believe he loved me, knew I loved him, but he left me anyway."

Were they still talking about God? Somehow Sophie doubted it.

CHAPTER 28

Wesley was crossing the hall when Thurman brought in the post on its silver tray. Wesley paused and idly fingered through letters to his mother, a new magazine for Kate, and a letter addressed to the Overtree family. He did not recognize the handwriting, but the Brussels postmark certainly caught his attention. He carried the letter into the parlour, but no one was about. He supposed he should wait for one of his parents to open it, but he was part of the Overtree family, after all, and something about the letter sent a prickle of foreboding over him, which made him want to read it immediately — and dread doing so at the same time.

Standing near the parlour window, he unsealed the letter, unfolded it, and read.

To my family,
A few lines to let you know I am alive. I regret you were given cause to think the worst. I have taken saber wounds in both shoulders, one severe. I hope I will not lose

*the arm. Your prayers are appreciated. I
was separated from my regiment for a time,
and briefly held as a prisoner of war, but
managed to escape by God's grace. I will
write with more details when I am able. For
now, I will recover here in Brussels along
with many of my men.*

Yours,
Captain Stephen Overtree
Cpl A.K.

Exaltation rose in Wesley's heart. To be the
bearer of such news to his grieving family! A
second later, his stomach cramped, as he saw
his hoped-for future with Sophie fading away.
A part of him wished he had pressed his
advantage while he could. Sophie had
warmed to him again, allowed him to hold
her hand, and tentatively smiled at him when
their paths crossed. He'd begun to believe it
would be only a matter of time before they
were together. Losing her now would rip the
heart from his chest. Perhaps he should have
convinced her to run away with him earlier,
but with the war barely over and a child on
the way it had not seemed wise. Besides, he'd
thought he had all the time in the world with
Marsh gone.

For one irrational moment, he considered
burning or hiding the letter, to keep the news
from Sophie as long as possible. It was foolish, of course.

Even he was not that selfish.

He went upstairs, found Sophie in the attic studio, and extended the letter toward her with little preamble.

"I thought you should see this first."

"What is it?" She wiped her hands on a cloth and accepted the letter. She read. Inhaled a sharp breath and looked up at him, wide-eyed. "He's alive!"

He nodded his head, watching her face closely.

She read the letter again, then slowly lowered it, resolutely meeting his gaze. "He's alive."

Again he nodded. So many words went through his mind, *"It doesn't mean the end for us . . . He doesn't even mention you or indicate his regard for you. He doesn't love you as I do — doesn't even pretend to. Let's leave now before he returns . . ."* But he said none of them.

"You haven't told anyone else yet?" she asked.

He shook his head. "No one was about when the post arrived."

"They'll be so happy."

"Yes. Of course they will. And . . . so am I."

"Are you?"

He forced a small smile. "I will be." He took her hand in his, glad she did not pull away, wondering if it was the last time he would be able to do so. *Please, God, no . . .*

"And you?" he asked.

She nodded, letter pressed to her chest. "Of course I am. It's the answer to my prayers."

Rising, she said, "Well, let's not keep this to ourselves another moment. You tell them. I don't trust my voice."

On their way past, Sophie insisted they stop at Winnie's room and tell her the news. For once the old goat seemed taken by surprise, her "sixth sense" apparently failing her. Winnie hugged Sophie and thanked God again and again.

Downstairs, his family were at first afraid to believe their ears or their eyes. But when everyone had read the letter and read it again, joy swept through their midst. Happy tears and embraces and praising God passed from one to the next.

"But it isn't even his handwriting," his mother said, a vestige of doubt creasing her brow.

The colonel nodded. "See the smaller initials here? *Cpl A.K.* — the corporal who wrote the letter as Stephen dictated."

Did that explain his impersonal tone? Wesley wondered. His failure to mention Sophie?

"Doesn't have the use of his hand, apparently," the colonel added. "Yet."

His mother grimaced. "He must be bad indeed. Poor Stephen."

501

"Prisoner of war . . ." Kate echoed, her voice tremulous. "I hope they weren't cruel to him."

"At least it doesn't sound as though he was held for long," his father said. "Though any delay in treating such severe wounds . . ." He grimly shook his head.

His mother said, "If only we could bring him home — or send Dr. Matthews to him there."

The colonel strode to the door, a man on a mission. "I will see what I can find out about his prognosis, who's treating him, and when he will be released."

"Thank you, Papa." His mother drew herself up. "In the meantime, let's all dedicate ourselves to doing what Stephen asks of us — and pray."

The next day they received another letter from Ensign Hornsby. Wesley waited impatiently while the family gathered and his father read it aloud.

"Dear Mrs. Overtree, Mr. and Mrs. Overtree, and family,

Hopefully by now, word has reached you that Captain Stephen Overtree is alive. Unfortunately, the bandsmen who comb the fields for wounded either did not see him, trapped beneath a horse as he was, or left him for dead in their hurry

502

to catch up with the troops already marching north to fight Boney at Waterloo.

He suffered a head wound and sustained saber wounds to his right hand and both shoulders — one very severe. (Perhaps his epaulets deflected the blow of one strike, but that is only a guess.) The surgeons believe his right side will heal, but are not certain they will be able to save his left arm. Perhaps if they had been able to operate sooner . . .

The captain is his usual stoic self, and rarely talks about himself, and certainly never boasts. But under the influence of laudanum I was able to pry out a little of the story, knowing you his family would be eager to hear.

Apparently a French patrol found him the following day, levered the horse off him (thankfully his legs were not crushed), and took him prisoner. After the battle of Waterloo, the French guard grew lax and the captain made his escape. He says it was easily done, as the French knew they were defeated and were more interested in going home than in guarding prisoners. I doubt it was as easy as he says, but he is modest that way. Even so, by the time he walked many miles toward Brussels, and collapsed near the edge of town, he was in a bad state indeed. We can thank God he is still alive.

When he was found, bleeding and insensible, and carried to one of the military hospitals, he had been stripped of anything of value that might have identified him — purse, letters, watch. Even his coat had been taken from him. Perhaps by one of his own company, who pick the pockets of the dead for what they can get, greedy vultures, as I mentioned before. All he had of a personal nature was a miniature portrait clutched in his hand. (He had shown it to me once before, so I recognized the portrait of his wife.) How relieved I was to find him at last — and alive.

I apologize for leading you to believe the worst. Please forgive me. My letter was well meant if premature. You will understand that the captain is in no fit state to write letters, nor will he be likely to hold pen and ink for some time, but if anything new develops, I shall write again. In the meantime, he will continue to recover, God willing, here in Brussels with other men of the 28th.

Sincerely,
Hornsby"

Portrait of his wife? Wesley wondered with a frown as his father finished reading. Where did Marsh get a miniature portrait of Sophie? He had a good guess. His brother had taken the woman without asking, why not the portrait? With effort, Wesley swallowed his resentment, and thanked God again that his brother was alive.

"Can one of us not go there?" his mother implored. "Help nurse him? Heaven knows what sort of condition that hospital is in — overcrowded filthy place, no doubt, and incompetent surgeons in the bargain."

His father soothed, "My dear, I am sure he is in good hands."

"I wished I shared your confidence, Alan," the colonel put in.

"I cannot go," his mother said. "Not and leave you on your own. Your health being what it is . . ."

"Of course you should not even think about going, my dear. No place for a lady. Nor should Sophie. Especially not in her condition."

"I shall go." The colonel rose and drew his shoulders back as though at attention.

"Papa . . . You are too old to go traipsing off to war-torn Belgium."

"Shall I go?" Wesley offered. "I suppose it's only right, the way Marsh has chased after me all these years."

Lieutenant Keith slowly shook his head. "I . . . don't think that's the best idea . . ." He glanced at Sophie, eyes wary.

"Why not?" Wesley challenged. Surely CK didn't think he would harm his own brother?

"Because it is dangerous, and one of the Overtree sons needs to stay in one piece. You are the heir, after all. Shouldn't risk it." Carlton Keith inhaled resolutely. "I am the best man for the job," he said. "If anyone goes, it should be me."

"You, Flap?" Wesley chided, irrationally irritated. "And what good will you do?"

"Wesley . . ." His mother admonished. "That isn't kind."

"If the captain does end up losing an arm, well, I know a thing or two about that, don't I?" Keith said. "And I am not as likely to call him disparaging names as you are."

Wesley put his hands on his hips. "I've seen your nursemaid skills, don't forget, and they leave much to be desired."

"That's enough, Wes," his grandfather said. "I'll brook no disrespect for an officer, especially one who gave so much for his country."

Mr. Keith rose. "Thank you, Colonel. Perhaps you might advise me on the best route and supply a letter of introduction should I encounter any obstacles, and perhaps to present to the officer in charge?"

"Immediately."

"And of course we shall fund the journey, Lieutenant," Mr. Overtree said. "That goes without saying."

"Thank you, sir."

Wesley bit back the retort on his lips, *He*

wouldn't make it far otherwise — never goes anywhere on his own shilling. Wesley knew it would reflect poorly on him to disparage the man willing to go and help the injured war hero. Was he doing it to impress Angela? He'd noticed the two spending time together. Well, there was a woman Wesley would like to impress as well.

That night, Sophie lay in bed, unable to sleep, reviewing the events of the day. She thought again of hearing the letter read. How her heart had leapt to hear her portrait had been found in Stephen's hand! Even as she hated the thought of all he had suffered, and was suffering still, she thanked God for the confirmation that Captain Overtree was indeed alive. She was thrilled at the news. Drop-to-her-knees grateful. And a little confused.

She had begun to wonder if Wesley might be right — that God meant for them to be together. But now this. . . . She felt dizzy at this reversal of fate and feelings. Her battered heart sore but beating a little faster at the thought of Captain Overtree's return.

If he learned she'd briefly entertained the notion of a future with Wesley, would he think her unfaithful — in thought if not in deed? And what about Wesley's accusation that Stephen had married her out of revenge? If he had, would he ever truly love her? Whatever

507

the case, knowing he was alive changed everything. She hoped Wesley realized that as well.

Even so, Sophie had been touched and impressed when Wesley offered to go to Belgium. But she had seen the look Mr. Keith had given her. Did he fear Wesley would do more harm than good, perhaps even intentionally? She would never believe it of him. Whatever Mr. Keith's motives, however, she was glad he was going to the captain's aid. He had also agreed to carry a letter she'd written to the captain, and promised to deliver it in person.

Sophie lay awake so long, she grew hungry again. Her stomach rumbled its protest. She supposed she could call for Libby and ask her to bring her something, but she hated to wake the kind maid when she had probably just gone to bed. No use in both of them being up.

She rose and wrapped her dressing gown as far around her as it would go, the ties covering her belly if the sides did not. Taking her candle, she went all the way downstairs to the kitchen larder and cut herself a wedge of cheese and a slice of bread. She ate them right there at the worktable with as much relish as if in a Royal Crescent dining room.

On her way back through the hall, Sophie found herself looking up to see if she could spot the squint holes in the musicians' gallery. There it was — the plaster mask on the gallery wall, its jester face grinning down at her. Sophie gasped. The eyes were glowing! A shiver scurried over her like spider legs. The eyes flickered another second, then faded. Someone walking through the secret passage with a candle?

Miss Blake would not be there at this hour. Then who was it . . . Winnie?

Sophie wasn't sure. Was she brave enough to investigate? She would at least position herself near the priest hole and see who emerged.

Grateful for her candle, she climbed the stairs, passed her own room, and peered around the corner but saw no one in the alcove. She crept to the corridor's end, feeling self-conscious and guilty, as if the ancestors staring so somberly down at her knew what she was doing. She worried a servant would see her sneaking around and suspect her of a late-night liaison. Or worse, one of the family. She looked over her shoulder to assure herself she was alone, then approached the hidden door. Dare she?

Gingerly, she positioned her fingers behind the filigree and pulled open the panel as she had seen Miss Blake do. The priest hole was dark, except for the dim moonlight from that high small window. She slipped inside and closed the door behind herself, heart pounding. For a moment she stood there, listening.

Her candle cast flickering light and shadows around the small room — the single bed, tiny table, and cross on the wall. She waited but heard nothing save a faint whistle of wind.

She told herself to relax. She was doing nothing wrong. No one had forbidden her to explore the hidden passages. If a neighbor was welcome to do so, would a daughter-in-law be any less so? She hoped not.

With this justification, she stepped to the pivoted timber beam and pulled it up, feeling a little stitch in her back as she did so. She would have to be more careful. A soft whisper of air guttered the candle. She waited to make sure the flame would remain lit before squeezing into the passage and allowing the timber to close behind her. She walked forward, as Miss Blake had done, then turned left at the T. She found the first squint and looked out, but saw nothing unusual. She walked on.

She came to another intersection of passages she didn't recall encountering the first time. Then again, she had been focused on following Miss Blake and not on any side passages not chosen. Or had she taken a wrong turn already?

She found herself at the top of a narrow flight of stairs. She heard a sound, something sliding open or closed, wood upon wood. A rush of air blew out her candle. Sophie's heart lurched. She stared at the red ember of wick until it faded to black.

Scuff. Another sound in the distance. Sophie held her breath. *Scuff-scuff.* Footsteps. Someone was in the passage with her. The slow footsteps were coming in her direction. . . .

Suddenly a hand clamped over her mouth and a body pressed against her back. She opened her mouth to try to scream, but then she recognized the voice whispering in her ear. "Shh . . . Sophie, it's me."

Kate. In the stairwell behind her.

What was she doing there? And who was coming down the passage?

Sophie stilled, and Kate removed her hand. The footsteps came closer. From where they stood, tucked into a little recess at the top of the stairs, she saw no bobbing light. Was it someone who knew the way so well, he or she needed no light? Or had his candle blown out as well?

Would the person be able to pass without tripping over Sophie's protruding slippers and abdomen? She tilted her feet to one side and willed herself slim.

The shuffling footsteps passed by. Sophie could see nothing. The darkness was that complete. She sensed a moving figure. A shuffling gait. The faint smell of woodsmoke.

She and Kate waited where they were for a minute or two until the footsteps faded away. Sophie thought she heard the quiet click of

511

the timber falling back into place, but couldn't be certain.

"Who was that?" Sophie whispered.

"I don't know," Kate replied. "I couldn't see anything. My candle blew out."

"Mine too," Sophie said. "What are you doing here?"

"Looking for Gulliver. Winnie is worried about him, and I thought I heard him mewing through the wall. What about you?"

"Your friend Miss Blake showed me the priest hole and this passage."

"She's the one who showed me as well. I wondered if she'd been in here when I spied that cobweb in her hair. I asked Winnie, but she said Angela has not been up to her room in months."

"And Angela told me you were too scared to venture any farther than the priest hole."

"I'm not the frightened young girl she thinks me." Kate stepped beside her, her shoulder pressing into Sophie's. "Let's follow and see who it is."

Sophie wasn't sure she was brave enough to pursue the shadowy figure, but she'd rather stay with Kate than stand there in the dark alone. "Right behind you."

She stayed so close to Kate that she stepped on the back of her heel. "Sorry," she murmured.

Then Sophie asked, "Where did you come from? Where do those stairs lead?"

"The kitchen. Shh . . ."

As they passed behind the family bed-chambers, the sound of muffled voices reached them. They paused to listen.

"Steal me blind, will you? I shall have my revenge."

A second voice replied, too quiet to make out.

The first voice added, "I warned you the last time not to take any more from me."

"That's Grandfather . . ." Kate breathed, surprise and concern in her voice. "But who is he talking to? I can't make out the second voice."

"I'm not sure," Sophie whispered. "What are they talking about?"

"I don't know, but it doesn't sound good."

Kate eased open the timber, slipped out easily, and held it for Sophie. She wriggled out, stumbling as she did so, and her shoes scraped the floor.

"Shh," Kate warned, then inched open the hidden priest hole door. From the corridor came the sound of rapidly retreating footsteps. "Uh oh," she whispered. "Do you think they heard us coming?"

"Probably, if we heard them."

Kate led the way to the colonel's door, still ajar. She knocked once, and opened the door wider. "Grandfather?"

Behind her, Sophie could only glimpse the top of his head over Kate's shoulder.

"Hello, Kate. What a surprise. What are you doing up this late?"

"I was worried about you. I . . . heard voices. And footsteps leaving your room."

"Did you? That's strange. One of the house-maids, I'd wager. Or perhaps I was talking to myself again."

"Are you all right?"

"Of course. Why wouldn't I be?"

"The conversation sounded . . . strange. Threatening."

"Threatening? No," he chuckled. "No one's threatening anyone, Kate. Just a little good-natured teasing. You know how I like to tease."

"Yes . . . Well, if you're sure you're all right."

"Perfectly sure. Good night, Kate."

"Good night." She shut the door.

Sophie whispered, "Did you see anything?"

"Not much. He was sitting alone at his tea table. I thought I saw him hide something in his lap, but I can't be sure." Kate looked up at Sophie with wide eyes. "Do you think someone is extorting money from him?"

"I doubt it. He didn't seem upset," Sophie pointed out, another theory forming in her mind.

Kate countered, "Maybe he just didn't want me to know."

"Well, let's leave it for now," Sophie said. "It's late. And he's a grown man — and a colonel in the bargain. I'm sure he can take care of himself."

"You're probably right." But Kate didn't look convinced.

The next afternoon, the family relaxed together in the white parlour. The colonel had gone out riding and Wesley to check on a tenant, for which Sophie was privately relieved. As the women knitted and Mr. Overtree perused the newspaper, Thurman appeared and announced Mr. Harrison's arrival.

Kate brightened immediately, and Sophie set aside her knitting, grateful for the reprieve.

The young man entered the room and bowed in greeting.

"Mr. Harrison," Mrs. Overtree acknowledged stiffly. "What a surprise."

"A pleasant surprise," Kate added with a smile.

"I had an appointment with Mr. Overtree," Mr. Harrison began. "To talk about his family history, but —"

Mr. Overtree rose. "Ah yes, for your history of the county. With all the excitement, I nearly forgot."

"I don't wish to disturb you, sir. I know you are celebrating the wonderful news about Captain Overtree." The young man held out a glass jug of ruby liquid. "My mother sends her good wishes and famed cherry cordial."

"How lovely," Kate murmured, meeting his gaze.

When Mrs. Overtree said nothing, her husband stepped forward, accepted the jug, and examined it approvingly. "Very much appreciated. Thank you, and thank your mother for us. Now, let's go into my study."

Mrs. Overtree frowned. "Is this really a good time, my dear? Perhaps later, when you are better rested?"

"Don't worry. I feel perfectly well. I have been looking forward to this interview. Our family has played an important role in the county's history, and it should be made known." He lifted the bottle with a twinkle in his eye. "And Mrs. Nelson's cordial should be enjoyed." He gestured for the young man to precede him from the room.

As the men left, Sophie dutifully reached for her half-finished baby bonnet. Noticing Kate stare after Mr. Harrison with soft eyes, Sophie hid a smile.

Later that night, Sophie lay in bed in nightgown and shawl, reading. She intended to stay awake until eleven, suspecting *someone* might pay another clandestine visit to Colonel Horton's room, since she and Kate had interrupted them the night before.

But suddenly she jerked awake, and realized she had fallen asleep. She hoped she wouldn't be too late. Quickly climbing from bed, she wriggled into slippers and stole into the corridor. She tiptoed around the corner to the colonel's room. Sure enough the door was ajar again, and she heard voices.

"Tomorrow night," the colonel said. "Remember. Can't let Janet find out."

"Janet? What about the vicar?" a female voice replied.

"He took a pony from me last week. He won't say a word. Our secret is safe."

"Very well. Good night."

Too late to hear more, Sophie pressed herself to the wall as the door opened. Sure enough, Winnie emerged, dressed in her usual blue frock and white collar, and quietly closed the door behind her.

She and the colonel were of an age, Sophie supposed. But it was still somewhat shocking. No wonder he'd said he didn't want his daughter to find out.

Sophie was almost certain Winnie would not extort money from the colonel, but she wanted to make sure she was not somehow taking advantage of the lonely widower, or preying on his sympathies.

"Hello, Winnie."

The nurse started. "Miss Sophie! What are you doing up and about this time of night?"

"Couldn't sleep. You?"

"Oh, em. I sometimes walk through the house at night. Take a bit of exercise, go past each of the children's rooms to make sure everyone is settled. Old habits from the past, I suppose."

"And do you check on the colonel as well?" Sophie asked, surprised at her boldness but feeling oddly protective of the old gentleman. He was her grandfather by marriage, after all, and she was fond of him.

"The colonel?" Winnie glanced toward the door she had exited as though just noticing it there. "Oh. Well. Sometimes. He is part of the family as well."

Sophie narrowed her eyes. "Winnie, what are you up to?"

The elderly woman looked at her in surprise, silvery brows raised high. "Up to? Nothing diabolical, I assure you."

"Then why sneak around? And what doesn't he want *Janet* to find out?"

The nurse winced. "Heard that, did you? I told him we ought to shut the door all the way, but he insists on leaving it ajar for propriety's sake. Worried about my reputation — at my age! But yes, he would prefer his daughter didn't know of our late-night . . . conversations. You won't tell, will you, my girl? I've kept your secret after all."

Which secret? Sophie thought but didn't voice the question. Remembering Stephen's assessment of the woman's foresight and seeing her knowing look, Sophie didn't doubt for a moment that Miss Whitney knew every last one of her secrets.

"And I appreciate it, Winnie. But Kate is suspicious too. I can't guarantee she won't say something, in hopes of protecting her grandfather."

"Protecting her grandfather?" Winnie hooted. "It will take more than a mere slip of girl to protect the colonel from me!" She grinned like a mischievous girl herself.

And with that unexpected pronouncement, Winnie turned and climbed the attic stairs, giggling as she went. And at that moment, Sophie thought she understood why uncharitable people sometimes questioned the woman's mental state.

CHAPTER 29

Stephen lay on a cot in the makeshift military hospital. He was exhausted, but the throbbing pain in his left shoulder made it difficult to sleep. He picked up the miniature portrait from the floor beside him and looked at it again. He had received a few letters from Sophie the day before, though they were several weeks old, written before battle but delayed in reaching him in Brussels. Her sweet, warm words filled him with hope for the future. Concerned as he was about his arm, Stephen was thankful to be alive.

He again remembered coming to his senses and finding himself half-buried by mud and a dead horse. Rain pummeled down like saber slashes, rousing him from his stupor. The hint of sunlight rising in the grey sky told him it was a new day. The quiet around him was unexpected, telling him the troops had moved on without him. Left him for dead. He seemed to remember a French cavalry horse rearing, hooves flying, and a stunning blow to the head. The dried gash and a large lump on his temple confirmed that memory. His head had stopped bleeding, but his right hand and left shoulder spurted blood with every move as he tried to push away the horse or wrench himself free. He wasn't going anywhere on his own strength. He prayed that someone would find him.

Soon footsteps and French voices approached. He'd been found all right. Perhaps he should have been more specific in his prayers.

He hadn't the strength to put up a fight, or he'd probably be dead. His French captors levered up the carcass and pulled him free. They taunted him and delivered a few jabs for sport but seemed to lose interest when he didn't resist. He knew enough French to understand some of what they said. *Don't bother. He's almost dead anyway.* He certainly felt that way.

He was thrown into a barn with another prisoner, who was in even worse condition than he was and died soon after capture. With a prayer for forgiveness, Stephen ripped strips of cloth from the man's shirt. He bound his hand and shoulders as best he could, which was not good at all, not to mention blindingly painful.

A few days later, his French captors forced him to march with them to another position, tying him to a tree at sunset while they built a fire and prepared a meager supper that they didn't share with him. Eventually their guard slackened, and Stephen was able to loosen his binds and slip free.

Trying to crawl with his bloodied, mangled arms was excruciating, so he struggled painfully to his feet and limped slowly down the road. Dizzy and disoriented, he would have given his inheritance for a glass of cool water. He didn't know how many miles he'd walked before collapsing in exhaustion.

He'd awoken in this hospital a week or so ago, with no memory of the surgeons working on him. And that he supposed was the greatest blessing of all. He'd heard too many screams from surgery tents after past battles to underestimate the horror and pain he'd been spared.

As he lay in his cot thinking back, the corporal who'd helped him write the letter to his family soon after he awoke came by with another small bundle of delayed mail. Letters had started finding him through military channels now that his whereabouts were known. Prayers from his parents, advice from the colonel, love from Kate, and . . . a letter from Wesley. With a frown, he unsealed it and noted the date. This letter had also been written weeks ago, before the family would have received the false report of his death.

Marsh,

I am back at Overtree Hall. I returned as soon as I could. I realized I was wrong to leave Miss Dupont, but did you give me time to correct my mistake? No. You swept in and took charge, as you always do. And to blazes with me, and with Sophie or her feelings. She loves me, you know. She has for a long time and still does. And I love her — even if I was slow to realize it. I also know the child she carries is mine. How could you do it? How could you pressure her into a rushed marriage without even trying to contact me first? To ask how I felt about her and give me a chance to do the right thing?

Did you give her reason to doubt me? Tell her I wouldn't marry her — convince her she had no other choice? I imagine you did, considering your resentment towards me. Whatever the case, you have ruined not only my life, but hers and our child's, too. She, of course, does not wish to betray you. Especially now that you are in harm's way, serving our country. And so she will be a martyr, and sacrifice her happiness for yours. To save face and the Overtree name.

Is this your revenge, Marsh? I "stole" a woman from you once and so now you are paying me back? Perhaps it is what I deserve, but Sophie doesn't deserve any of it. She deserves better than being a pawn *between us. Our child as well.*

But I will think of something. I will make it right.

W.D.O.

Doubts swamped Stephen. There was just enough truth in Wesley's letter to stab him with guilt and send him into a spiral of second-guessing. *Had* he acted in error? Acted selfishly? Hastily? He could honestly say he had not married Sophie out of revenge, but he had cast doubt on Wesley's character — given her reason to believe his brother would not return for months and would probably not marry her if he did. And he'd been wrong. Had he married her in vain? But even if he had, what could he do about it now? Marriage was sacred and divorce nigh unto impossible even if he could countenance the thought. What was Wesley suggesting he do to rectify the situation now — die? He would not oblige him.

Unless . . . Did Sophie wish the same — that he had died in battle? Had she been secretly disappointed to learn he was alive?

He pulled out her miniature portrait and looked at it again. Stephen had begun to think Sophie might — or might someday — return his love. But now? If what Wesley wrote was true?

He unfolded one of Sophie's letters and reread the sweet words. Had she written it *before* Wesley returned proclaiming he loved her and had always meant to come back for her? It seemed likely, as she made no mention of him in her letter. Unless she had another reason for failing to mention Wesley's return? Stephen had known his brother would show up at Overtree Hall eventually. But he'd truly not thought Wes intended to marry Sophie. If his brother was simply angry, Stephen could deal with that. He was used to disagreements and discord with him. But if Sophie agreed with his brother? Regretted their marriage? Stephen was not able to brush off such doubts as easily. He felt a sickly stab of self-pity and pushed it away. No doubt blood loss or laudanum was to blame for the foreign emotion.

Did Sophie wish there was some way to be released from their marriage? If she did, could he really blame her? Especially if he ended up losing an arm. Especially now that the father of her child was on the scene, declaring his love.

Stephen thought of sending a letter to Sophie — asking her outright if she preferred to be with his brother. But he was not yet able to write, and unwilling to dictate such a personal, mortifying question to another soul.

Several days after Mr. Keith left Overtree Hall for Belgium, Sophie looked through the letters on the silver tray. She sighed. Still no letter for her from Stephen. She prayed again for his recovery and for a safe journey for Mr. Keith.

With nothing else to distract her, Sophie found herself thinking about the initials she'd seen in the priest hole. That evening, she asked Kate, "Who is J.A.B.?"

"J.A.B.?"

"Yes. I saw those initials carved on a timber in the priest hole," she said, then added to herself, *and J.B. on a note in Wesley's room.*

Kate leaned forward with interest. "Really? I never noticed that." She considered a moment, then shrugged. "I suppose it must be Angela. She was christened Jane Angela Blake. But as Jane was her mother's name as well, she has always gone by Angela."

"Oh . . ." Then J was not "Jenny," Sophie realized.

"Personally, I've never understood why so many women name their daughters after themselves," Kate went on. "I am glad Mamma didn't name me Janet. How confusing that would be. But why do you ask?"

"Just curious."

Kate looked at Sophie with a sly twinkle in her eyes. "Show me the carving."

Sophie hesitated. "I don't know, Kate. It's late . . ."

Kate laughed and grabbed Sophie's hand. "Oh, come on!"

Taking a candle with them, they climbed

the stairs and crept down the corridor. Kate opened the hidden door in the wainscoting and ducked in first. Sophie followed, pulling the door shut behind them.

Kate lifted the candle higher and light swept across the narrow room.

"There . . ." Sophie pointed to the timber with the initials *W.D.O. + J.A.B.*

Kate stepped closer, then paused as a squeak pierced the quiet. Sophie cringed, her gaze darting to the farthest corner of the room. A mouse?

Tentatively, Kate stretched the candle toward the dark corner, and Sophie gasped. A creature huddled there — one much larger than a mouse. They heard another squeak, and then a rumbling sound like . . . purring.

"Gulliver?" Sophie asked in wonder.

The orange tabby lay in a nest of wood shavings, with squirming bundles of fur gathered around him — her, Sophie corrected herself. She counted, then shared a wide-eyed smile with Kate. "Six kittens. Gulliver must have moved them here since we were last inside."

"Oh, wait until Winnie finds out!" Kate cried. Kneeling, she set down the candle and extended her hand to Gulliver, letting her sniff it before smoothing the cat's head. "You've been a busy b . . . em, girl."

"Perhaps we should take them to Winnie's room," Sophie said.

"Right. We don't want Mamma to hear them."

"We'll need something to carry them . . . like a basket."

"Maybe a picnic basket?" Kate rose. "I'm sure I can sneak one past Mrs. John."

Sophie nodded. "You get the basket. I'll find Winnie."

"Won't she be in her room?"

"Maybe not . . ." But Sophie had a good idea where the woman would be.

Kate hurried off to retrieve a basket and Sophie started down the corridor. As she'd anticipated, she heard voices coming from the colonel's room, the door once again left ajar. But now she recognized both voices.

"Don't say I didn't warn you."

"You've nicked me, woman. Sink me, not again."

She tiptoed to the colonel's door and peeked inside the room, well lit by candelabra.

There sat Colonel Horton and Winnie at a small table covered in green felt, a glass of something at each elbow, a bowl of nutmeats between them, and a pile of sweets in the middle.

"Enough with these childish stakes. Let's play for real money."

"But what would Janet say?" Winnie gave him an impish smile.

He lifted a jar full of coins. "What she

doesn't know won't hurt her."

"I'll take all your money, just as I took all the sweets, and all the buttons."

"It's a risk I'm willing to take." The colonel grinned, maniacally wagging his eyebrows. He shook a pair of dice in his meaty hand, and sent them tumbling to the felt.

"Not again. I've thrown out."

Sophie pushed open the door. "Good evening, Colonel. Winnie."

The colonel sucked in a breath, and slapped his hand over the dice like a child trying to cover stolen biscuits.

But Winnie met her gaze evenly. "Evening, Miss Sophie. Don't worry, Colonel. Sophie is kind and won't go reporting us to the mistress — will you, my dear?"

"No, but you've got something else to hide from the mistress now. I was coming to find you. Gulliver is a female. She's had kittens!"

Winnie's mouth fell ajar.

The colonel whistled. "Don't let Janet find out."

"I thought he was getting fat!" Winnie exclaimed. "So that's why he — I mean, she — was hiding. Where are they?"

"Kate is fetching a basket to carry them up to your room."

Winnie rose to go, but Sophie held up a hand. "Wait! First things first. What exactly is going on here? Kate thinks someone is extorting money from her grandfather."

"Does she? Ha! That's a laugh," Winnie replied. "The other way around more like."

"You have the memory of a flea, woman," the colonel protested. "You're the one who took all the sweets and buttons and now are working away at my farthings."

"Farthings?" Sophie asked in concern.

He gestured toward the jar of coins. "Yes. Highfliers we are too. You see, my dear," the colonel said, "Miss Whitney and I sit together of an evening to pass the time, and play a little hazard. We're both of us a couple of lonely old souls, and it eases the ache." He grinned at the nurse. "Your visits are the bright spot of my day, Winnie. I don't think my dear Margaret would mind my saying that, now she's gone, but Janet would not approve."

Winnie shook her head and looked at Sophie. "No indeed. And if she knew I was spending time with her father, I'd be out on my ear in a heartbeat, loyal Stephen or no."

"But I ask you, what's an innocent game between friends?" the colonel said as though to a jury. "We only play for trifles. But I promised Janet that I wouldn't gamble anymore. Lost a bit in London, you see, in my younger days. And I wouldn't want her to think I'm slipping back."

"We return all the farthings into the same jar and use them again the next time," Winnie added helpfully. "Surely there's no harm in that."

"You didn't return the sweets," the colonel pointed out.

"Stephen gave those to me, and I won those back fair and square." Winnie returned her gaze to Sophie and gestured across the room. "Now, let's go meet the newest additions to my little menagerie."

Sophie grinned in relief and held the door for her. "You should have heard how it sounded. All this clandestine talk about stealing you blind, and having your revenge, and the vicar taking your pony."

"Oh, that last part about the vicar is true." Winnie winked. "But you didn't hear it from me."

Stephen was never more stunned than to look up and see Carlton Keith leaning his shoulder against the doorframe, ankles crossed at a jaunty angle, smug look on his face.

"Hello, Captain."

"Do my eyes deceive me or have I died and gone to blazes?" Stephen jested. "For I should never believe you an angel."

Keith grinned, then glanced around the shabby ward. "I would definitely not call this place heaven." He made a face. "That's why I'm here. To do everything in my power to get you home as soon as may be."

Relief flared and instantly faded. Except for

531

Wesley, his family would be eager to see him. But Sophie? He wasn't so sure.

"I am in no condition to travel, Keith. Nor will I be for some time. And when I am, I shall return to the regiment."

His former lieutenant studied his face. Surprise followed by understanding shone in his eyes. "Time to decide all that later, Captain. For now, I've brought you a few letters from home."

He pulled three from his pocket and handed them over. Stephen recognized his mother's handwriting, the colonel's, and Sophie's.

"Well," Keith straightened. "I'll leave you to read in private. Think I'll go and see who I have to bribe to get something to eat."

When he had left, Stephen opened Sophie's letter first, steeling himself as he read it.

Dear Captain Overtree,

How relieved we all were to learn you are alive. You cannot know how we worried and prayed and grieved during those dark days when you were missing and presumed dead. Mr. Nelson offered prayers of thanksgiving in church yesterday, and we all continue to pray for your recovery.

I hope Carlton Keith arrived safely and without delay. We were all so grateful that he offered to travel to Brussels to see that everything is being done for you that may be. And if it is possible to bring you home, so that we might nurse you here at Over-tree Hall under the care and direction of Dr. Matthews. Several in your family vied for the honor of coming to your bedside — myself among them, your grandfather most vocal of all — but various factors, such as your grandfather's age and my condition, caused us to be overruled.

You have probably heard by now that Wesley is here. You should know that he volunteered for the duty as well, saying it would only be right as you have so often come to his aid. But in the end, Mr. Keith made an impassioned argument that he should be the one to undertake the journey.

I feel I should say what I hope goes without saying. While we all pray that you will heal whole and strong and maintain the use of both arms, if God wills otherwise, we will accept that and welcome you home with our open arms. Here at Overtree Hall, there are arms enough to go round. Do come home, Captain. We long to see you.

> *Sincerely,*
> *Sophie*

We long to see you. . . . He thought again of Wesley's letter, describing Sophie's martyr-like determination to continue the ruse of their marriage. Was she really thankful he was alive? Did she truly want him to come home?

Stephen wanted to believe her encouraging words, but his brother's letter and his accusations continued to plague him with doubts. Would Sophie remain loyal to him for duty's sake, for the family's sake, and maybe even for God's, all while her heart longed to be with Wesley? His gut clenched at the thought.

If he fully recovered, perhaps he might apply to his superiors to be assigned guard duty on St. Helena to make sure Napoleon's second exile was his last. Such an assignment would keep him across the world for years, if not forever. And who knew? Perhaps he would die on the journey, and Winnie's prediction would come true after all. He winced at the melodramatic thought. What a sapskull he was. He really needed to wean himself off that laudanum, and the sooner the better.

CHAPTER 30

Sophie now shared her studio with a cat and six kittens. Though Kate had originally delivered the litter to Miss Whitney's room, for some reason Gulliver wasn't satisfied, and arduously carried each kitten one by one by the scruff of its neck to the room next door. Giving in, Winnie had relocated a low basket filled with soft bedding to the studio. She — as well as Kate and Miss Blake — visited often. Wesley, in turn, seemed to avoid them all.

A few days later, Sophie sat knitting in the white parlour when Wesley came in. Finding her alone, he crossed the room and sat beside her on the sofa.

Instantly uneasy, she said, "I'm sorry — Kate is sitting there. She has only gone to check on the kittens, but she'll be back directly." She glanced toward the door, then added softly, "Please don't say anything about the cats. Your mother doesn't know yet." She managed a smile, but he did not return the gesture.

He rose. "Then come with me to the church, and see my progress on the painting over the chancel archway."

She said, "I do want to see it — I'm sure it's wonderful. But I will wait and see it on Sunday with everyone else."

He crossed his arms. "You can't keep ignoring me."

"I am not ignoring you. I am simply treating you as a sister-in-law should."

"Like a leper, I think you mean." He picked up the twin to the little bootie she was knitting, and fingered the soft wool. He whispered hoarsely, "I am more than your brother-in-law, and you know it."

How small the tiny stocking looked in his long fingers. How heartbreaking.

The butler entered and announced, "A Mr. O'Dell to see you, madam."

Sophie's stomach lurched, and dread swamped her.

A moment later, her father's assistant stepped into the room, looking dapper in a new suit of clothes, his hair for once well groomed.

"Maurice! What are you doing here? Is my father all right? The children?"

"Yes, everyone is perfect well, if still reeling from recent, unexpected events." His gaze landed on Wesley, and his head reared back. "Mr. Wesley Overtree . . . What a surprise to

536

see you here, sir."

"And why should it be a surprise?" Wesley said coolly. "This is my home after all."

"Yes, but we thought you were in Italy. Didn't we, Sophie?"

"He returned. Earlier than expected."

"Ah! How . . . awkward for all of you."

"Not at all," Sophie said with a frosty smile.

"One big happy family, are you? Isn't that nice. So . . . where is your bridegroom? Oh, that's right. Off to war, while you two are snug here at home. How convenient."

"Not convenient at all," Sophie replied. "Captain Overtree has been injured. We pray for his full recovery daily."

Maurice *tsk*ed. "War is such risky business. I see now why you took your chances." He looked around the room and then smiled at her. "Well, are you going to invite me to sit down? Offer me tea? I don't exaggerate when I say I could drink a whole pot. Warm and dusty on the roads today."

"Of course." Embarrassed at her lack of tact, and his, Sophie avoided Wesley's gaze and rang the bell.

While they waited for tea, Kate and Mrs. Overtree came in, and Sophie's anxiety increased. She made the introductions with all the civility she could muster, but with no pleasure.

"How do you do, Mr. O'Dell," Mrs. Overtree said. "Any relations of Mrs. Overtree are welcome."

Sophie considered denying the family tie, but deemed it wisest not to comment. Maurice, however, did.

"Oh, we are not so closely related, ma'am. Not as closely related as I once thought we'd be. Thanks to your son, there."

Sophie felt her face heat. Heaven help her — Maurice *had* read Wesley's letter. Would he reveal all to her mother-in-law?

Mrs. Overtree narrowed her eyes. "You must refer to my other son, Captain Stephen Overtree?"

"Ah yes. The one she married."

"To what do we owe the pleasure of your call, Mr. O'Dell?" Mrs. Overtree regarded him coolly.

"Mr. Dupont and my aunt regret that they have not yet been able to visit Sophie, so I volunteered to do so in their stead. I was passing through the area, en route to fulfill a commission for Sir Cedric Fiennes. Perhaps you've heard of him? So generous. Even sent his fine traveling chariot to transport me in style."

"Why is Father not with you?" Sophie asked.

"Oh, I thought I could manage this commission myself."

Wesley sent her a knowing look.

Tea was delivered and Sophie began to pour, but her hand trembled. Noticing, Kate deftly took over the task, and Sophie's heart expanded with a little more love for the girl.

Maurice glanced around at the few paintings on the parlour walls. "I must say I am surprised not to see any of your work on display, Mr. Overtree. I know you spent a prolific season among us this winter."

"Oh? I have not yet seen his recent paintings." Mrs. Overtree daggered a look at her son.

"You would find them interesting, I think," Maurice said. "I suppose your son is naturally modest about showing his work?"

"Not usually, no."

"Ah, well. Perhaps the subject itself is modest. The Devonshire coast is a fertile area for artists. You will have to take a look at them one of these days."

"Indeed I shall."

Maurice returned his gaze to Sophie — that gaze that always had a way of making her uncomfortable, and all the more now. "You are in . . . robust health, I see, Sophie. Being with child becomes you. Everything is . . . progressing well, I trust?"

Sophie swallowed. "Yes. Thank you for asking. We hope Captain Overtree will return in time for the birth."

"Do we?"

"Yes."

For a moment longer he held her gaze, and Sophie feared he would continue on with his innuendo, or simply announce what he knew, or at least suspected. But instead he smiled and turned to Kate.

"Miss Overtree. A pleasure to make your acquaintance. And are you a budding artist, like your brother? I do hope he has painted your portrait. If he hasn't, I would be honored to do so."

"He has," Kate replied. "Though Sophie has painted another more recently. It's lovely . . ."

Sophie relaxed fractionally when Maurice turned his attention to Kate, but Wesley, she noticed, seemed to grow increasingly tense.

When Maurice finally took his leave, Sophie made her escape. But not before she heard Mrs. Overtree hiss to her son, "What was that young man going on about?"

Sophie didn't wait to hear Wesley's reply. She hurried upstairs, all the way up to the studio. Her sanctuary. There, she was drawn to the basket in the corner, where the kittens suckled, their little paws kneading their mother's belly, while Gulliver lay, languid and content. One little kitten popped off, asleep, and Sophie bent and picked it up. It was her favorite among them — tiny and grey with an unusual marking — a white patch that spotted its nose like cream. Cuddling it close, Sophie absorbed from the warm, soft body what comfort she could. God willing, she would soon hold her own child in similar fashion. What comfort that would be. What sweet consolation after all the strife surrounding the babe's existence and pending arrival. Sophie stroked the soft fur and prayed for her little one. What sort of childhood would he or she have? *Dear God, watch over us. Please protect my child. . . .*

Wesley'd had to control himself not to rebuke O'Dell and tell him to stop staring at his sister. Stop flirting with her too. For a moment he'd heard his own voice in the young man's flattery, and the realization sent a chill through him.

When O'Dell finally departed and Sophie left the room, his mother hissed, "What was that young man going on about?"

"Don't mind him, Mamma. He is a jackanapes. Sophie rejected him long ago and he is still bitter." *And vengeful,* he added to himself.

Her cool gaze met his. "I think it is time you showed me those paintings."

Wesley forestalled his mother yet again, and went upstairs to find Sophie. Things were getting out of hand. If O'Dell knew about him and Sophie, wasn't it only a matter of time until her father found out? And Wesley's recent paintings would certainly raise suspicions among his own family.

A surge of desperation flared through Wesley. Now that Keith had gone to see if he could bring Marsh home, this might very well be his last chance. He was running out of time to make Sophie see reason.

How could he convince her to realize and admit the truth: He loved her. Marsh did not.

Wesley let himself into the attic studio and found her staring out the window, cradling one of the kittens. She turned when he entered, mouth open in surprise.

Before she could object he said, "Sophie, listen to me. If I thought he loved you, if I thought there was a chance of happiness for the two of you, then of course I would never suggest you leave the man everyone sees as your husband. But he cares more for his regiment than he does for you. And when he recovers, he will go off with them for months — years — at a time. What sort of life would that be for you or our child? But I love you. And you love me. Don't deny yourself happiness because of my mistakes and Marsh's rash offer of marriage."

She gave him a dour look. "And my rash acceptance?"

"No. I don't blame *you*. Marsh made you doubt me — made you think you had no other choice. I wrote to him and told him how I felt. Told him that we love each another. And that you should not have to carry on this ruse of a marriage out of duty, or to protect the Overtree name."

She stilled, staring at him. "You shouldn't

542

have done that."

"Why not? He was wrong, and it isn't right you and I should have to suffer for it."

Sophie stepped away and returned the kitten to its mother, probably giving herself time to fashion a rebuttal.

Before she could, Wesley went on, "We could leave separately. You could say you are returning to your own family. And I . . . on one of my painting trips. Then we can meet and decide what to do next. Find a place to live here in England until the child comes and it is safe to travel. Or if you feel up to it, go somewhere now. To Italy, perhaps. Somewhere we might annul this ruse, and marry before the baby is born. We can still be happy. Live as husband and wife. Parents to our child. As it was meant to be. As it still *can* be."

She shook her head. "I am already married. I have a husband. His name is Captain Stephen Overtree. And I shall not betray him."

"But he is your husband in name only," Wesley insisted. "The marriage has never even been consummated."

She gaped at him, clearly stunned. "How do you know that?"

Triumph washed over him. "I was told about your sleeping arrangements, and guessed the rest. Non-consummation may not be grounds for annulment in England, but in another country . . ."

She frowned. "What sort of woman do you take me for? The captain is severely injured. And this is the news you would have await him when he returns? That his wife has run off with his brother?"

"We needn't tell anyone our plan, if you prefer to keep it quiet. For a time, at least."

"And you would never see your family again? Or lie to them for the rest of your days? And what about me? Am I to live as a kept woman in some isolated cottage somewhere, spurned by moral society, living for the few days a month you can get away to visit us? Never to see your parents or mine? You think a great deal too much of yourself, Wesley Overtree. That I would give up my family and yours and every last ounce of self-respect simply to be with you."

"Sophie . . ." He was taken aback. She had never spoken so forcefully before. "What a vile picture you paint. It won't be like that. We will have a loving home somewhere scenic with new landscapes to paint every day. Our precious, perfect child will grow up with a father and mother who love him or her. We can travel together. Paint together. Raise our son or daughter to love beauty and art."

She raised her hands. "You are heir to Overtree Hall. Do you forget it? How long would you stay with me? Would you give up all of this for some little cottage far from here?"

"Yes, I would."

She shook her head. "No."

"But you love me. I know you do."

"I did love you, Wesley. But that has changed. Everything has changed."

Wesley bridged the gap between them and grasped her shoulders. "But I love you. I need you."

His arms looped around her back, pulling her as close as her rounded middle allowed. He tried to kiss her mouth, but she turned her head and pushed at his chest.

"Wesley, don't. It isn't right."

He kept his arms around her, trailing his lips over her cheek. "Yes, it is. It will be."

"Good heavens. What is going on here?"

Sophie gasped and turned her head toward the door. *No.* The Overtrees had followed their son upstairs.

Mrs. Overtree stood there, her husband right behind her. "Let her go, Wesley."

Sophie's chest tightened, and she found herself suddenly dizzy. Wesley released her but remained close to her side.

Mr. Overtree's face slackened in incredulity. "Stephen is lying injured in a military hospital and you betray him like this?"

"I feared something like this would happen." Mrs. Overtree's cold eyes fastened on her.

"I did not betray him," Sophie protested.

Mrs. Overtree's mouth twisted. "No? What

do you call it?"

"This isn't what you think, Mamma."

"Dashed stupid, Wesley." His father scowled. "Could you not leave her alone?"

Wesley sighed. "Capital. Mamma blames Sophie. Papa blames me, and Stephen is the poor victim, when nothing could be further from the truth."

"Are you telling me nothing happened between you? When I find her in your arms. And you kissing her?"

"Nothing has happened. Not since she married Stephen. But we knew each other in Lynmouth. . . ."

Sophie pleaded, "Wesley, don't."

Mrs. Overtree whipped open the door with a bang. "It's time you showed us what's in that crate, Wesley. I'm through taking no for an answer. That O'Dell fellow was hinting at something unsavory, and it's time to have it over and done."

Mr. Overtree frowned. "What are you talking about?"

Wesley's jaw clenched. "You want to see those paintings, Mamma? Very well." He snagged Sophie's hand and pulled her along behind him. "Follow me. All of you."

"Wesley, no . . ." Sophie moaned.

"It's time for the truth to come out." He led her down the stairs and along the corridor to his rooms.

Behind them, his father called, "Wesley,

release Sophie. Be gentle with her!"

"I am not hurting her."

"Yes. You. Are," she panted out.

Wesley threw back the door to his studio, gestured them all inside, and closed the door behind him — perhaps afraid Sophie might flee the room. She was certainly tempted to do just that.

She saw the crate in the corner and dread mounted.

He pointed to it. "Read the delivery direction, Papa."

His father bent and squinted at it. " 'Mr. Wesley Overtree, Overtree Hall, Wickbury, Gloucestershire.' So?"

"And where it came from?"

"Lynmouth, Devonshire."

"This is the crate of paintings Stephen had delivered home from Devon for me. My paintings from the winter, weeks before he ever set foot in the county. I met Sophie long before he did," Wesley said. "He should never have married her."

"Is that what this is about — jealousy?" his father scoffed. "You're trying to prove you set your sights on her first?"

In reply, Wesley picked up a crowbar lying nearby — as though he'd been waiting for just the right time to reveal its contents.

With a creak and a groan and a splinter, he pried up the lid and laid it aside. He pawed out the paper wrapping and began pulling forth one canvas after another and lining them up along the walls.

Sophie's stomach wrenched, and she feared she would be ill. Her body flushed and perspired, and she could look at no one, her mortified gaze flicking from one portrait to the next and recognizing herself in more than she remembered posing for. From demure, reluctant poses, to private smiles and admiring glances, to the Grecian robes he'd insisted she don, and then slipped from one shoulder . . .

"I think we've seen enough," Mr. Overtree pronounced, his voice as dry as crushed November leaves, his expression as withering. "You said you knew Sophie from Lynmouth, but I didn't think you meant you'd known her . . . like this."

Sophie's face burned, and she ducked her head.

"I'm sorry, Sophie. I don't do this to embarrass you," Wesley said gently. "But yes. I knew Sophie first. I met her last year and spent more time with her this winter, before I left for Italy. We . . . fell in love. Don't look at her like that, Mamma. She was an innocent, proper young lady until I came along, I assure you."

"And the child . . . ?" his mother asked.

"Is mine, yes," Wesley replied.

"What?" his father's face contorted in disbelief.

"I didn't know she was with child. I left for Italy, and when Stephen came looking for me, he met Sophie and took advantage of the situation. He didn't even try to find me!"

Mrs. Overtree turned to her. "Why didn't you tell Wesley you were carrying his child?"

"He left before I gathered my courage to do so. I thought he might ask. Guess."

"Foolish girl."

"I left without warning, and she had no idea how long I would be gone," Wesley defended her. "She felt desperate and believed Stephen's assessment of my character — that I would not return, and could not be counted on to do the right thing even if I did. He fed her fears."

Mr. Overtree looked at his son in bleak disillusionment. "How could you, Wesley? How could you leave a girl whose youth and innocence you had seduced, with no help, ignorant of your address? You did what no gentleman of feeling would do."

"I did write. But that snake, O'Dell, hid the letter. But even if he had not, it would have reached her after she had already eloped with Stephen. For he lost no time in marrying her himself."

Mr. Overtree shook his head in disgust. "This is the *noble* character of the son I raised."

"Do not blame him alone, Mr. Overtree," his wife said. "I don't say Wesley is innocent, but what was he to think when a young woman spends time alone with him, posing *en dishabille*? Painters' models are known to be loose women."

"I was not a model," Sophie insisted.

Mrs. Overtree flicked a hand toward the canvas. "Evidence to the contrary."

"Only for Wesley."

Mrs. Overtree glowered at her. "Is it not enough that you slept with one of my sons? But then to prey on the sympathies of the other?"

"It wasn't like that!" Sophie cried. Her throat constricted, trapping the explanation inside: *"He offered to marry me. Insisted. Said it was his duty and his destiny . . ."* Instead, all that emerged from her mortified body were tears.

Mr. Overtree sighed. "Poor Stephen."

"Poor Stephen?" Wesley exclaimed. "What about me? What about Sophie?"

Mrs. Overtree gestured toward the bare-shoulder portrait. "She made her bed. Her choices."

"Did Stephen know you were with child when he married you?" Mr. Overtree asked.

"Yes."

"Did he know whose child you were carrying?"

"Yes."

"I can't believe it," he said. "What a sordid mess."

"Does anyone else know?" Mrs. Overtree asked. "Besides Stephen and those of us in this room?"

"I haven't told anyone," Wesley said. "Though Mr. Keith suspects the truth. As does O'Dell."

Sophie remembered the noise she and Stephen had heard when they were talking in the hall about her past with Wesley, thinking they were alone. And again later with Wesley, when he suggested sailing away to France or Italy together. Had Miss Blake been in the passage behind the squint, watching and listening? Or Winnie? Sophie inwardly groaned.

"It's possible someone else here knows," Sophie admitted, head bowed.

"Meaning Mr. Overtree and I are not the first to come upon you in such a compromising position?" Janet Overtree's eyes blazed.

"No, I didn't mean that," Sophie said. "But someone may have overheard Wesley and me . . . arguing."

"What a nightmare. We must endeavor to keep this within the family. And if we can spare Katherine, let's do. And my father! Heaven help us."

"Wesley, you must put all thoughts of her from your mind," his father said. "I cannot pretend to approve of what's happened. In fact, I am shocked and appalled. But what's done is done. Shall we add charges of adultery to your sins? Shall we invite yet more scandal to the Overtree name? No. Stephen is her husband. And you must abide by that. We all must."

"What am I supposed to do when the child comes?" Wesley threw up his hands. "Pretend I don't care? Give the babe a rattle and pat his head like a fond uncle and go on my way?"

"Yes. That is precisely what you must do."

"I won't. I can't."

"You will. Or you will drag us all down into the mud with you. What about your impressionable young sister? Her marriage prospects? And what about our friends and neighbors? Our church family? Our vicar? What are we to tell them, hmm? Are we to be shunned from the congregation that worships on our very grounds?"

"That's not my problem."

"Of course it is."

"Oh, what are we going to do?" Mrs. Overtree wailed. "We are ruined. All ruined!"

"Be calm, Mrs. Overtree. It isn't as bad as all that. Yet." Mr. Overtree looked from one to the other. "We will pray and consider what is best to be done." He gestured toward the paintings. "In the meantime, put those back in the crate and nail it shut. And, you two, stay away from one another. Do I make myself clear?"

At the door, Mrs. Overtree turned back with a final scathing look. "And don't think I didn't see those cats upstairs. Get them out of the house by day's end — or I will do it myself."

CHAPTER 31

Sophie remained in her room that night, not going down to dinner. She was too mortified to face them all, and too upset to eat. Libby brought her a light supper, but Sophie only picked at it.

Her mind still reeled from that awful scene with the Overtrees and from learning that Wesley had sent a letter to Stephen, telling him she and Wesley still loved each other. What else had he written? Had he intimated she regretted marrying him? Preferred to be with his brother? Her stomach twisted at the thought.

Sophie laid a hand on her uneasy abdomen, feeling a kick in reply. "I'm so sorry, little one," she whispered. "I have made a mess of everything." *Oh, God, please forgive me. Please bring something good out of all this bad.*

The next morning Sophie wrote a letter of her own. Then she counted the days it would take to reach Lynmouth, and how many for a reply to arrive. In the meantime, she stayed to her bedchamber as much as possible — having meals sent up on a tray and venturing down only when the post arrived.

Kate came by to check on her, concerned and curious, but Sophie simply claimed fatigue. She was certainly weary. Soul sick too.

At least Kate brought with her one piece of good news. Mrs. Overtree had given in to her daughter's pleas and relented, allowing the kittens to remain in the house until they were weaned. After that, Kate and Miss Blake would try to find homes for them all. They had asked Mr. Harrison to help them when the time came, and he'd agreed. But for now, Kate, Winnie, and even Miss Blake would enjoy Gulliver's offspring while they could.

One morning, Kate and Angela stopped by and invited Sophie to go upstairs with them to play with the kittens, but Sophie declined. She wanted to be on hand when the post arrived.

She went down to the hall at the usual time that afternoon. But instead of entering with a silver tray of letters, the butler entered with an announcement. "A Mrs. Thrupton to see you in the morning room, madam. If you are at home to callers?"

Her heart leapt. "Of course I am. Thank you, Thurman."

Sophie hurried in to the morning room. "Mavis! I am so happy to see you." Tears

555

filled Sophie's eyes and her face crumpled.

"Oh, my dear!" In a moment the dear woman's ample arms were around her, gathering her close to her soft bosom, and surrounding Sophie with the familiar smells of rosewater and freshly baked bread. "I came as soon as I got your letter."

Somehow her comforting presence made Sophie cry all the more. Her throat tightened and she struggled to speak. "His parents are so angry. And Wesley's pressuring me. And Captain Overtree won't answer my letters. Everything's ruined. Everything."

"There, there, my dear. We will work out what's best to be done. Come and sit down."

Sophie did so, telling the woman about Wesley's declaration of love, his determination to be together, and to claim her child as his own.

"And the captain?"

"I don't know. I've written to him, but he hasn't responded. I'm afraid he regrets marrying me, and will regret it even more now that his parents know the child I carry is not his. How mortifying for us both, but especially for him."

"Does he know his brother is home and repentant and . . . persuasive?"

"I mentioned he was home in my last letter. But I wasn't sure how much I should say about his brother. Not when he's so far away and there's nothing he can do."

Mavis took her hand. "Do you regret marrying the captain? Wish you'd taken your chances and waited for the painter?"

Sophie shook her head.

"What do you want to do now?"

"I don't know — so much has happened. I'm tired, Mrs. Thrupton. Tired of pretending. Tired of worrying. Tired of being pressured. I just want to sleep for a month. I worry what all this anxiety is doing to my baby."

Mavis patted her hand. "I'm sure your baby is perfectly well. I know that some folks say a mother's character and worries and cravings are passed on to the child she carries, but I think it's a great pile of claptrap. But so much anxiety isn't good for anyone, my dear. That is true. I hate to see you so unhappy."

"I fear what Wesley will do when the child comes. And then what the captain will do to him when he returns. If he returns. Will his parents even acknowledge their grandchild?"

"They should. And if it had to be another man's child, at least he is still of the family line. They ought to be happy he's an Overtree in blood as well as name."

"They are not happy at all."

Mrs. Thrupton took her hand, gazing steadily into her face. "I can't tell you what to do, Sophie. But I'll support you, whatever you decide."

"Thank you." Sophie inhaled deeply. "All I

know for certain is that I don't want to have my child here. Among a family I don't feel I really belong to — who seem more like disapproving strangers now than when I first arrived. Don't mistake me. I am fond of the grandfather and sister. And I cannot blame their parents for being disappointed and upset, but I can't abide the thought of his mother being on hand during the birth. I would be so tense, worrying every second I might do something else wrong."

"Do you . . . wish to go to Bath?" Mavis tentatively asked. "To your father?"

Sophie shook her head. "No. I do not wish to be beholden to my stepmother, who has made it plain she doesn't have room for my child."

"You know you are welcome to come home with me, if you like," Mavis said. "I hope that goes without saying. Though I don't flatter myself you'd be eager to leave all this for my snug cottage."

Sophie's heart lightened. "At the moment, I can think of nothing better! There's nowhere else I'd rather be. But I don't want to be too much trouble."

"Nonsense, my girl. I will be with you when your time comes. And Widow Paisley. And we can send for Dr. Parrish if need be. You'll be well looked after."

Relief washed over Sophie. And she smiled for what felt like the first time in weeks.

"Thank you! You are a godsend." Sophie bit her lip as she considered. "The Overtrees won't like me leaving this near my lying-in. And Wesley could make things difficult. So I'd like to keep it quiet for now, if you don't mind. I will tell them as I am leaving, or leave a note. But I prefer to avoid a drawn-out farewell. You must think me a terrible coward, but I cannot face another heated confrontation right now. My emotions are too frayed as it is."

"That's what pregnancy does to women. . . ." Mavis hesitated, then added, "Or so I understand. Strains our emotions as well as our bodies. But yes, at least leave a note so they don't worry."

Sophie nodded in agreement. Through the doorway, she noticed Kate and Miss Blake walk by, wearing aprons and bonnets, flower baskets and gardening shears in hand. Miss Blake glanced in, but Kate chatted on as she passed, unaware.

Once they had gone, Sophie continued in a lower voice, "May I meet you at the Wickbury coaching inn tomorrow? Have you enough money for the night? I will pay you back — the captain left money for any unforeseen needs that arose while he was away."

"Never you mind. I can manage. Might it be better if I hire a gig and pick you up here? A woman in your condition ought not carry a valise nor walk such a distance, especially alone."

"No, thank you. I'll be all right," Sophie assured her. She did not want horse hooves and carriage wheels crunching up the drive and announcing her departure. She doubted Mr. and Mrs. Overtree would put up much fuss. Probably bid her farewell and good riddance. But the colonel and Kate? Not to mention Wesley, with his impulsive, passionate nature? She dreaded a confrontation in front of the servants, and in the hearing of the vicar and any passersby.

"Very well, I will wait for you," Mavis said. "The coach leaves at eleven."

Fortunately, Kate remained occupied with Miss Blake, and Wesley in his own studio. So Sophie felt at liberty to quietly begin gathering her things — her knitting from the morning room, her sketchbook, the brushes Captain Overtree had picked out for her. Then she surreptitiously returned the novel and necklace Kate had lent her. She packed only her personal belongings and as few of the garments given her by Mrs. Overtree as possible.

She shut the valise she'd come with and slid it under the bed, in case any housemaid — or Kate — should pop in. Then she sat down to write three difficult letters.

Dear Mr. and Mrs. Overtree,

I have decided to take my leave of Overtree Hall and have my child in peace and among friends. I am sorry I caused strife among your family. I do appreciate your many kindnesses and generous hospitality while I remained under your roof, but I have no wish to fuel further tension. I am not leaving to be with Wesley, I promise you. As I'm sure you do, I think it would be best if he married a gentlewoman of excellent character from the best family. And the sooner the better.

Wesley has made some harsh accusations against Stephen about his method and motives for marrying me. But in my heart of hearts, I believe Captain Overtree married me with the best and noblest of intentions.

I regret causing him further inconvenience and pain, especially when he is injured and far from home and family. I will write to him as well, and hope my letter reaches him in Brussels. If it does not, I trust you will apprise him of the situation in the manner you think best. I know you hold me responsible, and I do not blame you for that. But as in any rift, rarely is one person solely at fault while the other is completely innocent. So I would ask that you be fair in your account of recent happenings, even though I have given you reason to dislike and mistrust me.

561

Regardless of what you think you saw, or the conclusions you may have drawn, I have never betrayed my marriage vows.

I will write to share news of the birth when I am able, in the event you are interested.

Sincerely,

S. Overtree

She wrote letters to Stephen and Wesley as well. Then she returned to the old schoolroom, gave the kittens a final pat, and gingerly straightened. Sophie slowly surveyed the room one more time. She looked at the dust motes floating in a shaft of sunlight and instead saw Stephen nervously showing her the new studio as his surprise, so hopeful she would be pleased. She looked again at the portrait of Stephen in uniform, remembering the precious hours they had spent together — him sitting, her painting. Smoothing back his hair, then suddenly realizing he meant to kiss her. . . .

Unbidden, a few moments spent there with Wesley returned to her as well. Painting side by side. Finding he'd repaired the portrait for her when she could not. Taking her in his arms. . . . But then his parents' shocked and condemning looks reappeared in her mind's eye, and she blinked the memories away.

Sophie was sad to leave the painting behind, but it was too large to take. Besides, she wasn't sure it belonged to her any longer —

the painting or the man. Especially if Stephen had received the angry, accusing letter Wesley had sent — telling him she and Wesley wanted to be together. No wonder Stephen had not written to her.

On her way past, Sophie left a little package outside Winnie's door. A ball of yarn for the cats, a packet of seed for her birds, and a pair of fingerless gloves Sophie had knit to keep Winnie's hands warm when she fed her birds in chilly weather.

Then Sophie returned to the bedchamber she had — almost — shared with Stephen, and memories both wonderful and regretful assailed her there as well.

In the morning, after the maid helped her dress and departed, Sophie decided to wear one article of clothing Mrs. Overtree had given to her — a billowy, full-length mantle, which would disguise or at least minimize her advancing condition. She laid a coin and a little drawing she had made for Libby on the dressing table, picked up her valise, and left the room.

Sophie placed the letters for Wesley and his parents where they would be sure to find them. And then, taking her valise and her letter for Stephen, she slipped from the house.

As Sophie crossed the drive, she felt a shiver creep up her neck. She looked over her shoulder and, sure enough, Winnie stood in her window, again dressed in black. Sophie knew by now that it was her dress of mourning. Of farewell. The woman solemnly raised a hand, and Sophie returned the gesture.

Then she stepped through the estate gate and turned down the road with a sigh of relief. She had made it away without incident. She was almost free . . .

Suddenly the rumble of horse hooves from behind startled her. Heart lurching, she stepped to the side of the road, drawing the mantle's deep hood over her head. Listening to the jingling tack drawing nearer, she hoped whoever was coming was simply a stranger passing by with a delivery of some sort.

Instead, when she glanced over, her stomach dropped to recognize Angela Blake at the reins of a small gig.

"May I give you a lift, Sophie?" She halted her horse and looked down at her expectantly.

Sophie studied her face. The redhead seemed a little smug, and a little sad, all at once.

"Were you . . . headed into the village this morning for some reason?" Sophie asked.

Angela gave her a hand up into the carriage. "No. Just had an inkling you might need a ride. I noticed you'd returned *Sense and Sensibility* to Kate, though I know you hadn't finished it, and that you'd gathered up your knitting as well. Not to mention whispering urgently with your visitor yesterday."

"Very observant," Sophie murmured.

Miss Blake urged the horse into motion. "May I ask why you are leaving Overtree Hall now, when you are so near your time?"

Sophie forced a smile. "I decided to depart while it is still safe for me to travel. I want to have my child at home. Mrs. Thrupton is a dear friend and has attended many a lying-in."

"Kate will be heartbroken, you know."

"Yes. But she has you."

"Do Mr. and Mrs. Overtree know?"

Sophie imagined that Mrs. Overtree was probably reading her letter right then and was thanking the Lord they were rid of her.

"I have left letters to inform the family," she said. "I could not wait for everyone to come down. I was in such a hurry. Mrs. Thrupton kindly came all this way to accompany me, but she has a business at home and cannot be away for long."

A knowing light glinted in Miss Blake's green eyes. "Found out, did they? And they blame you?"

Sophie swallowed a nervous lump in her throat and met the woman's gaze, without confirming or denying anything.

Miss Blake formed an apologetic little smile with her childish bow lips. "I am sorry, Sophie. Truly. I believe I understand how you feel."

"Do you?" Sophie murmured.

Miss Blake slid the reins into one hand and patted her arm. "You know I adore the Overtrees — well, most of them — but they can be most fastidious and not terribly forgiving." She added, "I don't mean Stephen, of course. He will not be happy to learn you've left."

"No. But Stephen isn't here."

"And Wesley is — is that it?"

Again, Sophie thought it wisest not to comment. "Could you let me down at the post office?" she asked. "I need to post a letter."

"To the captain?"

Sophie nodded.

Miss Blake held out her gloved hand. "I can do that for you."

Sophie hesitated.

Miss Blake sent her a wry glance. "Don't trust me, hmm? I promise you, you have nothing to fear where Stephen is concerned."

Angela halted on the High Street and handed Sophie the reins. "Hold these for me, will you? At least let me hop down and post the letter for you. Much easier for me, than for you in your present state."

Sophie reluctantly relinquished the letter, watched through the window as Angela posted it and climbed back into the gig. Then they continued down the street to the coaching inn.

The Devonshire Express was already in the

yard, while the guard and coachman made ready to depart. Sophie waved to Mrs. Thrupton, standing near the door, straw bonnet tied beneath her chin and carpetbag in hand. The woman's look of concern melted into a relieved smile upon seeing her arrive.

Mrs. Thrupton hurried toward the gig, with a curious glance at Miss Blake.

Sophie introduced the two women, and then Mavis helped Sophie down. She insisted on taking her valise from her and stepped away to hand it up to the guard, who was busy stowing baggage on top and rear of the coach.

Sophie watched the activity without really seeing it, thinking of the morning she, Mavis, and Captain Overtree had set off in a similar carriage for their elopement. How long ago it seemed. If she could go back in time would she make a different choice? Refuse his offer?

No . . .

She prayed he felt the same.

"Godspeed, Mrs. Overtree," Angela said.

"Thank you, Miss Blake. Take care of yourself."

"Of course I will. No one else has applied for the job." Angela picked up the reins. "Now I shall hurry back to the hall and see how the news is being received — and who needs comforting."

Wesley recognized Sophie's handwriting with

a twist of dread in his gut. It wouldn't be good news. He took the letter into his room and read.

Wesley,

I am sorry to leave without saying good-bye in person. But you can hardly blame me for that. I know you would make it difficult for me to leave, perhaps even try to forbid me or prevent me. You do not have that right. I am leaving to have my baby somewhere I will feel safe and loved and welcomed. I think it best for the child and certainly best for me at this time. Do not be concerned for my well-being or safety in traveling. Mrs. Thrupton accompanies me. I do not wish my child to become a pawn between you and your brother, if and when he returns. I will write to your parents to announce the birth when I can.

Please try to understand.

Sophie

Wesley threw down the letter in frustration. Yet could he really blame her for wanting to leave after the mortifying scene he and his parents had put her through? Why hadn't he restrained himself? Kept a level head? He might yet have convinced her to leave with him before the whole sordid thing came to light. He had only thought of freeing Sophie from Marsh, of establishing their prior relationship and his claim to the child. It was his child, after all. And no matter what Sophie said, it did give him some rights where she was concerned.

Yes, he should have handled things differently. But it was not too late. He would go after her. He noticed with irritation that she had refrained from mentioning her destination. Either Bath or Lynmouth, he supposed — and with Miss Thrupton as her companion, Lynmouth seemed most likely. Though the woman might simply be escorting her back to her family in Bath, so he couldn't be sure.

Wesley went looking for his sister, guessing Sophie may have confided in her. He found Kate in the morning room with Miss Blake. He hesitated upon seeing her there as well. He would prefer not to discuss the situation with Angela present, but was in no mood to wait.

Kate looked up at him, tears in her eyes. "Wesley! Sophie has left us."

He nodded and asked, "Did you know she meant to leave? Did she say anything?" He did not mention the note in his pocket, not wanting her to ask to read it.

"No, but Angela saw her at the coaching inn this morning with that friend who called yesterday."

"Oh and what were you doing in the village this morning?" he asked Angela.

"Giving her a ride, if you must know."

"And no doubt eager to do so. Did she say where she was going?"

"To her family in Bath, I believe. She said she wanted to have her child at home, and who can blame her for that? I am rather surprised she stayed as long as she did after Stephen left."

Had Sophie gone to Bath? Wesley inwardly groaned. Could he go to her there, with her family present? It would be awkward, to say the least.

He turned and left, considering how best to proceed.

Miss Blake followed him from the room. "You're not thinking of going after her?" she hissed, eyes narrowed.

"Perhaps."

Her freckled face puckered most unattractively. "Oh, just leave her alone," she snapped. "As you did me."

Wesley had no time for Angela's complaints, to listen to her dredge up all those past accusations and disappointments. He could hardly believe the woman still suffered from unrequited love after all these years. But there was nothing he could do about it now. His thoughts were consumed with Sophie.

Wesley went upstairs to his room, rang for the valet to bring down a valise from the attic storeroom, and then began gathering a few things for the journey. He could have waited for the valet to assist him, but he was in no mood to deal with the obsequious fellow.

When half an hour had passed, and Edgar had not returned, Wesley stalked from his room, determined to fetch the thing down himself. What the devil was taking the man so long?

Wesley rounded the first landing and began up the narrower attic stairs. Movement caught his eye from above, and he glanced up. He paused where he was, taken aback to see the old nurse standing at the top of the stairs, staring down at him. A valise — his valise — in her hands.

"Is this what you're looking for?" she asked, an eerie gleam in her eye.

"Yes. How did you . . . ?"

"I told Edgar I would bring it down to you, but you have saved me a trip."

Wesley frowned and continued up the stairs, irritated at the interfering old woman.

"Thank you," he murmured disingenuously, and reached for the valise.

She held it tight. "Going after your brother's wife? That's a dangerous game, Master Wesley. One that can only end badly. Stay away from her, or it will not go well with you."

He scowled. "Is this another of your *false prophecies*?"

"No. Just a feeling in my bones. Something bad is going to happen."

Wesley shook his head in disgust. "You old

croaker. You don't scare me. You're off in your attic — everyone knows it. Except your pet, Marsh. I hear you told him he would die in battle, but he didn't. And I don't believe this little warning of yours either."

"I never said he would die. Only that he wouldn't live to receive his inheritance. But if something happens to you" — she shrugged, eyes glinting — "who inherits then?"

Despite himself, a chill went down Wesley's spine. He pulled his gaze from hers and yanked at the valise, just as she released it. The momentum nearly knocked him backward down the stairs. His heart clenched and he grasped for the railing, catching himself just in time.

The nurse did not blink. "Be careful, Master Wesley. We all make mistakes, but some falls are more deadly than others."

When Wesley trudged back downstairs, his parents were standing outside his bedchamber. Eyeing the valise he carried, his father slowly shook his head, and his mother's lips pinched tight. *Excellent,* Wesley thought. *So much for a stealthy departure . . .*

They followed him into his room and shut the door behind them.

His father began, "I take it you've heard that Sophie has left Overtree Hall?"

"I have. She wrote to me as well."

"I cannot say I approve of her sneaking off

like this," his mother said, "but perhaps it is for the best that she is absent for a time — put some distance between you."

His father gestured to the valise. "I can guess what you are planning, but I beseech you not to interfere."

"Don't follow her and make a bigger mess than we already have to deal with as it is," his mother pleaded. "Like it or not, Sophie is married to Stephen."

"As I am painfully aware." Wesley forked a hand through his hair.

"But don't you see?" his mother asked. "You have been given a second chance. You are free to marry anyone you like. A fine lady of excellent character from the best family."

"Your mother is right," his father said. "Perhaps it is time to find a wife of your own." His voice gentled. "If you married, your wife would help you forget Sophie. And the children the two of you bring into the world would comfort you in the loss of Sophie's child. You have your own heir to think of. The heir to Overtree Hall."

Traditionally, heirs were firstborn sons, but since the estate was not entailed, Wesley knew he would be able to choose his own heir someday, once he was master of Overtree Hall. However, there was no need to worry about who would inherit what for several decades to come.

His mother added, "Did you not once

admire Miss Blake?"

He puckered his face. "A hundred years ago, maybe. When I was young."

"Why not now? She is very pretty, in her way."

Wesley shook his head. "I don't know that I agree. She has a pleasantly shaped faced, I grant you. But all those freckles . . ."

"Wesley, be serious. I cannot believe you would object to a perfectly suitable marriage partner for so superficial a reason."

"It is more than that, Mamma, I assure you. Her sharp tongue does her no favors either."

His father wrinkled his face in disgust. "I would not be as fastidious as you for a kingdom, Wesley."

"He cannot help his sensibilities, my dear," his mother said. "Though I trust he is overstating his case to vex us, because he doesn't like us interfering." She turned back to him. "But do be reasonable, Wesley. Miss Blake would make you an excellent wife. I am sure she would have you, if you asked. She has long wished to marry an Overtree, I believe."

"Has she?" his father asked. "I thought she had seemed a little cool towards Wesley lately."

"Yes, she has," Wesley agreed. Though he didn't explain why.

His father gripped his shoulder — a surprisingly strong grip.

"Be that as it may be. Please honor us in

this by not going after Sophie. Stay here."

The nurse's warning echoed through Wesley's mind once again: *"Stay away from her, or it will not go well with you. . . . Some falls are more deadly than others."*

Wesley swallowed. "I shall . . . think about it," he allowed. "But I make no promises."

In the hospital ward, Carlton Keith sat on a rickety chair near Stephen's cot, drinking lukewarm tea and watching him with an expectant look. "Come on, Captain. I grow tired of this place. Why not finish your recovery within the comforts of Overtree Hall?"

Stephen huffed. "I don't know, Lieutenant."

"It's time you went home before Wesley gets into mischief — or convinces Sophie to do something she doesn't want to do."

But what if she did? Stephen asked himself. What if she still wanted Wesley? Did he even want Sophie to stay with him out of guilt or sense of obligation?

Yes, God help me. He wanted her no matter what.

But would he always wonder if she was thinking of Wesley, missing him, wishing it were him kissing her . . . ?

"All you have to do is go to the C.O. with the colonel's letter and I'm sure he will approve an early release."

"Stop pushing me, Keith. You're not my

commanding officer." He immediately regretted his sharp tone, and added evenly, "I'll . . .
think about it."

Later that night, Stephen climbed from his
cot, gritting his teeth against the pain. He
slipped from the ward and into the makeshift
chapel at one end of the hospital corridor.
There, he knelt before the little altar the
chaplain had erected.

He began to pray for Sophie, and for God
to help him accept losing her if Wesley had
his way. As distasteful as the scandal would
be, he would not want her to be unhappy her
entire life.

"Thy will be done, Lord. . . ."

But he soon found his mind wandering to
memories of Sophie's increasing warmth
toward him. Her sweet parting words and
encouraging letters. She had been fond of
him, at least, he thought. Had it been more
than that? Or merely gratitude?

Knowing Sophie must be near her time,
Stephen prayed for her safety in childbirth,
for the lives of both mother and child. *Let her
live, Lord, whomever she chooses.*

Stephen prayed for nearly an hour, asking
God for wisdom. For direction. He was
surprised at the peace that descended over
him, not a martyr-like "woe is me, she'd be
better off without me." Not a "let her go and
let God comfort" kind of peace, but a conviction to pursue his wife all over again. That it

was right — his right — to fight for his wife.

Was he not a commander of men? Had he not faced enemy after enemy in hand-to-hand combat and lived to tell the tale? Surely he could muster the courage to admit the truth to himself and to her: He loved Sophie body and soul and knew he would love and respect her and her alone far better than Wes ever could.

Stephen rose. He was determined to gather Sophie close, declare his love, and ask her to marry him all over again.

And as for his old nurse's prediction?

None of us knows the number of our days, Stephen thought, *but I have wasted enough of them.*

He returned to the ward, where Keith sat slumped in a chair, softly snoring. He tapped his shoulder. "You're right, Lieutenant," he said, picking up his grandfather's letter. "Let's go home."

CHAPTER 32

Three weeks after she left Overtree Hall, Sophie stood atop her beloved Castle Rock overlooking the valley on one side and the Bristol Channel on the other. The sun hung low in the sky, sending golden light over the water, over the rocks, over her canvas as she painted. It wouldn't be much longer until Mavis would forbid her to walk this far. As it was, she insisted on accompanying her. Just in case.

Mavis sat on a blanket, protected from the wind by a large gorse bush on one side and a rocky outcropping on the other. She had a flask of tea, a tin of biscuits, and her needlework, and sat contentedly enjoying all three. Now and again the wind would abate and a few bars of the tune she hummed would reach Sophie's ears. Mavis must have felt Sophie's gaze, for she looked up and smiled at her before resuming her work.

For the first several days after her return, Sophie had been too tense to relax and enjoy her favorite place — worrying Wesley might show up at any time. But he had not. And Sophie found herself not disappointed, as she might once have guessed, but relieved.

As the sun sank lower, Sophie wiped her brushes and hands and stowed away her palette. She straightened, and a sharp twinge struck low in her back. She winced and pressed a hand there, massaging the spot. The backache that had begun the previous night was now revisiting her with a vengeance.

Then a belt of pain seized her underbelly. Sophie groaned and bent over, waiting, hoping for the pain to pass.

This was no mere backache.

"Sophie?" Mavis hefted herself to her feet and hurried to her side. Looking into her face, she asked, "Have your pains begun?"

Sophie nodded.

Mavis put her hands on her shoulders and turned her toward the path. "Come, let's get you home."

Sophie leaned on Mavis as they went, praying, *Lord, please help me.*

Even as she prayed, she felt a subtle assurance that someone, somewhere, was praying for her at that very moment. And she had a good idea of who it was.

The following day, Sophie sat propped up in bed in nightdress and shawl, knowing the midwife would return soon as promised to check on her and her child. While she waited, Sophie reclined peacefully, exhausted but content. She could hardly keep her eyes from the bundled babe asleep in her arms. A little girl. Her little girl. With skin so pale, blue veins showed through, and a head nearly bald save for the softest downy fuzz. Sophie savored the sight of her, touching every one of her ten wee toes and ten delicate fingers with nails as thin as waxed paper. Her eyebrows and the shape of her eyes were like her own, while her nose and mouth reminded her of Kate. She was perfect, except for one thing. A minor thing, she told herself. Merely superficial.

The child had a strawberry birthmark on her neck.

In olden times, the suspicious thought such marks were the sign of a witch. The benevolent, simply that the mother had eaten too many strawberries. But presently, common wisdom said the mark was evidence of some unmet craving in the mother during her pregnancy.

After the birth the previous night, the old midwife had wiped the child clean and Sophie had noticed her focusing on one spot with special care, bending to peer closer as though at a stubborn stain clinging to the babe's skin. The infant chafed and squeaked in disapproval.

"What is it?" Sophie asked anxiously.

"Well, my dear. Your daughter is a beauty, and has a beauty mark. At least that is what I choose to call it."

"What do you mean?"

Widow Paisley angled the child toward Mrs. Thrupton for a second opinion. "See that? I thought it was blood, but it's not going anywhere."

Mavis ran a gentle finger over the spot. Sophie did not miss the shadow of concern cross her face before she smiled brightly. "Looks like a rose to me."

"A rose?" Widow Paisley repeated. "I'd say it looks more like a heart — wouldn't you, Sophie?"

Sophie peered closer. It did indeed.

"You know what that means, I suppose?" the midwife asked, a glimmer of humor in her old eyes.

Sophie shook her head.

"It means you craved love while you carried this wee girl — that's what."

Sophie felt warmth stinging her eyes and unexpected tears blur her vision. She could not deny the charge.

"And no wonder with her husband gone to war and recovering from his wounds in Brussels. But he'll no doubt return soon and make up for lost time." Mavis said it as though to explain things to the midwife, but Sophie knew she said it to reassure her as well.

"It's only a wee mark," the midwife said. "A cupid's kiss. A trifle. Why, I once delivered a young widow of a child with half his face a deep mulberry stain. Poor lad. Folks said it was because she mourned her slain husband." The midwife shrugged and traced the dainty red mark again. "This is nothing."

Sophie forced a smile. It didn't bother her personally. She thought every inch of her daughter perfect and perfectly beautiful. But with a mother's protectiveness, she hoped and prayed others would not taunt her little girl about it.

She wished she could talk to Stephen again — ask his opinion about names for a daughter. But with things as they were, she doubted he would express a preference one way or the other.

She decided to name her Mary Katherine. After her dear departed mother, Maria, and after Kate Overtree. She hoped Stephen would approve. And Wesley? She hoped he wouldn't object. Or insist he had the right to do so.

She dashed off a few lines to her father, but otherwise Sophie and Mary Katherine spent the majority of that first week sleeping, nursing, crying, and staring into each other's faces. Sophie had never felt so drained and weary, filled and fulfilled at the same time.

The following week, Mavis knocked on the door of the spare bedchamber Sophie occupied. "You have a visitor, if you feel up to it."

"Who is it?" Sophie breathed, hopeful and fearful all at once.

"Your father."

"Oh!" Pleasure washed over her. "Ask him in." She glanced around the room that had become hers, glad to see it tidy — easel near the sunny window and chaise longue and dressing chest against the wall.

Claude Dupont stepped inside and stood there, hat in hand, looking like an awkward schoolboy. "Hello, Sophie. I set out as soon as I received your letter. Are you well?"

Sophie nodded. "Come and see your grandchild, Papa." She angled the bundled babe toward him.

He stepped toward the bed, bent near, and studied the little pink face. "She's beautiful." He set aside his hat and held out his hands. "May I?"

"Of course," Sophie agreed, pleased he would want to hold her.

He carefully gathered his tiny granddaughter in his arms, looked into her face, and gently swayed of long experience.

"What will you call her?" he asked.

"I was thinking of Mary Katherine, after Mamma."

He glanced up swiftly, and she was touched to see tears brighten his eyes. "I think that an excellent notion. She would have liked that."

They shared a look of poignant empathy.

Eventually he handed the child back and sat on the nearby chaise, simply watching them. He wore an expression she had seen so often — her father surveying a scene with his artistic eye, measuring and planning and appreciating.

But there was unusual warmth there too. And again that unexpected gleam of tears. He said, "Sitting there like that, the sunlight from the window making your hair fairer yet, the little girl in your arms . . ." His voice thickened. "You remind me of your mother so much. How she looked. How she looked at you . . ." He wiped his eyes with the heel of his hand.

"Thank you, Papa."

"I'd forgotten how beautiful you are."

Sophie stared at him. Felt her mouth droop open. "Do you know, you've never told me that before."

"Haven't I?" He tucked his chin and shifted uneasily.

"Motherhood must agree with me," she said with a smile to put him at his ease.

He returned the gesture. "I'm glad to hear it. I admit I have been worried about you. Sophie, I apologize for leaving you alone so often the last few years. Not looking after you as I should have. Neglecting you."

"That's all right, Papa. I am not a child any longer."

"You will always be my child. And — as you will find out soon enough — Mary Katherine will always be your little girl. Your concern. If you don't believe me now, I'll remind you in about eighteen years."

He grinned, then sobered. "I've missed you, Sophie. Your marrying and moving away made me realize how much I depended on you. Maurice is talented, but he can't match your abilities in organization and dealing with wriggling children or unhappy patrons. Not to mention your ability to add life to the lifeless eyes I seem to paint."

Sophie warmed at his praise.

He cleared his throat. "I don't know what your plans are. I imagine you will have your hands full with Mary there for the foreseeable future. I did not expect you to leave Overtree Hall and come here in the first place, but if you decide to stay on, I hope you will consider returning to the studio. Working with me as my partner, rather than as my assistant."

She looked at him in surprise. And delight. Not delight at the prospect of working in the studio again, but that he should acknowledge her contributions and abilities.

"That is very generous, Papa. As you say, I don't know what my plans are at present. Captain Overtree is still recovering from his injuries in Brussels. And I am not sure if and when he will return to England or if his regiment might be sent elsewhere. Things in my life are uncertain. I don't know if . . ." She couldn't push the words over the sudden lump in her throat. *I don't know if he will even want me with him now that his parents know the truth. And if his duty keeps him from home? I wouldn't want to live in Overtree Hall again, not without Stephen there.*

But there was no need to burden her father with her troubles and worries. Instead she finished lamely with, "I don't know if I will have much time to paint. As you say, I will have my hands full with Mary."

A dozen questions passed behind his eyes, and in the wrinkle of his brow Sophie saw concern. Would her husband provide for her if she chose not to live with his family while he was off with the army? If not, how would she support herself in the meantime? At least she guessed those were her father's concerns. They were certainly some of hers.

Instead, he brightened. "Well, you have been busy working though, I see."

He gestured toward the easel and several canvases against the wall. "May I look?"

Sophie fidgeted. "If you like."

The first one he picked up was a new portrait she had painted of Captain Overtree, based on the preliminary drawings she had done at Overtree Hall. Her heart thudded to see his face, his blue eyes staring directly at her from beneath heavy brows.

Her father's discerning gaze swept the red coat and epaulets, the lines of the face, the scar, the eyes. "An excellent likeness."

"Thank you, Papa." She had worked hard to remember every detail and to depict his features correctly. She didn't want to forget his face. She glanced up, surprised to find her father no longer studying the portrait, but instead studying her.

"You love him, don't you. I can see it."

Her throat tightened. Tears warmed her eyes again. "Yes," she breathed. Though she doubted Stephen would believe it — especially after he heard Wesley's version of events — or his parents'.

Would he even come to see her there in Lynmouth once he returned? Perhaps she had been rash in leaving. If Mr. Keith was successful in securing his release and bringing him home, the captain would not want to travel again to see his wayward wife after a journey of such a distance. Not with his injuries. And she would not be fit to travel for at least a month. If Mavis had her way, she'd barely leave her bed in that time. Or even longer. Perhaps she should have stayed at Overtree Hall. But she quailed at the thought of being there, now that his parents knew her past and condemned her for it.

Her father set down the portrait and turned to regard the one on the easel, nearly finished.

"My goodness! Mavis Thrupton has never looked so lovely. And that's saying a great deal, considering how many artists painted her in her younger days."

"Thank you. That one is already sold, Papa," she added quietly, feeling a little sprout of hopefully not improper pride.

His brow furrowed. "Sold? My dear, Mavis has already been quite generous in inviting you to lodge here, I don't think —"

"No! Mavis didn't buy it," she quickly corrected him. "Of course she would be welcome to have it for nothing if she wanted. But a certain gentleman offered a very fine price, and she said I couldn't refuse. Not when I could paint another of her whenever I liked, living with the world-famous model as I do." Sophie grinned to recall Mavis's saucy comment.

"Which gentleman?" her father asked.

"Sir Frederick Nevill."

"Nevill?" Her father whistled. "He has a good eye, Sophie. That's a great compliment."

"Oh, I think it's more of a compliment to Mavis. He's come to admire her."

"Has he indeed? Well, good for her."

"Good for us both."

Even if the sale was not from a completely neutral party, Sophie's confidence and hope for the future was buoyed by her first sale — just a few days before the birth of her child.

Who knew? Perhaps she would sell others, take commissions of her own, and even support herself by painting, should worse come to worst.

Her father looked at another canvas, left out in the open to dry. "And this new landscape . . . It is quite good, Sophie."

"Thank you, Papa, but you needn't say so."

"It's true! Though as your father I suppose I am not purely objective. I like this perspective of Castle Rock. Would you mind if I displayed it in the studio? I've decided to stay on until Christmas, since I'm here already. There are a great many tourists about, taking in the sights on these fine, autumn days."

"Display it to sell, you mean?"

"Yes. If there is interest. If nothing else, it will draw people into the shop."

She nodded. "Of course. If you think it might help."

"Thank you. And I shall try not to burst my buttons when I tell people my daughter painted it."

Sophie had put off writing a letter to the Overtrees, fearing it might spur Wesley to come there, perhaps even to demand his paternal rights. And in those tender early days of motherhood, she had not been prepared physically or emotionally to face another confrontation. But her conscience would not allow her to put it off any longer. After her father departed, Sophie borrowed Mrs. Thrupton's lap desk, quill, and ink and wrote the promised letter to the Overtrees.

> *Dear Mr. & Mrs. Overtree and family,*
> *I am writing to announce the good news of the safe delivery of . . .*

Sophie paused. Was it presumptuous to refer to Mary Katherine as *their* grandchild? The girl was their flesh and blood, whether they considered her legitimate or not. Whether they considered her Wesley's child or Stephen's.

Sophie took a deep breath, dipped her quill, and continued.

> *your grandchild. She is healthy and strong, and reminds me quite a bit of your Kate. I have decided to name her Mary Katherine, after my own beloved mother and your dear daughter. I hope that meets with everyone's approval.*

She didn't specify whose approval she most wanted — Stephen's.

Sophie finished her letter, and then began a similar one to Captain Overtree. She wasn't sure it would reach him in Brussels, or if he was already on his way home. She prayed for him with every word she wrote, hoping he would believe her when she said she missed him with all her heart.

Chapter 33

Stephen leaned forward to look out the post-chaise window, then leaned back against the upholstered seat.

"Almost there."

He would be immensely relieved when they reached Overtree Hall at last. If he didn't travel farther than the adjacent church in the next twelvemonth, that would suit him perfectly well. He was worn out from days of travel by ship and carriage. Sore too. The wounds in his right shoulder and hand had healed, but his left shoulder was still bandaged and bound in a sling to help stabilize it for travel. All the jarring and lurching over the rutted roads of Gloucestershire sent daggers of pain through his arm and shoulder with every hole and sway. He gritted his teeth and prayed for strength. Only a few minutes longer.

He felt Carlton Keith's scrutiny on his profile and attempted to keep his expression impassive. He hoped the pain didn't show on his face.

"All right there, Captain?"

"I will be," he replied between clenched teeth, "as soon as we set down at home."

Perhaps he ought not to have been so stubborn in refusing the surgeon's offer of laudanum for the journey. But he wanted to be alert when he reached Overtree Hall. When he saw Sophie for the first time in months.

He wondered again how she and the child fared — she must have had the baby by now. No doubt letters containing the news were even now in a sack of post somewhere en route to him in Brussels. He prayed again for her and for the child, hoping they were both in good health.

He prayed, too, for kindness, gentleness, patience, and self-control in dealing with his brother.

The hired chaise turned the corner, and there it was — tall, stately Overtree Hall, its stone façade glowing golden in the afternoon sunlight. There the church, the dovecote, and entrance gate. When the chaise passed under its archway, Stephen closed his eyes to relish the familiar, missed sound of carriage wheels on the pea gravel drive.

At last the chaise lurched to a halt. Outside the guard hopped down, opened the carriage door, and let down the step.

Keith said, "Let me go first, Captain, and lend a hand."

"I'm all right," Stephen insisted and pushed himself up and through the door. When his feet hit gravel, his legs wobbled and his head spun. Perhaps Keith had been right. *Pride goeth before the fall,* he thought, and felt about to topple.

Keith took his arm. "Steady on, Captain. You'll get your land legs in a moment."

Ahead, the front door opened and the footman James exited. On the man's heels, his family, not waiting for a formal entrance, spilled out after him. There his father, his sister, his mother, her arms outstretched. But no Sophie. She might still be confined to her bed, he realized, remembering that a month of bed rest was often prescribed after birthing.

"Stephen! Thank God. Welcome home."

His father looked the same as Stephen remembered, but he noticed how thin his mother looked, and the shadows under her eyes. He kissed her cheek. "Hello, Mamma."

He shook his father's hand, then turned to his grandfather as he puffed down the stairs to join them. The colonel ignored his hand and pulled him into an embrace, slapping his back and his shoulder in the bargain. Stephen winced.

"Careful there, Colonel," Keith said.

"Oh! Forgive me. What an oaf. I completely forgot for a moment."

The throbbing shoulder allowed Stephen

no such luxuries.

Kate threw her arms around his neck. "I missed you, Stephen."

He planted a kiss on her head. "And I you."

She released him, her face shining. "I shall return directly," she said. "But I promised to tell Angela the moment you arrived." She hurried off across the drive in the direction of Windmere.

Wesley came languidly down the steps, surveying him head to toe. "You don't look on death's door to me. Surprised they invalided you back to England."

"Oh, Grandfather has his ways as you know."

Stephen glanced toward the door once more, his heart eager and reluctant at once. He told himself not to be disappointed she'd not come out to greet him.

"And . . . Sophie?" he asked, hoping to sound casual.

His mother looked at his father, then back to him, a worry line between her brows. "She is not here."

"What do you mean she is not here?" He whirled on his brother. "What did you do?"

Wesley raised his hands. "Nothing."

Keith said under his breath, "Doesn't mean he didn't try."

Wesley lifted his chin. "I merely told Mamma and Papa the truth. After that, she chose to leave."

Anger coursed through Stephen. "You selfish wretch . . ." Poor Sophie! How mortifying for her.

Their father said soothingly, "Come into the house, Stephen. Let's everyone remain calm, and we will explain the situation as best we can in private."

"Where is she? Has she had the child? Is she well?" His concerned questions tumbled out one after another as he followed his parents into the house and through to the parlour.

"I am sure she is well," his mother asserted. "She promised to write when the child was born. Calm yourself. Unfortunately, the letter she posted to you in Brussels before she left has been returned here, undeliverable."

"You didn't mention a letter to me," Wesley objected.

His mother's expression remained flat. "No, I did not." She turned to the hovering Thurman. "Please send for Dr. Matthews directly."

"Very good, madam."

She returned her gaze to Stephen. "I shall bring you the letter. But first — a bath and dinner."

"Hear, hear," Keith agreed.

Stephen thought about demanding to read the letter first and insisting that he didn't need to see yet another doctor. But at the moment he was too weary to protest and allowed his Mamma to take care of everything, as much for her sake as for his.

After a bath, clean civilian clothes, and a
good meal, Stephen felt a little better physically. Dr. Matthews arrived and examined
him somberly, without his usual unruffled
ease, but in the end, declared he thought both
arms would heal in time, though the mobility
of the left one would always be limited and
he did not envy the aches and pains that were
sure to plague Stephen every time the weather
changed when he grew older.

His mother, finally satisfied all had been
done, brought the letter to him in his bedchamber. Her hand lingered on his and rare
tears shone in her eyes. "I am so glad you are
safe."

He squeezed her hand. "Thank you,
Mamma. And thank you for praying for me."

She nodded. "I did. Every day." She stepped
to the door, then turned back. "Sophie did as
well."

She held his gaze a moment longer, and
then left him. Too weary to do anything else,
Stephen stretched out on the bed that had
been his grandparents' — that had been
Sophie's — and read her letter.

Dear Captain Overtree,
By the time this letter reaches you in that
distant place, I will long have left Overtree
Hall. I have decided to return to Lynmouth

with my dear friend Mrs. Thrupton and have my child there. I think I would be more comfortable with her at such a personal, vulnerable time, than here among people I have known so briefly. Especially as you are not among them. I hope you will understand and not think the worst of me.

Regretfully, I have become a cause of strife among your family. I am sorry for that. I regret inflicting further worry and pain, especially when you are injured and far from home. What a way to repay your kindnesses to me!

Don't mistake me — your family has been very good to me and provided well for me while I was with them. I grew quite fond of your grandfather and of Kate especially. But things deteriorated when Wesley returned and have become awkward and uncomfortable. Please believe me when I tell you I am not leaving to be with Wesley but rather to avoid him.

Your parents suspect there is something between us. And I admit that when we were told you had died, I briefly thought some future relationship with him might be God's will. But once we learned you were alive, I knew I was wrong and resisted his entreaties. I was sincerely relieved to learn you were alive — are alive — and will someday return to England. I realize that when you *hear from Wesley himself, or from your parents about me, you may wish to find some way to wash your hands of me forever. But I nurture no such wish to be freed from you. Please believe me. No matter what you may hear, I have never betrayed my marriage vows, nor will I. I wish I could promise you a happy, strife-free return to Overtree Hall, and be there to warmly welcome you home. But I fear I have tainted my chances of happiness there forever. I don't know what the future holds. In great part, that is up to you. But for now, I feel it best for the child, and for me, to live elsewhere.*

I will write to share news of the birth when the much-anticipated event occurs. I know you are a man of faith, and I would covet your prayers for a safe delivery.

Yours sincerely,
Sophie

Oh, Sophie, he thought, his heart aching for her in more ways than one. He thanked God that the letter laid to rest his doubts about her wanting to be with Wesley. And he would lay to rest *her* doubts about his feelings for her as soon as he could.

Stephen rested the next day at his mother's insistence. It felt good to be coddled, to be warm in bed and well fed. But he knew himself, and knew the idle pleasure would soon wear thin. He would travel to Devonshire as soon as he felt a little stronger. In a day or two, even though he knew his parents would protest.

And Wesley? Stephen would keep his plans to himself for now.

Miss Blake stopped by to wish him well. Mr. Keith joined them and the three talked and teased for several minutes. Then Stephen sobered and said, as much for Angela's benefit as for Keith's, "Well, Lieutenant, I am in your debt."

"How's that, Captain?"

"You coming all that way to Brussels like that to bring me home."

"Aw. I'd say that about makes us even, sir. Almost." He winked.

"It was very brave of you, Mr. Keith," Miss Blake added, eyes warm with approval.

Carlton Keith held her gaze with a dreamy grin and murmured, "Definitely worth the trouble . . ."

The next day, Stephen insisted on dressing and going downstairs. He ate breakfast with his father and grandfather and then gave in to Kate's plea for a game of draughts in the parlour. When Miss Blake arrived, he happily relinquished the game to her.

Wesley came in, followed by Mr. Keith, who played a gentle tune on the pianoforte. Stephen was impressed with his ability — disability or not.

Later, his mother entered the room, looking a little brighter than she had upon his arrival. She drew up short in the doorway, looking from face to face.

"My goodness," she breathed. "What a blessing to have everyone together again."

"Not quite everyone, Mamma," Kate spoke up before Stephen could. "We're missing Sophie."

Yes, he was certainly missing her.

Thurman brought in the day's post, including a letter addressed to his parents.

His mother read it first, then looked across the room at Stephen. "It's from Sophie. She is well, never fear."

Keith abruptly stopped playing to listen.

"What does she say, Mamma?" Kate asked eagerly.

His mother deferred to him. "It's written to all of us," she said. "May I read it aloud?"

Stephen nodded, though a part of him would have preferred to read it in private. But it wasn't his letter to hoard.

"Dear Mr. & Mrs. Overtree and family,

I am writing to announce the good news of the safe delivery of your grandchild. She is healthy and strong, and reminds me quite a bit of your Kate. I have decided to name her Mary Katherine, after my own beloved mother and your dear daughter. I hope that meets with everyone's approval."

Kate let out a little squeal. "How wonderful!"

His mother continued,

"Please share the news with all the family for me. I will write to Captain Overtree myself, but as I am uncertain if he may already be en route back to England, Lord willing, I don't know if a letter shall reach him. If not, I trust you will pass on the good news for me.

Sincerely,
Sophie"

Relief washed over Stephen. Sophie was well. The child healthy. He was gratified to know she had written to him personally, though he had left Brussels before the letter could arrive. He noticed she made no mention of her plans to return, nor asked Stephen to visit them. But he would. As soon as he was physically able.

The colonel leaned near and whispered, "I'm going upstairs to share the good news with Miss Whitney."

That surprised Stephen, but he said nothing as his grandfather excused himself and left the room.

His mother reached over and extended the letter to him, but before Stephen could reach it, Wesley stood and snatched it from her. He turned the folded sheet over and looked at the postal markings.

"Lynmouth. Dash it, Angela. You told me she went to Bath, but I should have known better."

"Wesley . . ." his father warned. "You promised not to interfere."

"I made no promise, Papa. I said I would think about it and I have. I'm going."

Stephen rose and grabbed his arm. "Stay away from her, Wesley."

Wesley shook him off. "I will not. I plan to be on the next Devonshire Express."

"Not if I have anything to say about it."

"You don't."

"Stop it," Mrs. Overtree commanded, frowning thunderously. "I cannot believe the two of you. This girl has made you lose your better sense. Cast a spell on you both."

"Mamma, what are you talking about?" Kate protested. "Don't speak unkindly about Sophie."

"I had hoped to spare you, Katherine. Such topics are not proper for innocent ears. Why don't you and Angela walk into the village, or to Windmere."

"Mamma, no. I am not a child any longer."

"I believe I will stay as well, Mrs. Overtree," Angela said. "I am not such an innocent either, I assure you."

Their mother huffed. "Angela, I know you mean well, but this is family business and doesn't concern you."

"Oh, but it does. In its way."

Stephen noticed the challenging glare she directed at Wesley. Wesley sullenly met her gaze but looked away first.

Angela then glanced quickly at Mr. Keith, sitting motionless at the pianoforte. She took a deep breath and began, "I have remained silent too long. I cannot sit by and say nothing while you vilify Sophie — blaming her, just as my father blamed me."

"What do you know about it?" their mother snapped.

"Enough. I know about her and Wesley. I heard them speaking together. From the squint." She turned to face Wesley, expression as brittle as ice. "You showed me the hidden passages when we were young, remember? And from the squint in the hall, I heard you begging Sophie to run off with you. But she refused you. She showed more strength of character than I ever did."

Confusion, dread, and alarm flashed through Stephen in rapid turns.

Wesley crossed his arms but refused to meet her gaze.

Angela released a ragged breath. "I wish she were still here, so I could apologize. I was not always kind to her. I admit I was jealous.

Was it not enough that she married one Over-tree? Did she need to have the other one chasing after her as well?"

Angela shook her head. "Wesley is not the innocent party here, Mrs. Overtree. Nor is Sophie the first woman he's left with child and abandoned. My father said I must have done something to lead him on, to give him the idea that I was a woman of easy virtue."

"Never!" Kate exclaimed.

Angela shrugged and went on, speaking as though Wesley were not standing right there. "Perhaps I did. I was in love with him, after all. And I once thought he loved me. I would have forgiven him, said yes to him five years ago when he left me with child."

Shock washed over Stephen. Kate gasped. His mother grabbed his father's hand.

Angela continued, "I would have said yes to him the following year, when I gave up my child to a foundling home." She let out a cracked little laugh. "I would have said yes last week — I am sorry, Mr. Keith, but it's true — so strong is his effect on weak-willed women like me. But today? Today I wash my hands of him. He will never change."

Wesley slowly shook his head, a disgusted twist to his lips, but he said nothing.

Angela returned her gaze to his mother. "I am sorry, Mrs. Overtree. I know you idealize your eldest son. I don't say this to hurt you, though I know it does." She turned to his sister. "I'm sorry, Kate. I know you've looked up to me, and now I have disillusioned you. Disillusioned you all."

Kate's eyes filled with tears.

Wesley frowned. "That's enough, Angela. You've had your revenge. I hope you're happy."

She whipped her white face toward him, lips tight. "Do I *look* happy?"

She inhaled slowly and drew back her shoulders, reining in her emotions, but Stephen did not miss the tremble of her chin. He had known of Miss Blake's youthful adoration of Wesley.

Noticed how her eyes followed him, how she'd hung on his words, and tried too hard to gain his attention. And yes, Stephen had been disappointed when she'd switched her attentions to his brother. But that had been years ago. He did remember worrying about her when she suddenly left for an extended absence with a relative, but he'd never thought the rumor he'd heard could be true. And he certainly never suspected that his brother had taken advantage of his old friend. And worse yet, had heartlessly abandoned her, forcing her to abandon their child.

Stephen turned to her. "I am so sorry, Angela. I didn't know."

"I know you didn't. No one did — save Wesley, my aunt, and my father. Would you have rescued me, as you did Sophie?"

Stephen met her glistening gaze, his heart aching for her. "Yes. Had it been in my power to do so. I would have made Wes do his duty by you."

"Which is why I never told you," she said coolly, "I didn't want him to be forced to marry me. I foolishly held out hope that he would marry me out of honor and love. What an imbecile I was."

"No, Angela. You are not to blame."

"Wesley, tell me this isn't true," their mother implored. "Miss Blake is a gentleman's daughter. Our neighbor . . ."

Wesley said, "I offered to help her. But she said she didn't need my help."

Angela's lip curled. "I didn't want your *money.* I wanted your love. But no . . ."

His father's face turned a dangerous shade of purple. "By God, he will do his duty now, Miss Blake, if it's the last thing he does."

Angela rose. "Thank you, Mr. Overtree. But you are five years too late." She turned, head held high, and strode from the room.

Mr. Keith followed her out, stunned and anxious. "Miss Blake, wait . . ."

Stephen turned on Wesley. "How could you abandon her like that? Have you no feeling? No conscience?"

Wesley threw up his hands. "She waited to tell me until the eve of my departure! I was leaving to study under Signor Tofanelli for the year. The timing was impossible. Was I supposed to give up my life's ambition?"

Stephen shook his head in disgust. "You never deserved Angela, and you certainly don't deserve Sophie."

"That's for her to decide," Wesley retorted. "She didn't exactly wait here like the devoted wife to welcome you home, did she?"

"Shut up, Wesley," their father snapped.

"Sophie left because we humiliated her and blamed her unjustly," their mother said, expression guilty and pained. "Me most of all."

"And to avoid your repugnant advances," Stephen accused. "So stay away from her. She's my wife."

"Nothing a trip to Italy or France can't fix. I know your sham of a marriage has never even been consummated."

Stephen felt like a French saber had struck him once more, stunned and hurt that Sophie had revealed their secret. He met his brother's gaze and said with more confidence than he felt, "An oversight I plan to address as soon as time allows."

Wesley reeled back his fist and struck. Stephen instantly ducked, and Wesley's fist landed only a grazing blow to his jaw.

"Wesley, don't!" Kate cried.

Anger erupted, but hearing his sister's horrified shriek, Stephen restrained himself — barely — from striking back. "Shall we step outside, Wes," he said. "Settle this like gentle-

607

men, though I doubt you know the definition of the term."

"Stephen, no," his mother pleaded.

Keith charged back into the room. "Sorry, Captain, that's my privilege." He slammed into Wesley like a battering ram, head first.

Wesley grunted, and the two men went flying, crashing to the ground.

Keith sat atop Wesley pinning him with his knees, and landed a punch to his face. "I can't believe I once thought you the better man." His voice hitched. "Miss Blake? How could you?"

Wesley took advantage of Keith's emotional state and single arm, and shoved him to the side. He rolled out from under Keith and lurched to his feet.

Keith scrambled up as well. "She says she'll have no husband because you've ruined her. And ruined my chance at happiness in the bargain." He reeled back his fist again.

Stephen grasped Keith's shoulders from behind, trying to forestall his attack. He knew his slight, soft brother was no match for his enraged former lieutenant — missing an arm or not. *Lord, help us.* He prayed none of them would succeed in killing the other. Especially in front of his mother and sister.

Keith lunged again, jerking them both forward. Flame seared Stephen's shoulder, and he felt his stitches tear and pain knife deep. He fell to the floor.

"Stephen!"

He opened his eyes to find his mother and sister kneeling beside him.

"I'm all right." He grimaced and sat up, his shoulder screaming and his vision dotted.

Wesley wiped blood from the corner of his mouth and scowled at Keith. "You are welcome to Angela, CK. Not that she'd have a one-armed drunkard like you. Sophie is the woman I want. Now if you'll excuse me, I have a coach to catch."

"The devil you do," Stephen called after him, trying to lunge to his feet. But his father kept hold of him, his grip surprisingly tight.

"Hush, Stephen," his mother commanded. She pulled back his coat. "Oh no. You're bleeding."

Stephen protested, "If anyone goes to Sophie, it will be me."

"You're not going anywhere, my boy," his father insisted. "At least not until Dr. Matthews takes another look at your shoulder."

"Yes, my dear. Send for him, quickly."

His father drew himself up. "Mine is the fastest horse. I will go for Dr. Matthews myself."

"No, not all that way. Think of your chest —"

"My chest is fine, woman. I am through thinking of it. I am thinking of Stephen now. You are not the only one who needs to feel useful."

She blinked in surprise, clearly taken aback. "Very well, my love," she said gently. "If you think it best."

"I do."

It was the first time in years Stephen had heard his father stand up to her. Perhaps it had been what she was waiting for.

Stephen acquiesced, cursing every minute the physician took in reaching Overtree Hall, and his tedious examination. The stitches in his left shoulder had reopened during the skirmish, and his parents insisted he wait until the doctor restitched, redressed, and bound the wound. The doctor prescribed a day or two of bed rest, but Stephen refused. Thankfully the tear was superficial, and the physician concluded that the muscle beneath was intact and mending nicely.

"Papa, I have to go. I love her. And who knows what Wesley might say to try to persuade her otherwise."

"If she could be so easily swayed, she isn't worthy of you," his mother said.

"I happen to agree with poor Miss Blake in this instance," his father said. "Sophie possesses great strength of character. She will not be persuaded to do anything she doesn't want to do."

Stephen prayed that was true.

He was willing to accept God's will. Or hers. But not Wesley's.

CHAPTER 34

Nearly six weeks after Mary's birth, Mrs. Thrupton finally relinquished her protective watch-care and allowed Sophie to go for a walk alone. She had been cooped up indoors too long and longed to enjoy the remaining autumn sunsets before winter's chill returned.

She did not bother with easel and paints. She only wanted to walk, to see, to absorb, to breathe. Reaching Castle Rock, she simply stood there on the precipice, cape flapping around her, hair whipping in her face, watching the sun lowering on the horizon over the sea. She had done the same dozens of times over the years, but now she stood there with a new stillness. A new gratitude. A new appreciation for the one who had created this spot, and that sun, and her, and her daughter. Everything. He had created the whole vast, astoundingly beautiful world and yet knew ordinary little her personally. Loved her. Sent His Son for her. Sent Captain Overtree too.

"Thank you," she breathed. "Thank you

for Mary Katherine. For Stephen. For allowing me to reflect just a tiny bit of your creative power in the talents you have given me. Whatever happens with Captain Overtree, please help me to raise my daughter and live my life in a way that pleases you — that adds a little stroke of glory to your vast display."

It rained hard that night, but the next day broke sunny and beautiful.

Her father walked up to Mavis's and delivered the welcome news that he had sold her landscape painting, and for a very good price.

Sophie beamed in pleasure. She and Mary Katherine would be all right on their own for a time, if need be.

Late that afternoon, leaving her baby with trusted and doting Mavis for the second time, Sophie struck out along the cliff path, her legs a little stiff from her first long walk the day before, after so many weeks of idleness.

She had neared Castle Rock before she glanced up and noticed a man standing on its summit. Her heart lifted. Was it him? Had he come?

The man turned and she saw his face.

Wesley.

She stopped on the path where she was, heart sinking. Had Stephen given up? Was he not coming for her after all? Or not able to? Sophie turned, deciding to hurry back the way she had come before Wesley saw her. She

612

knew he would show up at Mavis's door, but she would rather not face him alone. But she had no more than turned, when she stopped again. A second man was approaching from the other direction.

Stephen.

"Sophie!" Wesley's voice, calling her from behind. From the past.

Yards ahead, Stephen raised a hand, his other bound in a sling. She raised hers in turn, barely resisting the urge to run to him, which would not be safe on the narrow path high above the sea, slick from last night's rain.

She glanced over her shoulder. Wesley strode quickly toward her. She stood there, feeling more and more trapped as the brothers neared, closing in on her.

"Stay back, Wesley," Stephen commanded.

"I don't take orders from you, Captain Black."

"You do if you value your life."

Worried for them both, Sophie turned toward Wesley, searching for the words to release him — and convince him to release her — once and for all.

"Wesley. It's over. You have to let me go."

"Not without a fight," he growled.

"That can be arranged." Stephen fisted his good hand.

Sophie knew Stephen could easily defeat his brother in any fight under normal circumstances, but at the moment, with the captain's arm bound, his face pale, and his legs slightly trembling, Wesley might for once have the advantage.

"Stephen, don't. Your shoulder."

Wesley lunged past her and pushed Stephen's chest. Stephen grabbed him in a wrestling hold, sling forgotten. They struggled back and forth, grunting and cursing, heedless of the cliff and turbulent sea far below.

"Stop it!" she shouted. "Before you both get yourselves killed."

Stephen's grip loosened at her words, and Wesley shoved hard. Stephen lost his footing and they both fell. Sophie screamed.

Arms clutching each other, the two men tumbled over the edge, Wesley slamming into a boulder protruding from the cliff side and stopping their fall, Stephen stretched headfirst down the slope.

Sophie dropped flat on the path and reached down, wrapping her arms around Stephen's legs. She had hold of him, and he had hold of Wesley as he clung to the rock.

The rock shifted.

Fear for his wife gripped Stephen's heart. "Sophie, don't. Let go," he called in warning.

"I won't."

"You're not strong enough to pull us up. It's all right, love. Let go."

"I won't. If you go, I go."

"No! Think of your child. Our child."

The rock shifted again, loosening. It would not bear their weight indefinitely.

Wesley gritted out, "You can't save me this time, Marsh. All you'll do is wreck your arm and pull Sophie down with us."

Stephen tightened his grip, muscles trembling. "Hang on. I've got you."

"Not for long. She's made her choice. Now, let go."

Stephen felt his stitches straining and his grip on his brother weakening. Was this the future Winnie had warned against? Would Wesley die here today, leaving Stephen their father's heir? Rather than his own death being imminent?

No, Lord. I don't want it. Not like this. Help me save him. . . . Pain burned through his shoulder and down his arm. He wouldn't be able to hold on much longer.

A scramble of rocks from above, and Stephen felt himself drop lower as Sophie slid forward.

She panted, "I'm . . . slipping."

Stephen pressed his eyes close. *God, no. . . .* He would not risk her life.

Heart breaking, he released his brother.

Wesley fell away from his grasp down the steep slope. *Lord have mercy on his soul.*

Stephen forced himself to look. Wesley slid, then rolled, then jerked to a stop. A stubborn gorse shrub several yards down snagged him with its sinewy arms and thorny branches.

The thing was apparently stronger than he was. Surprise and relief filled him. *Thank you, God!*

With Sophie's help, Stephen clawed his way back up to the path. His torn sling blew away in the wind.

"Don't move, Wes," Stephen called down to him. "We'll go find a rope and come back to pull you up."

"I'm not going anywhere," Wesley replied, humor and fear thinning his voice. "At least I hope not."

Together Stephen and Sophie hurried back to the village for a length of rope and help. Half an hour later, with the aid of two strong men, they pulled a sheepish, scratched, and bruised Wesley to safety.

The three of them returned to Mavis Thrupton's cottage. As they walked in awkward silence, Sophie longed to put her hand in Stephen's but resisted, afraid to goad Wesley into another fight.

At the door, Mavis looked in surprise from one man to the other, but quickly regained her composure. She sternly told them to be quiet, because the baby was sleeping. Then she looked significantly down at the men's boots, muddied in the fight, along with their outer coats. Both men took the hint and removed coats and boots inside the entry porch — Stephen struggling with his injured arm but managing without help.

Wesley had cuts on his face and hands. Mavis ordered him to sit at her table while she cleaned the wounds and applied salve.

While they were thus occupied, Sophie drew Stephen aside and said, "Wesley is right about one thing. I have made my choice. I hope you know that."

"I still like hearing it."

"Now I need to ask you to do something difficult for me. I need to ask you to let me take Wesley in first to meet Mary Katherine. I feel as though I need to resolve things with him. Let him say his piece, to me, to her, before I introduce you. Will you trust me?"

"I trust you completely, Sophie. But Wesley?" He shook his head. "Not at all."

"You can stay right here. In calling distance, if need be. But I doubt you have anything to worry about. And I don't think we'll be long."

"Very well. If you think it best."

"All right, Captain, your turn," Mrs. Thrupton announced, cloth in hand and patting the back of the chair Wesley had just vacated. He acquiesced.

Sophie turned to Wesley. "Will you come in and meet Mary?"

He stilled. "Of course I will. It is why I came here after all. Well, one of the reasons."

Sophie opened the bedchamber door and held it open for him. She walked to the cradle and scooped up her daughter in her arms, then turned and presented her to her natural father.

"Here she is."

Wesley leaned near, his golden-brown eyes taking in every feature. "Well, look at you, young lady. You're right, she does look like Kate. Oh . . ."

His brows lowered as his attention was snagged by the purplish-red mark on her neck.

"That is . . . unfortunate. For a girl, I mean." He could not quite hide a wince at seeing it.

"It is only a birthmark," Sophie said.

"I know. It's just . . . Ah well. At least it is on her neck and not her face. A well-placed collar or shawl shall easily conceal that little flaw, never fear." He raised the blanket to Mary's chin and kissed her perfect cheek.

Then his eyes shifted to Sophie, his expression more sorrowful and humble than she had ever seen it. "I am sorry, Sophie. Sorry for everything. When I thought I was about to die, so many regrets filled me. So many mistakes. . . ." He wearily shook his head.

"It's all right," she whispered. "God has turned our mistakes into something good. Something better than I deserve."

"Don't say that. You deserve every good thing life has to offer. Someone better than me. But are you sure this is what you want? *Marsh?*"

"Never more so."

Wesley sighed and lifted his palms. "Well then, I surrender. Let's not keep him waiting."

Taking the child awkwardly in his arms, Wesley used his shoulder to push the door open wider. "Marsh? Come in here, if you please."

Captain Overtree rose from the table, left arm wrapped, but forgoing a sling. He entered the room, looking from one to the other. Then his eyes lit on the child.

Wesley held Mary out to him, as though a gift. An offering. "Here she is, Captain. Your daughter." His voice hitched as he said it, and Sophie's heart twisted in reply.

Stephen's eyes flashed to his brother's, and a look passed between them. He held out his large hands and gingerly accepted the bundled infant, carefully gathering her in his arms.

"Hello, Mary Katherine. How beautiful you are." He gave his brother another look, begrudging humor in his eyes. "Lucky for her she looks like you rather than me."

"Do you think so? I think she looks like Kate, as Sophie said."

"Yes, I do see a bit of Kate in her."

Wesley inhaled. "Well, I shall leave you. I hope you three shall be very happy."

Stephen asked, "And what about you? Will you go home and make things right with

Angela?"

"I will try. But how can I, really? Seeing Mary now gives me an inkling of what Angela went through because of me. What she gave up. Forever . . ." Again he shook his head.

Confusion flared. "What do you mean?" Sophie asked.

When Wesley hesitated, Stephen murmured, "I'll explain later."

Wesley drew himself up. "I will at least apologize. *Truly* apologize. Even if I had a mind to do more than that, I imagine CK has won her over by now." He managed an unconvincing grin. "Not my week with women."

"And after that?" Stephen asked.

"Oh, I think I might sail back to Italy, now that Napoleon is exiled again. See if my Mona Lisa is still out there somewhere."

"If you think that's the best course."

Wesley gave his brother a wry look. "I'm surprised you aren't prodding me to stay home and do my duty by the estate if not Angela."

"Are you really surprised?"

"Ah. Want me gone, do you? And the more miles the better?"

"For now, yes."

Wesley's gaze rested on the child once again. "I won't forget Mary. In fact, I shall bring her something back from Italy. A christening present, perhaps. I will strive to

620

be a proper uncle to her."

"That is good of you."

He shrugged. "I haven't accomplished the feat yet. I may need some time first. Some distance." He pressed a kiss to Mary Katherine's brow, then turned to Sophie and pressed a twin kiss there.

He whispered, "I wish you happy, Mrs. Overtree."

"Thank you, Mr. Overtree."

Stephen added, "Take care of yourself, Wesley."

"I shall. I had better — CK won't be tagging along to keep me out of mischief this time, and you won't be there to bail me out of trouble."

"No."

"As it should be. You have new concerns to attend to."

"Yes. Thank God." Stephen shifted Mary to one arm and held out his hand.

Wesley shook it. "I hope you will endeavor to deserve her."

"Indeed I shall."

When the door closed behind Wesley, Sophie turned almost shyly to Stephen.

He sat down on the upholstered chaise and deftly and gently repositioned the infant on his lap. He'd obviously had experience helping to care for his much younger sister.

She asked, "What do you think of her?"

"I think I am falling in love all over again."

Sophie dipped her head as self-conscious pleasure ran over her.

He pulled forth a little fist that had been trapped in the swaddling blanket. "Such long fingers. Like her mother's."

He loosened the blanket further, exposing her full face and neck.

Sophie held her breath, waiting for him to notice the strawberry birthmark.

His finger traced the spot. "Ah . . . a kiss from God. A special sign of favor."

"Do you think so?"

He nodded. "Whatever it is, it's precious. She is precious. Perfect."

Relief warmed Sophie. "Mavis said I must have craved strawberries while I carried her. And the midwife said the birthmark is in the shape of a heart." She swallowed. "And that means I craved . . . love . . . while I carried her."

He looked up and held her gaze, intensity smoldering in his eyes. "Oh?" Then he looked down and pressed a kiss on the rosy heart.

Sophie's breath caught to see his scarred cheek so close to her little girl's birthmark. Stephen, with his scarred face and body, apparently found the mark endearing. She could have kissed him then and there.

"Heart-shaped, you say?" he mused aloud, eyes on Mary Katherine. "I'd say it's shaped like lips." His voice lowered. "Perhaps her

Mamma craved a sound kissing while she carried you, hmm, my little beauty?"

Sophie's pulse raced to hear his words, and her chest tightened. Again she dipped her head to hide her flush, then looked up at him from beneath her lashes. "I . . . cannot deny it."

His eyes flashed to hers, warm and glimmering with hope.

"Sit with me, my love." He secured Mary in one arm, and Sophie sat on the chaise beside him. He reached a hand toward her, gently stroking then cupping her cheek. "My Sophie . . ."

"I am yours, yes. And dearly wish to be."

His gaze held hers like an embrace, then moved slowly over her face before settling on her mouth. He ran his thumb over her lower lip, and a tingle of pleasure whisked up her spine.

"You don't know how I've missed you," he said.

"Oh, I think I have an inkling, Captain."

He leaned forward, pressing a kiss on her forehead. Then he placed a warm kiss to one of her cheeks, then the other.

She lifted her chin, hoping, hinting . . .

He murmured, "Surely you might call me Stephen by now?"

"Kiss me, Stephen."

"My three new favorite words."

He lowered his mouth and touched his lips

to hers softly, then again more firmly. He held her face, his long fingers threading into her hair. Then he angled his head and deepened the kiss.

Safely nestled between them, Mary let out a little cry of protest.

Hoping the child would remain content a while longer, Sophie ignored the first squeak and pressed her mouth to her husband's. She knew it was almost time to feed Mary again, but oh, she wanted this kiss to go on and on.

He broke away first, resting his forehead against hers.

"Is she all right?" he whispered.

"Yes, just hungry. Blasted timing." She managed a shaky chuckle.

"Shall I leave you?"

Sophie bracketed his face with both hands and slowly shook her head. "Never again."

She rose and took Mary, stepping to the cradle to retrieve a muslin cloth. She glanced back at him over her shoulder. He sat on the upholstered chaise longue, propping one knee on its length, while his other stocking foot remained on the floor. Because Mrs. Thrupton had insisted he remove his muddied boots, he could at least relax and put his feet up while he waited for her to nurse Mary Katherine. But he did not look relaxed. In fact, he looked quite the opposite.

Feeling self-conscious, she wanted to turn her back. But she was the one who'd told him not to leave.

Hitting on an idea, she walked back to the chaise. "May we join you?"

His brows shot to his hairline and his lips parted. "I . . . of course. How will you . . . ?" He retreated as far against the backrest as he could.

She turned and sat down between his knees. Her back was to him, affording her a bit of privacy while staying near. In fact, they had never been in such an intimate position. She loosened the front flap of her gown, lowered the fabric cup of her corset, and positioned Mary to nurse. If he watched or averted his gaze, she could not tell, which was somewhat of a relief. It meant he could not see her blushing face either.

Mary latched on easily, and Sophie felt the sweet sting of milk coursing through her. They had become accustomed to one another, and Sophie was ever so glad those awkward early days of trial and error were over. As Mary began to suckle, Sophie's attention lifted from baby to the man behind her. She could almost feel his tension, his uncertainty.

Tentatively, she leaned back against him. Understanding her intention, he exhaled and some of the tension eased from his body. She slowly allowed herself to rest fully against him, her legs paralleling his on the chaise.

He slid his outside arm around her, drawing it up her arms, so they both shared Mary's weight. He gently eased her back more firmly against him. She found it comforting, holding her little one close, while being held close to her husband. She felt cherished. Protected.

She looked down and tried to see what he might see. Mary's content face, eyes closed, lashes against pale cheeks. Little red lips bowed over Sophie's white bosom, Mary's small fist, gradually relaxing open.

Could he hear the sounds of drawing and swallowing? She could, over the muffled beating of his heart.

Stephen raised his hand and ran a gentle finger over Mary's soft cheek and the curve of her neck. Then he bent and placed a kiss at the sensitive juncture of Sophie's shoulder and neck. A shiver of pleasure rippled through her.

He cradled her close. Cradled them both close. And Sophie closed her eyes to savor the warm wonder of his embrace.

Eventually, Mary's mouth popped off in a wet sigh of satisfaction.

Sophie kissed her soft, downy head. Then she repositioned her corset cover and bodice. She stood and held Mary at her shoulder, patting her back. She was more nervous now than when preparing to nurse Mary in front of Captain Overtree — this husband she was only coming to know.

What now?

He rose to his feet as well, his steadfast gaze holding hers.

A knock interrupted them, and Sophie jumped. She prayed Wesley hadn't returned.

Mrs. Thrupton's muffled voice came through the door. "May I take Mary for you?" she offered. "I thought she and I might call on your Papa for an hour or so, if that suits. . . ."

That would give them privacy, without fear of an audience in the next room, or the baby awakening at an inopportune moment.

Stephen murmured, "It's up to you. I'm in no hurry to send her away."

Sophie went to the door and cracked it open. "Thank you, Mavis. That is very kind." She settled the child into Mavis's arms.

"It's good of you, Mrs. Thrupton," the captain added.

"No trouble."

Mavis turned away, but not before Sophie saw the sparkle in her eyes and heard her coo to the child, "Better late than never . . ."

Sophie closed the door and turned to face him. Gripping her hands, she looked up at him shyly. "I, um . . ."

Stephen stood awkwardly, several feet away from her, a line between his brows. "Sophie, I don't want to rush you. Mary Katherine is only, what, five or six weeks old? We can wait. I would never want to hurt you."

"I feel perfectly well. But . . . perhaps we could be very careful?"

"Of course. I will be as gentle as I can, but I confess I have had little experience, so . . ."

"Well, thankfully we have our entire lives to practice."

His gaze flew to hers. "As you wish."

In two strides, he closed the gap between them, gathered her in his arms, and kissed her soundly. Her lips parted as she returned the pressure of his kiss. He melded his warm mouth to hers, her body to his, until her legs felt weak, and her heart . . . strong.

He was gentle with her and wonderfully patient. Her time with Wesley seemed like a distant and regrettable memory.

Late that night, the three of them fell asleep together — her and Stephen in the narrow bed, and Mary Katherine in her cradle beside them. As her eyes drifted closed, Sophie thanked God again for His forgiveness and self-sacrificing love — as well as her husband's.

Chapter 35

The following week, Stephen and his wife and daughter traveled to Overtree Hall in a hired chaise. He and Sophie held hands on the bench between them, and took turns holding the baby. Eventually, Sophie fell asleep against his good shoulder, lulled by the rocking of the carriage. He put his arm around her and held her securely against him, while he cradled Mary in the crook of his other arm. He felt more content than he had in his entire life.

He thought back with warm pleasure over their last several days in one of the hillside cottages, enjoying a makeshift honeymoon — thanks to Mrs. Thrupton's help with Mary Katherine. How he had relished sleeping with his wife curled against him when Mary slept. Or walking the child when she fussed in the wee hours, so his lovely, exhausted wife could rest.

Stephen hoped his parents would welcome Mary Katherine more warmly and eagerly than they had initially welcomed Sophie. And he prayed relationships would improve between his wife and his parents. The truth was, each one of them was partly to blame, himself included. But if they continued to condemn Sophie, he would not subject her to long or frequent periods in their company. Her happiness was too important to him. If necessary, they would visit now and again, but live in Lynmouth the rest of the time. At least until he recovered enough to return to duty. How he dreaded the prospect. He did not wish to leave his wife and daughter.

And what about Wesley? Stephen wondered. Would he remain true to his intention to step back and relinquish any claim to Mary Katherine, and be an uncle to her only, both publically and in private? He hoped so, or visits to Overtree Hall could be more tense and stressful yet, especially as Mary Katherine grew older.

Almighty God, direct our paths, he prayed. *Soften hearts. After all, you are the King of redemption and restoration.*

His parents were still away at a midweek service when they arrived at Overtree Hall. Stephen was glad for a little time to settle into their room, and feed and change Mary Katherine.

"Why do you not rest a while, my love?" Stephen suggested, after she'd nursed the baby. "We can wait and go down for dinner. No doubt Thurman will tell them we have arrived."

"I shall try to rest if you do," she said, Mary in her arms. "But I shan't hide in here — if you go down, so shall I."

"I didn't mean you should hide. The past is the past, thanks be to God."

She smiled tenderly up at him. "And thanks to you."

He helped her off with her pelisse, pressed an affectionate kiss to her cheek, and turned her toward the bed, shooing her toward its comforts with a gentle pat to her bottom. She put a few pillows around the sleeping Mary to keep her from rolling off the bed, then climbed in herself.

Perhaps he would join her as soon as he struggled his boots off. He didn't want to ring for Edgar. At the moment, he wanted only to enjoy Sophie and Mary Katherine in this room. Their room. He found himself remembering those restless nights he had slept in the dressing room — or tried to. More than once he had to run a cold cloth over his face and neck. Those lonely nights were over, thank the Lord.

He remembered the first time he saw her hair down, longing to run his hands through it. To tangle his fingers in its golden strands and gently draw her near for a slow, leisurely kiss. He found his heart rate accelerating at the thought. He might need cold water from his washstand yet.

He confessed, "Do you know many nights I lay in that dressing room — tormented by the thought of you on the other side of that door, a few yards away? Wanting to go to you. To kiss you. To be welcomed into your bed?"

Sophie smiled up at him and patted the blanket beside her. He didn't need to be asked twice.

He leaned down and kissed her. But a scratch at the door drew him upright again.

A housemaid timidly opened the door. "Sorry, sir. Ma'am. But Mrs. Hill sent me up with fresh water for your washstands."

Had the woman read his mind? At the moment, he would not thank her for interrupting.

"Hello, Libby," Sophie greeted. "Are you well?"

"Yes, ma'am. Welcome back, ma'am." The housemaid delivered the water, then asked him, "Shall I send up Edgar, sir?"

"When it's time to dress for dinner, then yes. But no hurry."

"Very good, sir." She bobbed a curtsy and slipped from the room.

Sophie bit back a worried grin, and whispered, "Do you think she knows what we were up to in here?"

"I don't care if she does," Stephen said. "We are husband and wife. It goes with the territory."

She grinned impishly. "And very glad of it I am."

"Why, Mrs. Overtree . . ." He leaned in for another kiss.

They went down for dinner half an hour early, taking Mary Katherine with them. As he'd hoped, the baby proved an effective diversion to ease Sophie's return.

"Thurman told us you'd arrived and were resting or we would have insisted on meeting this little lady earlier," his father began.

"Let me have a look at her," the colonel said, coming closer. "A bonny lass if ever I saw one."

His mother nodded. "Sophie is right. She does look like you, Kate."

"May I hold her?" his sister asked, holding out her slender arms.

Stephen obliged her, gingerly transferring the child. "Careful."

"Oh, look. She has a strawberry birthmark," his mother observed, leaning near. "Growing up, I had a dear friend with one of these on her cheek. The boys teased her about it — until I let them know in no uncertain terms that I would not tolerate such behavior."

"Perfectly true," the colonel spoke up with paternal pride. "She was only nine or ten, but my daughter could lay flat any boy in the parish."

"Woe to the man who crosses her even today." Mr. Overtree winked and put his arm around her.

"Pish."

"Well, Mary Katherine Overtree, you are very welcome," the colonel said, smiling into her little face. Mary cooed in reply and made a vague swat at his rather prominent nose.

When dinner was announced, Mrs. Overtree said, "Shall I ring for Mrs. Hill, and see if she might watch Mary Katherine while we dine?"

"No need, Mamma," Stephen said. "Winnie can do that."

"Winnie? I don't know that Nurse Whitney is up to the task."

"Nonsense, Janet," the colonel said. "She is perfectly capable. And I daresay she would enjoy nothing more."

"Do you think so, Papa? Well, then, I shall send for her."

"That's all right, Mamma," Stephen said. "I will take Mary Katherine up to her. I want to introduce her to Winnie myself."

"I'll go along if you don't mind," Sophie said. "I'd like to see her too."

"We'll join you for dinner as soon as we can."

Together they climbed the stairs to the attic, as eager as two children on their way to show a beloved grandmother a new prized possession.

They knocked softly and were invited in. "My boy! And Sophie! How delighted I am to see you again."

"Winnie, may I introduce you to someone?" He turned the bundled child toward his old nurse. "This is Mary Katherine Overtree."

"Ah! Master Stephen! I always knew you would find your rightful place in the end. And it is working out, all of it, you shall see."

"I already see. And I am thankful for my many blessings."

Winnie took the child in her arms, and instead of the added weight hunching her back farther, it seemed to straighten her spine. Eyes on the precious child, she murmured, "A beautiful family. An unexpected inheritance. Blessings meant for another are still blessings."

Stephen and Sophie shared confused looks at that cryptic remark.

Stephen cleared his throat, and began, "Then, apparently you already know that she isn't really mi—"

"Of course she is," Winnie snapped, eyes flashing. "And never let me hear you say otherwise. You're not too old for my stick!"

For a moment he feared the elderly woman was losing her better sense, but then he saw the glint of humor in her eyes.

He smiled. "I won't forget. I promise."

"Now, that's more like it."

Dinner was a somewhat awkward affair, everyone on his or her best behavior trying to be polite and friendly, while avoiding potentially awkward subjects like Wesley's involvement with Sophie, Sophie's leaving, and Miss Blake's revelation. Apparently, Wesley had returned to Overtree Hall a few days before, and had gone to Windmere to speak to Miss Blake, but no more was said on the subject.

"Sophie has sold her first two paintings," Stephen said, to break the strained silence.

Murmurs of approval rippled around the table.

"A Lynmouth landscape and a portrait to Sir Frederick Nevill himself. He declared her work most excellent. I'm no judge, of course, but I have to agree."

Sophie ducked her head, clearly embarrassed at his praise.

Eager to divert attention, Sophie asked, "What is the news here? And where is Mr. Keith?"

His grandfather replied, "Keith has taken a former officer he met in Brussels to have him fitted for an artificial arm like his."

Mrs. Overtree's nose wrinkled. "Not while we're eating, Papa."

"Oh, Janet, why not? The man is finally doing something useful."

"That is good news," Stephen agreed.

"We don't see Angela as often since . . . he left," Kate added sadly.

But Stephen doubted Mr. Keith's departure was the reason Angela felt less comfortable visiting Overtree Hall.

"We do see a great deal more of another neighbor though. Don't we, Kate?" their grandfather teased, eyes twinkling.

Kate blushed, but Stephen saw her dimples appear and knew the topic pleased her.

"Oh? Might this neighbor be a certain Mr. Harrison?" Stephen asked.

Kate grinned up at him. "It might indeed."

Stephen exchanged a look of surprise with Sophie. His mother, he noticed, did not utter a negative word about the young man — which said a great deal. Apparently she had revised her opinion of David Harrison. And hopefully of Sophie as well.

After dinner, the ladies withdrew to the adjacent parlour, leaving Stephen, his father, and grandfather in the dining room. Mr. Overtree had his usual small glass of port, while the colonel puffed on an after-dinner cigarillo.

His father began, "As you heard at dinner, you just missed your brother. He was here briefly to formally apologize to Miss Blake. But it was too little, too late." He set down his glass. "So I suppose this is as good a time as any to tell you of my decision."

"Oh?" Stephen asked, with a curious glance at his grandfather, who appeared as solemn as his father did.

"Yes. I cannot in good conscience allow your brother's actions, his blatant disregard for duty and family — and every good Christian impulse — to go on unanswered. I have you and Katherine to think of, not to mention Miss Blake and other ladies like her. I also have to consider the estate itself, the house and land and tenants — its future. I can no longer fool myself, or allow your mother to sway me for a little more patience where Wesley is concerned. No. Were the estate entailed, I would have no choice — it would go to Wesley in its entirety after my death. But the estate has never been entailed and I may do with it as I think best in my will. This has not been an easy decision, but I believe it is the right one. I have decided to disinherit Wesley as heir and future master of Overtree Hall. Yours are the hands to steer the estate, Stephen. Assuming you are willing."

Stephen's heart beat dully at the grave pronouncement. "You know I am always ready and willing to help, Papa. You needn't make me your heir. I have my military career to think of, and —"

"My military career, I think you mean," the colonel interrupted. "My aspirations for you." He grimaced. "I should not have forced my chosen career on you, nor made service a condition of the trust I offered you. I'm sorry.

I knew, deep down, it was never what you wanted." He lifted a hand. "Don't mistake me. You made me proud and served with valor. You always put your heart into anything you undertake. That is your nature. You commit without looking back, whether it be a career, a faith, a wife, a child . . . I admire that about you, my boy. And I know you will commit yourself in the same way to the preservation and improvement of this great estate."

"But, Colonel . . . I am not yet thirty. I am no quitter. I don't wish to let you or the army down."

"I think a certain French saber has done that for you. That coupled with Boney's exile. His last, if I don't miss my guess. You might live on your half pay, but why should you, when you are heir to Overtree Hall? If your country still needed you, that would be one thing. But the war is over. For good, this time, God willing. You can sell your commission. Settle down. You have a wife to think of now. A daughter."

"Yes, I have."

"I am sorry, you know," his father said. "About the way we treated Sophie when she first arrived, and after the scandal with Wesley came out. She isn't the woman your mother and I would have chosen for either of you. But I understand why you did it. I hope Sophie will understand our concerns and forgive us in time."

"And Mamma?" Stephen asked.

"Well, she may take a little more time to get over the whole ordeal." He lifted a consoling palm. "Don't mistake me. We admire you and respect what you did. And realize it is Wesley who is truly to blame for the situation in the first place. Not you. Hence our discussion here this evening."

"Does Wesley know of your decision?"

"Not yet. The lawyers are working on the papers as we speak." He sighed. "Unfortunately, it is more of a blow to your mother than to Wesley himself, who will probably be relieved to be freed of the responsibility . . . though not the financial benefits that come with it."

Stephen suggested, "Perhaps you might rewrite the trust, Colonel. Leave Wesley a little something to soften the blow."

His grandfather inhaled. "It did cross my mind. But I wasn't sure it would be fair to you."

"I didn't serve to receive your money."

"You served to please me. I know. And you have. I will not countenance leaving it all to him, but I would consider dividing it between the three of you — you, Wes, and Kate."

"That is very kind of you, Grandfather."

"*Pfff.* Not really. I may spend it all yet myself if I live long enough," he teased. "A third of nothing is nothing."

"You might have told me that before I rushed headlong into that French saber," Stephen replied. And the two former military officers shared knowing grins.

In the white parlour, Mrs. Overtree, Sophie, and Kate sat together waiting for the men to join them.

Sophie had long ago guessed Wesley had broken Angela's heart, but she had been stunned and grieved when Stephen had told her about the child. Now she said tentatively, "I was sorry to hear Miss Blake visits less frequently. She is . . . in good health, I trust?"

"I believe so," Kate said with an uneasy little smile. "When I saw her in church on Sunday, I assured her she is more than welcome here, so hopefully she will call again soon."

Mrs. Overtree changed the subject. "I have been thinking that we ought to host a christening dinner. Mary Katherine hasn't been baptized yet, I trust?"

"No. Stephen wanted to wait and have her christened in the church here, with all of you in attendance."

"Very thoughtful. Yes. It is a little unusual, waiting this long. But not unheard of to wait even longer, say, during an especially cold winter. No one wants to carry a little lamb out in the frigid weather, especially after being doused with water. Who shall serve as her godparents?"

"I was thinking Kate might, as her name-sake. And . . . you and Mr. Overtree, per-haps?"

Her eyebrows rose. "Very good. Have you been churched yet?"

"I was. Mrs. Thrupton insisted upon it."

"Excellent. We should send out cards an-nouncing the birth." She looked at Sophie. "Have you any visiting cards upon which we may write Mary Katherine's name and date of birth? Or perhaps we should use the baptism date, so there is no . . . confusion."

"No. I'm afraid I haven't any cards."

"What a pity. I doubt there is time to have them printed. Ah well. I will at least send my cards to some dear friends and neighbors, to let them know we will be receiving afternoon callers. I shall ask Mrs. John to have biscuits and tea ready. Many of our neighbors will wish to see Stephen's" — she hesitated — "the newest Overtree."

"It's all right, Mrs. Overtree," Sophie said gently. "Mary Katherine is and shall be Stephen's daughter. Henceforth and forever."

"Good. Well. That's good then. Easier. For everyone." She shifted on her chair, then glanced down and brightened. "There you are!"

To Sophie's surprise, a grey cat arched against Mrs. Overtree's skirt, and the woman bent down to stroke it. Sophie recognized the white patch that spotted the cat's nose like cream — the smallest of Gulliver's kittens, now an adolescent.

"Mr. Harrison helped us find homes for the others," Kate explained with a fond smile. "But Mamma couldn't give this one up."

"Now, Kate, you know Mrs. John needed a good mouser. And besides, it would have been uncharitable to turn out the poor creature."

Sophie bit back a grin as the cat's rumbling purr grew louder. "And how is Gulliver?" she asked.

"Already up to her old tricks," Kate replied. "Sneaking down the old passage from Winnie's room and out the scullery door. No doubt visiting her beau in the churchyard."

The grey cat curled up next to her chair, and Mrs. Overtree straightened, taking charge of the conversation once more. "May I ask how Wesley reacted? We know he went to see you, but he would say nothing of it while he was here. He didn't put up a fight?"

Sophie paused to consider how best to answer. She said evenly, "He met Mary Katherine, agreed she looks like Kate, and handed her to Stephen." All true, though the explanation left so much unsaid. Perhaps it was for the best.

The parlour doors opened, and Mrs. Overtree turned. "That was quick."

But it was not the men come to join them

643

— it was Angela Blake. The footman announced her, then departed, closing the door behind himself.

"I hope you will forgive the intrusion," Angela began. "But I knew you would have eaten already and I couldn't wait to meet the newest Overtree."

"We are very happy to see you, Angela," Kate said. "You know you are always welcome."

Mrs. Overtree rang the bell and sent the footman to ask Winnie to bring down the child.

While they waited, Angela handed Sophie a wrapped package.

"I've brought a little something for her."

"Thank you, that was very kind." Sophie accepted the gift and unwrapped the tissue. Inside was a small baby blanket embroidered with white hollie point lace. "It's beautiful. My goodness. Did you do this needlework yourself?"

"I did, yes. A long time ago. But it hasn't been used — never fear."

"I wouldn't mind if it were. It's lovely. Thank you." Had Angela embroidered all that delicate white work for her own child? Only to give the child away to a foundling home before the blanket might ever be put to use? A hollow ache filled Sophie's chest at the thought of losing Mary Katherine like that. She silently prayed that Angela's child, wherever he or she was, had been placed in a caring home and was growing up content and healthy.

Winnie brought in Mary Katherine. The old nurse looked spry and smugly met Mrs. Overtree's cool glance.

"Miss Blake would like to see her," Sophie explained.

Winnie nodded and laid the child in Angela's arms.

"She's beautiful . . ." Angela breathed, tears welling in her green eyes. "She looks so much like —"

"Sophie says she looks like Kate, and we all agree," Mrs. Overtree interrupted in a burst, her composure so ruffled that she'd called her daughter by the disapproved-of pet name.

Angela blinked up at her, lips parted. Then looked back down at the little girl. "Yes, I see it now. You are perfectly right." Her eyes lingered on the child's face a moment longer, then she lifted a determinedly bright face to Sophie.

"Have you heard my news?"

Sophie shook her head.

"Mr. Keith and I are engaged to be married."

Sophie gaped. "Are you indeed? That is wonderful news."

"Is it? I think so, though not everyone agrees. My father berated me for 'not landing one of those Overtree boys,' as though that had *ever* crossed my mind." Fragile humor shone in her eyes.

Sophie gave her a gentle smile for brave effort.

"We thought of eloping, as did you and Stephen. What is good for the captain is good for the second in command, after all. But my father insists on a proper wedding. He sees me only a few days a month but suddenly takes an interest in my affairs."

Sophie lifted a cautioning hand. "Don't regard us as the standard bearers, I beg of you." She chuckled in self-deprecation and was pleased to see the woman manage a tentative grin.

Angela said, "Father *is* glad to know there will be a man about the place to manage things during his absences." Her grin widened. "And so am I."

Sophie leaned over and pressed the woman's hand. "Mr. Keith will be an excellent help to you and an excellent husband. I am very happy for you both."

When Stephen left the smoky dining room ahead of the other men, there stood Winnie outside the door, eyes clear and bright, Mary Katherine in her arms. It was good to see her on the main level again, in the company of others. She stood in quiet conversation with Sophie, but both women looked up in anticipation as he exited. Had they been waiting for him?

Winnie searched his face. "He told you then?"

Stephen held the dear woman's gaze. "He told me."

Her eyes lit in triumph. "Did I not tell you? I said you would not receive your rightful inheritance. You shall have your brother's and he shall have yours, or at least a portion of it."

Stephen looked at her in surprise. "Now how did you know that detail? The colonel only just decided it."

"Did he?" Winnie said innocently. "A lucky guess — that's all."

Stephen winked at Sophie and said, "Told you she has second sight."

Sophie grinned. "Oh, I don't think it's second sight so much as squint sight, but no need to quibble."

"And now the two of you shall be happy," Winnie proclaimed. "Or should I say the three of you." She planted a kiss on the small charge in her arms.

Stephen had rarely seen his old nurse look younger or more pleased with herself.

"You predict a happy future for us, do you, Winnie?" he asked with an indulgent grin.

"Hah. You don't need to be a prophet to know that. You have already had to fight to stay together. The battle is half-won."

Stephen raised his eyebrows. "Half-won?

And here I thought my fighting days were over."

"This is real life, Master Stephen. Happily ever after takes effort. But you two will triumph. I believe it with all my heart."

"I am excessively glad to hear it."

His grandfather came out of the room and drew up short at the sight of them clustered together.

"Ah, Miss Whitney. I see you have your hands full." He glanced over guiltily to make sure the parlour doors were closed. "I suppose that means our game is off for tonight?"

"Game?" Stephen asked in surprise.

"Yes, Colonel. I am otherwise engaged and couldn't be happier."

"As I see." He smiled warmly at her.

Stephen's brow furrowed. Beside him, Sophie whispered, "I'll explain later."

"It's been too long since there's been a wee one in this house," Winnie said. "Thought I'd outlived my usefulness. But see here — it's as if Master Stephen knew all along and that's why he arranged for me to stay on when others would have sent me away. Perhaps he is the prophet and not me."

His grandfather clapped his back — but not too hard. "And all this from the young man who once told me he doubted he would ever marry, let alone have a family."

"God had other plans, apparently," Stephen said, uncomfortable with all the attention.

Sophie looked up at him, eyes shining, and squeezed his hand. "And I am thankful indeed He did."

EPILOGUE

Stephen, Sophie, and Mary Katherine remained at Overtree Hall through Christmas and Epiphany. Then they returned for a few months to Lynmouth where they first met. They let a house overlooking the channel and harbor, not far from Mrs. Thrupton's cottage and her father's studio. There they spent time with them both. There Sophie painted, as motherhood allowed.

Stephen, for his part, corresponded with his father and Mr. Boyle to keep abreast of affairs at Overtree Hall in his absence, walked the cliff-side paths with Sophie, learned to love the rugged landscape as she did, and simply enjoyed time alone with his two cherished females.

Sophie had become more comfortable and confident about painting openly, believing herself talented and beautiful. It was the accomplishment Stephen was most proud of.

With his grandfather's blessing, Stephen had sold his commission to embrace a life he had never expected but was blessed to call his own: heir of Overtree Hall, husband to Sophie, and father of Mary Katherine Overtree.

On a brisk March evening, a year after they first met at that craggy precipice, Stephen and Sophie stood atop Castle Rock, watching the sun sink low and kiss the water, gilding the sky. Stephen drew his beloved wife close, leaned down, and kissed her warmly. The cold, buffeting wind seemed a distant whistle and suddenly almost balmy.

"Happy, Mrs. Overtree?" he asked in a contented drawl.

"Perfectly, Mr. Overtree. How could I not be?" she teased. "It is our destiny, after all — did not Winnie say so?"

"Let's leave her out of this, shall we? A man doesn't like to think of his childhood nanny when he's making love to his wife."

She grinned, took his face in both of her hands, and proceeded to kiss him with such maddening sweetness that he soon forgot everything else.

Later, they walked back hand in hand along the cliff-side path to reclaim their daughter, snug with Mrs. Thrupton, who took great pleasure in taking care of her. Then together they continued down the steep path to their winter home, Mary Katherine secure in Stephen's arms.

Inside they built up a fire in their bedchamber. A fire sparked on the cliff side a year ago. On the wall hung two matted portraits, sharing a frame. The rescued painting of Sophie, beside her more recent portrait of him, drawn by her own hand and no longer hidden from view.

Stephen's gaze rested on the portraits a moment longer, and he breathed a prayer of thanksgiving. Then he gathered his wife and child in his arms and kissed the painter's daughter.

AUTHOR'S NOTE

I first visited Lynton and Lynmouth, twin villages in North Devon, England, when I was working on another book (*Lady Maybe*), which required a cliff-side setting. I traveled there with an old friend, Sara Ring, and we fell in love with the dramatic coastal landscape within Exmoor National Park — also the setting of the novel *Lorna Doone* by R. D. Blackmore. We enjoyed the scenic harbor town of Lynmouth and stayed in the wonderful Castle Hill Guest House in Lynton, perched on the hill above. We spent a few idyllic days there, finding the villages and landscape lovely and the local people warm and friendly. We learned that the area was indeed a favorite among poets and artists in the nineteenth century (and probably to this day). So when I began mulling an idea about a painter and his daughter, well, it seemed only natural to choose this setting.

Sara and I hiked out to the majestic Valley of Rocks on a narrow path atop steep green slopes that plunged down to the sun-streaked water below. I remember well the bracing wind, the windsurfing gulls, the prickly yellow gorse, regal rocks, and the stunning vistas receding into the horizon. Sara took many photos of it all. Stop by www.julieklassen .com to see a few of them.

And Mavis Thrupton? While strolling along the harbor, I saw a charming whitewashed ice cream stand with *Mavis Thrupton's of Lynmouth* emblazoned on it and instantly knew I'd found a name for a sweet character. (Not that I have a soft spot for ice cream or anything. . . .) If you visit the area, have a cone for me. Also be sure to ride the water-powered Lynton & Lynmouth Cliff Railway. Established in 1888, it was too modern to include in this novel, but it rewards those not afraid of heights with beautiful views.

Claude Dupont and Wesley Overtree are fictitious, though most of the other artists mentioned in the book are real. Overtree Hall is not an actual place, but I based it loosely on stately Chastleton House (with its secret room) in Oxfordshire. As well as Great Chalfield Manor in Wiltshire with its stone-mask-covered squints. (Again, see photos on the Research page of my website.)

Please know that I am not an artist. And therefore, I humbly beg indulgence for any painting details that may not be quite right. I am indebted to artist Alice White, who reviewed the book and gave me helpful input, but any remaining errors are mine, all mine. I also relied on a website called Pigments through the Ages (www.webexhibits.org/pigments/intro/oil.html), which helped me identify paint colors and methods in use at the time.

If you noticed anything familiar about chapter fifteen's scene of Sophie sketching Captain Overtree's face, you must be a fellow Charlotte Brontë fan. That scene was partly inspired by Jane sketching Mr. Rochester's face in our beloved *Jane Eyre.*

Speaking of Janes, you may have also noticed the echo of two lines borrowed with love from Jane Austen's *Sense and Sensibility* and *Pride and Prejudice.* Similarly, chapter three's description of the wedding attire Mavis gives Sophie (*the soft silk shawl, white shot with primrose, with embossed satin flowers, and very handsome fringe*) is a description of the simple wedding dress of Jane Austen's friend, Anne Lefroy, found in the book *Jane Austen and Marriage.*

Anglicans may realize that I abridged the wedding service from the Book of Common Prayer. This was done for brevity's sake — no offense intended.

Besides taking copious amounts of pictures for me, Sara Ring also spent several evenings during our trip brainstorming the initial plot of this book. Thanks again, Sara. And grati-

655

tude goes to her daughter, Katie, for helping me input corrections on an early draft.

I want to thank Anna Paulson, talented author-in-the-making, who served as my intern and was so helpful in research, brainstorming ideas and solutions, fleshing out scenes, and naming the cat, Gulliver. It's been a pleasure to work with you, Anna. You have a bright future ahead of you.

I also want to thank my husband, Brian, who helped me write an "epic" battle scene. (Sorry I had to trim it down, honey.) History buffs will notice that we compressed and simplified it for fiction's sake. The 28th North Gloucestershire Regiment of Foot was a heroic British infantry regiment from 1782 to 1881. Its record bears further reading if you're interested in military history. (See 28thglos.co.uk, glosters.org.uk, etc.) Note that, in reality, reports about Quatre Bras did not reach England ahead of the news of the victory at Waterloo. But for the sake of the story, I think we can imagine Colonel Horton receiving information ahead of the general population through his connections.

Thank you to Cari Weber, first reader, trusted sounding board, and amazing friend.

Thank you to author-friend, Michelle Griep, for her insightful critiques that leave me smarting and snickering.

Thank you to Ceri Tanti, from Wales, who reviewed the manuscript in advance to help me avoid American vs. British errors and anachronisms.

Thank you to my agent, Wendy Lawton, for her input and encouragement.

Thank you to my entire team at Bethany House Publishers, who support me in so many ways: Raela Schoenherr, Charlene Patterson, Jen Veilleux, Noelle Buss, Amy Green, Anna Henke, David Horton, Steve Oates, Jim Parrish, Carissa Maki, and especially my editor Karen Schurrer. Also a shout-out to designer Jennifer Parker, who creates such beautiful covers.

Last, but never least, thank you to you, my readers. Can't wait to meet you online or at a book signing someday soon.

DISCUSSION QUESTIONS

1. Did you enjoy the book overall? What was a moment or scene you particularly liked?

2. What historical detail most surprised you about the book (e.g., army practices, marriage laws, the serious consequences of illegitimacy)?

3. How did you view the rivalry between Stephen and Wesley Overtree? Did you experience similar sibling competition growing up?

4. Many problems in the book result from lack of communication and concealment of truth. Have either of these caused you pain or problems in the past? Were you satisfied with how truth came to light in the novel?

5. Painting brings both sorrow and healing to characters in the book. Has some form of

artistic expression ever helped you or others you know cope with hardship?

6. Did you have a favorite main character (or secondary character) in this story? What did you like about him or her?

7. What did you think of Winnie's unintentional "prophecy" about Stephen's future? How much power should the words of others hold over us? How can well-meant words influence a person's life (especially a young person's) both positively and negatively?

8. Stephen loathes his facial scar until Ensign Hornsby reminds him how he received it — in protection of Hornsby's life. Other physical issues in the story, such as Lieutenant Keith's missing arm and the baby's birthmark, are also shown from different perspectives. How does the book contrast the differences between the outward appearance and the heart?

9. Sophie and Stephen each shoulder responsibilities for others — Sophie by helping her father in his studio, and Stephen by assuming his older brother's estate duties. How does this affect each one's character and identity? Can you relate?

10. The book centers on the theme of keeping an oath, "even when it hurts." In the midst of doubt and conflict, Sophie and Stephen fight to maintain their marriage vows. Have you ever kept a promise at high cost? What are the difficulties and rewards of doing so?

ABOUT THE AUTHOR

Julie Klassen loves all things Jane — *Jane Eyre* and Jane Austen. A graduate of the University of Illinois, Julie worked in publishing for sixteen years and now writes full time. Three of her books, *The Silent Governess, The Girl in the Gatehouse,* and *The Maid of Fairbourne Hall,* have won the Christy Award for Historical Romance. *The Secret of Pembrooke Park* was honored with the Minnesota Book Award for genre fiction. Julie has also won the Midwest Book Award and Christian Retailing's BEST Award, and has been a finalist in the Romance Writers of America's RITA Awards and ACFW's Carol Awards. Julie and her husband have two sons and live in a suburb of St. Paul, Minnesota. For more information, visit www.julieklassen.com.